Hugh MacLennan's Best

Hugh MacLennan's Best

*A selection of the famous author's best work –
published and unpublished – including poetry,
essays, journalism, travel writing, and excerpts from
all of his novels.*

Selected and Edited by Douglas M. Gibson

A DOUGLAS GIBSON BOOK

M&S

Thanks are due to Macmillan of Canada for permission to reprint from the
following books: *Two Solitudes, Each Man's Son, The Watch That Ends the
Night, The Return of the Sphinx,* and *Voices in Time.* All of these titles are
available in paperback. All of the essays in this book, with the exception of
"Trudeau and Nixon" (which appears here courtesy of the editor of
Maclean's magazine) and "The Maritimes," are to be found in
The Other Side of Hugh MacLennan: Selected Essays Old and New, edited by
Elspeth Cameron, and published by Macmillan of Canada.

McClelland & Stewart Inc. are the publishers of *Barometer Rising*
(available in paperback) and of *The Colour of Canada.*

For permission to reprint all of the remaining material not currently
available elsewhere in book form, and for providing the frontispiece
photograph, thanks are due to the estate of Hugh MacLennan.

Canadian Cataloguing in Publication Data

MacLennan, Hugh, 1907–1990
    Hugh MacLennan's best

ISBN 0–7710–5593–5

I. Gibson, Douglas.   II. Title.

PS8525.L45A6 1991   C813'.54   C91–095187–X
PR9199.3.M334A6 1991

Printed and bound in Canada on acid-free paper

A Douglas Gibson Book

McClelland & Stewart Inc.
The Canadian Publishers
481 University Avenue
Toronto M5G 2E9

Printed and bound in Canada by John Deyell Company

CONTENTS

ACKNOWLEDGEMENTS

In compiling this anthology I have received help from many quarters. First, from the MacLennan family represented by Michael Ogilvie and by the literary executor of Hugh MacLennan's estate, Shirley Woods. Friends of the family such as the Hon. Heward Grafftey have continued to provide support and encouragement for the project.

In the difficult business of making the selections I owe a special debt to Ronald Sutherland and Constance Beresford-Howe. Without their advice the chosen passages would undoubtedly have been more idiosyncratic, and less representative.

I thank Macmillan of Canada, the holders of the copyright of most of Hugh MacLennan's books, for their permission to quote the selected passages listed elsewhere, and the stalwarts at McClelland & Stewart who helped push the book through the publication process, especially the tireless Gail Stewart. Special thanks go to Eleanor Sinclair for her dedication to the task of copy-editing the manuscript.

Above all, I owe a great debt to Elspeth Cameron. Her essay selection, *The Other Side of Hugh MacLennan*, was a source of inspiration, while her biography, *Hugh MacLennan: A Writer's Life*, was unfailingly useful. Indeed, compiling an anthology of this sort without a reliable biography to act as a compass would be an almost impossible task. All students of Hugh MacLennan and his work owe her a great deal.

On the domestic front I am grateful for their support and forbearance to Beverly, Meg, and Katie.

As is customary in these matters, I accept full responsibility for any errors that may be found in the pages that follow.

D.M.G.

INTRODUCTION

This book is a tribute to Hugh MacLennan. I have approached its creation as a friend of Hugh's for more than twenty years as his editor and publisher, and as a staunch admirer of his work in all of its surprising variety. My chief hope for this anthology is that it will give its readers such enjoyment that they will be inspired to read – or to reread – all of the books briefly represented here.

In making this anthology I had the pleasure of reading everything that Hugh MacLennan published, and much that has never been published in book form. I received helpful advice and suggestions from many people, whom I list in the Acknowledgements. At the end of the process I found myself pleasantly troubled by an embarrassment of riches. To the reader disappointed not to find here a favourite passage from one of the novels, or incredulous that an especially delightful essay is missing, I apologize for the exclusion. To anthologize is to choose, and here the choosing was hard. In fact, I have come to regret that I have only one book to devote to this marvellous writer.

"This marvellous writer." That phrase is untypical of the editorial style in the rest of the book. There, my role has been to introduce each piece with a brief sentence or two, perhaps referring to the events of MacLennan's life at the time or to similar passages elsewhere, then to leave the excerpt – without benefit of adjectives – to speak for itself.

This Introduction, then, may be the place to throw away such reticence (so characteristic of Hugh MacLennan himself) and to speak of his contribution to our national literature. Margaret Laurence, who was almost uniquely qualified to comment, has written: "MacLennan was our first truly non-colonial writer, writing faithfully out of his own perceptions of his land

and his people. In this way, his writing has reached beyond geographical boundaries, and belongs both to Canada and to a universal area of literature. His books will endure."

Others recognized his central role as a pioneer who showed by his example that to be a Canadian novelist was a noble calling. Let one personal anecdote serve as an illustration. I remember the winter day when he delivered the manuscript of *Voices in Time* to me at the Château Versailles in Montreal, where a committee of the Writers' Union of Canada was meeting. I insisted that he drop in to say hello to this group of a dozen senior Canadian authors, and after much persuasion, because he was reluctant to disturb them, he went in, shyly. Everyone in the room stood up and applauded.

This book is for those who would like to know what he did to earn that applause, as well as for his already wide audience of admirers.

Claude Bissell of the University of Toronto, one admirer, has made the flat assertion, "No Canadian writer has contributed so much to national self-awareness and understanding." It is extraordinary now to recollect that when Hugh MacLennan wrote *Barometer Rising* in 1941, it was regarded as an act of almost foolhardy courage to set a novel in Canada. But with that book and with *Two Solitudes*, the 1945 novel that gave every caring Canadian a new expression to ponder, Hugh MacLennan was in the forefront of hacking out a path to a national literature. And his later novels, from *The Watch That Ends the Night*, which held me spellbound as a schoolboy in Scotland reading of Jerome Martell's escape down the river from the lumber camp, to *Voices in Time*, whose Portuguese edition confronts me as I write today, have touched hundreds of thousands of readers here and abroad.

But even that is only part of Hugh MacLennan's contribu-tion – he will be remembered with gratitude as a teacher, a generous adviser, a caring husband, a man for whom the word "courtly" might have been invented, and as a friend to many, including writers of all generations. As an essayist he has been among the world's best, writing excellent and much-quoted pieces on everything from hockey to Captain Bligh. Some of those essays reflect his unmatched skills as a writer about the

Canadian landscape – gloriously demonstrated here in the short excerpts from *The Colour of Canada* or the longer ones from *Rivers of Canada*, and in the wonderful, much-quoted opening to *Two Solitudes*. Like his novels, the essays reveal him as a writer engagé, a writer dealing with vital political issues. Hugh MacLennan was notable for his willingness to tackle the great themes, the questions that shape our lives to this day. He was writing about French and English relations in Canada in 1945. As early as 1960, he was writing essays about what he called "the Americanization of Canada." It is worth recalling here that it was MacLennan's essays that taught the American critic Edmund Wilson that there was indeed "a Canadian way of looking at things . . . a point of view surprisingly and agreeably different from anything else I know in English."

That "Canadian way of looking at things" is a very personal one and the things Hugh MacLennan looks at in this book are so varied that we are left feeling with some awe that he can write well about anything under the sun. His unrivalled record of five Governor General's Awards – three for fiction, and two for his non-fiction essay collections – remind us of his extraordinary range.

He can write about a funny encounter with a trigger-happy barfly in Arizona, and link it with sixteenth-century religious debates in England. He can describe the torture chambers of the Gestapo, or the eerie shuffling of the homeless Kulaks in Leningrad, and also write a ribald story about Cape Breton nicknames. He can take us to sunny Wimbledon, or to a steamy New Jersey arena by night. And just as deftly he can write about chopping wood in his beloved Eastern Townships.

At the same time he can make Canada and its history spring to life in our senses: he can make us see the yellow foam above the Fraser in flood at Hell's Gate; hear the bagpipes blowing as Sir George Simpson's giant Hudson's Bay canoe is paddled to the Lakehead; feel the impact of the Halifax explosion – or of Jerome Martell's bayonet stuck in the German soldier's throat; or smell the scent of new-mown hay in St. Marc in *Two Solitudes*.

And, of course, he can make us laugh. The fact that his novels have serious themes has blinded too many people to the fact that he is very funny indeed. "Orgy at Oriel," several other essays included here, and many episodes in his novels make that abundantly clear. In his life he was good company, a fine, amusing story-teller. I hope that this selection will provide the reader with that same sense of enjoyment.

The organization of this book is very simple. Starting with excerpts from MacLennan's earliest work, the book moves chronologically to the latest work. The editor's role is to introduce each piece briefly in the hope that the chronological arrangement will show how Hugh MacLennan's writing developed. In that way this book may perhaps be seen as a useful companion volume to Elspeth Cameron's excellent biography, *Hugh MacLennan: A Writer's Life* (University of Toronto Press, 1981).

Usually the excerpt is four or five pages long. Sometimes it is self-contained: an essay; a description of a river from *Rivers of Canada*; an incident from a novel; a memorable scene described in a way that reveals one of the many facets of the author's skill.

When Hugh MacLennan died in November 1990, editorials in newspapers across the country mourned Canada's loss. Some paid tribute to his ability, as one who had lived in every decade of this most turbulent of centuries, to notice and call attention to the important movements in our world. Others spoke of his pioneering role in creating a literature that belonged to Canada, and recalled Robert Kroetsch's poetic description of Hugh MacLennan as "the cartographer of our dreams."

At the end of this book I hope that everyone will feel as David Helwig did after reading his essays:

"MacLennan is one of those writers whose personal goodness and decency shine through all his works. His generosity of spirit is such that after a couple of hours spent with one of his books, the world seems a better place."

Douglas Gibson
Toronto, June 1991

Hugh MacLennan's Best

Beginnings

Valedictory

At Dalhousie University in Halifax Hugh MacLennan was the 1928 winner of the Governor General's Gold Medal and the class valedictorian. His speech deals with the gifts of leisure and freedom from outside pressures that allowed Dalhousie's students time to have ideas, and to change them "steadily at the rate of about once a month." Then he becomes more personal:

It is from these two things – this leisure and this freedom – that whatever intellectual advances we have made have had their beginning. But in after years, when we think back on these years we have spent here together, thinking, perhaps, that they have been the happiest of our lives, it will not be in these terms, I think, that we will reflect on them. Rather we will be seeing the little things, things of everyday that passed into our lives unconsciously and remained there. The quiet talk with our friend over the winter fire; the crowds laughing together at the football matches; the sun making shadows in the rafters of the library – another time, perhaps, we will be glad to remember these things, but it is hardly fitting to speak of them now; for each man knows them best for himself. . . .

Poetry

From his teenage years Hugh MacLennan wrote poetry of a romantic kind. He continued this practice through his years as a Rhodes Scholar at Oxford (1928-32), where he entertained hopes of having his poems published in "a small volume."

Off Halifax Harbour

I smelled the balsam in the air
And the good sea-fog in every spar,
And knew my pines were standing there
And my town beyond the harbour-bar.

The mist hid every ugliness
As the ship went ghosting up the Bay,
And in her flowing silver dress
Like a sleeping maid my city lay.

Oh, I know a town in Italy
Vine-clad amid its ancient hills,
That all the world has gone to see
And that all the world with wonder fills.

And a town in England's meadows deep
Where all day long the chiming bells
And mellowing walls seem half-asleep,
Where the richest hope of England dwells.

But the sea has throbbed against my brain,
And the spicy winds have tossed my hair,
And I have watched the moonlight rain
On waves and the pine-wood, crouching there

Like a spell-bound, ghostly worshipper,
In night's mysterious robings clad. . . .
To none but a fool should my town seem fair,
– But her sea and pines have made me mad!

These Laid the World Away
("We buried them together, our officer
and an English Lieutenant." –
German soldier's letter, July 1917)

Here lie two youths, once beautiful and swift,
That knew the music of the summer sky;

But, being young they squandered nature's gift
And wrought great deeds because their faith was high.

O Faith! God's mightiest boon that moveth mountains,
Take here these two, our cheapest, easiest gift,
Forgetful of their earth, its hills and fountains,
And of themselves, once beautiful and swift.

Flight

O eager, anxious, wondering little soul!
– Like some small child, with wide-flung questing arms
(Hearing Life's whisper thro' his being roll),
That runs, wide-eyed, deep-fraught with vague alarms,
Back from the dark; and finds his little room,
The hearth-fire glowing on the carpet's flowers,
His mother's needles, clock-like in the gloom,
Clicking away the comfort – drowsy hours –
Even so, my little soul (remembering well
How Certainty and Sleep together dwell
In that old room where he forgot his Care),
Back from the winds of your own thoughts you came,
Yearning for drowsiness, the hearth-fire's flame,
And thoughtless comfort, fleeing – Oh, to where?

Oxyrhynchus

In October 1932, Hugh MacLennan went to Princeton to study for a Ph.D. in Classics. His thesis, completed in 1935, dealt with the detailed records of a town in ancient Egypt whose decline imitated the decline of the Roman Empire.

INTRODUCTION

The growth and collapse of the Roman Empire, that astounding cycle in which a brilliant culture in the cities rose, waned and passed finally into the darkness of a quasi-feudal system in which the village-unit became in most regions more vital than the city, presents to us now, as it has presented to all generations since the Renascence, a series of questions which somehow must be solved if our own culture is to survive.

It has long been evident that if we are to interpret the growth and decline of the Roman Empire we must study the history of the provinces. This has, of course, been done. And the results of the study of the Roman provinces make it clear that it is in the relationship between the towns and the rural districts that some of the most important keys to the secret of the collapse of Rome lie concealed. Therefore, if we could investigate the history of a single provincial town we might be able to see the main picture in a more exact perspective.

Oxyrhynchus was the name of a town and of a small district in Roman Egypt. The purpose of this work is to trace from a social and economic standpoint the history of its growth and decline through the seven centuries during which it was subject to the Caesars. My reason for the choice of this particular town is a simple one: owing to the accidental discovery of a great many papyri on its site we have more information about Oxyrhynchus than about any other town of corresponding size in the entire empire. Egypt was not, perhaps, a typical province, but it was a vitally important one. And because Italy, and Rome herself, depended so largely on this province for its corn supply, the fate of Egypt was closely linked to that of the Empire as a whole. Of Egypt proper, Oxyrhynchus was at least as typical as Peoria is typical of the American Middle-West. So, to survey this town is more or less to look at Roman provincial life through the large end of the telescope.

Civilization has always been supported by the patience of the poor, and nowhere were the poor more patient than in Roman Egypt. Rostovtzeff, at the conclusion of his great *Social and Economic History of the Roman Empire*, intimates that Rome perished because her civilization was not of the masses but of a single class; that she fell because the upper classes, degenerating through the centuries, not only failed to absorb the proletariat but were themselves absorbed by the masses. This inevitable, organic decay in the Roman system is fully and pitilessly illustrated in the Oxyrhynchus papyri, and the poignancy of the story is enhanced by the fact that the writers of these documents were not men of letters. They were, in fact, innocent of any knowledge whatever of the general implications that lay in their own simple affairs.

The inhabitants of the province of Egypt constituted one of the main supports of Roman greatness, but with the exception of the people of Alexandria, they generally lacked the refinements which were the fruits of the Roman system. It is true that there was a theatre in Oxyrhynchus, and baths and a gymnasium in accordance with the Greek tradition. Certain of the citizens read the classical literature of Greece. But the average man was debarred from the enjoyment of these things, and in Egypt he probably had less opportunity to better his station than his counterparts had in other less servile provinces.

Even after the grip of the central government weakened, exploitation continued in a new and more rigorous form, for some of the local citizens enriched themselves during the chaos of the third century, and through the two centuries following reduced their own people to a state bordering on serfdom. In the final period, just before the Arab invasion, a handful of landed proprietors lived high and extravagantly, but the price of their fine living was the virtual enslavement of the people in the district.

Although this study cannot be used with complete freedom as a basis for conclusions applied to the Empire as a whole, it is still safe to say that a great deal of it is applicable. Certainly the Oxyrhynchus papyri have been of enormous service to modern scholars in their task of investigating the general history of the late Roman Empire.

In the third century A.D. conditions in Oxyrhynchus and the "nome," the wider district around it on the west bank of the Nile, were in marked decline:

Although by the end of the second century no great internal upheaval had occurred in the empire, it is safe to say that by that time the course of the next four hundred years had been practically determined. Essential reforms had been neglected too long and the bureaucracy had become securely entrenched.

That the main cause of the chaos in the third century was the degeneration and virtual breakdown of the Roman economic system is well known. Documents from Oxyrhynchus not only show the results of this breakdown but also indicate many of the circumstances which caused it. The entire nome suffered, and the city suffered most of all. Yet it is manifest that the bourgeoisie of Oxyrhynchus (and presumably of most towns in the empire) had to a great extent brought catastrophe on their own heads and on those of their descendants. As Rostovtzeff has pointed out in the introduction to his *Social and Economic History*, the legislation during the first two centuries of Roman rule had nearly always favoured the bourgeoisie and had generally been controlled by them. Few successful attempts were made to protect the agriculturists who formed the backbone of society. One of the most common anxieties voiced in the documents was the "fear of becoming a wanderer." Farmers evicted from their land owing to failure to pay taxes or meet mortgages were given little protection either by the central government or by the cities of their own districts. It is no wonder that they were eager to form the nucleus of the many revolutionary armies which tore the empire to pieces during this century.

There can of course be no easy explanation for the anarchy of this time. Yet, there is little doubt that these wars were to a considerable extent incidents in the age-old struggle between the town and the country, and that they were inflamed by the attempt of Roman society to retain unlimited private enterprise in commerce, coupled with the absolute political authority of a Caesar. The papyri show only too clearly how the bourgeoisie were incapable of anything more than sporadic reforms and were unwilling to sacrifice momentary advantages to gain an ultimate security. During the middle of the third century, when nothing but a miracle could have saved the urban civilization they prized, we see them using depression and anarchy to gain an upper hand over their own neighbours. This process of mutual destruction not only thinned the ranks of the bourgeoisie, but precipitated one crisis after another and finally produced barbarism.

Later MacLennan writes: "The Landlords, like pike who have emptied a fishpond of its smaller denizens, began to cast hungry eyes on each other." His disgust with these "capitalists" was clear, and implied, in Elspeth Cameron's words, "a relationship between the pattern of decline in Ancient Rome and the events that had resulted in economic crisis in his own time." The thesis – written between 1932 and 1935 – was produced at the height of the Depression.

Originally published by Princeton University Press in 1935, the thesis was reprinted by a Dutch publishing house in 1968. This contradicted Hugh MacLennan's modest assessment of the value of his work among the scraps of papyri: "If an African scholar fifteen hundred years from now were to do a similar job on the waste-baskets of Regina, his would be an effort comparable to mine, and he would probably discover neither more nor less."

Barometer Rising

In the 1930s Hugh MacLennan wrote two unsuccessful, and unpub-
lished, novels; one was set in Europe, the other in the United States. It
was Dorothy Duncan, the American he met in 1932 and married four
years later, who suggested that he set his next work in Canada. At
that time, such a setting was sufficiently unusual that when Barome-
ter Rising was published in the fall of 1941, it began with this
Foreword from the author:

It seems necessary to offer more than a conventional statement
about the names of the characters in this book, since it is one of
the first ever written to use Halifax, Nova Scotia, for its sole
background. Because there is as yet no tradition of Canadian
literature, Canadians are apt to suspect that a novel referring to
one of their cities must likewise refer to specific individuals
among its characters. If the names of actual persons, living or
dead, have been used in this book, it is a coincidence and no
personal reference is intended.

Nova Scotia family names have, nevertheless, been employed;
to avoid them would have been too definite a loss. Since there is
no great variety in Scottish given names, the combinations are
inevitably repetitious. The characters are, it is hoped, true to
their background, and nothing more.

Eight days are involved in the story: Sunday, December second, to Monday, December tenth, in 1917.

The opening chapter introduces us to Neil Macrae, and to Halifax:

SUNDAY

Four o'clock

He had been walking around Halifax all day, as though by moving through familiar streets he could test whether he belonged here and had at last reached home. In the west the winter sky was brilliant and clouds massing under the sun were taking on colour, but smoke hung low in the streets, the cold air holding it down. He glanced through the dirty window of a cheap restaurant, saw the interior was empty and went in through the double doors. There was a counter and a man in a soiled apron behind it, a few tables and chairs, and a smell of mustard. He sat on one of the warped stools at the counter and ordered Bovril and a ham sandwich.

"You English?" the man behind the counter said.

"No. I used to live around here."

"Funny, I thought you were an English fella. You been over there, though?"

"I just got back."

He glanced restlessly over his shoulder before he let his muscles relax, but there was no need for caution in a restaurant like this. No one he had ever known in Halifax would be seen in the place.

"You been away long?" the restaurant man said. He poured steaming water over the glutinous Bovril essence after he had ladled it into a thick mug.

"Quite a while."

The man set the drink on the counter and began cutting slices from a loaf of brown bread.

"Guess you been in the war, too," he said. "I was in it myself for a while but I didn't get very far. I got to Quebec. My wife thinks that's funny. She says, when you got in the army you started moving backwards before you even began." He pulled a thin slice of boiled ham loose from a pile on a plate and slapped it on the bread.

"What was your outfit?" he said.

The customer stared at the counter without answering and the restaurant man shifted his feet uneasily.

"I was only asking. Hell, it's no skin off my ass."

"Never mind. I was with a lot of outfits, and I didn't sail from here in the first place."

"Mustard?" When he received no answer the man passed the sandwich over the counter. "A lot goes on in town these days. You'd be surprised."

The sandwich was eaten in a fierce silence, then he swallowed the Bovril in one passage of the cup to his mouth. He drew a deep breath and asked for more, and while the restaurant man was supplying it he asked casually, "Are you still in with the army around here?"

"No. They let me out on account of varicose veins. That's why I only got to Quebec."

A tram rumbled around the corner in the gathering shadows of the street and its flanges screamed on the uneven rails. The young man jerked nervously at the sudden noise and cleared his throat. All his muscles had tightened involuntarily, giving him a rigid appearance like an animal bunched for a spring. He remained taut and this physical tenseness invested his words with a dramatic value he did not intend.

"There's a chap I knew overseas," he said. "I was wondering if you'd ever heard of him. Alec MacKenzie . . . Big Alec, we called him."

"I knew a man called Alec MacKenzie once, but he was a little fella."

"Do you know Colonel Wain?"

The man shoved the second cup of Bovril closer to his customer. "How would a guy like me be knowing colonels?"

"I didn't mean was he a friend of yours. I meant, did you ever hear of him?"

"There's one Colonel Wain here in Halifax." He glanced at the younger man's thin and shabby overcoat. "But you wouldn't be meaning him, either. He's pretty rich, they say."

"So?" He picked up the mug and drained it slowly, then stood straight and looked at himself in the mirror behind the counter. The war had made as big a change in him as it seemed to have made in Halifax. His shoulders were wide, he was just under six feet tall, but his appearance was of run-down ill health, and he knew he looked much older than when he had left three years ago. Although he was barely twenty-eight, deep lines ran in parentheses around his mouth, and there was a nervous tic in his left cheek and a permanent tension in the expression of his eyes. His nails were broken and dirty, he carried himself without confidence, and it seemed an effort for him to be still for more than a moment at a time. In England he would have been labelled a gentleman who had lost caste.

He buttoned his coat and laid some coins on the counter. He turned to leave and then turned back. "This Colonel Wain . . . is he in town now?" he said.

"I saw his picture in the *Chronicle* last week some time," the restaurant man said. "I guess he must be."

When he left the café he turned toward George Street and slowly began the climb toward Citadel Hill. When he reached the last intersection he continued across the pavement, then upward along a wavering footpath through the unkempt grasses which rustled over the slope of the hill. He pulled himself up slowly, with a jerky nervousness that indicated he was not yet accustomed to his limping left leg, which seemed more to follow his body than propel it forward. At the top of the hill he stopped on a narrow footpath that outlined the rim of the star-shaped moat which defended the half-hidden buildings of the central garrison. An armed soldier stood guard over an open drawbridge giving access to the military enclosure. Over it all rose a flagpole and signal masts.

He turned about and surveyed the town. A thin breeze was dragging in from the sea; it was a soundless breath on the cheek, but it made him feel entirely solitary. Though it was early December, the winter snow had not yet fallen and the thin soil had frozen onto the rocks, the trees were bare and the grass was like straw, and the land itself had given up most of its colour.

The details of Halifax were dim in the fading light but the contours were clear and he had forgotten how good they were. The Great Glacier had once packed, scraped, and riven this whole land; it had gouged out the harbour and left as a legacy three drumlins . . . the hill on which he stood and two islands in the harbour itself. Halifax covers the whole of an oval peninsula, and the Citadel is about in the centre of it. He could look south to the open Atlantic and see where the park at the end of the town thrusts its nose directly into the outer harbour. At the park the water divides, spreading around the town on either side; to the west the inlet is called the Northwest Arm, to the east it is called the Stream, and it is here that the docks and ocean terminals are built. The Stream bends with the swell of Halifax peninsula and runs inland a distance of four miles from the park to a deep strait at the northern end of town called the Narrows. This strait opens directly into Bedford Basin, a lake-like expanse which bulges around the back of the town to the north.

He followed the footpath and looked for familiar landmarks, walking around the moat until he had boxed the compass. From here even a landsman could see why the harbour had for a century and a half been a link in the chain of British sea power. It is barricaded against Atlantic groundswells by McNab's Island at the mouth of the outer harbour, and by the smaller bowl of George's Island at the entrance to the Stream. It was defended now against enemy battle squadrons by forts set on rocky promontories running over the horizon into the sea. It was fenced off from prowling submarines by a steel net hung on pontoons from McNab's to the mainland. This harbour is the reason for the town's existence; it is all that matters in Halifax, for the place periodically sleeps between great wars. There had been a good many years since Napoleon, but now it was awake again.

The forests to the far west and north were nothing but shadows under the sky at this time of day. Above the horizon rim the remaining light was a turmoil of rose and saffron and pallid green, the colours of blood and flowers and the sheen of sunlight on summer grass. As his eyes shifted from the dull floor of the distant sea to this shredding blaze of glory crowning the continent, he felt an unexpected wave of exultation mount in his mind. Merely to have been born on the western side of the ocean gave a man something for which the traditions of the Old World could never compensate. This western land was his own country. He had forgotten how it was, but now he was back, and to be able to remain was worth risking everything.

After sunset the hilltop grew colder. The colours died quickly and as the landscape faded into darkness the street lights of the city came on. They made bluish pools at intervals along the narrow thoroughfares that fanned away from the roots of the hill, and all the way down to the waterfront the life of Halifax began to reveal itself in flashes. Barrington, Granville, and Hollis streets, running north and south, were visible only at the intersections where the inclines plunging from the hill to the waterfront crossed them, and at these corners pedestrians could be seen moving back and forth, merged in irregular streams.

Children were playing a game with a whole block of a George Street slum for their playground. They darted in and out of his vision as they pursued each other in and out of doorways and back and forth across the street. Here and there in the withered grass along the slope of the Citadel the forms of men and girls lay huddled, scarcely moving; they clung together on the frozen ground in spite of the cold, sailors with only a night on shore and local girls with no better place to be.

Halifax seemed to have acquired a meaning since he had left it in 1914. Quietly, almost imperceptibly, everything had become harnessed to the war. Long ribbons of light crossed on the surface of the water from the new oil refinery on the far shore of the Stream, and they all found their focus in himself. Occasionally they were broken, as undiscernible craft moved through the harbour, and he suddenly realized that this familiar inlet had become one of the most vital stretches of water in the world. It still gleamed faintly in the dusk as its surface retained a residual glow of daylight. Ferryboats glided like beetles across it, fanning ruffled water in their wake. A freighter drifted inland with a motion so slight he had to watch a full minute before it was perceptible. Its only identification was riding lights; no one but the port authorities knew its home port or its destination. While he watched, its anchor ran out with a muted clatter to the bottom and its bow swung to the north.

Then the Stream became static. The smoke of Halifax lay like clouds about a mountain; the spire of St. Mary's Cathedral cut George's Island in two; the only moving object was the beam of the lighthouse on McNab's, circling like a turning eye out to sea, along the coast and into the harbour again.

He descended the hill slowly, easing his left leg carefully along the dirt path. Down on the street the contours of Halifax were lost in the immediate reality of grim red brick and smoky stone. In the easy days before the war he had winced at the architecture, but it no longer bothered him. Halifax was obviously more than its buildings. Its functional aspect was magnificent, its solid docks piled with freight to the edge of deep water, Bedford Basin thronged with ships from all over the world, the grimy old naval and military buildings crowded once more with alert young men. However much he loathed the cause of this change, he found the throbbing life of the city at once a stimulation and a relief.

For twelve hours he had been back, and so far he had been recognized by no one. He stopped in the shadow of a doorway and the muscles of his face tightened again as his mind returned to its endless calculations. Big Alec MacKenzie had returned from France – and so had Wain. The colonel had probably been back for more than a year. The problem was to find MacKenzie before he himself was discovered by Wain. If only he could get to Big Alec first. . . . He began to smile to himself.

When he reached Barrington Street and the shops he found himself in a moving crowd. Girls with English faces brushed by him in twos and threes, sailors from a British cruiser rolled as though the pavement were a ship's deck. Although most of them were walking the main street because they had no better place to go – soldiers, dockworkers in flat cloth caps, civilians – they did not appear aimless. Even their idleness seemed to have a purpose, as though it were also part of the war.

By the time he had walked to the South End where the crowds were thinner, he realized that underneath all this war-begotten activity Halifax remained much the same. It had always looked an old town. It had a genius for looking old and for acting as though nothing could possibly happen to surprise it. Battalions passed through from the West, cargoes multiplied, convoys left every week and new ships took over their anchorages; yet underneath all this the old habits survived and the inhabitants did not alter. All of them still went to church regularly; he had watched them this morning. And he was certain they still drank tea with all their meals. The field-gun used in the past as a curfew for the garrison was fired from the Citadel every noon and at nine-thirty each night, and the townspeople took out their watches automatically twice a day to check the time. The Citadel itself flew the Union Jack in all weathers and was rightly considered a symbol and bastion of the British Empire.

Grinding on the cobblestones behind a pair of plunging Clydesdales came one of Halifax's most typical vehicles, a low-swung dray with a high driver's box, known as a sloven. This one was piled high with bags of feed and it almost knocked him down as the driver brought it around to level ground. He cursed as he jumped clear of the horses and the driver spat and flourished his whip, and the lash flicked in a quick, cracking arc over the sidewalk. The sloven moved north onto Barrington Street as the horses were pulled in to a walk. Traffic slowed down behind it, a few horns sounded and the column stopped behind a stationary tram.

His leg pained after the sudden pull on his muscles and he walked more slowly until the soreness abated. Images flashed through his mind and out again . . . shell-shock simultaneous with a smashed thigh and no time to be frightened by either; the flash of destruction out of the dark; who knew until it was experienced how intense the molten whiteness could be at the heart of an exploding chemical? . . . Naked when they picked him up, unconscious . . . and afterwards memory gone and no identity disk to help the base hospital.

The English doctor had done a fine job in mending his thigh and a better one in saving his reason. This, at least, had been no accident; more than twenty centuries of medical history had been behind that doctor. Even though his world was composed now of nothing but chance, it was unreasonable to believe that a series of accidents should ultimately matter. One chance must lead to another with no binding link but a peculiar tenacity which made him determined to preserve himself for a future which gave no promise of being superior to the past. It was his future, and that was all he could say of it. At the moment it was all he had.

A motor horn sounded and he leaped convulsively again. Every time a sudden noise struck his ears his jangled nerves set his limbs jumping and trembling in automatic convulsions which made him loathe his own body for being so helpless. He stopped and leaned against a lamppost until the trembling stopped. Like a fish on the end of a hook, he thought, squirming and fighting for no privilege except the opportunity to repeat the same performance later.

People moved past him in both directions, laughing, talking, indifferent. Were they too stupid to care what was happening to the world, or did they enjoy the prospect of a society in process of murdering itself? Did he care himself, for that matter; weren't any emotions he had left reduced to the simple desire for an acknowledged right to exist here in the place he knew as home? He had long ago given up the attempt to discover a social or spiritual reason which might justify what had happened to himself and millions of others during the past three years. If he could no longer be useful in the hell of Europe, then he must find a way to stay in Canada where he had been born.

He took his bearings when the trembling in his limbs subsided and was astonished to see how far south he had walked. Had the years in London made him lose all perspective of distance? He walked slowly to the next corner and knew he had reached his objective. But now he was here he felt nervous and unreasonably disappointed. He surveyed the cross-street to his right as though he were searching casually for his bearings, but he knew every inch of it and every doorway as far up the hill as he could see.

It seemed to have lost all its graciousness, and yet nothing was actually changed. Then he realized that he had been remembering it as it was in summer with the horse chestnuts and elms and limes towering their shade over the roofs, with the doorways secluded under vine-covered porches, with everything so quiet that it always seemed to be Sunday afternoon. Actually there was little difference; winter had always made it look bare, stripped as ruthlessly as the rest of Halifax. There was no town anywhere that changed in appearance so quickly when the foliage went.

He fumbled for a cigarette and lit it slowly, looking carefully in all directions as though he were deciding which way to shield himself from the wind. Then he began the steep ascent of the hill, his movements furtive and his hat pulled low over his left eye. He stopped at the crest and stood panting, hardly believing that after so much time he was really here, that the red house opposite had stayed just as he remembered it, that the trees still crowded its windows and the high wooden fence shut the garden away from the eyes of passersby.

At least the war had not dulled his trained appreciation of good architecture. Among the many nondescript Victorian houses of Halifax, this one stood out as a masterpiece. It was neither gracious nor beautiful, in a way it was almost forbidding, but it so typified the history and character of its town that it belonged exactly as it was: solid British colonial with a fanlight over the door, about six feet of lawn separating it from the sidewalk, four thick walls and no ells or additions, high ceilings and high windows, and shutters on the inside where they could be useful if not decorative. It had stood just as it was for over a hundred years; it looked permanent enough to last forever.

To cross the street and knock on the door, to take a chance on the right person opening it, would be so easy. Just a few movements and it would be done, and then whatever else he might feel, this loneliness which welled inside like a salt spring would disappear. Spasmodically he clasped one hand with the other and squeezed it hard, then turned back down the hill and followed it to Barrington Street.

There was nothing more he could do today. Sunday was the worst possible time to hunt for Alec MacKenzie or anyone else too poor to own a telephone. He walked north to the junction of Spring Garden Road and waited for a tram. Evening service was under way in St. Matthew's Church and the sound of a hymn penetrated its closed Gothic doors. "O God of Bethel by whose hand thy people still are fed . . . Who, through this weary pilgrimage, Hast all our fathers led. . . ."

The girls went by in twos and threes, sailors rolled past, evening loafers lounged against the stone wall of the military cemetery opposite, a soldier picked up a girl in front of the iron gate of the Crimean monument. "God of our fathers, be the God of their succeeding race." With a muffled sigh the congregation sat down.

A tram ground around the corner and stopped, heading north. Fifteen minutes later when he left it he could hear a low, vibrant, moaning sound that permeated everything, beating in over the housetops from the sea. For a second he was puzzled; it sounded like an animal at some distance, moaning with pain. Then he realized that the air was salty and moist and the odour of fish-meal was in his nostrils. The wind had changed and now it was bringing in the fog. Pavements were growing damp and bells and groaning buoys at the harbour-mouth were busy. When he reached his room in the cheap sailor's lodging he had rented that morning he lay down, and the sounds of the harbour seemed to be in the walls.

Inside the Wain house that evening, Penny Wain prepares to receive dinner guests, including some formidable relatives:

At a quarter to nine the doorbell rang, a prolonged jangling sound from the basement as half a dozen bells answered the puller by the front door. Before Penny could reach the hall, Alfred Wain and his wife Maria had let themselves in and were taking off their coats.

"'lo, Penelope," Alfred muttered absently. "Where's your father?"

"He's not back yet. How are both of you?"

"Not very good," Alfred said.

Aunt Maria's voice blared out like a trumpet. "Nonsense, there's nothing the matter with you. Penelope, why weren't you in church? There was a terrible sermon." She squinted at herself in the long mirror and patted the sides of her pompadour with a pair of powerful hands. "I ran into Mrs. Taylor this evening as we came out, that woman I was telling you about in the Red Cross. She's dreadful. People like that shouldn't be allowed to take part in the war."

Alfred was already on his way to the living-room, muttering as he went. "Geoffrey works too much. He's almost as bad as you, though I must say there's some sense to his job." He stood in front of the fire and rocked on his heels, while his hands, cupped behind his back, hoisted the tails of his jacket so that the hot fire could toast his buttocks. He was a gangling man with mutton-chop whiskers and a squeaky voice; he rarely did any work and his chief interest was the Presbyterian church in which he was an elder. There, twice a week and once at Wednesday prayer-meeting, he snored through sermons he later condemned, but he could estimate the collection value of any congregation to within half a dollar.

Aunt Maria stalked into the living-room and sat down in Geoffrey Wain's armchair, which she adequately filled. "Why is your father still working, Penelope?"

"I'm afraid that's one of the things I can't tell you, Aunt Maria."

"Nonsense, you mean you don't choose to. You're all the same. And look at Roddie. I wouldn't be surprised to see him turn out the worst of the lot."

There was a moment in which the room held no sound but the noise of Aunt Maria's breathing, which permeated it. She was a powerful woman with curly grey hair, ruddy cheeks, deep chest and a bosom that projected like a battlement. Although she was always dowdily dressed, nothing less than a crinoline could have concealed the contours of her thighs, which looked potent enough to appease a Hercules.

The clocks ticked noisily; there was a distant moan from the harbour buoys. Then Aunt Maria's voice broke out again. "Cecil has the grippe but Jim and Mary will be here. Who else is coming?"

"I've asked Major Angus Murray," Penny said.

"Who?" Her aunt stared. "Well, of all the things!"

"Eh?" said Alfred. "Who was that?"

"That man," Aunt Maria explained. "That Major Murray everyone knows about." She turned to Penny: "Is this your father's idea of a joke on us?"

"No." Penny got up from the arm of the chair where she had been sitting and moved toward the door. She hoped she had heard footsteps outside. "It was my idea," she said. "I thought he might enjoy it."

On Tuesday evening Neil Macrae is roaming the streets:

As he continued his walking of the pavements he felt at last that they belonged to him, and that Halifax for all its shabbiness was a good place to call his home. The life he had led in Europe and England these past two years had been worse than an empti-ness. It was as though he had been able to feel the old continent tearing out its own entrails as the ancient civilizations had done before it. There was no help there. For almost the first time in his life, he fully realized what being a Canadian meant. It was a heritage he had no intention of losing.

He stopped at a corner to wait for a tram, and his eyes reached above the roofs to the sky. Stars were visible, and a quarter moon. The sun had rolled on beyond Nova Scotia into the west. Now it was setting over Montreal and sending the shadow of the mountain deep into the valleys of Sherbrooke Street and Peel; it was turning the frozen St. Lawrence crimson and lining it with the blue shadows of the trees and buildings along its banks, while all the time the deep water poured seaward under the ice, draining off the Great Lakes into the Atlantic. Now the prairies were endless plains of glittering, bluish snow over which the wind passed in a firm and continuous flux, packing the drifts down hard over the wheat seeds frozen into the alluvial earth. Now in the Rockies the peaks were gleaming obelisks in the mid-afternoon. The railway line, that tenuous thread which bound Canada to both the great oceans and made her a nation, lay with one end in the darkness of Nova Scotia and the other in the flush of a British Columbian noon.

Under the excitement of this idea his throat became constricted and he had a furious desire for expression: this anomalous land, this sprawling waste of timber and rock and water where the only living sounds were the footfalls of animals or the fantastic laughter of a loon, this empty tract of primordial silences and winds and erosions and shifting colours, this bead-like string of crude towns and cities tied by nothing but railway tracks, this nation undiscovered by the rest of the world and unknown to itself, these people neither American nor English, nor even sure what they wanted to be, this unborn mightiness, this question-mark, this future for himself, and for God knew how many millions of mankind!

The tram came and he boarded it. Then he sat quite still looking sideways out the window to keep his face away from the passengers, as the car bore him north to his lodgings.

On Wednesday, night falls on Halifax:

A small troop of cavalry had been detailed to patrol the streets to watch for windows emitting light. There was no good reason for this order except the uneasy state of the official mind, which had resigned itself to the strategic failure of Passchendaele and another winter of war. A handful of men on horses went through the dark streets at a slow trot and occasionally one of them blew a bugle.

Maria Wain heard the bugle and the trotting horses and opened her shutters to look out. The troop halted and a man got off his horse, crossed the sidewalk and rang her doorbell. When they had gone, Alfred Wain, asleep in his armchair before the fire, stirred and sniffed. "Maria, what was that?"

"Soldiers. They said we had a light showing."

"Humbug!" he said, and closed his eyes again.

An hour later, Penelope and Roddie Wain heard the horses' feet and Roddie was careful to turn out his bedroom light before peering out. He looked down on the caps and shoulders of the horsemen trotting past, and saw the glint of moonlight on the bugle of the boy riding beside the leader. After they had passed, he came downstairs with wide eyes to find his sister.

Penelope, tired and worried and unable to sleep herself, told him to go back to bed; then, discovering that he would be certain not to sleep in any case, she made him produce his schoolbooks and went over his lessons one by one until they were all checked and Roddie was heavy-eyed. She then went up to his bedroom and tucked him in, and sat on the edge of his bed listening while he talked about the war. He could hardly remember when it had begun, but he horrified her with his precise and detailed knowledge of it. He could repeat from memory the tonnage and gunnage of every vessel in the navy and was looking forward to six years from now when he would be old enough to enlist. She had noticed that every one of his school scribblers had a picture of a soldier or a sailor on the cover, or a British bulldog standing on a White Ensign draped over the stern of a battleship while a Canadian beaver crouched in the corner and sharpened its teeth. As she heard him talk, she marvelled at the skill of the propagandists. Living in a great nation virtually guaranteed by the United States, the present crop of publicists seemed determined to convince Canadians that their happiness would be lost forever if they should aspire to anything higher than a position in the butler's pantry of the British Empire.

Roddie finally showed signs of sleepiness and she left him alone. The house was still now, so still she could hear in every room the ticking of its many clocks, but over everything seemed to throb the overtones of Neil's voice.

All that night the streets of Halifax remained dark and empty of traffic, and the whole town, this clearing in a forest fronting the sea, was utterly silent. Yet a panorama of history, vital and in the main unperceived, flowed through the minds of the seventy thousand people who at that moment inhabited the region marked on the map as Halifax peninsula.

In beds down the long wards of military hospitals lay hundreds of Canadians, some suffering, some bored, some asleep. They had gone to France from the prairies and the west coast, from Ontario and Quebec and the Maritimes, and soon they were going to be discharged back to the cities and the solitudes. Just as soon as they were well enough to exist without help they would be going home. But the war had altered the vision of them all, breaking some and healing the gashes it had made in others by enlarging their consciousness. They could never be the same again, nor could the land they had returned to inhabit.

On the ships anchored in Bedford Basin, men were talking in most of the languages of the Indo-European and Slavonic systems, playing cards and telling each other how it was in the places thousands of miles away from which they had come. Here in Bedford Basin, if thought had any meaning at all, Stockholm and Haugesund existed, and Rotterdam, Antwerp, Lisbon, Genoa, Marseilles, Odessa, and Cape Town. There were Lascars from Calcutta and Bombay, Latin Americans from Rio and Montevideo, Yankees from Boston, sailors from all the ports and havens of England. They were on ships anchored in an indentation of the coast of Nova Scotia, and they knew that one in every five of the ships was doomed to destruction. They wished they were in a port where there were lights and music and women, where a man could raise a thirst and forget the unreality of his skill; they wished they were almost any place in the world except here, bounded by the stars and the empty, inviolate North American forest surrounding them.

In the lighted offices of the Dockyard and the stately rooms of Admiralty House, and in various unnamed buildings along the waterfront, uniformed men on night duty were at work, tabulating orders and registering information. The official wireless crackled incessantly, and N.C.O. messengers came and went from the wireless room, delivering slips of paper to various officers. Incoming messages were read and filed, and notes of the movements of enemy submarines were emended in the light of later knowledge. Intelligence knew that a German submarine had just stolen out of the Bay of Biscay and was heading for Hell's Hole, that another was lying on the bottom near Queenstown waiting for the destroyers to go away, that still another was moving westward toward the shipping lane that passed Cape Race. They knew that a small British squadron was advancing into the Atlantic to meet a convoy at a secret rendezvous. The information was noted, tables and charts were checked and positions of shipping revised; minor alterations in projected courses were planned.

And in the consciousness of thousands of the generality of citizens who were still awake there lurked as their constant companion a brooding anxiety they rarely uttered, for they pictured sons, brothers, husbands, fathers, sweethearts somewhere in the lines about Arras or Ypres, and yet all were thankful that they were still able to be worried and that another day had passed without the receipt of a private letter from His Majesty.

The war had changed these people, too, but only slightly; it had merely splashed over their lives a little of the hatreds and miseries of the great cities, for quite unwittingly they lived tonight as they had done for years, with their thoughts and actions mainly determined by the habits they had inherited from their forefathers, from the Loyalists who had come here generations ago from the United States because they preferred King George to the new freedom, from the English who had settled in Halifax when their time of service in the garrison was up, from the Irish who had escaped the potato famine seventy years ago, from the Highlanders who had lost their clans at

Culloden. They lived in Halifax in an anomalous permanency, still tied to England, suffering when she did but rarely partaking of her prosperities, unreconciled to be Americans or even Canadians, content for the moment to let their status drift with events, convinced that in being Nova Scotians they possessed a peculiar cause for satisfaction, an excellence which no one had ever troubled to define because no one outside the province believed it existed, and everyone on the inside took it for granted.

On Thursday morning, December 6, 1917, the minutes tick away towards the Halifax Explosion:

Eight-fifteen o'clock

... There was now only one vessel moving north toward the upper harbour, the French munition ship *Mont Blanc*. An ugly craft of little more than three thousand tons, she was indistinguishable from thousands of similar vessels which came and went during these days. She was inward bound, heading for Bedford Basin to await convoy. Moving very slowly, she had crawled through the opened submarine net and now was on her way up the Stream, past the breakwater, George's Island, and then the South End docks. She had been laded a week ago in New York with a cargo consigned to a French port, but only her crew, the Admiralty authorities, and the captain of the British cruiser in port to command the convoy, knew what her main cargo was.

Men on the motionless ships in the Stream watched her pass and showed no interest. The previous day they had all received orders not to move until further notification, but none had been told they were giving sea-room to a floating bomb.

The cruiser's captain came on deck to watch the *Mont Blanc* pass and estimate the speed she would be able to produce. He was about the only person in the vicinity of Halifax to take any overt notice of her passage up the harbour.

The *Mont Blanc* moved so slowly that her bow seemed to push rather than cut the water as she crept past the cruiser. The pilot was proceeding cautiously and the cruiser's captain observed this with satisfaction. What was not so satisfactory to him was the manner in which the cargo was stowed. Her foredeck was piled with metal canisters, one on top of the other, held down with guy ropes and braced at the sides by an improvised skeleton of planks. The canisters and visible parts of the deck glistened patchily with oil. The after-deck was clear and some sailors in dungarees were lounging there out of the wind.

"I wonder what she's got in *those things?*" the captain muttered to his Number One. "Petrol?"

"More likely lubricating oil, I should think, sir."

"I doubt it. She's not a tanker, after all. Might be benzol from the colour of it. How much speed would you say she's got in her?"

"Ten knots at the most, I'd say."

"Doubt if it's even that. I wish they'd realize that a munition ship ought to be faster than the general run of ships. I can't have a cargo like that keeping station with the rest of them. She's got to cruise on the fringe, and she needs about three extra knots to do it."

But the *Mont Blanc* glided on up the harbour with little sound or evidence of motion except for a ripple at the bows and a thin wake. She was low in the water and slightly down by the head. A very sloppily laded ship, the cruiser's captain decided. She passed awkwardly onward, the pilot pulling her out to the exact centre of the channel as the harbour narrowed. The tricolour flapped feebly from her stern as she floated in, and as she reached the entrance to the Narrows, bells sounded in the engine-room calling for a still further reduction in speed.

Eight-forty o'clock

. . . The *Mont Blanc* was now in the Narrows and a detail of men went into her chains to unship the anchor. It would be dropped as soon as she reached her appointed station in the Basin. A hundred yards to port were the Shipyards and another hundred yards off the port bow was the blunt contour of Richmond Bluff; to starboard the shore sloped gently into a barren of spruce scrub. During the two minutes it took the *Mont Blanc* to glide through this strait, most of Bedford Basin and nearly all its flotilla of anchored freighters were hidden from her behind the rise of Richmond Bluff.

Around the projection of this hill, less than fifty fathoms off the port bow of the incoming *Mont Blanc*, another vessel suddenly appeared heading for the open sea. She flew the Norwegian flag, and to the startled pilot of the munitioner the name *Imo* was plainly visible beside the hawse. She was moving at half-speed and listing gently to port as she made the sharp turn out of the Basin to strike the channel of the Narrows. And so listing, with white water surging away from her fore-foot, she swept across the path of the *Mont Blanc*, exposing a gaunt flank labelled in giant letters BELGIAN RELIEF. Then she straightened, and pointed her bow directly at the fore-quarter of the munitioner. Only at that moment did the men on the *Imo's* bridge appear to realize that another vessel stood directly in their path.

Staccato orders broke from the bridge of the *Mont Blanc* as the two ships moved toward a single point. Bells jangled, and megaphoned shouts came from both bridges. The ships sheered in the same direction, then sheered back again. With a violent shock, the bow of the *Imo* struck the plates of the *Mont Blanc* and went grinding a third of the way through the deck and the forward hold. A shower of sparks splashed out from the screaming metal. The canisters on the deck of the *Mont Blanc* broke loose from their bindings and some of them tumbled and burst open. Then the vessels heeled away with engines reversed and the water boiling out from their screws as the propellers braked them to a standstill. They sprawled sideways across the Narrows, the *Mont Blanc* veering in toward the Halifax shore, the *Imo* spinning about with steerageway lost entirely. Finally she drifted toward the opposite shore.

For a fraction of a second there was intense silence. Then smoke appeared out of the shattered deck of the *Mont Blanc*, followed by a racing film of flame. The men on the bridge looked at each other. Scattered shouts broke from the stern, and the engine-room bells jangled again. Orders were half-drowned by a scream of rusty metal as some sailors amidships followed their own inclination and twisted the davits around to lower a boat. The scurry of feet grew louder as more sailors began to pour out through the hatches onto the deck. An officer ran forward with a hose, but before he could connect it his men were ready to abandon ship.

The film of flame raced and whitened, then it became deeper like an opaque and fulminant liquid, then swept over the canisters of benzol and increased to a roaring tide of heat. Black smoke billowed and rolled and engulfed the ship, which began to drift with the outgoing tide and swing in toward the graving-dock of the Shipyards. The first trembled and leaped in a body at the bridge, driving the captain and pilot aft, and there they stood helplessly while the tarry smoke surrounded them in greasy folds and the metal of the deck began to glow under their feet. Both men glanced downward. Underneath that metal lay leashed an incalculable energy, and the bonds which checked it were melting with every second the thermometers mounted in the hold. A half-million pounds of trinitrotoluol and twenty-three hundred tons of picric acid lay there in the darkness under the plates, while the fire above and below the deck converted the hollow shell of the vessel into a bake-oven.

If the captain had wished to scuttle the ship at that moment it would have been impossible to do so, for the heat between decks would have roasted alive any man who tried to reach the sea-cocks. By this time the entire crew was in the lifeboat. The officers followed, and the boat was rowed frantically toward the wooded slope opposite Halifax. There, by lying flat among the trees, the sailors hoped they would have a chance when their ship blew up. By the time they had beached the boat, the fore-deck of the *Mont Blanc* was a shaking rampart of fire, and black smoke pouring from it screened the Halifax waterfront from their eyes. The sailors broke and ran for the shelter of the woods.

By this time men were running out of dock sheds and ware-houses and offices along the entire waterfront to watch the burning ship. None of them knew she was a gigantic bomb. She had now come so close to the Shipyards that she menaced the graving-dock. Fire launches cut out from a pier farther south and headed for the Narrows. Signal flags fluttered from the Dockyard and the yardarms of ships lying in the Stream, some of which were already weighing anchor. The captain of the British cruiser piped all hands and called for volunteers to scuttle the *Mont Blanc*; a few minutes later the cruiser's launch was on its way to the Narrows with two officers and a number of ratings. By the time they reached the burning ship her plates were so hot that the seawater lapping the plimsoll line was simmering.

The *Mont Blanc* had become the centre of a static tableau. Her plates began to glow red and the swollen air inside her hold heated the cargo rapidly toward the detonation point. Launches from the harbour fire department surrounded her like midges and the water from their hoses arched up with infinite delicacy as they curved into the rolling smoke. The *Imo*, futile and forgotten, was still trying to claw her way off the farther shore.

Twenty minutes after the collision there was no one along the entire waterfront who was unaware that a ship was on fire in the harbour. The jetties and docks near the Narrows were crowded with people watching the show, and yet no warning of danger was given. At that particular moment there was no adequate centralized authority in Halifax to give a warning, and the few people who knew the nature of the *Mont Blanc*'s cargo had no means of notifying the town or spreading the alarm, and no comfort beyond the thought that trinitrotoluol can stand an almost unlimited heat provided there is no fulminate or explosive gas to detonate it.

Bells in the town struck the hour of nine, and by this time nearly all normal activity along the waterfront had been suspended. A tug had managed to grapple the *Mont Blanc* and was towing her with imperceptible movement away from the Shipyards back into the channel of the Narrows. Bluejackets from the cruiser had found the bosun's ladder left by the fleeing crew, and with flesh shrinking from the heat, were going over the side. Fire launches surrounded her. There was a static concentration, an intense expectancy in the faces of the firemen playing the hoses, a rhythmic reverberation in the beat of the flames, a gush from the hose-nozzles and a steady hiss of scalding water. Everything else for miles around seemed motionless and silent.

Then a needle of flaming gas, thin as the mast and of a brilliance unbelievably intense, shot through the deck of the *Mont Blanc* near the funnel and flashed more than two hundred feet toward the sky. The firemen were thrown back and their hoses jumped suddenly out of control and slashed the air with S-shaped designs. There were a few helpless shouts. Then all movement and life about the ship were encompassed in a sound beyond hearing as the *Mont Blanc* opened up.

Nine-five o'clock

Three forces were simultaneously created by the energy of the exploding ship: an earthquake, an air-concussion, and a tidal wave. These forces rushed away from the Narrows with a velocity varying in accordance with the nature of the medium in which they worked. It took only a few seconds for the earthquake to spend itself and three minutes for the air-expansions to slow down to a gale. The tidal wave travelled for hours before the last traces of it were swallowed in the open Atlantic.

When the shock struck the earth, the rigid ironstone and granite base of Halifax peninsula rocked and reverberated, pavements split and houses swayed as the earth trembled. Sixty miles away in the town of Truro windows broke and glass fell to the ground, tinkling in the stillness of the streets. But the ironstone was solid and when the shock had passed, it resumed its immobility.

The pressure of the exploding chemicals smashed against the town with the rigidity and force of driving steel. Solid and unbreathable, the forced wall of air struck against Fort Needham and Richmond Bluff and shaved them clean, smashed with one gigantic blow the North End of Halifax and destroyed it, telescoping houses or lifting them from their foundations, snapping trees and lampposts, and twisting iron rails into writhing, metal snakes; breaking buildings and sweeping the fragments of their wreckage for hundreds of yards in its course. It advanced two miles southward, shattering every flimsy house in its path, and within thirty seconds encountered the long, shield-like slope of the Citadel which rose before it.

Then, for the first time since it was fortified, the Citadel was able to defend at least a part of the town. The air-wall smote it, and was deflected in three directions. Thus some of its violence shot skyward at a twenty-degree angle and spent itself in space. The rest had to pour around the roots of the hill before closing in on the town for another rush forward. A minute after the detonation, the pressure was advancing through the South End. But now its power was diminished, and its velocity was barely twice that of a tornado. Trees tossed and doors broke inward, windows split into driving arrows of glass which buried themselves deep in interior walls. Here the houses, after swaying and cracking, were still on their foundations when the pressure had passed.

Underneath the keel of the *Mont Blanc* the water opened and the harbour bottom was deepened twenty feet along the channel of the Narrows. And then the displaced waters began to drive outward, rising against the towns and lifting ships and wreckage over the sides of the docks. It boiled over the shores and climbed the hill as far as the third cross-street, carrying with it the wreckage of small boats, fragments of fish, and somewhere, lost in thousands of tons of hissing brine, the bodies of men. The wave moved in a gigantic bore down the Stream to the sea, rolling some ships under and lifting others high on its crest, while anchor-chains cracked like guns as the violent thrust snapped them. Less than ten minutes after the detonation, it boiled over the breakwater off the park and advanced on McNab's Island, where it burst with a roar greater than a winter storm. And then the central volume of the wave rolled on to sea, high and arching and white at the top, its back glossy like the plumage of a bird. Hours later it lifted under the keel of a steamer far out in the Atlantic and the captain, feeling his vessel heave, thought he had struck a floating mine.

But long before this, the explosion had become manifest in new forms over Halifax. More than two thousand tons of red hot steel, splintered fragments of the *Mont Blanc*, fell like meteors from the sky into which they had been hurled a few seconds before. The ship's anchor soared over the peninsula and descended through a roof on the other side of the Northwest Arm three miles away. For a few seconds the harbour was dotted white with a maze of splashes, and the decks of raddled ships rang with reverberations and clangs as fragments struck them.

Over the North End of Halifax, immediately after the passage of the first pressure, the tormented air was laced with tongues of flame which roared and exploded out of the atmosphere, lashing downward like a myriad blow-torches as millions of cubic feet of gas took fire and exploded. The atmosphere went white-hot. It grew mottled, then fell to the streets like a crimson curtain. Almost before the last fragments of steel had ceased to fall, the wreckage of the wooden houses in the North End had begun to burn. And if there were any ruins which failed to ignite from falling flames, they began to burn from the fires in their own stoves, onto which they had collapsed.

Over this part of the town, rising in the shape of a typhoon from the Narrows and extending five miles into the sky, was poised a cloud formed by the exhausted gases. It hung still for many minutes, white, glossy as an ermine's back, serenely aloof. It cast its shadow over twenty miles of forest land behind Bedford Basin.

After the explosion, Neil Macrae is slapped back into consciousness by Angus Murray in the heart of the devastated North End of Halifax:

He felt Murray's arm across his shoulder.

"There's nothing the matter with you. You're an old soldier. When that ship went up you went flat on your face. Dove right off the doorstep into the street. Now – do you remember?"

"Yes, I remember now."

"We've got to dig Alec out – he's buried under the house somewhere. His wife's there too."

Neil smelled smoke and the acrid stench of an unfamiliar gas. Murray's twisted face lengthened and shortened in front of his eyes and then gradually quivered into steadiness as he recovered his focus. Murray was covered with dirt and his coat and uniform were torn, but he was uninjured. The street had disappeared. It was almost impossible to tell where the MacKenzie house had begun or ended. Every building in a space of three hundred acres had been smashed and hardly a single wall was standing. Alec's house had no intact planking larger than a door; it was split to kindlings and deluged with a fine dust of pulverized plaster. The main roof-beam stood upright, straight as a flag-pole in the heart of the wreckage, and by some vagary of the shock, the horsehair sofa on which Neil had spent the night was standing on its four legs on top of an upturned bath-tub which had been hurled through the toppling wall of a neighbour's house and now was resting twenty yards from its original position.

"Alec – where are you, MacKenzie?" Murray was already looking under broken beams and trying to heave some of the loose timber free. Neil's eyes ranged dizzily over the slope of the hill. It was a devastation more appalling than anything he had witnessed in France. The wooden houses had been punched inward and split apart, some of them had been hurled hundreds of feet; furniture, clothing, and human bodies were littered in swathes and patches among this debris. The trees and lampposts lining the street had disappeared, some of them uprooted and flung, others shorn or snapped jaggedly and lying where they fell, still others tangled with the general wreckage.

"Where are we, in front of the house or behind it?" Murray was looking in bewilderment at the wreckage.

Then Neil remembered that he and Murray and Alec had just been leaving the house, Murray and himself on the sidewalk and Alec still indoors.

"The place is catching fire! We've got to get a move on!"

"I'm all right now," Neil said. Where had these flames come from? With a sound like bracken igniting in thousands of campfires, the entire North End was taking fire. He felt sore places on his own scalp and along the back of his neck and saw that Murray's hair was singed. The flames – they had come from the sky, sharp torches spouting downward out of the atmosphere. But the fire was on the ground now. A flame three feet high was crackling in the wreckage of Alec's house.

Murray lifted his arms and let them fall limply to his sides. He turned back wearily to the wreckage to see if some of it could be cleared away.

Neil's ears were now hearing separate sounds and distinguishing them, the crackling of the flames and the cries of hidden voices, women and children screaming from under smoking heaps of timber and plaster and bricks. From a pile of rubble twenty feet off he saw a human hand wave feebly, then sink back and be still. And blackened figures were emerging everywhere, some of them crouching in the ruins and others crawling clear on hands and knees. They were like ants suddenly scrambling into daylight after their hill has been overturned. They were like soldiers crawling out of shelters into the smoking, heaving earth after a bombardment has passed.

Then suddenly he felt all right. It was as though the prospect of shock had torn at his nerves all these months and now he found his nerves better than he had hoped. The most appalling shock a mind could conceive had come and passed and he was all right. He leaped forward to the edge of the flames, and Murray grunted as he reached his side.

"I think he's under here. Help me lift this beam. Bloody hand of mine's useless."

Neil bent and heaved on the beam but it would not give. Some of the side-wall still pinned it at one end. He picked up a heavy board that once had been a door-jamb, inserted it under the beam and pressed. The beam yielded, lifted a few inches and slithered to one side, making a triangular gap four feet across at its base. Neil crawled through the aperture; his legs slipped and he dropped on all fours to the cellar floor. The place was filled with smoke and dust and he could see nothing. He shouted once and heard an answering groan. Then Murray's muffled voice came down from above. "Don't get yourself trapped down there!"

The dust was choking him and wherever he moved he stumbled over something. He reached in his pocket and pulled out a match and struck it against the seat of his pants. Immediately an arrow of flame darted away from him; there was a quick flash and shock and a noise like thunder. Gas escaping from a broken main had entered the foundation and formed pockets in the wreckage and his match had touched off the train. The ruins jerked upward and separated, then settled back noisily with a sound of cracking wood. Something knocked him to his knees but he was not hurt. As he rose, he saw patches of daylight above him and realized that the exploding gas had scattered some of the wreckage.

"What the hell are you doing down there?"

He heard Murray's voice, near and urgent, shouting from above, and squirmed out through a jumble of planks, tearing his clothes and his skin. He was almost back at the street level and Murray was sweating at the same plank they had tried to lever before. Then a low moan sounded near them and when Neil had cleared out a few loose boards he saw Alec's face.

The big man was crouching like Sampson, with spread arms

holding apart two beams which crossed over his shoulders like a pair of shears. His face was distorted and the sweat was already washing a tide of dust down to his neck. He moved his head and seemed to be nodding toward something under his feet. Murray came over and together he and Neil pressed the beams farther apart. Then Neil crouched and got into the space between Alec's legs and found Annie lying there unconscious. Getting his feet under her arm-pits and lying on his back, he pulled backward with his elbows as props until he had drawn her clear. There was no visible wound on her body and she was still breathing.

Then he turned to help Murray and for a second the two men were immobile as they strained on the beams which sheared down on Alec's shoulders. All around them the ruins were on fire and the flames were already close about Murray's legs. Neil finally gave a lurch forward and the shears yielded. As they slithered sideways off Alec's back, the big man's face twisted and he gave a low cry, and then fell forward insensible. "God," Murray muttered. "There was a spike in one of those beams! It got his lung."

They pulled Alec and his wife clear of the fire and Murray cut the coat off Alec's back with a piece of broken glass. It was a deep wound, and the blood looked arterial. Murray gestured toward Annie and Neil bent and tore off her skirt. Murray ripped it into sections and made a pad which he bound across the wounded back with Alec's own belt. Then he sat back on his haunches and rubbed the sweat off his forehead. "If we move him we'll probably kill him. If we leave him here, he'll burn. Oh Christ – is there anything on wheels around here?"

Neil sat still and panted. Figures of stunned and wounded people were crawling and stumbling in and out of foundations and ruins, appearing and disappearing in the smoke. There was no sense or direction in their movements and their number never seemed to change. He shook his head and coughed. "Where's the nearest hospital?" he said.

"God knows if any hospitals are left."

Two Solitudes

Two Solitudes was published on January 17, 1945, to such enthusiastic reviews that by noon of that day the entire first printing was sold out. In tackling the grand theme of friction between English- and French-speaking Canadians, Hugh MacLennan changed the language of political debate. Sadly, while the phrase "two solitudes" remains in common use, few of those who use it so glibly remember the rest of the Rilke quotation from which it comes, "Love consists in this, that two solitudes, protect, and touch, and greet each other."

The novel opens with what is perhaps the best-known passage in Hugh MacLennan's work:

PART ONE   1917-1918

1

Northwest of Montreal, through a valley always in sight of the low mountains of the Laurentian Shield, the Ottawa River flows out of Protestant Ontario into Catholic Quebec. It comes down broad and ale-coloured and joins the Saint Lawrence, the two streams embrace the pan of Montreal Island, the Ottawa merges and loses itself, and the mainstream moves northeastward a thousand miles to the sea.

Nowhere has nature wasted herself as she has here. There is enough water in the Saint Lawrence alone to irrigate half of Europe, but the river pours right out of the continent into the sea. No amount of water can irrigate stones, and most of Quebec is solid rock. It is as though millions of years back in geologic time a sword had been plunged through the rock from the

Atlantic to the Great Lakes and savagely wrenched out again, and the pure water of the continental reservoir, unmuddied and almost useless to farmers, drains untouchably away. In summer the cloud packs pass over it in soft, cumulus, pacific towers, endlessly forming and dissolving to make a welter of movement about the sun. In winter when there is no storm the sky is generally empty, blue and glittering over the ice and snow, and the sun stares out of it like a cyclops' eye.

All the narrow plain between the Saint Lawrence and the hills is worked hard. From the Ontario border down to the beginning of the estuary, the farmland runs in two delicate bands along the shores, with roads like a pair of village main streets a thousand miles long, each parallel to the river. All the good land was broken long ago, occupied and divided among seigneurs and their sons, and then among tenants and their sons. Bleak wooden fences separate each strip of farm from its neighbour, running straight as rulers set at right angles to the river to form long narrow rectangles pointing inland. The ploughed land looks like the course of a gigantic and empty steeplechase where all motion has been frozen. Every inch of it is measured, and brooded over by notaries, and blessed by priests.

You can look north across the plain from the river and see the farms between their fences tilting towards the forest, and beyond them the line of trees crawling shaggily up the slope of the hills. The forest crosses the watershed into an evergreen bush that spreads far to the north, lake-dotted and mostly unknown, until it reaches the tundra. The tundra goes to the lower straits of the Arctic Ocean. Nothing lives on it but a few prospectors and hard-rock miners and Mounted Policemen and animals and the flies that brood over the barrens in summer like haze. Winters make it a universe of snow with a terrible wind keening over it, and beyond its horizons the northern lights flare into walls of shifting electric colours that crack and roar like the gods of a dead planet talking to each other out of the dark.

But down in the angle at Montreal, on the island about which the two rivers join, there is little of this sense of new and endless space. Two old races and religions meet here and live their separate legends, side by side. If this sprawling half-continent has a heart, here it is. Its pulse throbs out along the rivers and railroads; slow, reluctant and rarely simple, a double beat, a self-moved reciprocation.

The next chapter takes us down to the farmland on that "narrow plain," to the fictional parish of Saint-Marc, to meet one of the "old races and religions" in the person of Father Émile Beaubien, the parish priest:

. . . Thinking about the war, Father Beaubien's dark face set into a heavy frown. So far Saint-Marc had kept fairly clear of it. Only one member of the parish had volunteered, and he was on a spree in Trois Rivières when the recruiting sergeants got him. He was no good anyway, always missing masses. But this year the English provinces had imposed conscription on the whole country, trying to force their conquest on Quebec a second time. Conscription officers had been in the neighbouring parish of Sainte-Justine and had taken young French Canadians out of their homes like thieves to put them into the army.

The priest's solid jaw set hard. His superiors had ordered him not to preach against the war and he had obeyed them. He did not question their wisdom; they knew more than he did. But at least his parish knew how he stood. He thought of the war and the English with the same bitterness. How could French Canadians – the only real Canadians – feel loyalty to a people who had conquered and humiliated them, and were Protestant anyway? France herself was no better; she had deserted her Canadians a century and a half ago, had left them in the snow and ice along the Saint Lawrence surrounded by their enemies, had later murdered her anointed king and then turned atheist. Father Beaubien had no fondness for the Germans and no wish for them to win the war; he knew nothing whatever about them. But he certainly knew that if a people deserted God they were punished for it, and France was being punished now.

He turned back towards his presbytery and paused on the lawn to pick up an acorn dropped from his great oak. As he did so the silence was cracked again by a pair of gunshots down in the marsh. The priest held the acorn in his palm, looking at it, then he polished it firmly between his thumb and forefinger. This nut was like his own parish of Saint-Marc-des-Érables. It was perfect. You could not change or improve it, you could not graft it to anything else. But you put it into the earth, and you left it to God, and through God's miracle it became another oak. His mind moving slowly, cautiously as always, the priest visioned the whole of French Canada as a seed-bed for God, a seminary of French parishes speaking the plain old French of their Norman forefathers, continuing the battle of the Counter-Reformation. Everyone in the parish knew the name of every father and grandfather and uncle and cousin and sister and brother and aunt, remembered the few who had married into neighbouring parishes, and the many young men and women who had married the Church itself. Let the rest of the world murder itself through war, cheat itself in business, destroy its peace with new inventions and the frantic American rush after money. Quebec remembered God and her own soul, and these were all she needed.

Suddenly, as he went back to his porch, the priest heard the trotting hooves of a horse coming down the road into the village from the direction of Sainte-Justine. Shortly before dinner he had seen Athanase Tallard and Blanchard, Tallard's farm manager, drive past on their way out of the village. Now they were coming back, having met the afternoon train from the city at Sainte-Justine. Father Beaubien felt a twinge of uncertainty as the horse's hooves beat nearer.

Athanase Tallard was the only limit, under God and the law, to the priest's authority in Saint-Marc. Since the days of the early French colonization, the Tallards had been seigneurs. For more than two hundred years social opinion in Saint-Marc had depended not only on the parish priest, but also on whoever happened to be head of the Tallard family. Most of their seigniory had been broken up during the latter half of the nineteenth century and they collected no more rents. But the family still seemed enormously rich to the rest of the parishioners. Athanase owned by inheritance three times more land than anyone else in Saint-Marc, and he hired men to work it. He also owned a toll-bridge over a small tributary river at the lower end of the parish, and this brought him far more money than came from his crops. In many respects his surface authority was as great as that of the priest himself, and his manner of a great gentleman increased it.

The people of Saint-Marc had always been proud of the Tallards. They were of their own stock and neighbourhood, yet they had always amounted to something in the outside world. In the historic days of the eighteenth century they had been noblemen. A Tallard had been a seigneur and officer in the colonial army of France at the same time a kinsman of the same name, back in Europe, lost the battle of Blenheim to the Duke of Marlborough. Another Tallard had won a skirmish against the English redcoats in the Rising of 1837. But along with other institutions, they had gradually become more prosaic. Since the confederation of the provinces into the Dominion of Canada just after the American Civil War, a Tallard had always sat in Parliament in Ottawa.

Unlike most French Canadians, they had never been a prolific family. Athanase himself was an only child, and after two marriages had only two sons. Although Catholics, they were traditionally anti-clerical, and apt to make trouble for their priests. Saint-Marc still talked about the grandfather of Athanase, who had once chased a priest through the village with a whip.

The horse came into Father Beaubien's view, trotting fast and pulling Tallard's best carriage. Four men were in the vehicle, two in front and two behind. It stopped before Drouin's store and Blanchard dropped off, touching his cap to Athanase before he turned to enter the store. Then the carriage drove on past the presbytery as Tallard looked and nodded to the priest, dipping his whip with a graceful flourish. The priest returned the nod and the carriage went on beyond the village along the river road.

Suddenly Father Beaubien's big hands flexed, open and shut, Recounting the scene in his mind, he realized now that the two men in the carriage with Athanase were English Canadians. Their faces as well as their clothes showed it clearly. He dropped his hands to his sides and walked quietly down the path to the road and looked after the carriage. The road ran straight for a mile and he could see the carriage diminish to a small black speck before it turned at a tall maple tree and disappeared. The priest frowned. They had not entered the Tallard property. It was the Dansereau place they were visiting, and it was up for sale because Dansereau was a childless widower who had contributed heavily to the new church and now was in debt. . . .

Marius Tallard, the elder son of Saint-Marc's leading family, discovers a gift for oratory while addressing an anti-conscription crowd in east-end Montreal. Exhilarated by success, he walks his girl-friend home through the dark streets:

He turned and without looking back he went along the way he had come. Alone in the dingy street, a sense of relief and exhilaration came over him. He looked up at the sky. The moon was entering its last quarter, surging through a wrack of cirrus cloud high above the dark roofs. Even in the city the spring air was sweet. He found himself remembering Saint-Marc as it looked from the ridge behind the parish on such a night as this.

He stopped at the corner to wait for a tram. And then he saw the soldier who had been at the meeting. The man had followed him, and now he was waiting. Marius looked the other way, but the fellow came and stood close beside him. He took a quick glance up and down the street, but there was no one in sight within a couple of blocks. An arc lamp overhead made a bluish splash of light on the pavement, and across the street another lamp brought out the stripes on a barber's pole.

The soldier edged in against him. "Listen, you goddam peasoup, you're too fast with your mouth. Sure, I followed you. Somebody's got to shut that trap of yours."

Marius was trembling. He had no defence against physical violence. "I don't know what you mean," he said in English.

"No? Well, I'll tell you." The soldier came closer, taking his time. The smell of stale whiskey was on his breath. "I been over in France. See? There's a war on there. And a lot of French guys from right here was in my outfit. They're doing a job. And back home bastards like you kick them in the ass. Yellow sons of bitches like you stay here and shoot their mouths off."

Marius turned and looked at the soldier's face. Everything he most hated about the English was in it. He saw hardness and coldness, a supreme ability to outrage others, a way of forcing themselves on more sensitive people, but never letting themselves be touched in the process.

"Why don't you run?" the soldier said. "You're so yellow you look green."

Once Marius had seen a lumberjack just out of the woods handle a man in Saint-Marc who was drunk on *whiskey blanc*. He drove out with his foot now the way the lumberjack had done and caught the soldier on the shin. The man hopped back, lifting his leg to ease the pain. Before he could shout Marius hit him and the soldier went down. Marius fell on him, his knees taking the man in the face. He heard the soldier's front teeth crack and his skull snap on the sidewalk. He got up and stared at the limp body. A little splutter of blood started out of the soldier's mouth. Marius began to tremble violently, afraid he had killed the man. He looked quickly up and down the street, saw a figure moving toward them about two blocks away, then bent and placed his ear against the soldier's chest. The man stirred and tried to grip his neck with his arm, but Marius broke loose and got to his feet again.

He stood panting, his black hair over his eyes and his felt hat on the pavement a few yards away where it had fallen. The soldier was stirring like a knocked-out boxer trying to grope his way to his feet. Slowly he sat up, his mouth open and red with blood, bracing himself with his hands.

Marius watched him for a moment, then he picked up his hat and walked quickly away. The sight of the man's bleeding mouth, the sound of the cracking teeth, blazed and roared in his mind until he could see and hear nothing else. He looked back at the first intersection. The soldier was on his feet, swaying unsteadily, and a policeman was asking him questions.

Marius turned quickly to his left and began to run. He kept on running for three blocks, his hat in his hand, the echo of his pounding feet banging back at him from the housefronts. Suddenly he darted into an alley and then he stopped, doubled over and gasping until the wind returned to his lungs and he was able to walk again. He put on his hat, adjusted his coat, turned up his collar and pulled his hat down over his eyes. Under his coat his shirt was wet against his back. He put his hands in his pockets and began to walk west until he reached Saint-Denis Street. Here under the brighter lights he was no longer alone. A few drunks and loafers and late workers were still around, and a prostitute accosted him as he passed her. He boarded a tram and took a seat in the middle, alone in the long car with the wicker seats yellow as straw in the light.

He felt wonderful. He felt as if he had broken all the chains that had held him all his life. His chest swelled under his coat as he filled it with more and more air, and a smile appeared on his mouth, cutting deep wrinkles on either side of it as his thoughts rolled.

After tonight they would certainly try to get him. They might even print in the English papers that he was a wanted man. But no one would get him. Now or any other time. He would go to his lodgings and pack his bag and disappear. Montreal was a great city and there were many places to hide. It would have been better if he had found the money two weeks ago in Saint-Marc. But he would still be all right. There were plenty of people ready to help him, to help anyone who was determined to keep out of the army in order to defy the English and assert his rights as a French Canadian. And he would be doing even more than that. He was saving himself for his career, a career that he knew now would be a crusade.

Athanase Tallard, father of Marius and young Paul, sits as a Quebec Member of Parliament in Ottawa. He is returning from there by rail:

The fields, beautiful in the afternoon sun, slipped past the train. They were running through French parishes now, and on both sides of the train there were familiar figures with bowed shoulders going about their work, an essential part of the general landscape. French Canadians in the farmland were bound to the soil more truly than to any human being; with God and their families, it was their immortality. The land chained them and held them down, it turned their walk into a plodding and their hands into gnarled tools. It made them innocent of almost everything that existed beyond their own horizon. But it also made them loyal to their race as to a family unit, and this conception of themselves as a unique brotherhood of the land was part of the legend at the core of Quebec. Even when it exasperated him, Athanase was still proud of it.

Across the aisle two men were talking in English. Out of carelessness or indifference their voices were plainly audible.

"This whole province is hopeless," one of them was saying as he swept the scene through the windows with his hand. "They can't think for themselves and never could and never will. Now in Toronto we . . ."

Athanase's lined face remained motionless as he listened to them. The satisfaction in their voices as they talked about Quebec spread like grease.

"Labour's cheap here. That's one good thing. But my God, trying to do any business here gets you so tangled up with priests and notaries you don't know where you are! Now in Toronto . . ."

Athanase swung his chair around and turned his back on them. If there had been the slightest suggestion of kindliness, the least indication of a willingness to believe the best of Quebec in such men as this from Ontario, Canada's trenchant problem would cease to exist. He let his brows fall into a frown now and he deliberately breathed deeply as though in search of fresh air to fill his lungs. Little by little he managed to pull his thoughts back to himself.

Huntly McQueen represents the Canadian business establishment, then based in St. James Street in Montreal. MacLennan's portrait reminded many readers of Prime Minister Mackenzie King. It is interesting to note that the full extent of the Prime Minister's reliance on his dead mother for advice did not emerge until his private diaries were released, long after this imaginative account was created:

At precisely two minutes to nine-thirty on Monday morning, Huntly McQueen stepped out of his Cadillac town-car and entered the Bank Building in Saint James Street. He was dressed in a dark suit, a black coat, a black hat, a dark blue tie very large in a winged collar. In the tie he wore a pearl pin.

He passed through a pair of bronze doors, was saluted by the ex-sergeant of Coldstream Guards who stood there in livery, and entered a marble atrium as impersonal as a mausoleum. He joined a group of middle-aged and elderly men waiting for an elevator at the far end of the atrium. They were all dressed exactly like himself. Nods passed between them, they stepped into the elevator, shot each other a few more discreet glances as though to make certain that nothing important had happened in their lives over the weekend, then stared straight ahead as the cage moved upward.

On the second floor Sir Rupert Irons got out. He had a heavily hard body, was square in the head, face, jaws and shoulders; his hair was parted in the middle and squared off to either side of his perpendicular temples. His face was familiar to most Canadians, for it stared at them from small, plain portraits hanging on the walls of banks all the way from Halifax to Vancouver. Even in the pictures his neck was ridged with muscles acquired from a life-long habit of stiffening his jaw and pushing it forward during all business conversations.

On the fourth floor MacIntosh got out. He shuffled off toward his office, a round-shouldered, worrying man who carried in his head the essential statistics on three metal mines, two chemical factories, complicated relationships involving several international companies controlled in London and New York, and one corset factory.

On the seventh floor Masterman got out, to enter the offices of Minto Power. Although Minto harnessed the waters of one of the deepest and wildest rivers in the world, there was nothing about Masterman to suggest the elemental. He was a thin, punctilious man with a clipped moustache, a knife-edge press in his dark trousers, and a great reputation for culture among his associates in Saint James Street. He was one of the original members of the Committee of Art. He also belonged to a literary society which encouraged its members to read to each other their own compositions at meetings; he was considered its most brilliant member because he had published a book called *Gentlemen, the King!* The work was an historical record of all the royal tours conducted through Canada since Confederation.

One floor higher, Chislett got out: nickel, copper and coal, a reputation for dominating every board he sat on, and so great a talent for keeping his mouth shut that even McQueen envied it.

The elevator continued with McQueen to the top floor. The thought crossed his mind that if an accident had occurred between the first and second floors, half a million men would at that instant have lost their masters. It was an alarming thought. It was also ironic, for these individuals were so remote from the beings they governed, they operated with such cantilevered

indirections, that they could all die at once without even ruf-
fling the sleep of the remote employees on the distant end of the
chain of cause and effect. The structure of interlocking directorates which governed the nation's finances, subject always to an
exceptionally discreet Parliament, seemed to McQueen so delicate that a puff of breath could make the whole edifice quiver.
But no, McQueen smiled at his own thoughts, the structure was
quite strong enough. The men who had ridden together in the
elevator this morning were so sound they seldom told even their
wives what they thought or did or hoped to do. Indeed, Sir
Rupert Irons was so careful he had no wife at all. They were
Presbyterians to a man, they went to church regularly, and Irons
was known to believe quite literally in predestination.

The elevator stopped to let McQueen out. His own preserves
occupied half the top floor of the Bank Building. Beyond a
sizeable reception room there were half a dozen small offices in
which carefully selected executives did their work. McQueen's
private office was in the far corner, reached through the room of
his private secretary.

His round face smiled abstractedly at the switchboard girl and
the typists as he went through the large room. It was his practice
to enter his office by this route rather than through the private
door from the outside hall to which he alone had a key, but he
never lingered on his way. As he opened the door to his secretary's room she looked up brightly. "Good morning, Mr.
McQueen."

"Good morning, Miss Drew."

"It's a fine day."

"Yes," he said. "It may well turn out a fine day." He let a cool
smile fall in her direction before he went into his own office,
where he took off his hat and coat, hung them methodically in a
cupboard, straightened his tie, pulled his coat down in the rear,
and stood looking out the window as he did every morning
before he settled down to work.

McQueen's office overlooked one of the panoramas of the
world. Its windows opened directly on the port of Montreal,
and from them he could look across the plain to the distant
mountains across the American border. The Saint Lawrence, a
mile wide, swept in a splendid curve along the southern bend of

the island on which the city stood. Everything below the window seemed to lead to the docks, but there were few ships in them now. Since the war most of the ocean-going craft sailed under convoy from Halifax. The few vessels that were visible were all painted North Atlantic grey, with guns under tarpaulins pointing astern.

McQueen's satisfaction constantly renewed itself through his ability to overlook all this. He felt himself at the exact centre of the country's heart, at the meeting-place of ships, railroads and people, at the precise point where the interlocking directorates of Canada found their balance. Saint James Street was by no means as powerful as Wall Street or The City, but, considering the small population of the country behind it, McQueen felt it ranked uniquely high. There was tenacity in Saint James Street. They knew how to keep their mouths shut and take the cash and let the credit go. They were bothered by no doubts. They had definite advantages over the British and Americans, for they could always play the other two off one against the other. Americans talked too much and the British made the mistake of underrating them. McQueen smiled. That gave the Canadians an advantage both ways. More than one powerful American of international reputation had lost his shirt to Sir Rupert Irons.

McQueen turned from the window, letting his glance rest casually on the furnishings of the room before he became immersed in work. By the window was an oversized globe on a heavy wooden stand. Behind his desk was a relief map of Canada, ceiling-high, dotted with coloured pins at various points to indicate where his enterprises and interests were located. An oriental rug covered the floor. Opposite his desk was an oil painting of his mother, with fresh flowers in a bowl beneath it.

Because of the manner of its furnishing, this office had acquired something of a romantic reputation in Saint James Street. Some men considered it eccentric. Few were permitted to enter it, and those who did exaggerated the luxury of its furnishings afterwards. It did nothing to lessen the respect in which McQueen was held as a man who kept his mouth shut about all important matters, talked freely of trivialities, and was uncannily successful.

A change of expression appeared on his face as he crossed to his mother's portrait. Every morning Miss Drew put a dozen fresh flowers in the cut-glass bowl on the small table beneath it. The flowers were never arranged quite to suit him, and now he spent some time moving the stem of each daffodil until the effect met his approval. He looked up at the picture. His mother's was a small, sad face, lips tight, hair in a frizz over her forehead, neck enclosed by the sort of dog-collar made fashionable by Queen Alexandra. Her face as a whole distilled a Scottish kind of sternness, a Scottish melancholy that finds pleasure only in sad ideas. Except when he was alone in the room, McQueen never even glanced at the portrait, but whenever he had a decision to make he shut everyone out and communed with the picture, and after he had looked at it long enough he was usually able to feel that his mother was silently advising him what to do. It was the most closely guarded of all his secrets.

Now he turned to his desk and his expression changed again. His eyes, widely set and intelligent in his moon-face, became opaque in their blueness. His lips compressed themselves. Deliberately he read through his mail and the letters crackled as he thumbed them through. When he reached the bottom of the pile he buzzed for his secretary.

Miss Drew opened the door soundlessly and stood waiting. She was fifty, she wore nothing but tweeds winter and summer, her hair was dull grey and she had been with him since the beginning of his career in Ontario twenty years before. He suspected that she knew the details of his enterprises as well as he did himself. But not the sense of balance, the delicate grip of the whole; not the logical feel for cause and effect that pulled the future out of mystery and sometimes caused McQueen to wonder if he were a genius.

The English-speaking newcomer to Saint-Marc, Captain Yardley, becomes popular with the Tallard family, especially young Paul, and with the rest of the community. But when his daughter Janet joins him with her children, the war in Europe reaches all the way to Saint-Marc:

It was a day in early July when Janet Methuen stood in Polycarpe Drouin's store with a letter in her hand from His Majesty the King, via the Canadian Ministry of Defence. She read it through, and when she had finished she lifted her head and looked around the store, seeing nothing. She began to walk forward and bumped into the side of the Percheron model, her arms hanging at her sides, the letter in one hand and the envelope in the other.

Drouin came from behind the counter. His voice was soft and kind, his face wrinkled, his eyes friendly. "You are all right, Madame?"

Janet turned her head rigidly and saw his tap-like nose and the wrinkles about his eyes blur and then waver into focus. She saw him look at the letter in her hand and immediately she lifted her chin. She was as pale as unbleached muslin.

"I get you a drink, maybe?" Drouin said.

She heard her own voice, like a scratchy phonograph in another room, "I'm quite all right, thank you." But she continued to stand without moving.

Drouin went to the kitchen behind the store and returned with a glass of water, spilling some of it in his hurry. When he offered it she gave him a frozen smile. "I'm quite all right, thank you," she repeated tonelessly.

Her mind kept repeating a phrase she had read months ago in a magazine story: "I mustn't let people see it. . . . I mustn't let people see. . . . I mustn't let . . ." The words jabbered in her mind like the speech of an idiot.

Drouin looked sideways at the only other person in the store, a farmer who had come in to buy some tar-paper. Their eyes met and both men nodded. The farmer had also seen the long envelope with O.H.M.S. in one corner.

"Get a chair, Jacques," Drouin said in French. "The lady wants to sit down." But before the man could get one to her, Janet went to the door and walked out. The silence in her wake was broken as the chair hit the floor. Drouin shook his head and went around behind the counter. "That's a terrible thing," he said.

"Her husband, maybe?"

"The old captain says her husband is overseas."

The farmer scratched his head. "When I saw that letter this morning," Drouin went on, "I said to my wife, that's a bad thing, a letter like that. You never hear anything good from the government in Ottawa, I said."

The farmer was still scratching his head. "And she didn't cry," he said. "Well, maybe she don't know how."

Drouin bent forward over the counter in his usual jack-knife position, his chin on the heels of his hands. After a time he said, "You can't tell about the English. But maybe the old captain will be hurt bad," he added, as though he had just thought of it.

Out on the plain the sun was overcast by smoke from distant forest-fires to the north. On the river the hull of a lake boat was lifted chunkily by the mirage. An iron-wheeled cart clanked slowly past Janet, but she was unaware of the farmer standing in the front of it, holding the reins. The tobacco stains in his heavy moustache were orange in the eerie light. His cart held a load of steaming manure. After it had gone by, Janet stopped and drew several deep, panting breaths of hot air. She looked about and saw that she was no longer hemmed in by the sides of houses and the faces of strange people. She touched her eyes with the back of her hand and took the hand away dry. Then she began to walk very fast down the road to her father's house. All the stories she had ever read in which one of the characters received bad news of a bereavement began to chase each other through her mind. Idiotically, they got out of control, they became herself. She was each of the characters in turn, bravely keeping her personal grief from intruding on others, she was nothing but memories and the things which had made her what she was.

At school, years ago in Montreal, she had been a shy girl without money among girls whose families were rich. She knew none of them, but they had all grown up together. When they looked pointedly at her clothes and asked where she came from, she had not been able to answer because they made her feel that she came from nowhere. Her father was at sea nearly all the time, sailing around the world, and her mother moved from one port to another to be near him while he was ashore. Before Janet had been in the Montreal school a fortnight she realized that proper people go to sea as passengers on a liner, not as sailors. From then on her father's profession was never mentioned; it was better to speak of her mother, who had been born in England.

Ursula Yardley's values were those of her class, and her class had always been the colonial civil service. Her father had upheld the white man's burden in the minor colonies and did everything so correctly he was incapable of doing anything really well, looking forward always to the day when he could retire to Sussex. She never lost the conviction that she had married beneath her, nor that she must somehow inform everyone she met in Canada of her social status in England. But John Yardley's salary had never been ample enough to permit her to take Janet back to the old country to live in the manner to which her mother had been accustomed. So she had moved restlessly about the Empire, finding it better to be poor in the colonies than at home. She died in Montreal while Janet was still in school, proud because her daughter was finally being accepted by the right families, but regretting to her last breath the fact that she had never been able to return to England.

Janet's sense of inferiority remained long after her marriage to Harvey Methuen. She found she had married more than the boy with whom she had fallen in love at a dance; she had joined a tribe. The Methuens felt themselves as much an integral part of Montreal as the mountain around which the city was built. They had been wealthy for a sufficient number of generations to pride themselves on never making a display. Instead, they incubated their money, increasing it by compound interest and the growth of the Canadian Pacific Railway. They were all Scotch Canadians who went to a Presbyterian church every Sunday and contributed regularly to charities and hospitals. They served as governors of schools and universities, sat as trustees on societies founded to promote the arts, joined militia regiments when they left the Royal Military College, and had the haggis piped in to them at the Saint Andrew's Day dinner every winter.

Methuen women never ran to beauty because too much in the way of looks in a woman was distrusted by the family. They were expected to be irreproachable wives and solid mothers of future Methuens, not females who might stimulate those pleasures the men of the family believed had caused the ruination of the Babylonians, Greeks, Romans, French, Italians, Spanish,

Portuguese, Austrians, Russians and various other minor races of the world.

No Methuen found it possible to feel inferior to the English in any respect whatever; rather they considered themselves an extension of the British Isles, more vigorous than the English because their blood was Scotch, more moral because they were Presbyterians. Every branch of the family enjoyed a quiet satisfaction whenever visiting Englishmen entered their homes and remarked in surprise that no one could possibly mistake them for Americans.

The tribe accepted Janet and considered her a good woman, but she had never been able to feel at ease with them. At Harvey's side she had felt secure, for Harvey was greatly respected by the tribe and none of them believed he could ever do anything wrong. But since the war Janet had felt more than ever unsure of herself. Harvey was so filled with self-confidence; he had such an easy way of laughing; he was the only one who was able to joke with her and make her smile in spite of herself. After he left for overseas she missed the positive direction he gave her, and she was sure she could never uphold the standards her position in the family required.

Again and again she had a recurrent dream in which she entered General Methuen's library in the big house on the side of Mount Royal and saw her father-in-law sitting very straight in his leather armchair next to the red draperies under the gilt-framed landscape in which a French-Canadian farmer drove a white horse and a black horse through the snow. He was reading the *Strand Magazine*, and in her dream her skirt dropped to her ankles and exposed her thighs in tights like those of a chorus girl. General Methuen never spoke in her dream. He sighed heavily as he went on with his reading and pretended not to notice.

Janet had always known Harvey would be taken from her and she would be left alone again. As she walked fast along the river road this thought beat repeatedly at her mind, confused with scenes from the magazine story, with her mother's tight, lined face, with her own voice like a phonograph record repeating endlessly, "I mustn't let people see it. . . . I mustn't let them see. . . . I mustn't . . ."

Suddenly Daphne and Heather were there on the road before her. She stopped when she saw them, her hand at her lips. They must have come from the clump of maples at the corner of her father's land. "I mustn't let them see," the voice in her mind repeated. Then another figure darted from behind the trees and she saw it was young Paul Tallard. His dog was at his heels and he was carrying something in his hands that looked like a dead bird. Janet let her hands drop to her sides. Paul was a nice boy even if he was a French Canadian and had an impossible woman for a mother.

"Look, Mummy!" Heather called. "Look what we've got!"

The dog began to bark as he ran down the road to Janet. He frisked about her legs and she nearly tripped over him. Then she found herself standing in the middle of the road with the three children around her. Daphne was an ash-blonde, very straight and neat, taller than the other two. Her clean middy blouse made a sharp contrast with Heather's dirty smock, streaked where brown mud had been carelessly wiped from the palms of small hands. Paul's hands were also dirty. He stood with large liquid eyes looking up at her, offering the dead bird for her to see.

"Napoléon found it in the bog," he said.

"But he didn't kill it," Heather interrupted, her voice rising with excitement. "He just found it. Look, Mummy, at his leg. He's a heron, isn't he?"

Paul thrust the bird forward and she saw that one of its feet was missing.

"He stands on one leg anyway, so he didn't need his other foot," Paul said.

"Or is it a crane?" Heather said. "Which is it, Mummy?"

"It's a blue heron," Daphne said, standing apart from the tight group made by Paul, Heather and the dog. "We had it in school."

Janet scarcely heard what they said. She looked over their heads and saw nothing. Then Heather said, "What's the matter, Mummy?"

"Nothing. Why should anything be the matter?"

"Oh, I don't know exactly."

"Is there a letter from Daddy?" Daphne said. "If there isn't, there ought to be."

Janet felt she was swaying, the earth lurching under her, and her knees were numb. "Run along now," she said. "Don't go into the bog again."

"But Mummy, why not?" Heather said. "It's fun in the bog."

"It's dirty, Heather. And you always get so filthy. Why can't you be like Daphne?"

"But, Mummy!"

She was walking down the road again, the children following.

"Why isn't there a letter from Daddy?" Daphne said. They were near Yardley's gate now. "Daddy's a major," she heard Daphne explain to Paul. "He's in France."

"I know it," Paul said. "It must be wonderful to be a major."

When Janet turned into the gate she saw that her father had visitors on the porch. Yardley was sitting on a chair with his wooden leg crossed over his good knee, and Athanase Tallard and Mrs. Tallard were on either side of him. Janet turned to the children. "Run along now and play."

"But can't we really go into the bog any more?" Heather said.

"Oh, go anywhere. But run along."

Napoléon began to bark shrilly as he went chasing a red squirrel down the road, his tail high and his ears back and flapping. The squirrel shot up a tree and Napoléon stood underneath barking steadily. Paul dropped the bird and went after him, Heather gave a shout and followed, and Daphne turned to her mother. "Heather's awfully noisy, don't you think so, Mummy?"

Janet passed her hand over her forehead. "Do run along and play with them like a good girl," she said. As she went up the drive everything blurred before her eyes. Vaguely, his image staggering in a haze, she saw Athanase lift himself from his chair as she reached the steps, and she heard her own voice asking him not to bother. No, there was no mail this morning, none at all. No, don't bother, please don't anybody bother, she was going upstairs to her room to write letters.

As she opened the house door the coolness of the interior bathed her hot skin. She walked carefully upstairs, thinking about placing her foot on each tread, and by the time she reached her bed she was panting. She dropped onto the bed with relief, and as an easing of her tension set in she could hear the conversation from below as it floated up in the still air. Kathleen laughed heartily once or twice, and there was a chuckle from Mr. Tallard as her father's twangy voice went through one of his innumerable stories.

"Well, this horse I was telling you about was called Okay, and I never saw a stallion with a better name. He could stud like a rabbit and never lose a second off his pace, and the fella thet owned him made a nice sum of money, considering it was in Nova Scotia. Calvin Slipp, his name was, and he was the hardest-shell Baptist I ever saw come out of the Annapolis Valley. And thet's a Baptist to end all other Baptists forever. Calvin was a horse-doctor by trade, and a mighty smart one, and man, if you played poker with him on Saturday night you lost your shirt. He used to take Okay all around the Maritime Provinces to the fairs and exhibitions, year after year, till he got the piles so bad he couldn't sit his sulky and had to hire another driver. . . ."

Upstairs Janet listened in spite of herself with a feeling of horror. How often he had embarrassed her in Montreal with his stories! She hated herself for disapproving of him, for she loved him and he had always been gentle and kind to her. But there he was telling a story like that, with the Tallard woman listening and she upstairs with her whole world collapsed and the future breaking over her with wave after wave of horror. She turned on the bed and murmured, "God give me strength! Oh, God help me!" with her teeth clenched. How could she tell her children that their father was dead? Her beautiful children, her beautiful, beautiful children!

Through the open window floated the inexorable monologue of her father's voice. "Now right there in thet same town was another Baptist named Luther Spry, and I guess maybe he was even harder-shelled than Calvin ever got around to being, for he was a deacon in the church. Luther was a racing man himself, owned a livery stable in the back part of town, and he had a mare name of Mademoiselle. In her own way she was just about as good as Okay, so the boys naturally were thinking what a great thing it would be if Okay could be put to the mare. Thet way they'd have a world-beater. But the trouble was, Calvin hated Luther's guts ever since the time Luther beat him out for being deacon in the church, and Calvin said he'd see Mademoiselle covered by a cart-horse before he'd let Okay get so much as a sniff of her. So the boys figured . . ."

Janet pulled herself off the bed and went into the bathroom to look at herself in the mirror. Her face was still the same. She closed her eyes and pressed her fingers over them until they hurt so much she couldn't stand the pain. Then she washed her face in cold water. Still her senses remained paralysed. This moment, the most terrible in her life, stayed with her, it wouldn't go away, it didn't get larger or smaller, but it remained unreal. She continued to stare at herself in the glass, wondering if this was insanity, this paralysis of feeling. She dried her face and returned to the bedroom.

"So just after moonrise," came her father's voice, "Luther and the boys came into Calvin's backyard with Mademoiselle on the end of a halter. It was a real nice October night, the way you get them down home in a good fall, with most of the leaves off the trees, and their feet were rustling in the leaves and the moon was making shadows through the bare branches. Mademoiselle began to whinny and Okay was inside the stable stamping around and kicking his stall the minute he got wind of her, and next door in the Baptist church the organ was going full blast and the whole prayer-meeting was singing 'Rescue the Perishing' as loud as they could. The boys had to laugh, knowing Calvin was in there singing thet hymn. So they unlocked the stable door . . ."

Janet leaned from the window but she was unable to see the figures on the porch because of its shingled roof. It was easy to imagine them down there, her father's wooden leg cocked over his good one, Kathleen leaning toward him in that intimate way Janet always detested, Mr. Tallard with the ironic smile that baffled her completely.

"Man, but Okay gave thet mare a beautiful cover! The sweetest ever seen in thet town. And next morning when Calvin went out to the stable . . ."

Suddenly Janet screamed. The sound pierced the heavy atmosphere and rested in the spine of everyone within earshot.

She screamed again, and then she began to cry, "Stop! For heaven's sake have pity and be quiet!"

She jerked herself away from the window and fell onto her bed, her whole body wracked by dry, shaking sobs. Through it all her eyes remained dry. She heard her father's wooden leg tapping as he hurried upstairs, but she kept her head on her outstretched arms when he entered the room. She felt his hand on the back of her head and heard him uncrumple the letter on the bed beside her, while the sobs kept shaking her whole body.

"Janet," he said softly. "Janet child!" The bed sagged as her father sat down beside her. He lifted her easily and held her in his arms and she tried to turn her face away from him. After a moment he tried to make her look at him, and for a second she did, but her eyes closed as soon as they met his own. Her lips kept opening and closing, and behind them her teeth remained tightly clenched.

"Go on and cry, Janet," he whispered softly. "You must."

For a long time they remained like that, but Janet did not cry. A breeze sprang up from across the river and the smoke in the air moved out of the valley. A hay-wagon rumbled down the road, dropping fragments of its load in a trail behind.

The second part of the novel – from 1919 to 1921 – begins with the return of the troops:

The war had been over for six months, and now the first battalions were coming home.

Some of them had lived through half a week of the first gas attack, breathing through rags saturated with their own urine while they fought the Germans before Ypres. Some had existed in the cellars of Lens for weeks, gnawing their way underground through the town like rats, wall by wall; and each new cellar had meant grenades and the L-shaped rip of bayonets. Some had seen the top of Messines Ridge blossom like a fire-shot black flower into the sky, carrying with it the shredded limbs of a whole division of Germans mixed with thousands of tons of dirt. Some had gone up the slope of Vimy and fought all day with the Prussian Guard they had been told would be dead when they got there, and at the next dawn they had seen each other's helmets encased with sheet-ice from rain that froze as it fell. Some had stood up to their necks in cold water stained with blood and human excrement while they waited for hours to crawl a few yards closer to Passchendaele. Some had been drunk on sacramental wine found when they had dived into a hole in the ground to escape bombardment, and so had discovered that they were in the crypt of a church, that the occupied ground was a village, that the village was the objective of a three-months offensive. Some had crawled like snakes through the standing grain east of Amiens after the break-through of August 8, 1918. Some had seen friends loosen and fall around the coal piles of Mons on the last morning of the war, then had gone in past them to gut the last snipers of the war with their bayonets. Some had marched at attention across the Rhine bridges into the clean untouched German towns. Some had won medals. Some had acquired trench foot, scars, clap, gas-burns, syphilis and hallucinations that came in the night. Some had learned a peculiar peace through an ultimate knowledge of themselves. And now, having done the whole duty of a soldier, they were coming back to the middle classes, to the farms and forests and the wooden railroad towns, to the gaunt stone cities like Toronto and the sprawling wind-swept ones like Winnipeg. They were coming home to a land still so near the frontier that in most of it everything was black or white, uncomplicated, where wickedness was barely intelligible unless it were sexual.

They were returning to what they thought was good because it had been familiar. When their ships drew in to Halifax, they smelled their country before it rose to them over the horizon, and their nostrils dilated to the odour of balsam blown out to sea from the evergreen forests that cover most of Nova Scotia like a shaggy hide. On the train through the Maritime Provinces they smelled the orange peel, Lysol, spittoon and coal-smoke staleness of the day coaches, and they looked through the windows with their rough khaki collars open, sweating into the stale air the sharp, animal smell of massed soldiers. They saw, as if for the first time, how empty the country looked, how silent it was. They noticed the towns like collections of grey and brown wooden boxes scattered as if by a hand's gesture in the clearings, dirt streets running through them and perhaps a short stretch of asphalt near the brick or sandstone post-office. They noticed the red brick or board railroad stations, nearly every one the same, in Truro, Springhill, Amherst, Sackville, Moncton, Newcastle, Campbellton and Matapedia. They saw the little Nova Scotia trout streams, each one shallow and freshly splashing over amber-coloured stones. They saw the Miramichi, wide and steel-grey, curving flat calm out of the spruce forests. When they woke up the next day they saw the Saint Lawrence, smooth and opaque like a strait of the sea. Then the train rumbled over the bridge and ran through the factories into Bonaventure Station in Montreal.

That afternoon they paraded through the city, and on the reviewing-stand on Sherbrooke Street generals with red tabs and red officer-faces and politicians with grey faces and silk hats saluted them under the Union Jack, the country having no flag of its own. And the soldiers marched at attention through the crowds, only their eyes preserving the traces of what they had done and where they had been. For most of the battle-tension had relaxed now; nearly all of it was gone. They were returning to the human race, floating upward into the illusion of the middle classes again. Now that they were home the last realities were fading. The war was becoming what their minds made it; not the broken instants, the clawing into the earth, the stepping out into ultimate loneliness when the earth jogs up through the feet and legs into the brain and makes each step forward a new thing; not the feel in the arms and shoulders as the bayonet slips into the belly without resistance, or stupidly sticks on bone with a trivial sound, the action so different from what it ought to be: the enemy's face not what was expected, the instant so mind-destroying that the felt knowledge comes that the mind is nothing, the man nothing, only the fear and the outrage real, the moment so private no one can communicate it – only afterwards to look into the eyes of another and understand that he knows it too, and knows that any words about it will be stupid, for words are human and have a history, and this has none. But now the war was slipping back into pictures again, almost into the same pictures the civilians and the advertisers had made of it, whole pictures fabricated by the mind, not broken moments; place-names and dates and what the corporal said to the sergeant-major, the mind going back to its builder's work, curing itself by making war what it never was.

So today they marched through Montreal, and the pipers played them along with "The Blue Bonnets" and "The Hundred Pipers," and before the French-Canadian regiment the band played the "Sambre et Meuse." In the English section of town the crowd had always been behind the army, had worshipped the idea of it. In a war it had never made, the country had given everything, doubling and raising and redoubling the ante again and again until all it was and ever hoped to be was forgotten, as the stakes were piled up on the table for the great powers to manipulate into a victory. The country had suffered a quarter more action-deaths than the United States out of a population a fourteenth as large. Now it was over, and thank God. Now the whole duty of colonials was done, the surviving troops were home, now the future could rest with the great powers till the next time. . . .

A generation later, another war is about to break out; Paul Tallard, after years in Europe, has married his childhood friend Heather Methuen, and has completed a novel:

He was thoughtful for nearly a minute; the burning wood cracked loudly and a violent gust of wind made the windows rattle. He got up and looked out. Cap Chat was buried in darkness under the rushing wind and there was nothing to see. Coming back to the fire, he crouched again. "Well, one thing is certain. The same brand of patriotism is never likely to exist all over Canada. Each race so violently disapproves of the tribal gods of the other I can't see how any single Canadian politician can ever imitate Hitler – at least, not over the whole country. But when the war comes . . ." He stopped and shrugged his shoulders.

Keeping her eyes on the fire and her voice quiet, she said, "I suppose you meant what you said about the Navy?"

"I suppose so. Why not be frank? I've made up my mind."

"My father was killed in 1918. I can't even remember him." She turned. "Oh Paul – do we really have to get into it again?"

"We'll be in it, all right." He got up. "Let's not talk about it.

It just pulls the guts out of me. If you've grown up in a minority you can never feel simply about war. Quebec will enter it trying to save her legend. Many will go to it. Some like Marius will begin remembering each separate insult the English threw in their faces the last time. Some like me will have to feel for Quebec and feel for the whole country at the same time. No – let's not talk about it."

"Paul?"

He looked down at her. She was curled on the edge of the hearth, staring into the fire. When he answered the changed inflection in her voice she still looked away from him.

"I've finished your manuscript," she said.

He waited, but for a time she said no more. All day Heather had been brooding over what she would say to him about his book. Each knew how tightly their future was bound up with the quality of this manuscript. "Well," he said finally. "do you think it can be published?"

"I don't see why not." She was still watching the fire. "Parts of it are wonderful. Your style is simply marvellous. I forget it's you when I'm reading."

"But something is the matter with it. Something fundamental. You've spotted it. I can tell from your voice."

His calm, factual tones made Heather's hopes sink. This book of his had completely baffled her. She was no professional critic, but her work with the museum in New York had involved a good deal of editing and she had helped write a small textbook for art classes in schools. She had something of a professional approach to any form of written words. His theme was ambitious. Many sections had extraordinary power and descriptions were new and vivid. But the balance was not right and the whole was curiously unsatisfying.

They discussed the book for nearly half an hour, and he took the manuscript and went over specific sections with her. At the end of that time she knew what had puzzled her.

The book was too ambitious for him. She herself had been dazzled by the scope of the design. The young man of 1933, intended to type a world in disintegration, had seemed so important that she had not questioned the validity of his plan.

Now she saw that the trouble lay in the fact that Paul's emotions and mental analysis had not coalesced.

"Look," she said suddenly, "I read somewhere that the novelist's principal aim is to celebrate life."

"I suppose it is."

"That's what you do best of all. Every time. Your characters are all naturally vital people. But your main theme never gives them a chance. It keeps asserting that they're doomed."

He frowned thoughtfully. Then he remembered a discussion he had had with his tutor in Oxford. "Maybe I shouldn't have chosen a European scene. Of course, Europe is the focus . . ." He jumped up and began walking back and forth. "My god!" he shouted, "I've been a fool! A year's work! Heather – I've wasted a year's work!"

She looked at him in excitement. Her thoughts were on the same tack as his own. "Paul, why didn't you set the scene in Canada?"

He stopped in the middle of the room. "Because no world trends begin here. I thought of it, but – everything that makes the world what it is – fascism, communism, big business and depressions – they're all products of other people's philosophies and ways of doing things. A book about Canada – it would be like writing of the past century!" Having said this he wondered if it were really true. He sat down before the fire again, staring into it. Must he write out of his own background, even if that background were Canada? Canada was imitative in everything. Yes, but perhaps only on the surface. What about underneath? No one had dug underneath so far, that was the trouble. Proust wrote only of France, Dickens laid nearly all his scenes in London, Tolstoi was pure Russian. Hemingway let his heroes roam the world, but everything he wrote smelled of the United States. Hemingway could put an American into the Italian Army and get away with it because by now everyone in the English-speaking world knew what an American was. But Canada was a country that no one knew. It was a large red splash on the map. It produced Mounted Policemen, Quintuplets and raw materials. But because it used the English and French languages, a Canadian book would have to take its place in the English and

French traditions. Both traditions were so mature they had become almost decadent, while Canada herself was still raw. Besides, there was the question of background. As Paul considered the matter, he realized that his readers' ignorance of the essential Canadian clashes and values presented him with a unique problem. The background would have to be created from scratch if his story was to become intelligible. He could afford to take nothing for granted. He would have to build the stage and props for his play, and then write the play itself.

Suddenly he began to talk. He got up and paced back and forth across the floor. He lit cigarettes and threw them into the fire half-finished and lit some more. Heather had never heard such a deluge of words from him. As she listened she felt sick from apprehension. He was telling her that his present book was a total failure, that he could do nothing to save it.

Then, as abruptly as he had begun to talk, he stopped and knelt beside the fire. It had burned down until the logs were glowing coals. After a time he took a deep breath and turned to her. His face seemed several years older than it had been an hour ago, but his eyes were bright. He laughed in sudden irony.

"And what have I discovered tonight?" he said. "Something the whole world has known for centuries. An artist has to take life as he finds it. Life by itself is formless wherever it is. Art must give it a form." He laughed again. "So – after all these years – I learn tonight what my job is!"

Then casually, so casually she did not realize what he was doing, he picked up the manuscript and dropped in into the fire. With a cry she reached forward to save it, but the flames shot up and covered the papers. He took her by the arms and drew her back. "No," he said, "that's finished. Burn the mistakes. Otherwise they'll haunt you permanently."

She was frightened by the resignation in his voice, appalled by the fact that he was destroying what had taken him a year to create. She watched the mass of papers burning and her face became hot from the flames. Slowly they curled and shrivelled into quivering layers, blackening from the edges into the centre, and she knew she was watching more than an unfinished book going up in smoke. She felt she was watching the fire burn up the next two years of her own life.

"An Orange from Portugal"

The success of his novels did not bring Hugh MacLennan instant wealth. Money was to remain a constant problem for him, and he had to interrupt his work on his novels to give lectures, to speak on the radio, and to write articles and essays.

Happily, he proved to be a gifted essayist, and many of these occasional pieces continue to provide delight. In 1978 a selection of the best of these essays, The Other Side of Hugh MacLennan, *edited by Elspeth Cameron, was published. Its appearance caused William French in* The Globe and Mail *to note: "MacLennan's work as an essayist has been overshadowed by his reputation as a novelist, but that's an injustice that should be corrected by* The Other Side of Hugh MacLennan." *The earliest of his essays in that book was "An Orange from Portugal," which first appeared in* Chatelaine *in 1947:*

I suppose all of us, when we think of Christmas, recall Charles Dickens and our own childhood. So today, from an apartment in Montreal, looking across the street to a new neon sign, I think back to Dickens and Halifax and the world suddenly becomes smaller, shabbier, and more comfortable, and one more proof is registered that comfort is a state of mind, having little to do with the number of springs hidden inside your mattress or the upholstery in your car.

Charles Dickens should have lived in Halifax. If he had, that brown old town would have acquired a better reputation in Canada than it now enjoys, for all over the world people would have known what it was like. Halifax, especially a generation or two ago, was a town Dickens could have used.

There were dingy basement kitchens all over the town where rats were caught every day. The streets were full of teamsters, hard-looking men with lean jaws, most of them, and at the entrance to the old North Street Station cab drivers in long coats would mass behind a heavy anchor chain and terrify travellers with bloodcurdling howls as they bid for fares. Whenever there was a south-east wind, harbour bells moaned behind the wall of fog that cut the town off from the rest of the world. Queer faces peered at you suddenly from doorways set flush with the streets. When a regiment held a smoker in the old Masonic Hall you could see a line beginning to form in the early morning, waiting for the big moment at midnight when the doors would be thrown open to the town and any man could get a free drink who could reach the hogsheads.

For all these things Dickens would have loved Halifax, even for the pompous importers who stalked to church on Sunday mornings, swinging their canes and complaining that they never had a chance to hear a decent sermon. He would have loved it for the waifs and strays and beachcombers and discharged soldiers and sailors whom the respectable never seemed to notice, for all the numerous aspects of the town that made Halifax deplorable and marvellous.

If Dickens had been given a choice of a Canadian town in which to spend Christmas, that's where I think he would have gone, for his most obvious attitude toward Christmas was that it was necessary. Dickens was no scientist or organizer. Instead of liking The People, he simply liked people. And so, inevitably, he liked places where accidents were apt to happen. In Halifax accidents were happening all the time. Think of the way he writes about Christmas – a perfect Christmas for him was always a chapter of preposterous accidents. No, I don't think he would have chosen to spend his Christmas in Westmount or Toronto, for he'd be fairly sure that neither of those places needed it.

Today we know too much. Having become democratic by ideology, we are divided into groups which eye each other like dull strangers at a dull party, polite in public and nasty when each other's backs are turned. Today we are informed by those who know that if we tell children about Santa Claus we will probably turn them into neurotics. Today we believe in universal justice and in universal war to effect it, and because Santa Claus gives the rich more than he gives the poor, lots of us think it better that there should be no Santa Claus at all. Today we are technicians, and the more progressive among us see no reason why love and hope should not be organized in a department of the government, planned by a politician and administered by trained specialists. Today we have a super-colossal Santa Claus for The Customer: he sits in the window of a department store in a cheap red suit, stringy whiskers, and a mask which is a caricature of a face, and for a month before every Christmas he laughs continually with a vulgar roar. The sounds of his laughter come from a record played over and over, and the machine in his belly that produces the bodily contortions has a number in the patent office in Washington.

In the old days in Halifax we never thought about the meaning of the word democracy; we were all mixed up together in a general deplorability. So the only service any picture of those days can render is to help prove how far we have advanced since then. The first story I have to tell has no importance and not even much of a point. It is simply the record of how one boy felt during a Christmas that now seems remote enough to belong to the era of Bob Cratchit. The second story is about the same. The war Christmases I remember in Halifax were not jolly ones. In a way they were half-tragic, but there may be some significance in the fact that they are literally the only ones I can still remember. It was a war nobody down there understood. We were simply a part of it, swept into it from the mid-Victorian age in which we were all living until 1914.

On Christmas Eve in 1915 a cold northeaster was blowing through the town with the smell of coming snow on the wind. All day our house was hushed for a reason I didn't understand, and I remember being sent out to play with some other boys in the middle of the afternoon. Supper was a silent meal. And then, immediately after we had finished, my father put on the great-coat of his new uniform and went to the door and I saw the long tails of the coat blowing out behind him in the flicker of a faulty arc light as he half-ran up to the corner. We heard bagpipes, and almost immediately a company of soldiers appeared swinging down Spring Garden Road from old Dalhousie. It was very cold as we struggled up to the corner after my father, and he affected not to notice us. Then the pipes went by playing "The Blue Bonnets," the lines of khaki men went past in the darkness, and my father fell in behind the last rank and faded off down the half-lit street, holding his head low against the wind to keep his flat military cap from blowing off, and my mother tried to hide her feelings by saying what a shame the cap didn't fit him properly. She told my sister and me how nice it was of the pipers to have turned out on such a cold day to see the men off, for pipe music was the only kind my father liked. It was all very informal. The men of that unit – almost entirely a local one – simply left their homes the way my father had done and joined the column and the column marched down Spring Garden Road to the ship along the familiar route most of them had taken to church all their lives. An hour later we heard tugboat whistles and then the foghorn of the transport and we knew he was on his way. As my sister and I hung up our stockings on the mantelpiece I wondered whether the vessel was no farther out than Thrum Cap or whether it had already reached Sambro.

It was a bleak night for children to hang up their stockings and wait for Santa Claus, but next morning we found gifts in them as usual, including a golden orange in each toe. It was strange to think that the very night my father had left the house, a strange old man, remembering my sister and me, had come into it. We thought it was a sign of good luck.

That was 1915, and some time during the following year a boy at school told me there was no Santa Claus and put his case so convincingly that I believed him.

Strictly speaking, this should have been the moment of my first step toward becoming a neurotic. Maybe it was, but there were so many other circumstances to compete with it, I don't know whether Santa Claus was responsible for what I'm like now or not. For about a week after discovering the great deception I wondered how I could develop a line of conduct which would prevent my mother from finding out that I knew who filled our stockings on Christmas Eve. I hated to disappoint her in what I knew was a great pleasure. After a while I forgot all about it. Then, shortly before Christmas, a cable arrived saying that my father was on his way home. He hadn't been killed like the fathers of other boys at school; he was being invalided home as a result of excessive work as a surgeon in the hospital.

We had been living with my grandmother in Cape Breton, so my mother rented a house in Halifax sight unseen, we got down there in time to meet his ship when it came in, and then we all went to the new house. This is the part of my story which reminds me of Charles Dickens again. Five minutes after we entered the house it blew up. This was not the famous Halifax explosion; we had to wait another year for that. This was our own private explosion. It smashed half the windows in the other houses along the block, it shook the ground like an earthquake, and it was heard for a mile.

I have seen many queer accidents in Halifax, but none which gave the reporters more satisfaction than ours did. For a house to blow up suddenly in our district was unusual, so the press felt some explanation was due the public. Besides, it was nearly Christmas and local news was hard to find. The moment the first telephone call reached the newspaper offices to report the accident, they knew the cause. Gas had been leaking in our district for years and a few people had even complained about it. In our house, gas had apparently backed in from the city mains, filling partitions between the walls and lying stagnant in the basement. But this was the first time anyone could prove that gas had been leaking. The afternoon paper gave the story.

DOCTOR HUNTS GAS LEAK WITH
BURNING MATCH – FINDS IT!

When my father was able to talk, which he couldn't do for several days because the skin had been burned off his hands and face, he denied the story about the match. According to modern theory this denial should have precipitated my second plunge toward neurosis, for I had distinctly seen him with the match in his hand, going down to the basement to look for the gas and complaining about how careless people were. However, those were ignorant times and I didn't realize I might get a neurosis. Instead of brooding and deciding to close my mind to reality from then on in order to preserve my belief in the veracity and faultlessness of my father, I wished to God he had been able to tell his story sooner and stick to it. After all, he was a first-class doctor, but what would prospective patients think if every time they heard his name they saw a picture of an absent-minded veteran looking for a gas leak in a dark basement with a lighted match?

It took two whole days for the newspaper account of our accident to settle. In the meantime the house was temporarily ruined, schoolchildren had denuded the chandelier in the living-room of its prisms, and it was almost Christmas. My sister was still away at school, so my mother, my father, and I found ourselves in a single room in an old residential hotel on Barrington Street. I slept on a cot and they nursed their burns in a huge bed which opened out of the wall. The bed had a mirror on the bottom of it, and it was equipped with such a strong spring that it crashed into place in the wall whenever they got out of it. I still remember my father sitting up in it with one arm in a sling from the war, and his face and head in white bandages. He was philosophical about the situation, including the vagaries of the bed, for it was his Calvinistic way to permit himself to be comfortable only when things were going badly.

The hotel was crowded and our meals were brought to us by a boy called Chester, who lived in the basement near the kitchen. That was all I knew about Chester at first; he brought our meals, he went to school only occasionally, and his mother was ill in the basement. But as long as my memory lasts, that Christmas of 1916 will be Chester's Christmas.

He was a waif of a boy. I never knew his last name, and wherever he is now, I'm certain he doesn't remember me. But for a time I can say without being sentimental that I loved him.

He was white-faced and thin, with lank hair on top of a head that broke back at right angles from a high narrow forehead. There were always holes in his black stockings, his handed-down pants were so badly cut that one leg was several inches longer than the other and there was a patch on the right seat of a different colour from the rest of the cloth. But he was proud of his clothes; prouder than anyone I've ever seen over a pair of pants. He explained that they were his father's and his father had worn them at sea.

For Chester, nobody was worth considering seriously unless he was a seaman. Instead of feeling envious of the people who lived upstairs in the hotel, he seemed to feel sorry for them because they never went to sea. He would look at the old ladies with the kind of eyes that Dickens discovered in children's faces in London: huge eyes as trusting as a bird-dog's, but old, as though they had forgotten how to cry long ago.

I wondered a lot about Chester – what kind of a room they had in the basement, where they ate, what his mother was like. But I was never allowed in the basement. Once I walked behind the hotel to see if I could look through the windows, but they were only six or eight inches above the ground and they were covered with snow. I gathered that Chester liked it down there because it was warm, and once he was down, nobody ever bothered him.

The days went past, heavy and grey and cold. Soon it was the day before Christmas again, and I was still supposed to believe in Santa Claus. I found myself confronted by a double crisis.

I would have to hang up my stocking as usual, but how could my parents, who were still in bed, manage to fill it? And how would they feel when the next morning came and my stocking was still empty? This worry was overshadowed only by my concern for Chester.

On the afternoon of Christmas Eve he informed me that this year, for the first time in his life, Santa Claus was really going to remember him. "I never et a real orange and you never did neether because you only get real oranges in Portugal. My old man says so. But Santy Claus is going to bring me one this year. That means the old man's still alive."

"Honest, Chester? How do you know?" Everyone in the hotel knew that his father, who was a quartermaster, was on a slow convoy to England.

"Mrs. Urquhart says so."

Everyone in the hotel also knew Mrs. Urquhart. She was a tiny old lady with a harsh voice who lived in the room opposite ours on the ground floor with her unmarried sister. Mrs. Urquhart wore a white lace cap and carried a cane. Both old ladies wore mourning, Mrs. Urquhart for two dead husbands, her sister for Queen Victoria. They were a trial to Chester because he had to carry hot tea upstairs for them every morning at seven.

"Mrs. Urquhart says if Santy Claus brings me real oranges it means he was talkin' to the old man and the old man told him I wanted one. And if Santy Claus was talkin' to the old man, it means the old man's alive, don't it?"

Much of this was beyond me until Chester explained further.

"Last time the old man was home I seed some oranges in a store window, but he wouldn't get me one because if he buys stuff in stores he can't go on being a seaman. To be a seaman you got to wash out your insides with rum every day and rum costs lots of money. Anyhow, store oranges ain't real."

"How do you know they aren't?"

"My old man says so. He's been in Portugal and he picks real ones off trees. That's where they come from. Not from stores. Only my old man and the people who live in Portugal has ever et real oranges."

Someone called and Chester disappeared into the basement. An hour or so later, after we had eaten the supper he brought to us on a tray, my father told me to bring the wallet from the pocket of his uniform which was hanging in the cupboard. He gave me some small change and sent me to buy grapes for my mother at a corner fruit store. When I came back with the grapes I met Chester in the outer hall. His face was beaming and he was carrying a parcel wrapped in brown paper.

"Your old man give me a two-dollar bill," he said. "I got my old lady a Christmas present."

I asked him if it was medicine.

"She don't like medicine," he said. "When she's feelin' bad she wants rum."

When I got back to our room I didn't tell my father what Chester had done with his two dollars. I hung up my stocking on the old-fashioned mantelpiece, the lights were put out, and I was told to go to sleep.

An old flickering arc light hung in the street almost directly in front of the hotel, and as I lay in the dark pretending to be asleep the ceiling seemed to be quivering, for the shutters fitted badly and the room could never be completely darkened. After a time I heard movement in the room, then saw a shadowy figure near the mantelpiece. I closed my eyes tight, heard the swish of tissue paper, then the sounds of someone getting back into bed. A fog-horn, blowing in the harbour and heralding bad weather, was also audible.

After what seemed to me a long time I heard heavy breathing from the bed. I got up, crossed the room carefully, and felt the stocking in the dark. My fingers closed on a round object in its toe. Well, I thought, one orange would be better than none.

In those days hardly any children wore pyjamas, at least not in Nova Scotia. And so a minute later, when I was sneaking down the dimly lit hall of the hotel in a white nightgown, heading for the basement stairs with the orange in my hand, I was a fairly conspicuous object. Just as I was putting my hand to the knob of the basement door I heard a tapping sound and ducked under the main stairs that led to the second floor of the hotel. The tapping came near, stopped, and I knew somebody was standing still, listening, only a few feet away.

A crisp voice said, "You naughty boy, come out of there."

I waited a moment and then moved into the hall. Mrs. Ur-quhart was standing before me in her black dress and white cap, one hand on the handle of her cane.

"You ought to be ashamed of yourself, at this hour of the night. Go back to your room at once!"

As I went back up the hall I was afraid the noise had wakened my father. The big door creaked as I opened it and looked up at the quivering maze of shadows on the ceiling. Somebody on the bed was snoring and it seemed to be all right. I slipped into my cot and waited for several minutes, then got up again and replaced the orange in the toe of the stocking and carefully put the other gifts on top of it. As soon as I reached my cot again I fell asleep with the sudden fatigue of children.

The room was full of light when I woke up; not sunlight but the grey luminosity of filtered light reflected off snow. My parents were sitting up in bed and Chester was standing inside the door with our breakfast. My father was trying to smile under his bandages and Chester had a grin so big it showed the gap in his front teeth. The moment I had been worrying about was finally here.

The first thing I must do was display enthusiasm for my parents' sake. I went to my stocking and emptied it on my cot while Chester watched me out of the corner of his eye. Last of all the orange rolled out.

"I bet it ain't real," Chester said.

My parents said nothing as he reached over and held it up to the light.

"No," he said. "It ain't real," and dropped it on the cot again. Then he put his hand into his pocket and with an effort managed to extract a medium-sized orange. "Look at mine," he said. "Look what it says right here."

On the skin of the orange, printed daintily with someone's pen, were the words PRODUCE OF PORTUGAL.

"So my old man's been talkin' to Santy Claus, just like Mrs. Urquhart said."

There was never any further discussion in our family about whether Santa Claus was or was not real. Perhaps Mrs. Urquhart was the actual cause of my neurosis. I'm not a scientist, so I don't know.

CHAPTER · 5

The Precipice

Like Two Solitudes, The Precipice (1948) went on to win the Governor General's Award for Fiction. Unlike its predecessor, it has sunk into anonymity, and is little read nowadays.

Those who seek it out will find an interesting portrait of small-town Ontario and an exploration of the differences between Canadians and Americans.

It opens in Grenville, Ontario, a town based on Hugh MacLennan's visits to Port Hope, Cobourg, and Belleville:

In later years Bruce Fraser often asked himself how it had happened that a woman he had taken for granted most of his life, had casually watched at work in her garden next door, should ultimately seem to him the embodiment of all that was essentially female – easier to sense than to understand, durable, and possessed of a kind of private beauty he felt he alone could recognize. The time came when the thought of Lucy Cameron never failed to stir him.

But no such thoughts were near the surface of his mind that August morning in 1938 as he stood on the porch of his father's house in Grenville, Ontario, and watched her trimming the edges of her patch of lawn. Bruce was young enough then to think that ideas were more important than people. And besides, those were still the days of innocence in a little town like Grenville, where Canada breathed out the last minutes of her long Victorian sleep. They were the days when the well-meaning generation everywhere – in college common rooms, in the pages of the rough-paper magazines, in smoky apartments where beer-drinking was a ritual and a symbol of the times – were still so excited by the novelty of knowing the score that they could spend delicious hours proving to themselves that life was a dirty trick, measuring with logic and dialectic each year against its predecessor to prove how inevitable it was that the tide should keep flooding in. Now Italy, now Germany, now Spain, and soon the rest of us.

Bruce thought about the book he had been reading the night before, a book so full of social significance it had drugged him into a state of perverse contentment. If all the famous men in the world except a handful of Russians were knaves, fools, or conspirators, who could rightly blame him for being unsuccessful at twenty-four?

After days of rain the sun was out again and the sharp ozone from Lake Ontario was in his nostrils. Light shimmered on the water and redoubled itself, light vibrant and sensual as calling trumpets. On a morning like this, after two months in Montreal, even the old street where he had grown up seemed new.

Lack of experience made Bruce look even younger than he was, in spite of a rugged jaw which was oblong and very Scotch, bristly brown hair, and strong blue eyes. His youth showed in his tall, slim intensity and in his frequent expressions of startled surprise.

A dog barked next door and Bruce turned his head. It was a remarkably gracious house, he decided, as he did each time he came home. Massed ranks of phlox bloomed on either side of a low doorstep behind a curving border of petunias and sweet alyssum. The door itself had been painted a hue of turquoise blue, and a polished brass knocker hung in the centre of it below a wide-spreading fanlight. The walls were white clapboard with outside shutters of blue; dormers on the third storey broke the slope of the roof. But more than any other one thing about it, he liked the way the house clung to the ground, facing a street as quiet as Sunday.

It was an outward expression of the personality of Lucy Cameron. Seven years ago, when her father died, there had been no gardens and no colour, the splendid British colonial style of the house browned off by blistered tan paint, its lines unsoftened, its fences wood instead of the hedges that had taken their place. In those days it had seemed exactly the kind of house old John Knox Cameron would choose to live in, and to leave to the three daughters who were his only children. He would have been horrified, Bruce reflected, could he have guessed what Lucy would do with it on the strength of four years' salary from the only paying job she had ever held.

And yet she had done nothing new to the house at all. She had merely stripped off an imposed ugliness and restored it to its proper position in time, for it was one of the oldest properties in Grenville, built by a Massachusetts judge who had been driven out of New England at the time of the American Revolution, owned by his descendants ever since. It was a Scotsman who had married into the family three generations before who had added the brown paint and the harshness, for the Scotch and Scotch-Irish who had flooded into Ontario in the wake of the original Loyalist settlers had roughened everything they touched. It would be another hundred years before any part of English-speaking Canada could hope to be rid of what they had done to it.

Bruce left the steps of his porch and began to stroll up the narrow street. A century and a half ago someone had given it the name of Matilda Lane to honour a relative of George the Third, and the name had stuck. It seemed to Bruce more absurd than quaint, but he liked the street itself better than any other in town, for the elms that lined it, planted by the original settlers, had reached a noble height. Only here, in this lane running down from the King's Highway to the common at the edge of the lake, did Grenville seem in any sense mature. The branches of the elms soared up and out, dark grey under the mass of their leaves, and joined tips high overhead to make the lane like a cathedral nave open at both ends. It was constantly rich in changing lights. This morning the sunshine struck down, tangled in the branches, and dropped such a net of shadows onto the red paving-bricks of the street that he seemed to be wading through them as he walked.

He turned at the King's Highway and strolled back the way he had come. When he reached the Cameron house Lucy was working among her flowers. A shopping-basket lay on the grass behind her, and without noticing Bruce she moved slowly along the border as she looked at the petunias. Suddenly she bent down, carefully snipped off a dried seed pod, dropped it into a small envelope she took from a pocket, and shook the seeds loose. She was in profile to Bruce but he could see an expression of quiet, shy pleasure touch her face. He thought with some pity and even with a faint feeling of male superiority that any pleasures Lucy Cameron would ever have would be shy ones.

The Frasers had always been sorry for the Cameron women who lived next door. Bruce's mother was a happy, nerveless woman whose only grief was an operation which had made it impossible for her to have more than one child. His father was the best general practitioner in the county. Dr. Fraser's life had been clouded by the knowledge that he could have risen to the top of his profession in any of the cities of the country, had he not been compelled to support his parents after leaving medical school by establishing a practice in the first town where a vacancy had occurred. As a result he had concentrated most of his thwarted ambition on his son and was considered by Grenville a stern and highly respectable man.

But compared to old John Knox Cameron, Dr. Fraser's life had been almost licentious. John Knox had been hard even for an Ontario small town to take, where the Scotch-Irish are chocolate-brown with Calvinism. He had been dead for seven years now, but his ghost still haunted the house where he lived. His wife had died the year after her husband, in thankful relief, Mrs. Fraser was known to have said, and now his three daughters lived there alone. Jane, the eldest, was a church organist and a music teacher, known to be well on her way toward forty. Lucy, ten years younger than Jane, kept the house. Nina was only nineteen and she knew she was considered the prettiest girl in town.

Bruce waited for Lucy to turn around, but she was intent on her flowers, so he called out, "Hello, Lucy! How are you?"

She turned around, quick pleasure flashed into her face as she saw him and then was immediately checked, as though she thought she might create the presumption that he was equally pleased to see her.

"When did you get back?" she said.

"Last night."

"How was Montreal? And McGill?"

"All I can remember was the heat. If there were marshes instead of factories along the St. Lawrence the place would be famous for its malaria." He walked across the lawn to look at her flowers. "Your garden grows lovelier all the time."

She flushed with pleasure but her voice was matter of fact as she answered. "August is a dull month for gardens. I wish you could have seen it in June."

A cicada screamed from the tall grass on the common which lay between the foot of the street and the lake. Sunlight reflected from the white clapboards, and Bruce looked curiously toward an open window as he heard the tinkling of Jane's piano. He had once played the same piece himself, in the same room, and he grinned at Lucy as she read his thoughts. It was nine years since he had stopped taking lessons and Jane couldn't have been thirty at the time, but she had seemed to belong to his mother's generation then and she still did.

"You must get tired hearing those same things year after year."

"I do. Or I would if I hadn't stopped hearing them long ago. Nina complains about having to be quiet so much of the time in the house, but I never seem to notice." She bent down to pick up her shopping basket and dropped the shears and the envelope containing the seed pod into it. "If you're looking for Nina you might find her on the shore. She went down there with her dog."

"I wasn't looking for anyone. I'm lazy today."

Lucy stood with her basket on her arm. "I'm afraid I have to go along to King Street now. You're not going that way?"

"Not now. But maybe I could climb the back fence this evening?"

A trace of a smile touched her face and he thought it made her look charming and a little sad. "You won't be able to see the flowers in the dark," she said.

As she walked toward the King's Highway he watched her and wondered why he had never troubled himself to think about Lucy Cameron before. One took so many people for granted in Grenville; one accepted the stock judgments made of one's neighbours by the community and let it go at that. If Lucy would only give herself a chance, he thought, she could be an attractive woman. She moved with the quiet grace of a shy animal, yet in all her movements there was an air of conscious control, as though she hoped that whatever she did would escape notice. This same characteristic was even more marked in her face. It was an intelligent face, he thought; essentially a proud face. Her chin and the upper part of her head could have modelled a cameo, clean-cut and distant. But in the eyes and mouth unknown qualities brooded. Her large eyes were brown and widely spaced, with curving brows. Her lips were soft, warm, and sensuous. These features, together with her air of dignified solitude, combined to give her the prevailing expression of a woman who has never been recognized by others for what she knows herself to be.

Bruce turned and strolled down to the common. The grass was resilient as he walked under the trees and he felt a wall of coolness rise to meet him as he neared the lake. It was good to be back. Grenville was such a safe place, so stubbornly sure of itself and so full of humour when one knew it well. Certainly not a single one of the madmen who were making current history could support himself within its limits.

But even as the loveliness of the scene and the warmth of his returning affections invaded his mind, the restless, critical side of Bruce rose to meet them. Grenville was also a town of eight thousand people who had been stiff-necked from the day the first United Empire Loyalist had marked out his lot a century and a half ago, constantly right in its judgments but usually for the wrong reasons. Here was lodged the hard core of Canadian matter-of-factness on which men of imagination had been breaking themselves for years. Grenville was sound, it was dull, it was loyal, it was competent – and oh, God, it was so Canadian! The ferments and the revolutions of the past twenty years might never have existed so far as this town was concerned. Until the Grenvilles of Canada were debunked from top to bottom, Bruce decided, there would be no fun and no future for anyone in the country.

He reached the sand, picked up a flat stone warm from the sun, drew back his shoulder, and launched his whole body into the throw. The stone skipped over the flat blue water, splashing up a series of miniature rainbows, then tumbled, and sank. He stood on the edge of the shore for several minutes before he turned to stroll back under the trees of the common. He skirted a bandstand where once a fortnight in the summer a grocer, a hardware merchant, a shoemaker, a hotel-keeper, a freight-handler, and three clerks met to play marches and popular medleys while the children of Grenville came down to the common with their parents to listen. In one corner of the common near the foot of Matilda Lane he came to a neat, white belvedere, built two generations ago in honour of Queen Victoria's Golden Jubilee by the man who at that time had been the town's leading citizen.

Bruce climbed the steps into the belvedere and sat down for a smoke. Engrossed in his own thoughts, he forgot all about Grenville and the middle Cameron sister. Lines of poetry entered his head, were driven out by a sentence he thought he might use in an article he hoped to write for *The Canadian Forum*. He thought about Hitler and Chamberlain and the stupidity of the British Tories and his own unique ability to understand so much. Then he remembered that Nina Cameron was supposed to be somewhere on the beach, so he left the belvedere and walked down to the shore again.

There was no sign of Nina or her dog. The beach was empty as far as he could see in both directions. The water stretched over the horizon into the United States. Ontario might be the smallest of the five continental lakes, but to the people of Grenville its frontier seemed at least as absolute as an ocean.

Lucy Cameron's romance with Stephen Lassiter, an American manager at the local plant, creates tension at home, matched by the tension in the country:

Over the weekend the weather broke and a heavy gale rode inland off the lake. The Cameron house was so dark that lights had to be turned on during the day and a wind that had started far down the Mississippi Valley and then had been pushed eastward by a cold front moving from Hudson Bay tore over the rolling Ontario land. On Saturday afternoon Lassiter called Lucy to say that the power system at the plant had failed and that he would be working late that night and would have to work all day Sunday to complete his report to Ashweiler and he wished he could see her but he couldn't.

Tired from three late nights in succession, and from the strain of resisting the sense of guilt which Jane's close-lipped and forbidding silence spread through the house, Lucy rested and tried to interest herself in a novel. That night she went to bed early and fell asleep with the house trembling in the wind and the thunder of rapid waves hitting the beach in her ears.

On Sunday morning the whole country looked wet and flat. A few lonely cars swished over the King's Highway and the pavement was black in the rain. The wind had ceased, but the rain still fell, and just before eleven o'clock the sidewalks of King Street were filled with people walking under umbrellas to the churches.

There was tension in St. David's that morning, and Lucy noticed that a good many of the middle-aged men were wearing service buttons from the war. Most of the veterans had discarded the habit of wearing them years ago, but now they had taken them out of drawers, polished them and quietly fitted them into their lapels. She found herself counting their young sons who sat in the pews beside them, the ones in their middle teens who were still at school. Remembering Lassiter's tanned face, she noticed how the English and Scottish ruddiness predominated in the complexions of all these Grenville men. She found herself comparing the younger ones with their fathers. The fathers' faces looked heavier in expression than their sons' ever would. Not sad, but ponderously confident, more rugged and less sensitive, and the difference was not entirely caused by the difference in age. These youngsters were a new breed for Canada. Their features showed less stubbornness and perhaps less durability, but more refinement and more imagination. Across the aisle and several pews ahead she saw Bruce Fraser. He was one of the few men present who was in his early twenties, but there was no doubt that he was far closer to the sons than to the fathers. A world in which he would feel at home would be a very different place from the world John Knox Cameron and Jane had made for her.

Dr. Grant rose in the pulpit. He had been a chaplain in France and he was still close to the returned men. His powerful hands gripped the lectern, his short grey hair bristled, and his large nose seemed to grow larger still.

"Pour out thy fury upon the heathen that know thee not, and upon the families that call not on thy name: for they have eaten up Jacob, and devoured him, and consumed him, and have made his habitation desolate."

He preached for half an hour to these innocent people about the evil that was inherent in mankind. He was sick with anxiety about Hitler, and it was clear to him that Hitler would never have been allowed to reach power if the world had shared his own Presbyterian conception of wickedness. "They thought they could abolish evil by appointing committees of experts to deal with it."

After the service the three sisters went home to the usual Sunday dinner of roast beef and browned potatoes and a trifle for dessert. All the time they had been listening to Dr. Grant the roast had been cooking in a slow oven. During dinner the rain stopped and a changed wind sprang off the lake. About three o'clock Bruce came over and they all sat down to listen to a summer concert on the radio, but just when the last noisy surge of a Wagnerian overture was finished and Mozart's flutes began to sing into the room, they had to turn off the radio to receive callers.

Bruce went home and Jane poured tea for two elderly women and one white-haired man who stayed till half past five. By that time the sky had lightened, the clouds broke open, and the sun drove to the west in a blaze of ruddy gold. Robins appeared on the soaked grass of the lawn. They made quick running steps and froze with heads cocked to listen for worms, their beaks darted and then they shot forward over the grass again. The garden beds were spangled with white, lavender, and pink petals beaten from the phlox by the rain and the wind.

No one in the Cameron house mentioned Lassiter's name throughout the day, though all three sisters, each in her own fashion, was acutely conscious of his presence among them.

Lucy's uncle, Matt McCunn, is a most unusual son of Grenville:

Early in October Grenville felt its first frost. Waking shortly after dawn, Lucy got up and walked about her room. She saw the first rays of the sun striking red through the trees and colouring the wisps of hoarfrost on the grass of the common. It was the beginning of the season all Canadians love best, and for a short while, in the clarity of the air at sunrise, Lucy felt some of the weight of her depression lift. She went back to bed and fell asleep. When she got up for breakfast at eight o'clock the last of the hoarfrost had melted and she knew it would be a fairly warm day.

About mid-morning she walked northward out of the town. She left the houses behind her and then left the inland road and walked up through a footpath in a cropped field until she came in sight of the cottage where Matt McCunn lived. Here the land rose to a height of about two hundred feet, the fields bosoming upward in softly contoured slopes. It was not a range of hills, but an isolated eminence on a gently rolling plain, and it seemed higher than it really was because of the flatness of the surrounding country.

McCunn came out on the veranda as she approached and waved to her, then disappeared inside the cottage. By the time Lucy reached the steps he was out again with a glass in either hand. One contained whiskey and the other water. He handed her the water, saying he didn't like to drink alone.

"Well," he said offering her the lone rocker on the porch, "so the war didn't start after all! Never mind. It will in the spring. And that bloody fool Chamberlain has added two years onto the duration."

She sat down on the top step and felt the warmth of the sun on her shoulders. Her fingers touched the battleship-grey paint of the steps and it felt suave.

McCunn was in his shirt-sleeves but he looked tidy and well groomed. Lucy wondered whether or not Jane would revise her opinion of him if she ever came out here to see how he lived. McCunn's cottage was not very comfortable, but he kept it scrupulously clean and neat.

Her dark hair gleamed in the light as her eyes searched the fields rolling down to the lake-shore plain. From here Grenville looked like a cluster of trees with four steeples and the cupola of the post office resting among their tops and shining in the sun. Beyond the town, the lake shimmered deep blue under a cloudless sky.

"Well, Lucy," said McCunn.

She looked up at him, her forehead wrinkled slightly, but she managed to smile. "Well, Uncle Matt."

McCunn sipped his whiskey and looked at her gently. "Why don't you get in bed with the big bastard?" he said quietly.

She flushed. "You certainly manage to reduce everything to bare essentials."

"Why not? Isn't it what you wanted me to say – only maybe in politer words? Your expression showed it the minute I saw you."

"You manage to read faces easily."

McCunn grinned and crossed his legs. "Any woman's, Lucy. It's my talent. That's why they unfrocked me. I made them too uncomfortable."

The familiar pattern was repeating itself. McCunn's genius for irrelevancy, for building up a fantasy world resting on a limited amount of acute observation, was beginning to develop.

"Did they really unfrock you?" she said drily. "I never quite believed that story, you know. I think you just retired."

He grinned. Knees spread, head on one side, he set his glass on the floor. His face, incongruous under the noble dignity of his white hair, looked innocent and rather childlike.

"You're not happy here, are you, Lucy?"

"For the first time I'm willing to admit I'm not."

A tender expression followed the grin on his face. "You know something? In spite of it all, I love Grenville. I always did and I always will."

"You seldom talk as if you did."

"Whom the Lord loveth, he chasteneth."

She laughed quietly.

"No," said McCunn. "Don't laugh. The people here are bright and clean, they've got the whole future before them and they've got savour. They're warm, Lucy. That's the funny thing about them – under the surface they're warm. I don't mean the ones like Jonathan Eldridge. But our Highland people – I learned this in the ministry – they really want to do the will of God. But the information they got on that subject all came from John Calvin, and all he told them was what not to do. Now me, I always thought John Calvin was a son of a bitch, and that's the main reason why they unfrocked me."

She looked at him without comment.

McCunn chuckled. "But they're a lusty lot here. In spite of everything they're lusty. You'd be surprised, if you knew them as well as I do. Don't judge them by Jane and your father. Those two just happen to be the incarnate images of the kind of morality the rest of them pretend to believe in but really don't. A lot goes on here, and a lot more people get tousled than you think. The fact is, the town has always thought Jane and your father a mighty peculiar pair." He gave her a sideways look, took another pull at the whiskey and laid the glass down again. "I used to watch the people from the pulpit in the old days," he said with another grin. "The young girls with their plump arms and shining morning faces, the young men with necks and shoulders like prime young bulls looking up the earnest way they do as if they wanted me to know how eager they were to do the right thing. It was a touching sight to see. But then I'd look at their parents. And I'd see your father in his old pew on the middle aisle, waiting to hear me say something he could disapprove of. And then I'd get sore. So one day I told the congregation right out what was the trouble with the whole lot of them."

Again McCunn stopped to pick up his glass. He took a long pull and half emptied it, then wiped his lips with a handkerchief and laid it down again. His eyes began to twinkle as he looked over the slope of the fields to the church steeples rising above the trees of the town.

"That morning I told them something no preacher ever dared say from a pulpit in the whole of Canada. I told them the Province of Ontario was so innocent the only sin they could understand was the sin of fornication. I said they put so much stress on it, the worst kind of crook could cheat them and exploit them, and they'd never be quite sure he was a crook so long as what they called his morals looked okay. Why right here in this town, I said, there's one of the biggest skinflints and widow-cheaters that ever lived. But so long as he keeps out of the law courts he's going to get by, for he don't drink, he don't play cards and he'd be scared to look at a woman sideways so long as anyone from his home town was within fifty miles to tell someone else he did it." McCunn stopped and eyed her again, very pleased with himself. "Of course, I was talking about Jonathan Eldridge, and they all knew it. But I didn't stop there. From now on, I said, when I preach about sin – and I'm going to do it aplenty – I want it clearly understood I'm thinking about what the old ones do in their business hours, and not what the young ones do in the hammocks behind the ivy. Little children, I said, looking at a young couple in the second pew, love one another."

McCunn stopped, shook his head and rubbed his hand over his face as Lucy's level eyes watched him.

"Do you expect me to believe you preached a sermon like that?" she said.

"As sure as my name means a son of a bitch – and in Gaelic that's what it does mean, with a root right back to Sanskrit, that's what I preached. You asked me why they unfrocked me. I've told you. Of course, they brought up some more reasons besides. They also said I was divisive." There was a long silence. "Now, did what I say make sense, or didn't it?"

Again she laughed quietly. Uncle Matt really was preposterous enough to have preached a sermon like that in a Presbyterian church.

"Lucy," he said, "everybody thinks I'm a fool. Well, what is a fool? Generally it's a man who isn't shrewd. I admit I'm not shrewd. But there are times when being shrewd doesn't get you anywhere, and you're at one of those times now. The whole world is, for that matter. You want to do something perfectly natural. Why don't you do it? You don't because of how your father and Jane brought you up. Those two were shrewd. And what did it get them?" His voice suddenly became angry. "God help a people if they think sex is the only important sin there is, for the day will come when they find out they've been lied to and cheated, and then they'll cut loose and make a mockery of sex and go straight to hell the way the Romans did. Don't forget, Lucy – the old Romans were puritans too!"

Bruce Fraser, now with the R.C.A.F., visits New York for the first time:

Like so many Canadians before him, Bruce Fraser came down to the United States in 1940 on the defensive, subconsciously determined not to be lured into discontent with his own country. After stepping off the Montreal train into Grand Central at seven-thirty in the morning he began to walk around the city.

His first impression led to astonishment when he discovered that New York, in addition to being stupendous, was also friendly.

It was late afternoon by the time he found the upper reaches of the Fifth Avenue shopping district. Some time during the day the old inherited attitude had disappeared. As he walked north with alert steps he was pleased when people noticed his new Air Force uniform with the Canada shoulder-flashes. The light in Fifth Avenue was faintly golden. New York was at its best; it was beginning to reveal the pastel quality of a fine autumn evening.

He paused in front of Van Cleef and Arpels to look at unset rubies which lay on a bed of satin in a box window, a great single jewel surrounded by a garland of lesser ones, lying only a few inches from his eyes. It was like observing a queen naked, near and naked to tempt her subjects, surrounded by her women and guarded by an invisible wall. Bruce wondered how much they cost. Then the puritan side of his nature was assuaged by the consideration that these imperious stones, valuable enough to support a family in comfort for years, would probably be bought by a newly rich merchant who feared inflation, to be hidden in a bank vault or hung about the sinewy neck of a faded wife.

He smiled to himself and continued his walk. A faint odour blended of numerous perfumes clung to the humid air, and once again he became conscious of many women. As he walked north the avenue opened up before him, running into the Plaza with buses and taxis and cars and people. The hard faces, the indifferent faces, the happy faces, the beautiful women, the spoiled women, the women looking forward to being loved, the women no man would ever love again – he saw them all with a clarity that generally needs fatigue or drink or even drugs to make it sharp; he saw moving in front of him a tall, lithe girl with tawny hair, slim hips, wide shoulders, and beautiful rhythmic legs; he reminded himself that he had never in his life talked to a girl who looked and carried herself like that, and wondered what kind of life had bred such an Athenian self-confidence, and how a man like himself would seem to such a girl if he could ever meet her.

This was a new kind of perspective for Bruce. He had always taken it for granted that most people his own age would find him interesting, and he had always felt a mild superiority to Americans in general, without knowing anything about them except what he read in the newspapers and magazines.

This section of New York continued to take him aback. He had expected no such grace or dignity in an American city, for until today the only other one he had seen was Detroit. So far as he could tell, nearly every important building on Fifth Avenue except the churches and hotels existed solely for business purposes, and it was almost a shock to see such grace of design in buildings used for earning a living. The astonishing thought occurred to him that there must be people here who considered that business itself was beautiful.

It was now a quarter to five. Lucy had asked him to come to their apartment at six to be in time for cocktails before dinner. He still had more than an hour to kill.

As he turned east into Fifty-ninth Street the feeling of vitality continued to bear him along. All day he had been feeding on the power and self-confidence of New York, lapping up all of it he could absorb. From a stationery shop came the good smell of clean stacked paper and fresh cards. He paused to examine the bright jackets of new novels in a bookstore window. A refrain sang through his mind in time to the drive of the traffic: "They'll never beat us, we'll knock hell out of the sons of bitches, they'll never beat us." It was the first time in six months that he had felt this way about the war. It was peculiar to come down to New York, which was supposed to be in a neutral country, and have the city make him feel like this.

The traffic was thick when he reached the darker, more serious air of Madison. He went into a flower shop where the chrysanthemums looked so fresh and fluffy he would have ordered a couple of dozen of them if he could have afforded it, but the export of Canadian currency was so closely controlled just then that he had to be satisfied with half a dozen. The clerk promised to send them out at once.

When he left the flower shop the air seemed much darker. The sunshine was still bright on the tops of the buildings on the eastern side of the street, but on the pavement there were no shadows. More people: a woman in a black dress with a lifted face, tightly squeezed hips and a high bosom, a string of graduated pearls around her neck, and perfectly slimmed legs; their eyes met for an instant, he felt the impact of a cosmic disillusionment, and then she was past. Two laughing girls. A white-haired gentleman with a black Homburg and an erect back. A Mediterranean type gesturing happily to his wife. A woman in a mink coat coming out of a Gristede's with two bags of groceries in her arms.

Suddenly Bruce felt very tired. He had absorbed all of New York his senses could take for a while. North of Fifty-ninth Street he turned into a restaurant with a bar at the front, sat down in a dark corner and ordered a rye and soda.

The drink warmed, softened, and loosened him. He glanced at a solitary girl near him who was sitting with a drink in front of her, apparently unconscious. The barman was talking to the proprietor about horses. Bruce leaned back with his eyes half closed and whole sequences of New York scenery began to jump through his head. He wondered how much of the city he had really seen that day. He smelled again the pickles, spices, and fresh fruit which had delighted his nostrils that morning on Third Avenue. He smelled subways. He remembered the curious procession of shipping clerks pushing racks of women's dresses somewhere on Seventh. Popcorn and peanuts – where had he smelled them? He remembered the sharp bite of salt air when he walked up from the subway in Bowling Green just before noon, and the old lady on the Fifth Avenue bus, the one who had got on just above Washington Square, who had bent toward him across the aisle to say, "I just want you to know I feel grateful."

Uncle Matt McCunn, Grenville's black sheep, has had an interesting war:

Matt McCunn told the crews of the various ships on which he served that if he had received a stripe for every time he was torpedoed he would have been a vice-admiral by the end of 1942. As it was, he never rose higher in the merchant service than quartermaster; he was considered too old to be worth training into an officer. But even if McCunn had been younger he would probably have stayed where he was, for his heart was in every fo'c'sle and privates' mess in the world. So long as there were people anywhere who rejected the idea of success, he was with them.

He was first torpedoed off Newfoundland in the fall of 1940 on a former Greek vessel which had been put on the fringe of the convoy because she would have been the smallest loss if she was hit. McCunn was glad to see the ship go, for she was the worst he had ever sailed on, so badly balanced that the best quartermaster in the world couldn't keep her wake from looking like a corkscrew. McCunn walked off her and onto the deck of a destroyer without even wetting his feet, and he was in Halifax four days later. Another ship went down under him the next April, in the night, and during the twenty minutes he spent in the water he nearly froze to death. His worst season was the winter of 1942, when he was torpedoed five times, three times on a single convoy.

After that voyage McCunn spent several months in a boarding-house in Liverpool, but he got restless again and went up to Scotland, and in Leith signed on a vessel for the Mediterranean. He knew as well as anyone that Malta convoys were the worst in the war, but by this time he was beginning to feel himself indestructible and he was interested in warmer water than the north Atlantic. He made Malta on one convoy in which his ship and three others were the only merchantmen out of twenty-four to get through. He saw a bomb hit the *Formidable* and a second later the whole carrier flash into a moving sheet of flame, then sail on, and an hour later receive planes back on her deck. That, he said to himself, is what comes of having men on the bridges with straight stripes on their sleeves.

Later he watched a large bomb curve down for the *Rodney* and disappear just under her forefoot, then the sea jerk as though somebody had kicked it underneath, rise in a mushroom of water a hundred and fifty feet high, and the *Rodney* walk through it and come out with her decks streaming and all her guns firing, lashing out with all nine sixteen-inchers on her long foredeck at a formation of torpedo planes. McCunn had never seen a sixteen-inch gun fired before, much less at an airplane, and he thought with exhilaration that if they were using H.E. in shells that size against aircraft this must be the hottest convoy action of the whole war, and by God, here he was in the middle of it! Looking around at one after the other of the merchant ships in his convoy being hit as he leaned on the rail, he found himself admiring the feathery wakes made by torpedoes in the blue Mediterranean, the wild flaming arcs of struck planes, the big Royal Navy ships handing it back, and he couldn't help comparing this scene favourably with the Atlantic where he had never seen a better ship than the *Revenge* and attacks were always made at night with corvettes and destroyers exploding millions of dead fish to the surface for every submarine they touched. The Mediterranean seemed a very good sea for a war. McCunn found himself enjoying the sheen of sunlight on the white plumes of bombed-up water, almost hoping that a twisting, turning Heinkel would get through so there would be another bomb-burst and another plume of water glistening in the sun against an azure sea.

That night when his ship docked in Malta and the let-down set in and a crowd of half-starving Maltese worked frantically to get the cargo out of her before the dive-bombers returned in the morning, McCunn wondered if he might just possibly be going crazy. It was a bad sign when a man enjoyed the sight of a torpedo coming at him. A friend of his in the old war had become the same way he was now, so shell-happy he had thought himself immortal until he stopped taking cover, and the same shell-burst which had relieved McCunn of one of his most prized possessions had killed the man because he had made no attempt to get out of the way.

On his return to Gibraltar, McCunn managed to get himself transferred to a vessel bound for Alex around the Cape. The long voyage made in complete safety rested him and gave him a hankering for the shore. He had been in the war for more than three years without seeing a single German, with the exception of a corpse which a wavy-navy lieutenant-commander in charge of a corvette had hoped would be accepted as evidence for a sinking, and that had been two years ago in Greenock where the body had arrived preserved in ice. So in Alexandria he got himself transferred again, this time illegally, to a special unit of Americans who had volunteered to convey supplies to the partisans in Yugoslavia. The Americans called him Pop and the officer in charge had no idea what to do with him when he discovered, after the unit was under way, that McCunn was not the interpreter he had been given to understand he was and could speak no word of any language but his own.

McCunn stayed with them, however, and when they landed at night in a cove not far from Dubrovnik and went inland with a group of Dalmatian shepherds guarding a straggly caravan of donkeys and mules, he was glad to leave the sea behind. For the first time he felt close to the war and close to the Germans he had fought in the last one, and he could climb as well as any of the younger men. But he had to be silent on this strange march, and so he began to think of Grenville, and thinking of Grenville to be a little homesick, almost for the first time in his life.

In New York, Stephen Lassiter learns about loneliness:

As he put on his hat and coat and snapped off the lights he knew he was tired and he also knew he would not be able to sleep for hours. He stepped into the elevator, dropped to the ground floor and walked out into the rain. A few taxis were swishing up Madison and their sound made him think how wonderful New York could be on a rainy night when you were alone with the buildings in the long empty streets. He felt good again, eager to go somewhere and do something. What? It was too late to go back to Gail, for she was sure to be asleep already. He caught a taxi cruising downtown and gave the driver an address in the Village.

Was that actually where he wanted to go? It was a little place Gail had discovered, where Povey Bartt played the piano, with Eddie Soper on the clarinet and Sol Gold on the drums. The real music never got loose there until after midnight. Gail said Bartt's was a new kind of jazz – a genuine white man's jazz, she called it, close to the New Orleans idiom, but under Bartt's hands it came out differently. Stephen had been down there only once before and had annoyed Gail by talking while Bartt played. She insisted the man was as important an artist as anyone you could hear in a season at Carnegie Hall. And maybe she was right. Anyway, it was a good place to go now, a place to sit and be alone and have nobody bother him.

He paid the driver, went in, checked his coat at a hole in the wall where a dark face emerged from a faint yellow glow, and found a table near the band. The room was nearly dark, bare, ugly, and more than three-quarters empty on account of the rain. While he waited for his drink and a sandwich, a Negro improvised on the piano, playing an imitation Basie not quite good enough to pass for the original. Gail called this one of the places where the musicians worked for love and marihuana.

The Negro finally slid away from the piano and the white men came in one by one, settled themselves at their instruments and began to play, taking their time, feeling their way into the music. A waiter appeared with a drink and a sandwich, put them on the table and Stephen began to eat, noticing little change in the music since the coloured man had left, apart from the support of the clarinet and the drums. And then, so gradually it was something he felt in the pit of his stomach, felt it lying there alive and moving, the loneliness began.

He could hear it in the high trilling in the treble of Bartt's piano, the right hand poised like a five-beaked vulture over the same group of keys, endlessly poised while the left spent an infinite brooding patience as it beat out the rhythm, exploring fantastic harmonies which always promised to be something new but which always – cruelly, relentlessly, logically as fate – came back to where they had started as Bartt stripped away the delusion of hope and revealed that nothing had changed at all.

Stephen stared up at him, saw the man's eyes bright with marihuana, saw how he needed it, the relapsed ease it gave his whole body, saw how he used it and made it work for him, how with the drug he could accept what he was doing and love it.

The loneliness jetted out in piercing personal agony on Soper's clarinet. It was visible, it was something you could touch in the posture of Sol Gold crouched among his drums like a sharp-nosed animal confident in danger, the flaring lapels of his striped double-breasted jacket pointing upward to his narrow shoulders, the shoulders marking time in contemptuous non-chalance, vast Asiatic eyes deep and softly smiling on either side of his great hook of a nose.

Stephen finished his drink and beckoned the waiter for another one. He was mindless; the music had saturated him. Now every whorehouse and station hotel and backroom from Utica to Flagstaff was present in that half-dark box of a place, was displayed as if under glass in the arc-lighted bareness of Stephen's mind, every whorehouse, station hotel, and saloon in the dead hours of the morning when time stops and the continental night pales before the morning stars and the whistles of freight trains wail from town to town across the American plain. Cones of light shine down over the green baize of the crap game. Cones of light make the poker table a phantasmal altar. Rows of bottles brood behind the bar under the mirror that reflects *Custer's Last Stand* from the opposite wall, while the hard-faced men, every face with its own variety of the same expression, sit above shirt-sleeves and loosened collars in organized disorder. They have been there for hours. A single waiter shuffles about soundlessly refilling their glasses, the dice rattle in the box, flash white on the green and stare up at the light with black eyes. The cards shuffle, the spittoon splashes over. Upstairs the springs of three brass beds jingle steadily while a brakeman, a telegrapher, and a traveller in women's hosiery silently fornicate three girls whose names they do not know except by the framed pictures which hang above each bed – *September Morn, Rosebud, Salome.* Downstairs there is a roar as someone is given the hotfoot, a loose laugh, and through the light-cone at the card table a voice snaps, "Pipe down you sonofabitch." The door leading upstairs opens and the brakeman comes in; he looks relaxed and easy, pushes back a cowlick from a moist forehead and grins knowingly as he slumps over to the bar. His pants tighten across his fat buttocks as he sets his elbows.

Stephen closed his eyes and clutched the glass in front of him, lifted it and poured the rest of the drink down his throat, opened his eyes again and beckoned to the waiter. Then he stared straight ahead at the musicians as the waiter went off with the empty glass.

It is three o'clock in the morning. Where is it three in the morning, aside from a worn old song? Everywhere. The loneliness is all there is, Bartt's piano has captured it all and translated it into Stephen Lassiter's soul. It is three o'clock in the morning and suddenly the wooden timbers of the back room begin to tremble as a freight on its way from Evansville to St. Louis crashes through the town, the whistle wails four times for the crossing where the Ritz Café faces across Main Street to

Hergesheimer's hardware, the empties rattle out of town and silence again, silence creeping like white mice out of the plain into the open streets of the wooden town. And at that moment an American boy looks up from the crap game with his hands in his empty pockets and a dream in his eyes. No words, he never needed them and he never will, only the dream in his eyes as he listens to the train and wishes to God he were with it, wishes he were out of this town and guesses it's time for the road again, maybe St. Louis, maybe Chicago, who knows but maybe New York itself, maybe this is the break, the apartment high above the Christmas-tree lights of Park Avenue and the limousine waiting below, the girl, and the top of the world.

From the piano Povey Bartt tells it all because he has seen it all already: the American boy with the dream in his eyes. Bartt sees him thirty years from now with the pouches under his eyes, without the dream but still with the hope, here in the same backroom on the fringe of the light-cone where the tobacco smoke is rising. And Bartt knows the skill of all these men and loves them for it: their skill with cards, with electric wires, with jumping pistons and turning wheels, their skill with anything lifeless their hands can touch, and he sees that their skill is part of the vastness of the continental loneliness that bred itself into the seed their fathers and grandfathers carried about from town to town along with the knowledge that there is nothing they or anyone else can do about it, nothing but what the freight train does, go on and on and on until it stops in another town exactly like the one it left. And Bartt loves them. He knows them and they know him, for he is with them and always has been, and without him where is their meaning? He was with them when the Conestoga wagons rolled westward out of Council Bluffs, he was down in the Lehigh Valley when Lil met Sawed-off Pete, he was in San Francisco when the earth trembled under the cribs. When the cops come in to break it up he will be there, his left hand weaving the heartbeat of the bass to the shrill pain of the quivering right, and his rhythm will continue as long as America, for when he dies, another will be there in his place.

One close look at Povey Bartt shows he is dying now. He is small, hollow-chested, with high cheekbones and a flush over the bones, black hair parted in the middle but still stiff and untamed, his face a white and smiling triangle over the keys, over the gentle, wise, brooding hands with the signet on the fourth finger of the left.

"Waiter, what time is it?"

"Four-twenty. It's four o'clock in the morning."

Stephen got to his feet and rubbed his eyes, staggered and leaned his head against the side wall. The beating in his head – was it the liquor or his blood pressure. Or was it that goddam music that never stopped?

Each Man's Son

Hugh MacLennan was born on the twentieth of March, 1907, in Glace Bay on the island of Cape Breton. His father, "Dr. Sam," was a much-respected doctor there. It was to Cape Breton, and to that time, that Hugh MacLennan returned in the setting of his 1951 novel, Each Man's Son:

AUTHOR'S NOTE

Continents are much alike, and a man can no more love a continent than he can love a hundred million people. But all the islands of the world are different. They are small enough to be known, they are vulnerable, and men come to feel about them as they do about women.

Many men have loved the island of Cape Breton and a few may have hated her. Ericson was probably the first to see her, Cabot landed on her, and after Cabot came the French. She seemed harsh and frigid to the first-comers, but the moment the French saw her their imaginations were touched and they called her the Royal Isle. After a while they built on her eastern rim the master fortress of Louisbourg to dominate Nova Scotia and guard the St. Lawrence.

When the wars began, the English and the New Englanders came up to Cape Breton and for a time she was as famous as Gibraltar. Louisbourg fell, the French were driven out, the English and Americans went home and for a third of a century the island was vacant again.

Then across the ocean in the Highlands of Scotland a desperate and poetic people heard of her. They were a race of hunters, shepherds and warriors who had discovered too late that their own courage and pride had led them to catastrophe, since it had enabled them to resist the Saxon civilization so long they had come to the end of the eighteenth century knowing nothing of the foreman, the boss, the politician, the policeman, the merchant or the buyer-and-seller of other men's work. When the English set out to destroy the clans of Scotland, the most independent of the Highlanders left their homes with the pipes playing laments on the decks of their ships. They crossed the ocean and the pipes played again when they waded ashore on the rocky coast of Cape Breton Island.

There they rooted themselves, big men from the red-haired parts of the Scottish main and dark-haired smaller men from the Hebrides, women from the mainland with strong bones and Hebridean women with delicate skins, accepting eyes and a musical sadness in their speech. For a long time nothing but Gaelic was spoken in the island until they gradually learned English from the handful of New England Loyalists who came to Nova Scotia after the American Revolution.

To Cape Breton the Highlanders brought more than the quixotic gallantry and softness of manner belonging to a Homeric people. They also brought with them an ancient curse, intensified by John Calvin and branded upon their souls by John Knox and his successors – the belief that man has inherited from Adam a nature so sinful there is no hope for him and that, furthermore, he lives and dies under the wrath of an arbitrary God who will forgive only a handful of His elect on the Day of Judgment.

As no normal human being can exist in constant awareness that he is sinful and doomed through no fault of his own, the Highlanders behaved outwardly as other men do who have softened the curse or forgotten its existence. But in Cape Breton they were lonely. They were no part of the great outer world. So the curse remained alive with them, like a sombre beast growling behind an unlocked door. It was felt even when they were least conscious of it. To escape its cold breath some turned to drink and others to the pursuit of knowledge. Still others, as the Puritans of New England had done earlier, left their homes, and in doing so found wider opportunities in the United States or in the empty provinces of western Canada.

But if the curse of God rested on the Highlanders' souls, the beauty of God cherished the island where they lived. Inland were high hills and a loch running in from the sea that looked like a sleeve of gold in the afternoon sun. There were trout and salmon streams lined by sweet-smelling alder, water meadows and valleys graced by elms as stately as those in the shires of southern England. The coast was rugged with grey granite or red sandstone cliffs, splendid with promontories, fog-bound in the spring when the drift ice came down from Newfoundland and Labrador, tranquil in summer, and in the autumns thunderous with evidences of the power of the Lord.

So for several generations the Highlanders remained here untouched, long enough for them to transfer to Cape Breton the same passionate loyalty their ancestors had felt for the hills of home. It was long enough for them to love the island as a man loves a woman, unreasonably, for her faults no less than for her virtues. But they were still a fighting race with poetry in their hearts and a curse upon their souls. Each man's son was driven by the daemon of his own hope and imagination – by his energy or by his fear – to unknown destinations. For those who stayed behind, the beast continued to growl behind the unlocked door.

Daniel Ainslie was one of those who stayed. In the year 1913 he considered himself a freethinker, a man who was proud because he had neither run away nor sought a new belief in himself through hard liquor. But he did not know – how many of us can understand such a thing – that every day of his life was haunted by a sense of sin, a legacy of the ancient curse.

Even when he tried to find strength by denying God's existence, he lived as though the hound of heaven were snapping at his heels. Even when he displayed his knowledge and intelligence as a priest displays his beads, he felt guilty because he knew so little and was not intelligent enough.

In one way or another he was forced to discover, as most of us do, that a man can ignore almost anything in his life except the daemon which has made him what he is and the other daemon which gives him hope of becoming more than any man can ever be.

After that stern opening, the book begins with an idyllic scene showing Mollie MacNeil playing on the beach with her young son Alan – a scene the grown Alan remembers as a cabinet minister in Ottawa in The Return of the Sphinx:

The shadow of a promontory lay forward on the sea like that of a giant resting on his elbows with the back of his neck to the late-afternoon sun. Facing the sun over the water was a second-quarter moon, white in the cobalt mass of the sky.

Two small figures sat in a cove under the promontory, a woman and an eight-year-old boy. The red smock of the mother, the white shirt and green pants of the boy – the pants secured by cloth braces with large white buttons – were bright between the cliff and the giant's shadow on the sea. The tide was moving into the cove and now the water was breaking not many yards from the boy's feet. The whole place was awash with sound as the cliff caught and magnified the noise of the wind and water, echoed the screams of sea birds and reverberated with the occasional thunder of a big wave. Feeling the air rushing cold out of the sunshine into the shadow, suddenly conscious of the rise of the whole sea, the boy turned to his mother.

"The tide's coming in, isn't it?" He was proud of his knowledge. For a few moments he watched to see if the next wave would obliterate the mark of the one before. "What makes it change like that?"

She pointed to the white wafer of the moon. "There is what does it."

He looked at her with bright surprise. "The moon? How?"

"It pulls the water up the shore and then lets it go back again."

"Mummy, that's just another of your stories." His eyes were twinkling.

"No, it isn't. I read it in a book. All the stars in the sky pull on each other all the time. In every direction at once. The earth is pulling on them, too. That's what we're on – the earth. And when the moon comes around on our side of the earth it pulls and pulls and the whole sea is lifted up against the land and that's what the tide is."

He looked up at the moon and again at the water, and as she

watched his face she wondered what he was thinking about. She was pleased because she had been able to answer such important questions so well. He watched the moon for a long time and then turned back to his play. It was no ordinary child's castle he had built in the sand, she thought. It was like the picture of the castle he had seen in the book she was reading to him. There were four walls with towers on the corners, a courtyard within and a drawbridge over a moat. The drawbridge was a chip of driftwood which he had just finished inserting.

But the boy's attention wandered while she watched him. The sea and the sky were too big and he was getting sleepy. He turned his head as a gull flew out from the overhang of the cliff and then he looked far, far up the beetling rock to the flecks of white where birds rested in crevices of the rock.

Mollie MacNeil looked too young to have an eight-year-old son. Her body was slim and her pale skin made her seem fragile, just as the eagerness of her smile showed how vulnerable she was. She had a Celtic delicacy of skin with a rose flush over her cheekbones, and as she leaned back with her chin tilted towards the sky her face seemed even more fragile than her body. It was the younger-than-normal face of a woman who has lived for years with a child and for a child.

Without warning, a strident steam whistle blasted the air. There was nothing in sight which could send forth such a sound, but the scream of the whistle shot up into the sky and filled it. Birds flew crying out of their nests in the cliff as the noise hung wailing in the air, but neither the boy nor his mother moved. They knew the whistle came from the colliery half a mile inland and they heard it with only part of their senses. It had always marked hours in their lives.

When the sound died away she rose with apparent reluctance and pulled down her rumpled skirt. "There is the end of the day shift, so you know how late it is."

He watched her wrap a heel of bread in a piece of newspaper before putting it into a basket, along with a partly used jar of molasses and the empty bottle in which she had brought milk. Her dark hair and lovely eyes were reflected in his as she smiled.

"Think how good it will be when we get home this time! Did I tell you what we have for supper tonight?"

His face broke into a delighted smile. "Pork pie!"

"One whole one for you and another for me. I got them at the store only this morning so they'll be lovely and fresh." The wind riffled her hair and she pushed it back out of her eyes. "Come now, Alan. It is always longer going home."

"Will we stop at the spring in the woods?"

"Today there is no time for that. The spring is behind the doctor's house and that is on the other side of where we live."

"But you said it was the best water in the world."

"So it is, but we will save it for another day."

He turned to look back at the sea, trying to understand what his mother meant when she had told him about the moon. Then he saw something which had not been there before. It was a schooner emerging from behind a bluff of land; close-hauled on the starboard tack, it was standing out to sea against the humping waves.

"Look!" he said. "There is a really big ship. Where is she going?"

"She would be bound for Newfoundland, probably."

"What's that?"

"It's a great big island out there."

"I can't see it."

"Of course you can't. It is too far away for you to see it."

"Could Father see it if he was here?"

"Not even your father could see that far."

Dr. Daniel Ainslie, brooding about the difference between him and his Loyalist wife, Margaret, is travelling through Broughton on a Saturday night. Local custom dictates that it will be a busy time for him at the hospital:

As the mare took her time pulling the carriage along the main street closer to MacDonald's Corner, the crowds thickened on the sidewalk, but Ainslie looked straight ahead and saw no one. The first fights had not yet begun, but they took part farther up the street in the vicinity of the saloons. The shops were now closed, the coal carts and slovens were off the streets, the tram had already traversed the length of the town and gone on its way, and for the moment Ainslie's was the only carriage in sight.

The Presbyterian minister stood under a lamppost with one

hand scratching the small of his back and the other hooked by a thumb to his waistcoat pocket. He was brooding on the sermon he was going to preach tomorrow morning. He wondered if he should stop the doctor and ask him, as one scholar to another, if he thought it was going too far to warn the congregation against taking the promises of the New Testament too literally. For if God was love, what was to be done about Jehovah? But Ainslie passed the Reverend MacAlistair without turning his head.

Under the light of the next post was another man who wanted to speak to the doctor. He looked like a chubby walrus dressed in a bowler hat and a high white collar. Jimmie MacGillivray, the saloonkeeper, had a stomach-ache. He wanted to ask the doctor about an idea which had been scaring the wits out of him. Could a stomach-ache be sent as a punishment for sin? If it could be – and the Reverend MacAlistair said that was so – then there was no hope for the relief of Jimmie MacGillivray. For what more could a man do to keep the Sabbath holy than he was doing now? He made his daughters keep it, too. They cooked all the food for Sunday on the day before, put it on plates and the plates on the tables, and he even saw to it that they filled all the glasses in the house with water on Saturday night, so that not a tap was turned in the MacGillivray house on the Sabbath. But the stomach-ache was growing worse week by week, and the Reverend MacAlistair said this his sins would find him out. What more could he do? If only the doctor would look his way . . . but the doctor passed, still staring at the rump of his mare, and Jimmie turned away with a small moan.

At the next corner a crowd was gathering and as the fringes of it spilled over the curb Ainslie had to guide the mare to the far side of the street to avoid running down some of the men. This manoeuvre interrupted his thoughts and he looked for the cause of the disturbance. He could hear the broad voice of Mr. Magistrate MacKeegan . . . "'And by Chesus,' I said to her, Big Annie McPhee, six foot two with the beam of a potato schooner moreoffer, 'you whould come into my court and swear that a man the size of the prissoner wass able to rape the likes of you! By Chesus,' I said to her, 'you will get down on the floor and show me, or you whill get the hell owt of here and I whill haff you for perjury moreoffer.' And that" . . . MacKeegan's voice tailed off as Ainslie passed . . . "iss a hell of a lot more serious charge in my court than rapes iss, because perjury iss perssonal."

"Dear God," Ainslie muttered to himself. Now the crowds were so thick they spilled out into the street and he had to urge the mare on. Most of the men were miners who spent their days underground in the dark. He could tell at a glance how many years any one of these proud clansmen had spent in the pits. The young ones were defiant, cocky in the way they walked, and they pulled their rough caps down over their right ears like tam-o'-shanters. They were the ones who could be heard issuing a general challenge to a fight. The middle-aged ones were quieter, they moved slowly and talked little, seeming older than their age, and most of them were beginning to be plagued with sciatica and what they called the rheumatics. If a man had been in the pits beyond his fifty-fifth year, particularly in those mines with narrow seams, Ainslie's eye could measure fairly accurately how many more working years that man had before him. The young ones swaggered and the middle-aged ones could feel the break coming in their leg pains and their unspoken fears, but ultimately the mines would break them all. Those who survived accidents would become like the two white-haired men Ainslie passed near the corner, sitting side by side on the curb with sticks for support between their knees, their faces ennobled by the tremendous fact of survival, grave and white under the flickering arc light.

As the mare threaded her way through MacDonald's Corner, the T-shaped area of macadam which was the only social centre most of the miners had ever known, the place where Archie MacNeil had got his start, several of the men touched their caps to the doctor as he passed, and he answered them with nods or an occasional word. The mare turned right and began to pull up the hill that led to the hospital, pushing with her hind legs so that her rump muscles bulged and glistened with sleek highlights whenever a lamppost was passed. Halfway up the hill they met the Salvation Army band marching down, instruments glinting brassily in the lights, only the bass drum booming to keep the men in step, and twelve women in black bonnets with red ribbons clapping their hands as they followed. Ainslie scarcely noticed them, for the Army always established itself in the middle of MacDonald's Corner on Saturday nights, timing its first hymns to coincide with the moment the first drunks staggered up from the rum shops in the lower part of the street.

The mare reached the top of the hill where the hospital stood like a lighthouse over the whole town. Ainslie tethered the horse in the yard behind the building, picked up his bag and walked briskly through the yard and around the front to the steps. When he opened the door and smelled the familiar odours of the building he felt a sensation of pleasure that began to relax the tense muscles of his back. Here was his own world where his skill had made him a master. He saw Miss MacKay rustling starchily down the corridor to meet him. His feeling of certainty grew and he began to smile.

At the hospital, Dr. Ainslie's rest in the common room is disturbed by the welcome intrusion of Dr. Dougald MacKenzie:

Ainslie watched MacKenzie's large, lined thumb pressing the tobacco into the bowl of his pipe, and he wondered as he had often wondered before how a man with such huge hands had been able to perform thousands of careful, precise operations. He saw the long moustache, drooping at the ends, making its white splash against the ruddy cheeks, and thought about the change in MacKenzie's personality in recent years. When Ainslie had first met him, Dr. MacKenzie had been consciously the chief, a silent, earnest listener who was so absorbed in medicine he never seemed able to give a moment's thought to anything else. After giving up practice in the colliery to which he had been attached, he had remained as chief surgeon and director of the hospital which owed its existence to his energy and determination. At one time or another all the doctors in Cape Breton had come under his influence. But now he lived alone, and in his partial retirement he had taken to reading with the same quiet thoroughness he had once given to his work. It was the reading that had made him more talkative and self-revealing, less clinical and more given to speculation. There had been a time when Ainslie had believed MacKenzie to be a genius, but he knew now that the old man's mind was one which understood, rather than discovered.

"I suppose I ought to be going home," MacKenzie said without moving from his chair. "Since Janet died and the children went away that house of mine gets on my nerves. Some day you'll know what it's like to be afraid of going home in the dark."

MacKenzie's rich bass voice broke into a laugh and Ainslie watched the tobacco smoke rising in clouds over his stiff white hair. It was the head of an old Highland chief, but it was also the face of a man who had worked with Lister in the Old Country and against Lister's advice had deliberately chosen to return to his isolated island. That choice, and the hard years since he had made it, were all marked in the expression of his deep-blue eyes. Ainslie knew himself to be grateful to MacKenzie for many things which would never be told, but perhaps for nothing more than the sense he had given him of belonging to the great world of international medicine.

"It's the unnecessary nonsense that I grow weary of," he heard himself saying. "About a third of the work I do is unnecessary. Last night it was a hysterical old woman with indigestion. The night before I was had out by a blackguard who'd gotten into a brawl and wanted me to patch his eye. Och, I could brain them!"

"Why don't you?" MacKenzie smiled. "You can put a stop to that sort of thing any time you want to, and when you stop feeling sorry for yourself, you'll do it."

Ainslie flushed. "How? By barricading my surgery door?"

"No. There are other ways. The turning-point in my life was that flash explosion fifteen years ago in my colliery. Do you remember it?"

"Yes, I remember." The flush began to recede.

"Since that time I've saved myself a total of about three years of sleep. I'd been on my feet fifty-eight hours by the clock after that explosion and I'd just managed to get to bed when the surgery bell rang. I went down in my nightgown and there was Jumping Rorie MacNair with nothing worse than a cracked septum and a black eye. 'It took two of them to fix me, Doctor, honest to God' – that was how he introduced himself." MacKenzie paused. "Didn't I ever tell you that story?"

"No."

"I should have. I hauled Rorie inside by the scruff of the neck –

I could do it in those days – and I said, 'It's only going to take one man to fix you now.' And I made him stand in my surgery and begin to count the bottles with the Jolly Roger on them. When he got to twenty I said, 'Do you know what the skull and crossbones mean?' 'Indeed, Doctor, yes I do.' 'Do you know who signs death certificates when men die?' He knew that, too. 'Well, Rorie,' I said, 'think this over. The doctor is a very busy man. The doctor gets tired and needs sleep just like other people. And when the doctor gets wakened up by a rogue at three in the morning, only God Himself has the slightest idea what he might think of doing. Wouldn't it be an awful thing, Rorie, the next time you came in here like this for nothing, if you died knowing that the man who would sign your certificate was going to be me?'"

MacKenzie's right eyebrow cocked as he looked at Ainslie, his blue eyes twinkling. "It fixed him, Dan. What's more, it fixed the whole lot of them in my colliery. I never got so much respect in my life as I got after that."

Ainslie pulled himself to his feet, stretched and then began to laugh grudgingly, more at the old man's remembered pleasure than at the implications of the story, for any sense of fun had to rest in his mind for a while before it began to amuse him.

"It's time for me to have another look at Mrs. Morton," he said as he left the room.

All of Dr. Ainslie's skills as a doctor are required to deal with a young man from Newfoundland:

Now once more Ainslie's brain dimmed and for three hours he was out of the world. His sleep was so profound that it took him longer than usual to come out of it; he kept clinging to the borderline of consciousness because he felt so cool and peaceful he hated to return. He was home in the Margaree Valley where he had been born, it was the Queen's Birthday and he was a boy of fifteen walking down the slope of the hill from his father's house through John MacGregor's field to the river bottom. The meadow at the foot of the hills was stately with lone elms, the fans of their upper branches distinct in the first light, their trunks dim. The tall grass was heavy with dew and he felt the cold wetness come through his trouser legs as he walked through it. As he neared the stream a deer came out of an alder clump and bounded into the field ahead of him, stopped to stare and paw the ground with head held high, feeling safe because it was spring when no guns were fired. The deer's hide was wet with dew and there was a scar on his right shoulder from combat in a past rutting season. The sky lightened, and before the boy reached the river it was grey bright over the hill lines; then the whole landscape began to open up and now he could see the full sweep of the hills coming splendidly down the flanks of the valley to their final bend a mile below him where the river straightened and ran smoothly between meadows to the sea. The boy reached a spit of shingle from which the freshet had receded, walked out on it past a dead hawk with its eyes pecked out and found a washed-up spruce at the place where he wanted to fish. The spruce had been years in the river and its branches were worn as smooth as old bones. He dragged it away from the point and stood in its place with the mainstream at his feet, the water narrowed by the spit so that it poured deep without a ripple and ink-dark in the first light. He secured a homemade fly to his leader and the sound of his reel tore brassily across the monotone of the stream as he made the first trial casts to lengthen his line. The smooth stones of the spit grew white as daylight increased, and by the time he had his second trout, red clouds were splintering out of the east in advance of the rising sun. He remembered Homer's line about the rosy-fingered dawn and was proud of the Margaree, for here as in the ancient Troad the dawn was exactly as Homer had described it. The moist air was fragrant with alder, the cleanest, most innocent smell in the world, and when his rod bent double and the line screamed out for the third time he knew he had a grilse instead of a trout. The grilse broke water once so far down the pool it seemed to have no connection with him at all. The deer returned and stepped noiselessly over the white stones about twenty yards to windward and drank. The reel clacked as the boy wound it in, sang out again, clacked and sang. Then its noise disappeared as the entire valley opened up, the hills rolling back like the Red Sea before the Children of Israel into a light-flooded plain loud with the movement of men in armies, and Dr. Daniel Ainslie opened his eyes.

"I'm sorry, Doctor."

He was back in the hospital again and the air was not cool with alder but stuffy with the smell of the tobacco he and MacKenzie had smoked, compounded with a sharp stink of carbolic sneaking in the open door. The voice of a nurse, so Gaelicky it made two syllables out of every one, actually did sound sorry. A voice like hers sounded sorry all the time.

"I did not want to trouble you, Doctor, with you so tired, but Dr. Weir says the patient is getting too much for him to handle."

Ainslie jumped to his feet. "Confound it, why wasn't I wakened earlier?"

"Och, Doctor, but it iss not the OB case at all, it iss the young Newfoundlander. I think he iss going crazy."

"Is he bleeding?"

"He tried to tear off the bandages, but without hands he could do little harm to himself. Another patient called out, and when I went into the ward, there he wass with his teeth into the gauze. Now he hass the whole ward awake."

"You say Dr. Weir is with him?"

"Yes, Doctor."

Ainslie sat down, scuffed off his slippers and reached for his shoes. "He's probably a little drunk from the ether. However, I'd better take a look at him. People like that with high thresholds of pain sometimes get beside themselves when they panic. Is everything else quiet?"

"There hass been nothing to bother *you* with, Doctor, but of course it iss Saturday night."

Ainslie grunted as he worked his toes into his shoes. The Margaree was still close to him and he hated to leave it.

"Dr. MacMillan hass been busy," the nurse went on. "He iss new and not used to it, and he wass very nice to them, I must say."

"They're lucky they had him to deal with instead of me."

"Indeed, Doctor, that iss just what I said to Red Whillie MacIsaac when he came into the outpatients."

"So he was at it again, was he?"

The nurse was relieved because the doctor she feared more than any of the others seemed to be so congenial tonight.

"Indeed he wass, him and Mick Casey again. They started in

front of Jimmie MacGillivray's and before it wass over it spread all the way up to MacDonald's Corner. Everybody it seems got in on it tonight." She failed to notice that the doctor had begun to frown as he tied the laces of his shoes. "It wass real disgraceful, Doctor. They say Magistrate MacKeegan talked them into it. They were so drunk they were ready to kiss each other, but MacKeegan said loudly why should he spend two dollars to see Archie MacNeil in the ring when he could see Casey and MacIsaac fighting in MacDonald's Corner for nothing, and after a while MacKeegan himself would have been in it only Big Alec McCoubrie reminded him of his position. We had two broken noses, one broken jaw and compound fractures of two ribs altogether. But everything is quiet now."

"Everything?" Ainslie said dryly and walked past her out the door.

He could hear the boy's cries before he reached the open door of the ward. When he entered he saw the heads and shoulders of patients sitting upright in their beds. Only the night lights were burning and the ward was a forest of shadows. Young Weir's white jacket rose from a bedside and approached him with a what-have-you shrug of the shoulders, but he cut the houseman short before he could speak.

"You'd better rest, Weir. I'll take over."

He sat on the side of the Newfoundlander's bed and with quiet strength forced the boy to lower his right wrist. Then he felt the pulse with his finger high on the forearm. It was fast but steady, though the boy's whole body was shaking so violently the bed shook with him. Ainslie put his hand on the forehead and felt the sweat.

"It's not easy, is it, lad?"

The boy sobbed again and his body gave a convulsive twist.

"You can't go on like this, you know."

The boy started up wildly, his chest bursting Ainslie's hands away. "Only a week ago I was 'ome in Newfoundland and look at me now since I come 'ere! I want to go 'ome." He lifted his bandaged stumps and shook them at the doctor. "What kin I do with these?"

"You can lay them on the bed and rest them." Ainslie's hand returned to the sweating forehead and remained there. His fingers felt the trembling nerves begin to relax. Suddenly he smiled. "What's your name?"

The boy swallowed before he spoke. "Bill Blackett." Then for nearly half a minute he lay still, his mind roaming through fear, shock, the lingering delusions produced by the ether and the cloudy effect of the sedatives he had been given.

"With a fine name like that," Ainslie said, "you're going to be famous."

The boy gave a twisted grin. "Blackett ain't so much, but 'ome in Blow-Me-Down they do call me Billy Foreskin."

"What did you do to earn that?"

"Nuthin' I done, zurr, but I got a long 'un."

Ainslie smiled. The quivering in the boy's nerves was less noticeable now. "Can you read and write, Bill?" he said.

"No, zurr, I ain't smart."

"Ever been to school?"

"I were out in the dories when I were eight."

"How do you know you aren't smart," the doctor said, smiling, "if you never went to school?"

"I were none too smart in the dory, thet were what my old man said."

"Don't believe what he said. Believe in yourself, Bill."

"With thim squatten 'ands?"

Ainslie bent forward. "Listen, my boy – you aren't too badly off at all. I've saved four fingers, and on your right hand, too. Did you think I'd turn you loose with no hands?" In the night light the doctor's face became lined and concentrated as once again he merged himself with the patient and moved forward toward the boy's need. "Those four fingers – you think about them. Tonight they became the most important four fingers in the world." He paused as he saw the stare of wonder flicker upwards towards hope, and then he continued in a voice so low the man in the next bed could hear nothing but a murmur. "Before you get out of hospital, you're going to begin to learn how to read and write. All you need for reading is your eyes – and you've got fine eyes, much better than mine. For writing all you need is two fingers of the four you've still got. The day will come when you'll think this accident was the luckiest thing that ever happened to you."

Blackett looked up, then shook his head. "Doctor, I were a fool about them cables with Tom, but I ain't a fool enough to call these squatten 'ands lucky."

"That's just where you're wrong. This accident is going to compel you to get an education. So long as you had your hands, there was nothing in front of your bows but coal-heaving or the dories. But now, Bill, you're going to be man of brains because you've got to be."

It took a while for the shocked mind to grasp even a partial meaning in the doctor's words. Ainslie watched the boy's face quietly and at last he saw the lips part in a slow smile.

"My old man can't read or write neether."

Ainslie smiled back at him.

"My brother Garge knows 'ow to run a motorboat, but last election 'e made 'is mark, same's me." The smile turned into a wide grin. "Doctor, you ought to know Garge, for he's real smart. Last election 'e got two dollars out of the Liberals for voting five times, and seventy-five cents from the Tories for voting twice."

"There couldn't have been many votes left in Blow-Me-Down after that.".

"It weren't in Blow-Me-Down Garge done thet, Doctor, it were in Port-aux-Basques."

"Forget about Garge," Ainslie said. "Think about what you can do yourself for a change. Garge is going to envy you some day."

Ainslie sat by the bedside for another five minutes, speaking occasionally. His quest with the patient had taken his mind out of Cape Breton to a dark grey coast so clean and pure that men, whose crops must rise out of corruption, could grow scarcely a vegetable on it. He saw the outport villages of Newfoundland perched on stilts in nooks of the granite cliffs, square grey huts under a grey sky with sudden blinks of green and yellow emergent over the ocean. He heard the dragging surge of water in Bonavista Bay. He remembered his first glimpse of yellow dories lifting and disappearing in the shelving Banks' roll under a cold mist of rain and the mate of the bark pointing at them, shouting over the scream of a sticky halyard block that those men fished all winter long with bare hands, adding that they couldn't navigate but smelled their way through the fog like seals. He remembered the Newfoundland doctor whose entire practice depended on a motorboat because there were no roads in the district, a thick-set man with bowlegs and wind-burned cheeks, telling him there was less fuss in taking the leg off an outport Newfoundlander without anaesthetic than in removing the tonsils of a city man with all the innovations of a modern operating-room.

"I saw your home once," Ainslie said.

"You seed Blow-Me-Down, zurr?"

"A long time ago. I was younger than you are now. I only saw it from the sea." Ainslie got to his feet, wondering if the place he remembered really had been Blow-Me-Down. "Now turn over and go to sleep. And when you wake up, remember – you're going to learn to read and write."

The ward was silent as Ainslie left it. This time he did not trouble to remove his shoes when he reached the common room, but stretched out in the chair, expecting to be called within the hour. He was wrong. He slept until eight o'clock and then he was wakened by a smiling nurse who was bearing his breakfast on a tray.

Archie MacNeil, Alan's father, is in a sweltering arena in New Jersey, preparing for a fight under the care of his trainer, Charley Moss. The best fighter to come out of Cape Breton is now past his prime; he does not know that his own manager, Sam Downey, has bet against him:

Archie crossed the room to a row of hooks and fumbled in the pocket of a jacket hanging from one of them. He came back with a snapshot in his hand and held it out to Moss.

"That iss the boy," he said.

Moss squinted at the picture through the smoke of his cigarette. "Yeh. He's a nice-looking kid."

"He iss why my wife will not come to me."

Moss handed the snapshot back and shrugged. "Women are only good for one thing. It's something to remember." He turned to the table. "Come here under the light. It's time for the bandages."

Archie held out his right hand and Moss wound the bandage

over the knuckles and wrists with expert care. Then he bandaged the left and Archie clenched his fists and knocked the bandages solid until they seemed like parts of his hands. The door opened with a creak of rusty hinges and one of the semifinal boys came in, followed by the bald-headed seconds supplied by the arena. The fighter's right eye had a mouse under it and his nose was bleeding, but he was pleased because he had won the decision.

Moss picked up a faded green dressing-gown with ARCHIE MACNEIL in a flourish of white letters on the back, and Archie put it on.

"Okay," Moss said, "let's go."

"I whill do my best, Charley."

"You better had. It's all you got left."

As they went out and down the sloping concrete aisle the circus roar of the crowd pounded against the steamy walls of the arena. The crowd was in darkness and suddenly the familiar roar came out of it savagely. But it was not for them; it was for Packy Miller, who had entered the ring from the other side and was dancing about, caparisoned in a shiny black silk dressing-gown, shaking hands with himself and showing his grin. Archie looked at this exhibition with scorn. He crawled through the ropes and went straight to his corner, and his back was turned when Miller cavorted over to give him some more of his grin and slap his shoulders with his bandaged hand.

"Get back where you belong," Moss snarled at him, "before I paste you one myself."

Miller's theatrical grin changed to an equally theatrical scowl and Moss turned back to Archie, well pleased. "That'll bring the bastard out fast," he muttered.

Archie sat down and let Moss massage his legs. Under the lights it was even hotter than he had expected and he hoped he would not have long to wait. At the same time he found it was easy to sit down. Across the ring Miller was dancing and scuffing his toes in the resin, snapping punches at the air and jumping backwards into the ropes and coming off them with his chin down and his arms driving. Archie opened his mouth wide and yawned to fill his lungs. He felt old. Once he had danced around like that before a fight but now he felt none of the old tension. He wanted to knock Miller out and go home. He wanted to sleep in cool air. He realized that an announcer with a voice like a hog caller's was baying his name, weight and birth-place, and he got up and bowed curtly. The only applause he got was the sound of shuffling feet, but he was used to being unpop-ular and did not care. It was fully two years since he had fought with a crowd behind him. When Miller's name was bayed, the mob roared.

Archie got up and stood erect, then walked to the centre of the ring with Moss beside him to listen to the automatic instruc-tions of the referee. Before they turned back to their corners Moss needled Miller once again and Miller made a rush at him which was blocked by the referee. Then Archie was alone in his corner waiting for the gong, with Charley's salt-and-pepper hair sticking up over the apron at his feet and Charley's voice snarl-ing at him to keep his left going. In the opposite corner Miller was acting as though he needed all his will-power to keep from exploding.

Suddenly Archie felt better. Miller was going to come out fast and he would nail him. He was going to win this for Charley Moss. He loved Charley Moss, by Chesus, he did. Looking sideways he saw Sam Downey's pale noseless face for the first time that night. Downey was in the middle of the front row with a cigar in his hand. Archie stared at him and licked the back of his right glove, then the gong rang and he slid forward, saw Miller rushing with his chin down and drove his left into the swarthy face, followed it with a short right to the body that spun Miller halfway around, knocked him back with another left, danced, feinted and split Miller's lips with a left as straight as a piston. He saw the whole face as exposed as a full moon, heard Charley's scream behind him and let go with the right. It smashed in solid and the next thing he saw was Miller on his haunches with a line of blood trickling out of the corner of his open mouth.

He stepped back and felt the ropes chafe his spine. By Chesus, it couldn't be as easy as that!

Then he saw Miller on one knee holding his right glove down on the canvas and he knew he was coming up and was still strong. He saw Miller's grin indicating to the crowd that he was all right and remembered the measurement of his neck. But in spite of that size-eighteen neck, Miller took a count of nine before he got up and Archie saw, as he slid forward, that the Pole's eyes were none too steady. He snapped a left into his face and liked the feel of its impact, but immediately Miller went into a crouch with nothing showing but arms, elbows, gloves and the top of his head. Archie crossed his right and felt a stab of pain and wondered if he had broken a knuckle on Miller's skull. He slammed another right into the pork-barrel body and felt pain again, but he did not believe he had broken any bones in his hand. He decided to work over Miller methodically, but the pork-barrel body exploded against him and his head snapped back in a cloud of stars as Miller butted his jaw in the clinch. Archie felt ashamed to be caught by a butt in the first round, shook loose and went after Miller in a rage. He found nothing but arms and elbows and he seemed to have been punching for hours before the gong ended the round.

"You crazy bastard" – Moss was snarling into his ear – "quit slugging and box him!"

"Work on my legs," Archie muttered. "They feel like they wass nothing in them."

He felt Charley's skilful fingers kneading his calves, but there was no sign of returning life. By Chesus, wass this the time they all waited for, the time the legs went? He told himself he must be careful, but in the next round he let himself be lured into another flurry which ended with Miller wrestling him hard against the ropes. He kept snapping his left into the face in the third round, and in the fourth Miller missed such a theatrical swing that he fell down with the momentum of his own blow. By the end of the fourth Archie was well ahead on points and Miller had failed to land a single solid punch. But Archie came back to his corner shaking his head.

"He iss still strong."

"Keep your left going," Moss muttered. "That's all you got to do."

"By Chesus, I feel like there iss nothing inside of me whatef-fer."

"Maybe there ain't, but there's enough for tonight. This bum is worse than I thought he was." Moss looked down at Downey in the front row and jerked his thumb towards Miller's corner. "How do you like him?" he snarled, so loudly that men three rows behind Downey heard him.

Through a haze of sweat Archie saw the pork-barrel body opposite and could almost feel its strength across the ring. There were six rounds left and he was so tired his loose legs were quivering. That neck on Miller, by Chesus it wass not a neck at all. His head grew out of his shoulders like a gorilla's.

Archie was thinking about the neck when Miller got into a series of clinches in the next round and he had to keep his head off his chin. It was a bad round of boxing without a single clean punch, but when Archie came back to his corner he told himself desperately that the fight was half over and he was still ahead. He felt water splash over his face and shoulders and gulped for air, but the harder he fought for it the less air there seemed to be. Suddenly Charley's face was right there in front of his eyes and Charley was telling him to go in and finish it this round. The gong rang and he did not move. He felt a stab of pain in his left buttock and sprang up from the prod of Charley's penknife and for a moment his head cleared.

Miller was in front of him, chin down as usual, forehead wrinkled, black curly hair sodden with sweat. Archie's left shot out and cut Miller's eye. Another and another left, and Miller staggered back with Archie feline and lethal after him. There was a surge from the crowd, a surge like the noise of water when the tide turns, and Archie knew that support was coming to him at last. Miller heard it too, and in one single lucid moment Archie had time to think what a fool this boy was, for though he had just been shaken, Miller picked this moment to charge. Archie's left flashed out and landed solid. With Miller rushing, that shot would have been decisive if there had been any real snap behind the glove. As it was, it stopped Miller upright and glassy-eyed and the right followed with all Archie had left flickering up through his legs and shoulders and coming out with a bang on Miller's jaw. Archie stepped back with trembling knees and a white coldness clamping his forehead and knew he was through. Miller rolled heavily on the floor and got his elbows under his chest. The referee was counting as slowly as he could and get away with it. Miller tottered up, turned his back on

Archie and grabbed the ropes with both hands. Archie went after him and for several seconds stood there, his brain clouded, not knowing what to do, no reflexes working as he found himself confronted by Miller's back. He swung his right and it landed feebly on Miller's hulking shoulders. Then Miller bent down like a crab, lurched around, grabbed Archie by the waist and hung on. By the time the clinch was broken, he was at least as fresh as Archie was. The round petered out in fumbles and clinches and Archie's legs were weaving when he went back to his corner.

"My luck iss run out on me!" he gasped to Charley Moss and began rolling his head for air.

It was two rounds later before Miller was sufficiently recovered to make a fight of it, two rounds in which the men had lurched around the ring while the crowd booed them. Now Miller was strong again. He wrestled Archie against the ropes and got in four slugging body slams. As Archie staggered, Miller kept after his body, clinched again and savaged the scar tissue over Archie's eyes with the palm of his glove. If Miller was in front of him now, Archie did not know it. The roar of the crowd was something he remembered having heard a long time ago. He saw nothing but the red haze which kept renewing itself in front of his eyes and he felt hardly any pain from the reverberating shocks pounding against his ribs and stomach and the sides of his head. Even now Miller was unable to land a clean punch, but the pounding told. When Archie went down he seemed to be taking an endless time about it. As he lay on a heaving sea he heard a voice screaming that he was yellow. He crawled up out of the tumbling waters and a renewed reverberation told him he was on his feet again, but everything faded out quickly this time. A round later, when he foundered finally into the red thunder inside his own head, he had no knowledge of the fact that he had gone to the floor seven times and come up seven times before he fell for the eighth and last time.

In the front row under the lights, in the heat, smell and roar of noise, Sam Downey stared up at Charley Moss with his little mouth making a circle like a baby's as he sucked on his cigar. Three seats down the row a red-faced reporter leaned toward him and yelled, "What did you bastards do – dope him?"

Downey turned his noseless face and lifted his pudgy hands in a gesture of resigned disappointment. He took the cigar from his mouth and pointed it at the glaring lights over the ring.

"It's hot in here," he piped. "Archie comes from a cold country. He never could fight in heat like this."

Essays 1951–58

"But Shaw Was a Playwright..."

Throughout the 1950s, and beyond, MacLennan's constant financial problems impelled him to write many magazine and newspaper articles. Shortly after this article appeared in The Montrealer *in the summer of 1951, he began to teach at McGill. The position was a part-time one, and involved teaching two courses in English Literature a week. This did not remove all of the financial pressures on him, for the salary was so low that, in Elspeth Cameron's telling phrase, "even his publishers were horrified."*

It was shortly after my last novel made its Canadian debut that somebody said it again. I was in the bank in the act of drawing out a small sum of money, and I mean small. The extremely pretty, competent, and vivacious teller, as she began to count out the bills, said, "It must be wonderful!"

I looked over my shoulder, but the man who stood behind me in line was busy talking to the man who stood behind him, so I looked back at the girl on the other side of the wicket.

"What must be wonderful?" I said.

"Being a writer."

She counted the bills again. "I wish I could write. Just think of never having to get up in the morning like other people!"

"I'm up now," I said, but as I looked at the clock it didn't sound convincing. It was half past ten.

She shoved the bills toward me. "Think of sitting down and

writing something that everyone wants to read and then sitting back to watch the money come rolling in."

I looked at her sharply and wondered if she were mistaking me for the late Lloyd C. Douglas. I thought of telling her I had read only the night before that Sinclair Lewis, after one of the most spectacular writing careers in modern times, had left a mere fifteen thousand dollars, together with some real estate, when he died. But she was smiling at me as I pocketed the bills, and she really did think it was a wonderful thing to be a writer, and what was more, she thought everyone liked what I wrote. If she had been the manager of the bank it would have been the right time to ask for a loan.

"It's a shame to spoil such pleasant thoughts," I said. "But in the strictness of meaning I neither brew nor distil. If I did, then you could be sure that *everybody* would like my products and the money would really be rolling in."

She laughed as I made way for the man behind me. Perhaps it would occur to her later in the day to look up my file and discover the facts of my financial life. But I rather hoped she wouldn't. I could have told her the truth in unmistakable terms; by not doing so I was only living up to the tradition of my profession. Novelists move and have their living by recounting myths to the world. Our books stand or fall by their capacity or ineptness in persuading people that fictitious characters really lived and imaginary events really occurred. Who am I to explode myths concerning the arts?

On the other hand, people believe what they want to believe, and these myths are so well-worn and established that I doubt if any amount of evidence to the contrary will serve to explode them. What if she were to look up my bank account, which was never far from overdraft all the past winter? This charming and capable young teller would still be convinced that writing books was a fine way to watch the money come rolling in. She's seen it in the movies.

As a general rule, the thoughtful public believes that all poets are impractical, all painters are poor, and all novelists are rich. In a vague sort of way I thought so, too, once upon a time. But during the past twenty years I have come to know personally a number of poets and painters, as well as novelists, and I realize that of all the misconceptions generally held about artistic folk, the one which holds poets to be impractical is the silliest. Most of the poets I can think of are extremely shrewd.

An English poet whom I knew well at Princeton is now the head of the British Council in Italy and during the last war served in Military Intelligence in Scandinavia. One well-known poet in Canada has one of the sharpest and clearest legal minds in the country. Still another in France was an important leader in his country's underground during the war. A fourth poet friend of mine was well on his way to becoming president of a large university when he dropped dead at the age of forty-odd. In fact, I have finally reached the conclusion that the ability to write poetry has some strange connection with the ability to administer both men and affairs.

When Wallace Stevens was awarded the Pulitzer Prize for poetry I decided to look up the records for my own satisfaction. Stevens is either president or managing director or something of the like of a large Hartford insurance company. Of him Louis Untermeyer has written, " . . . Stevens is a stylist of unusual delicacy. Even the least sympathetic reader must be struck by the poet's hypersensitive and ingenious imagination." So there is a man of unquestionable talent who is also practical enough to rise to heights in the management of a company with world-wide financial interests. Let's look at some of the others.

David – one of the most beloved poets of all time – was also the greatest soldier-king Israel ever produced. Hadrian, an excellent poet, was the second-best administrator in the long history of Imperial Rome. Aeschylus was an extremely tough infantry soldier, far prouder of having stood in the line at Marathon than of writing the famous *Agamemnon* trilogy. Sophocles at one period of his life was a general of the Athenian republic. Horace was astute enough to acquire a life-pension from Augustus, although he had previously fought against him as an officer in Brutus's army. Vergil also won a life-pension from Augustus, an accomplishment as practical as his poetry was memorable.

Dante played an important role in the politics of Italian city states before he was exiled. Geoffrey Chaucer, gentle poet of *The Canterbury Tales*, served his king as a foreign diplomat, as comptroller of customs on wool and hides, and as clerk of the King's works. François Villon was a celebrated (and practical) thief. Shakespeare made a fortune as a theatre manager. Sir Philip Sidney was a general. Milton served for years in Cromwell's government and was at one time his secretary. Andrew Marvell became a member of Parliament. Goethe was for ten years the principal minister of state in Weimar. In our own day, to find one more example, T. S. Eliot has not only won a Nobel Prize, which is a considerable sum of money, he has also for many years drawn an excellent salary from one of England's largest publishing houses.

So for every Shelley, Heine, and Dowson you can give me on the side of impracticality, I will show you six more poets who knew how to take care of themselves, and command other men into the bargain.

As for the myth that all painters are poor, there is some basis for it – especially in our own day. For one thing, there are so many painters. We are told that more than two million people paint pictures in the United States alone, and clearly only a few of them can earn much money from their painting. Here it is not a question of whether or not painters are practical; the myth says they are poor. Well, it is true that many men who would have been worth large fortunes if they had possessed only a fraction of the price their pictures sell for now were poor enough while they lived. Geniuses like Cézanne and Van Gogh made little money, and Modigliani and Utrillo were always in debt. But again let's look at the record.

In Italy Raphael, Titian, and Michelangelo were patronized by noblemen and popes, and they could afford to live in the style of princes. In the Low Countries Rubens and Van Dyke displayed magnificence in their manner of living. Rembrandt could have lived the life of a rich Dutch burgher from the income he derived from his paintings had he not deliberately turned his back on the things of this world to search for his own private vision. In Spain Velasquez, Goya, and El Greco all rubbed shoulders with grandees and lived in fine style. Even in England, which has never been outstanding in the plastic arts, painters like Reynolds and Gainsborough fared much better financially than the most celebrated of British novelists. Today, without benefit of nobility, Picasso can sell anything he paints for an immense sum.

There are still a lot of hungry artists, to be sure, but we've been talking about top-flight poets and painters through time. It is the exception to find a ranking painter who went hungry, unless a bottle of wine or a tube of paint gave him more promise of pleasure than a loaf of bread.

But the myth which amuses me more than any of the others is the one that would have us believe that all novelists are wealthy. Where on earth did that one start? Relative to the rest of the arts, novel-writing is young, so one can't go as far back as Horace or even Titian to find examples to refute the belief. It is my own conviction that the people who hold it do so from nothing but wishful thinking. Most of them have never thought of composing music, painting a portrait, or even balancing words to make a sonnet, but they are convinced that a novel would be easy to write if only they could find time to get around to it. In fact, they are *going* to write a novel some day. It's the ace in the hole that will over-balance the budget and take the whole family on a trip around the world.

Scott Fitzgerald did nothing to lay this ghost-belief. He was undoubtedly a victim of it himself. When the money made on his first two books came rolling in, he spent it so fast that the news of his exploits could barely keep up with him. But when he died he was some tens of thousands of dollars in debt. That's the trouble with writing for a living. As Dorothy Thompson once said, you can't take out insurance on your brains.

Dostoevsky's works will be considered outstanding as long as people can read. He was even famous while he lived, yet he was seldom out of the hands of the pawnbrokers. Tolstoy never lacked for money, but he was born a nobleman and he gave a large portion of his royalties away in sponsoring a variety of impractical social schemes, including the shipment of Doukhobors to western Canada.

Balzac, the most prolific novelist who ever lived, wrote like a maniac to escape an appalling burden of debt incurred by his failures in the business life he portrayed so brilliantly in his books. Had he saved his earnings he would have been fairly well off; not rich as the great painters have been, but more than comfortable. Yet from his early twenties until his death Balzac was always in need of thousands of francs to raise him to the status of being worth nothing.

Dickens probably fared better financially than any other famous English novelist, but he was the exception which proved a rule in his outstanding nose for a dollar. It is more than likely, however, that he made more money as an actor (reading his own works) than he ever earned as a straight novelist.

It has been estimated by the Authors' Guild that there are, at the present time in North America, scarcely a hundred men and women who can live on the income from their novels alone. Some of them are now able to afford a secretarial staff which allows them to turn out a new book a year, but the majority of novelists whom you and I know by name spend an average of three years writing each book, on which they receive from ten to fifteen per cent of the retail price in royalties. And how many copies does the average full-length novel sell? About three thousand.

You will tell me that in the fields of painting and poetry I have used as examples not the average, but the outstanding. So I have. It is only in the realm of the novel that I can be specific in a quotation of averages. Besides, it is only in the field of novel-writing that so many people are so sure they can hit the jackpot if only they take time to try.

I don't know why I attempt to explode the myth which makes all novelists rich. The life of the writer is generally so quiet and solitary that he is greatly encouraged when he realizes that people who recognize him consider him quite a dog. "It must be wonderful to be a novelist and write something that everyone likes and then watch the money come rolling in." Indeed it must be.

Yet in another sense the life of a novelist *is* wonderful, for he is always dealing with and thinking about people. In time he even comes to understand them a little. So long as there are people about, it is hard to feel dull. Balzac's entire life was a quest for a fortune, but all his business schemes and all his negotiations were upset by his overriding fascination with human nature. Whenever he faced a new creature whom it was important to best in a deal, his genius was busy discovering how this strange man ticked. There were even occasions when he probably wilfully allowed men to cheat him in order to provide himself with knowledge of all the tricks and turns of a sharper's mind.

Such men as Balzac, Sinclair Lewis, Joyce Cary are not practical, in the manner of poets. They seldom make much money, but they do make good novelists and thereby enrich our understanding of man's relationship to men.

George Bernard Shaw? But he was a playwright . . . and that's something else again.

"Orgy at Oriel"

From 1929 to 1932 MacLennan's Oxford home was Oriel College. Some of his memories of those days, while sadly deficient in Matthew Arnold's "high seriousness," provided him with delightful material for humorous essays such as this one, which appeared in 1952:

Every man who drinks does so for reasons of his own, and I am not inclined to probe those reasons or make comment on the varying amounts it takes to satisfy them. But I insist that we need more joy in our drinking, and that good liquor should never have been brought into business. The day when cocktails and highballs were first included in a technique of salesmanship was an evil one. It marked the final triumph of puritanism in our culture. It gave us the idea that the "good" drinker is the man who looks, after his eighth glass, like a corporation lawyer being consulted by the board of a tar-roofing company. It reduced Bacchus from his role of liberator to that of an accomplice in a deal. It made us forget that without the orgy, societies become so bored they prefer war to peace and Mickey Spillane to Shakespeare.

Need I define an orgy? What we saw in *Quo Vadis* was not one; that was debauchery. The purpose of the orgy is to purify the soul. It is to fortify the spirit against the discipline and self-abnegation which a man must practise the rest of the year if he is to earn a living and keep out of jail. The Greeks, who knew everything, understood that without the orgy there is no middle ground between bedlam and Toronto.

Years ago – not too long ago but long enough for memory to

have enshrined the occasion – I had the good fortune to partici-
pate in an orgy conducted by men who had not yet sacrificed
the art of living to the god of efficiency. The place was my college
in Oxford and the occasion was a rare one. The college boat, for
the first time in seventy-five years, had triumphed on the river.
By ancient custom this called for what was known locally as a
"bump supper." In other words, an orgy. In other words, once
permission had been asked of the provost in Latin and granted
in Latin, the whole college was requested to get drunk.

Mine was a venerable institution, already more than six centuries old, and though it is called Oriel now, its original name
was The House of the Blessed Mary the Virgin. Its founder was
King Edward the Second "of famous memory," and every Sunday in chapel we prayed for his soul. Its visitor was the King, its
dean the man who is now Bishop of London, and in my last
year its provost was a stern Scotch Presbyterian of vast learning,
whose abilities had gained him a knighthood and whose schol-
arship had made him world-famous among those who are still
interested in Aristotle. Among the sons of the college were Sir
Walter Raleigh, of whom we were proud, Dr. Thomas Arnold,
of whom we were not proud, Beau Brummell, whom we envied,
Cardinal Newman, whose prose we admired, and Cecil Rhodes,
whose benefactions have changed the lives of several thousand
American and Dominion students, including my own.

In this institution there were no women. Not only were there
none in the college but there were none outside to whom we
could talk even if we wished. We lived austerely. Our rooms were
unheated, our food was English, we were supposed to do more
work in a single year than an American undergraduate does in
four. We were in perfect health, and though we numbered no
more than one hundred and sixty scholars and gentlemen-
commoners, we fielded two rugger teams, two soccer teams, and
two ground-hockey teams, and put four eight-oared shells on
the river every afternoon. It is true that occasionally we got
drunk. After Big Tom in Christ Church had struck his one
hundred and one bells at 9:10 every evening and the vast college
gates were closed and barred, there were occasions when students poring over texts in their rooms heard bibulous laughter
in the quadrangles below. But these were minor palliatives,

private parties or the aftermath of pub-crawls. The night no Oriel man of my time will ever forget was The Great Orgy, the binge so rare that it had come to us only after seventy-five years, small span though that may have been in the history of the college.

I wonder if I can indicate what that bump supper was like.

It began, as all good things should, with the blessings of religion. At seven-thirty one evening the college assembled in full dress in the hall. On the dais sat the provost and the fellows, together with the unfortunate crew of the boat which had earned us the orgy and in consequence were condemned to dine with the dons. Far happier was the rugger team, which had appropriated the table next to the door leading to the buttery, knowing in advance that every tray of wine borne forward would have to run its gauntlet to get through. We were drunk before the oarsmen had eaten their fish. But I am anticipating.

The orgy, as I said, began with the blessings of religion. So it was with the Greeks and so it was with us. The dean rose in his robes and silence fell. He closed his eyes and intoned a prayer imploring the Lord to fill our hearts with joy and gladness. The prayer was in Latin, but never have I been present when a prayer in any language was answered so quickly, for the moment the dean sat down the orgy got under way. It proceeded with the sureness of the passage of a celestial body through the sky to its pre-ordained climax.

By the time the dinner was over the venerable dining-hall looked as if a tornado had struck it. The dons, bombarded by potato balls, were hiding under the high table – all but the dean, who was a privileged don on this particular night. Wine glasses broke into fragments, bottles rolled under the benches, and a divinity student – his boiled shirt scarlet with wine, wine in his hair, and wine running out of his ears – was dancing on top of the high table under the portrait of Edward the Second. He ululated. He called down imprecations on the memory of St. Augustine. He announced that he was participating in a rite older than the Thirty-nine Articles of the Church of England, as indeed he was. He adjured us to follow his example. I never saw him after his subsequent ordination, but I doubt if any of his sermons have been addressed to a more rapt congregation.

When the hall was wrecked and the damask so wine-stained that it looked like an abattoir, the whole college poured out to the front quad, where a bonfire was laid. The noise we made rose over Oxford like the roar of a vast conflagration. Up to every pinnacle of the roof students swarmed bearing chamber-pots, that favourite symbol of the British undergraduate. Bottles of methylated spirits were sent up after them on cords, the pots were filled, the fires ignited, and soon the roof of the college was ringed with flame.

Meanwhile, on the ground a still more ancient ritual had begun. One hundred and sixty Englishmen, together with two Americans, one Australian, and one Canadian, in dinner jackets and boiled shirts, were dancing round the fire. Shadows plunged on the walls behind which Newman had meditated on the Holy Ghost and Rhodes had dreamed of empire. The dons had withdrawn to the safety of the senior common room in the second quad, and under the portico the senior scholar declaimed Latin verse. In the entrance by the porter's lodge the agile divinity student, still dripping with wine, was calling us on to a still greater show of vitality and power. One by one, every window in the front quadrangle crashed and fell in fragments as empty bottles hurtled through them.

My sense of time was not exact on that night and it may have been an hour after dinner or much later that the climax of the evening occurred.

Our new provost, as has been said, was a Scotch Presbyterian. He had granted the orgy because he understood the constitution of the college, but he had not joined in its spirit. He remained sober. He had retired, as custom prescribed, to the safety of the senior common room. What prompted him to leave that sanctuary, what impulse led him to the front quad where no don save the dean was supposed to be, we never knew. Suddenly we saw him in our midst, gowned and in full dress. It was obvious then that nothing, absolutely nothing, could save him. And nothing did.

A howl went up. A hunting-horn began to blow. The crowd stopped dancing and closed in. The provost disappeared under a mass of bodies.

Then like a flag the provost's pants appeared on high. The

man himself, still wearing his boiled shirt and gown, was lifted to his feet in order to observe what happened to his trousers. They were tossed and torn, the shadows of their flapping legs leaped fantastically against the walls, then they were committed to the flames. The hunting-horn blew again and one among us (he is now rector of another Oxford college) closed in with a fire-extinguisher. Our provost at last got the point. He turned and fled, the fire-extinguisher squirting at his shirt-tails. As he reached the arch leading into the second quad one of his most promising pupils threw the dregs of a claret bottle over his bald head.

After this moment my witness ceases abruptly. Somehow or other I found myself talking to the dean. I was telling him how much I liked him. I was complimenting him on the beauty of his voice in chapel and I may even have suggested that he consider me a catechumen for the Church of England, since his conduct that evening had persuaded me that his religion was more tolerant and joyous than my own. And all the time the dean was leading me quietly toward the front gate.

Then it happened. The little door in the great gate opened and a monstrous force impelled me outward. The door slammed shut behind me and against its four inches of oak and iron bars I was helpless. The dean had done his duty. Third-year men lived in digs out of college. They must be back in their digs by midnight or face the proctors. St. Mary's chime rang three times and I knew it was a quarter to twelve and that for me the revels were over. After reeling down the High Street I stopped a moment on Magdalen Bridge and saw the Cherwell trying to drink up the moon.

Next day the whole college of St. Mary the Virgin felt purer than it had felt in seventy-five years. It wanted neither wine, women, nor song. At eleven the next morning I entered the gate and as I looked around, the night before seemed like a dream. Already a team of glaziers had replaced the broken windows. The refuse of the bonfire had been cleared away and no broken glass was in sight. In hall the long refectory tables were grave and silent under the paintings. I set out to the provost's rooms for my weekly tutorial and at his door I encountered my tutorial mate. He was the scholar who had emptied the claret dregs on the provost's head the night before. But the provost, who undoubtedly remembers that night still, gave no indication that anything improper had occurred. He listened with his usual gravity to my essay on the Right and the Good. He was a great man. Though he had lost his pants, his dignity remained intact.

We need the healing grace of the orgy in this country but I confess myself at a loss to suggest what we can do about it. Even if our colleges possessed the wisdom of Oxford, we don't stay young forever. In middle age we frequent cocktail bars and backrooms, and babble at cocktail parties, and occasionally drink alone. These are pallid substitutes for the release of the orgy. It is no wonder we have as many wars as we do; war is the greatest orgy of all. Unfortunately it is also the most expensive and people and cities get hurt.

Then there is the matter of the women in our midst, who are probably more frustrated than ourselves. Perhaps there should be orgies for them. It's no new idea. In the eleventh edition of the *Encyclopaedia Britannica* I found this description:

"The Dionysiac Orgies, which were restricted to women, were celebrated in winter in spots remote from city life. The women met, clad in fawn-skins, with hair dishevelled, swinging the thyrsus and beating the cymbal; they danced and worked themselves into a state of mad excitement. The holiest rites took place at night by the light of torches. A bull, representative of the god, was torn to pieces by them, and his bellowings reproduced the cries of the suffering god. The women tore the flesh with their teeth, and the eating of raw flesh was a necessary part of the ritual."

Impractical? Immoral? I can only say that in those days divorce was not a problem.

From "Christmas Without Dickens"

A later essay from 1952 entitled "Christmas Without Dickens" concludes with this passage:

. . . After I came back from Oxford the unnatural pattern went on. Instead of being a day of joy, Christmas became a day of insight and experience. Sometimes I was in New York, sometimes at home where it was normal enough. But generally something happened and once – the most wonderful Christmas I ever spent – life seemed desperate before suddenly it changed. That was the one I spent in the hospital wondering whether my wife would live or die. That was the Christmas when I never thought of Dickens at all, but went back into time about as far as a man can ever go.

The struggle had been going on for days, each day harder than the one before. It was a fair Christmas, but I entered it with a foreboding I have never known before or since. Strain and imagination were telling. Everyone I passed, even beautiful girls, I seemed to be seeing as though they were old, their flesh shrunken as in the hour of their death. Sunlight flickered among the tree boles on the mountain and squirrels came down through fluffy snow to the hospital doors. A church carillon in the lower city was playing "Adeste, Fideles" and the faithful were coming from early Mass. I went into the hospital and the nurse's whisper was not reassuring. In the room I met with bare recognition. It was the same sight that had become so familiar: the tubes, the bottle dripping its liquid into the splinted arm, the rattle of desperate breathing. I sat down and time ticked on, empty and without significance.

Some time around noon the nurses got me out of there and I sat in the lounge at the end of the floor and looked down at the city in the sun and snow. Christmas dinner was brought but I ate only a few bites and pushed the plate away. I was the only person around until an interne came in and sat down and talked.

I was grateful for his thoughtfulness in sitting with me that afternoon instead of going home. After a time I left him and went back into the room. From a radio in the room next door came a faint sound of carols and I thought I could hear the story of the Nativity being retold. Perhaps I slept. Those days I hardly knew when I was asleep or awake, but all the time I was conscious of the desperate struggle for breath on the bed. I remember noticing it was dark in the room and that lights had come on outside. It was as dark, I thought, as eternity; as the low bottom of an anaesthetic; as the beginnings of time.

Then suddenly I sat upright with the feeling that something

had brushed me lightly and passed. Now, though everything was the same even to the sound of the breathing, the room felt different and an enormous pressure slid away and seemed to sink into the floor.

I went over to the bed, then turned as I felt a hand on my shoulder and saw the doctor's face.

"You'd better stay here tonight," he said.

It would have sounded worse than strange, it would have been wrong and shocking if I had said to him, who had the responsibility, that a few minutes before he entered the room I had felt death go out of it and life come back in.

That night I walked down the steep hill to Sherbrooke Street and when I got on the bus everyone looked young and their faces shone. A friend had asked me to a Christmas party and I looked in for a while but did not stay, for it was a Dickens party and the longer I stayed the more surely I felt like the skeleton at a Roman feast. I walked home and went to bed without dinner and as I fell asleep Handel's music sang through my mind – that exultant chorus that seems to express all the passionate hope of the human race – "O thou, that tellest good tidings to Zion – arise and shine, for thy light is come!"

The next day, as I knew would be the case, the doctor stopped worrying, too.

"The Shadow of Captain Bligh"

MacLennan could enjoy the jazz he described in The Precipice *but his true love was classical music. This wide-ranging essay, published in 1953, demonstrates the range of his interests; Haydn, Captain Bligh, Einstein, Mickey Spillane, and Albert Schweitzer all make an appearance here:*

Not long ago, in the same evening, I listened to my gramophone recording of Haydn's *Mass for St. Cecilia* and then went upstairs and began rereading the account of the mutiny on H.M.S. *Bounty* as written by Nordhoff and Hall. The grand cadences of the Mass kept sounding through my mind, and every now and then I stopped reading to let them swell and subside. I was rereading the book for a purpose and I didn't feel I could put it down. But the counterpoint made me realize with a sensation of shock that Joseph Haydn and Captain Bligh were contemporaries, that the society that had produced and honoured the one was the same society that had employed and respected the other.

Haydn's *Mass for St. Cecilia*, which was partially lost until Dr. Brand recovered it little more than a decade ago, and which hardly anyone had heard performed until it appeared recently in a recording of the Haydn Society, is certainly one of the most sublime works the human spirit has ever created. It seems to me worth all the music composed since the death of Beethoven. Beethoven himself was never able to sustain the power that is manifest here, for his struggle with himself and his medium was too great. Haydn's Mass, like the greatest work of Shakespeare, is at once majestic and intimate. Above all it seems effortless, and its joy and triumph are so breath-taking that no one who is moved by music can easily listen to it without reflecting that our modern world has produced no creative genius with his originality, his joyousness, or his power.

Yet Haydn was not unique in his time. His career overlapped those of Bach, Handel, Mozart, and Beethoven. Though his age acclaimed him a master, it occurred to nobody in the eighteenth century to think it miraculous that he was able to compose those immensely complex works, some of great length, in so short a time. The best of his contemporaries were equally prolific and worked with equal speed. Handel composed *The Messiah* in a few weeks and Mozart wrote one of his most famous symphonies in a few days. Compared to these eighteenth-century masters, a modern creative artist moves at a snail's pace. Our most famous poets will die leaving behind only a slim body of published verse. The average modern novelist takes from two to three years to write a single good novel. Our musicians – men like Sibelius, Stravinsky, and Vaughan Williams – have together, in their long lives, equalled only a fraction of Haydn's output.

How lucky Haydn was to have lived before the radio and the telephone, before civic societies which would have made exorbitant and unavoidable demands on his time and energy, before publicity and interviewers and income tax and traffic horns and metropolitan dailies – to have lived, in short, before the age of distraction.

But *Mutiny on the Bounty* reminded me of the other side of the eighteenth century. The very fact of Captain Bligh implies that the forces which have made ours an age of distraction are far subtler and less avoidable than technical innovations like the telephone and the radio. *Mutiny on the Bounty* should be required reading for anyone who is apt, like myself, to be romantic about past ages and to decry his own. For Captain Bligh was just as typical of the eighteenth century as Haydn was. When I bow before Haydn I must remember that Haydn accepted without question and apparently without remorse the fact that he lived in a world that contained Captain Bligh.

Nothing Mickey Spillane has ever written can be compared in horror to some of the factual scenes in *Mutiny on the Bounty*. Few passages in literature describe more revolting episodes than those of the *Bounty* sailors being seized in the gangway and flogged until the flesh hung in strips from their backs. With our modern knowledge of neurology, we know that the agonies of these poor creatures did not end when the boatswain's mate ceased swinging the cat. Such beatings damaged the nerve roots along the spine and condemned the victims to permanent suffering. What makes those scenes of torture so unbearable to think about is the added realization that they were not sporadic, were not the offshoots of a psychopathic movement like Nazism, but were standard practice in one of the most stable and reflective societies that ever existed. Captain Bligh's cruelty had the weight and approval of his entire society behind it. When the mutineers were later court-martialled, the court had no interest in determining whether Bligh had been cruel or not. It was interested solely in whether the accused had obeyed to the letter the harsh laws of the British Navy.

Haydn, Bach, Handel, and Mozart, sublime spirits full of mercy, with sensibilities exquisitely delicate, knew that men like Bligh were the mainstays of the societies they inhabited. Yet this knowledge, which to us would be a shame, felt personally, seldom if ever troubled their dreams or ruffled their serenity. The humanitarianism that disturbed Beethoven a generation later had not dawned when Haydn wrote the *Mass for St. Cecilia*.

Haydn reached his prime in the last moments when it was

possible for a creative artist to mind his own business in the sense that his conscience could remain untroubled by the sufferings of the unfortunate. If sailors were flogged to death and peasants had no rights, if a neighbouring country was ruined by famine or pestilence, if laws were unjust or princes cruel, none was Haydn's affair. He was compelled to no empathy in the suffering of others as modern artists are.

It is this awareness of personal responsibility for the welfare of strangers that makes uneasy all men of imagination today, that troubles their work and makes much of it seem tortured, that frustrates it, too, for seldom can a modern man of creative imagination do anything concrete to change the world he lives in.

Responsible only to himself, to his family, and to his God, Haydn enjoyed a freedom few artists have known since. The result was as glorious as it is inimitable. It is on most of his successors that the shadow of Captain Bligh has fallen and remained.

As Haydn represents the spiritual grandeur of the eighteenth-century imagination, Bligh represents its irresponsibility. In Bligh's own words, it was only through fear and cruelty that the stupid, the weak, the incompetent, the ignorant, and the unfortunate could be ruled and compelled to do what their masters considered to be their duty. Unless they were so compelled, the supporters of the system argued, there could be no fineness, no spiritual grandeur, no great literature or beautiful buildings, no masses for St. Cecilia. Civilization, as men of Haydn's day conceived it, could not exist if it yielded to the promptings of a social conscience.

When we realize this it becomes easier to reconcile ourselves to the fact that the world we live in is producing no more Haydns or Mozarts. In the nineteenth century men of imagination turned their attention to the miseries of the world they saw about them, accepted responsibility for it, and forever lost the peace and concentration of spirit which enabled the Haydns and Mozarts to devote the full force of their genius to the realization of the gifts God had given them.

Could a modern artist witness a public flogging and then go home and compose exquisite music? Could he even live quietly under a régime that permitted such atrocities and retain his own respect and that of others?

Merely to ask such questions is to answer them. Musicians who took no more active part in the Hitler régime than perform for a Nazi audience have had to spend years as outcasts before western society would accept them again. The social conscience of today demands the service of every artist alive, and does not forgive him if he refuses it.

On the other hand western society did not make outcasts of the physicists, chemists, and engineers who served Hitler. Until very recently science reserved for itself the same mental freedom that art enjoyed in Haydn's days. If politicians or monsters used the work of science for evil purposes, the scientists felt no personal responsibility. Enjoying such peace of mind, physicists and chemists have been able to devote the full forcè of their intellects to their work, and so their work has been more impressive than that of the artists who were their contemporaries. No wonder our age, when it looks for a genius to match Bach or Haydn, does not even stop to search among the ranks of the artists. It picks Einstein.

But when the atomic bomb fell on Hiroshima any number of scientists succumbed to a social conscience as the artists had done long ago. Einstein, Oppenheimer, and hundreds of others were overcome with a Hamlet-like self-questioning. If our world lasts long enough it will be interesting to see whether science in the next generation will be as original and productive as it has been in the last three. For a conscience, as Shakespeare knew when he created Hamlet, inhibits action and beclouds genius. Our collective conscience may not have made the modern artist a coward, but it has certainly made him a prisoner.

Consider in contrast to Haydn the life of Albert Schweitzer. Schweitzer began as a musician, and had he lived in the eighteenth century there is no knowing what masterpieces he might have composed. But his conscience would not permit him to devote his entire life to music, so he studied theology and became a minister of the Gospel. Then his conscience told him that preaching was not enough, so he studied medicine and became a doctor. His conscience then informed him that it was self-indulgent to practise medicine in a comfortable European city while there were millions in the world without medical care of any kind. So Schweitzer took his gifts to one of the most primitive parts of Africa. There he has lived and worked ever since, among men so elemental that they can know nothing of Bach or Haydn and cannot even guess at the greatness of the strange healer who came to help them.

Albert Schweitzer will die leaving behind him no tangible or audible monument, no record of objective achievement beyond a few books which are mere by-products of his life and interests. His enormous powers have been spread so widely in the service of others that neither as a musician, nor as a theologian, nor as a doctor-scientist, has his work, in itself, been such as to ensure his immortality. An earlier age would have said that Schweitzer had squandered his gifts on savages. But our age, rightly or wrongly, acclaims him as one of its noblest representatives because his life has translated into action, as hardly any other life has done, the highest aspirations of our social conscience.

No other modern artist I know of has made the total sacrifice of his talents that Schweitzer made; yet no modern artist (musician or poet or even the great individualist, Picasso) has been undisturbed by the social conscience of our day.

Critics who argue that the subject-matter of modern art is proof of the decadence of modern society don't really understand what they are talking about. Art has always been a reflection of the aspirations and obsessions of its time and the art of today is no exception. If it is haunted and distracted, if it is often ugly and even horrifying, it does not mean that the artists themselves are worse men than Haydn was. It means only they have not refused, as Haydn did, to accept responsibility for Captain Bligh. For all its horrors, the twentieth century is better than the eighteenth; no politician or dictator who has tried to defy its conscience has been able, in the end, to succeed.

Some time in the future art may reflect the tranquillity that Haydn knew. If it does so, it will not be because those artists of the future are likely to be abler men than artists of today. It will happen because, after this age of transition, the shadow of Captain Bligh has been removed from the whole world.

From "Fury on Ice"

MacLennan was a keen sportsman, and his novels include many convincing scenes of physical action, such as Archie MacNeil's last fight. This 1954 essay is his tribute to Canada's national passion – hockey:

Hockey night in Montreal. The crowds on their way to the Forum from buses, trams, and cars walk bowed against the winter wind – but who cares how cold it is? The colder the better, for hockey is a game that goes with frosty breaths, fur caps and overshoes, thick gloves that you beat together when the swirling players produce emotion so intense you couldn't stand it in July.

Inside the Forum the air is clear and cold – much colder than in most American arenas, but warm compared to Canadian rinks before the days of artificial ice. Overhead lights are blazing and the remaining empty seats show banks of grey, blue, or orange, according to price and location. Talk swells and echoes as the seats fill up – eight thousand, now ten, now fourteen thousand – until you look up and see that even the catwalks above the lights and the television cameras are black with people. Smooth, clean, and white, the ice spreads out between the waist-high boards, drawing everyone's eyes, for the ice itself is a part of the drama of this game and the coloured lines beneath the frozen water make its expanse seem larger than it is. There are three lines across the rink. A broad red one transversely bisects the ice and runs between the giant C's of the home-club's insignia in the exact centre of the rink. Between the red line and each of the two goals runs a line of deep blue. Besides being decorative, these three lines determine the offsides, red marking the limit for a forward pass by the defenders, blue for the attackers. The two goals at either end of the rink and a few feet out from the boards look very empty. Even a child could bat a puck into them now.

There is a stir in the crowd, a spatter of handclaps, then a rising thunder. From the players' benches in the centre on opposite sides of the rink the two teams debouch onto the ice.

Les Canadiens of Montreal, once known as the Flying French-men, are receiving the Red Wings of Detroit.

Gerry McNeil of Montreal and Terry Sawchuk of Detroit, bulky in their goalies' pads and swaying as they move, skate slowly to their cages, turn about, and face down the ice. From now until the game ends those nets will seem to shrink in size, because two men with nerves of steel and the reflexes of leopards – two men who have calculated shot angles to a fraction of an inch – crouch before them to keep the puck from getting past.

Now begins the invariable ritual that precedes every hockey game. We have seen it countless times but it always looks fresh. The warm-up begins and the players stream round and round their own halves of the rink, shooting at their own goalies, a pouring of red jerseys at the Detroit end, of white ones at the end defended by Montreal. With the warm-up come the famil-iar sounds – the ring and snick of skate blades and the special noises made by the puck. Against the goalie's pads the puck hits with a heavy thud; in close stick-handling it clucks; when it strikes the crossbar of the goal it gives out a loud clang; it makes a flat crack against the broad blade of the goalie's stick; and when it misses the goal and hits the boards it sends a reverberat-ing bang through the whole arena. These puck and skate noises excite the crowd like a bugle before a horse race, and thousands of men can almost feel their hands closing over a hockey stick as their recollections range back ten, twenty, perhaps even fifty years to a time when hockey was never played in a forum like this with red and blue lines, with artificial ice and comfortable seats and television, with French and English radio announcers reporting the game in frenetic voices to a listening nation and to hundreds of thousands of Americans.

A few minutes before 8:30 the referee and the offside judges glide onto the ice looking neat and small in their white jerseys and dark blue trousers. The teams line up, each on its own blue line facing toward centre ice, sticks held downward on the ice before them. The audience rises for the national anthem. The players look enormous because of their bulky pads and the added height given by skates. Their coloured jerseys and long coloured stockings are bright against the shining ice.

On the last note of music a roar bursts from the crowd, the alternate players skate off to the benches behind the boards, the goalies hunch forward, the centres bend for the face-off, the two wings and two defencemen on each side tense themselves, the referee gives a last look around to make sure there are no more than twelve men on the ice. Then, as he drops the puck, the black sweep hand of the huge clock at the end of the amphitheatre begins to revolve.

From now until the game ends that clock will share the drama. It will measure out sixty minutes of playing time, it will stop whenever there is a goal made, an offside, a penalty, or one of those outbursts of wrath or enthusiasm in the crowd vented by throwing rubbers and overshoes onto the ice. It will rest for ten minutes after the first period and for ten minutes after the second, but compared to the time clock of a football game, it will move fast. There are few delays in ice hockey, and such long ones as do occur are exciting, for they are generally caused by a Donnybrook.

The fact that there may be a Donnybrook tonight adds to the excitement of this rabid Montreal crowd. For these two clubs, Canadiens and Red Wings, are not only the best in the world this season; there is so little to choose between them that the smallest kind of break – a glancing puck, a screened shot, a penalty at a bad moment – will probably decide the outcome. It is said these teams hate each other. They don't really. They merely behave as the Dodgers and Giants would if they carried sticks and could crash into each other at a combined speed of forty miles an hour.

There is Ted Lindsay of Detroit, finest left wing in the game, truculent and jaunty; merely looking at him makes some people mad. His mate on right wing is big Gordie Howe, top point-getter in the league, his superb skating legs built like tree trunks. Once he was even-tempered and smiling, but since his nearly fatal accident a few years ago he has become one of the bad men in the league. On defence for Detroit are Red Kelly and Marcel Pronovost. Names like Pronovost, once found almost exclusively in the line-up of the Canadiens, are now dotted through American-based clubs. They are good names in hockey, for this game suits the Gallic *élan*. Kelly also has a good name for hockey and at present is the finest defenceman alive. This is one Irishman who would rather play than fight, for Kelly more than once has won the Lady Byng Trophy for gentlemanly play.

But this is a Montreal crowd and it worships its own heroes extravagantly. Ahead of them all is Maurice Richard, "The Rocket," who breaks the league's all-time scoring record (his own) every time he drives a puck through the goal posts. He, too, was once amiable, but ten years of being close-checked and nagged by lesser men have given him a trigger temper, and in the matter of collecting penalties, the Rocket is right up front with Lindsay and Howe. Richard is the Babe Ruth of hockey, as powerful and as unpredictable. Smouldering darkly, he glides in and out, often playing two or three nights without showing a spark of brilliance, but on the fourth night he will explode – and nobody ever forgets the sight. There never was a hockey player with the Rocket's power to focus a crowd's emotion and jerk their hearts out. I have seen him – what follower of the Canadiens has not? – go careening in on a single skate with one enemy wrapped around his neck and another dogging his elbows, his eyes blazing yet so cool for all his heat that he will draw the goalie a few inches away from the spot he has picked and blast the puck into it. No man ever lived who could get a shot away faster than the Rocket. And when he breaks through, he seems to do so by sheer force of passion.

On defence for the Canadiens are two happy warriors, huge Butch Bouchard and smooth Doug Harvey. Butch is the team's policeman, amiable as most French Canadians are if unprovoked, but when slashed so dangerous that the clinic prepares to receive his provoker. Among those on the bench who will shortly appear are Jean-Marc Béliveau, *le gros Bill*, mourned by the whole of Quebec City when he left his home town to play in the National Hockey League. Also on the bench is Boom-Boom Geoffrion whom I once saw score a goal while unconscious. Releasing a terrific shot from the blue line just as a checker crashed into him, he was knocked out an instant before the puck struck the net.

As for the two men who guard the goals, they seem miraculous to me. Other hockey players work in hot blood, but the goalie crouches and waits for pucks that flash at him at ninety miles an hour from point-blank range. I have seen a goalie led off the ice with nine teeth knocked out – and return ten minutes later to shut out the opposition. In 1936 I once saw two goalies, Normie Smith of the Red Wings and Lorne Chabot of the old Montreal Maroons, hold their forts intact from 8:30 on the Tuesday evening when the game began until about 2:25 the following Wednesday morning, when "Mud" Bruneteau won the game for Detroit with a screened shot. That Stanley Cup playoff – a Stanley Cup game can never end in a draw and if the teams are tied at the end of regulation play they continue until a goal is scored – lasted so long that we saw nearly three full matches for the price of one.

Now the charging lines sweep down on the defences. They crash in, the pattern of the attack is shattered, the puck shoots off into a corner. There is a scramble, then out of chaos a new pattern forms and the red jerseys of Detroit pour down into the white jerseys of the Canadiens, the puck darts from stick to stick, a shot at the goal, a deflection to the side of the net, another counter-attack and the puck is held in the Detroit end. A whistle blows, the first lines skate off and the second lines replace them. The puck is dropped again and the game goes on at the same furious pace; the goals are defended so expertly it seems impossible to score, and everyone knows that this is a game that can be decided in a single second. Somebody elbows someone into the boards, the referee signals the time-keeper and the little red light comes on beside the penalty clock.

Penalties are the climactic moments of a hockey game, for when one team plays for two or five minutes with a man short, the other throws in its first line for a power play. For the next two minutes the crowd utters a steady thunder of yells and jeers to ease its tension. The pace is frantic as the defenders work to keep the puck at the other end of the ice and the attackers battle for a goal. The shouting, gasping crowd shares all the passion of the wild struggle, feeling a part of its fury. Hockey is like that – it makes those who live it feel bigger, bolder, stronger, faster, and more reckless than they really are. A shot, a rebound, another shot, still another save, another scramble, a razzle-dazzle of rapid passes and another shot misses the goal and crashes into the boards. The defence breaks loose and lofts the puck down the ice and the attackers have to go back for it. In the brief moment it takes them to regroup and send another attacking pattern down the ice, the crowd glances up to the scoreboard to see how much longer the penalty has to run. Eighteen seconds more. High in the rafters announcers as excited as anyone in the arena are screaming in French and English the progress of the game. "He's going in there on the left side – a pass out – there's a scramble in front of the goal – Richard has it – he *SHOOTS – HE SCORES!!!*"

And when he does so, like an instantaneous *panache* of triumph, a red light blazes on behind the goal. Sawchuk digs the puck nonchalantly out of the corner of his net and bats it down to the referee at centre ice. He looks up at the clock and sees there are about forty-eight minutes left. Then he bends forward and faces down-ice again. The puck is dropped almost instantly and the game is under way again.

Natives of Spain and Mexico find incomprehensible the initial reaction of most foreigners to the bull-fight. Canadians feel the same way when strangers express horror at the violence of ice hockey. They even query the novitiate's assumption that the chief attraction is speed.

If you rave to a hockey player about the speed of the game, he is likely to inform you that speed is secondary to the ability to stick-handle, swerve, break your pace, and to stay on your feet after the shock of a body check; speed is by no means as important as all-round skating ability. No Canadian has won a world's speed-skating championship in the last quarter-century, but hockey players like Aurel Joliat and Toe Blake, who were never particularly fast, were nonetheless incomparably finer skaters than the men who race, just as cowboys are better all-round horsemen than jockeys. Speed-skating is only a kind of running on skates, but in hockey the skates of the player are so integrated with his body and brain that they become a part of his personality. The good hockey player never lurches, strains, or runs. Watch him closely and see how he glides.

During one of the relatively rare delays that hold up the progress of a hockey game, I watched Maurice Richard skating around in that restless way he has. For what must have been a half-minute, his blades never once left the ice. This kind of skating enables a hockey player to last for years despite the game's violence. Men like Elmer Lach and Milt Schmidt, in early middle age, could glide through a maze of hard-driving youngsters and appear the swiftest men on the ice when in fact they were taking their time. They moved from the hips rather than from the thighs and calves, and they drove hard only when putting on that extra burst of speed that took them through the defence. Even the huge Ching Johnson was this kind of skater, otherwise he could never have played NHL hockey in his fortieth year. Skating ability of this sort must be learned in childhood, and that is why men from this land of long winters dominate the hockey world. Of the great hockey players only Eddie Shore and the late Lionel Conacher developed skating technique after the age of fourteen.

The violence of hockey is another matter, for though some of it is encouraged by rink owners for its shock value, most of it is a part of the game itself.

Next to the Swedes and the Swiss, Canadians in their daily lives are probably as self-restrained as any people in the world. By comparison, Americans often seem as volatile as Latins. Yet the favourite sports of Americans are neat, precise games like baseball and college football. Baseball I dearly love, but after growing up with hockey, I find American college football as slow as an American finds a week-long cricket match; even its violence seems cold to me. But the violence of hockey is hot, and the game at its best is played by passionate men. To spectator and player alike, hockey gives the release that strong liquor gives to a repressed man. It is the counterpoint of the Canadian self-restraint, it takes us back to the fiery blood of Gallic and Celtic ancestors who found themselves minorities in a cold, new environment and had to discipline themselves as all minorities must. But Canadians take the ferocity of their national game so much for granted that when an American visitor makes polite mention of it, they look at him in astonishment. Hockey – violent? Well, perhaps it is a little. But hockey was always like that and it doesn't mean that we're a violent people.

We are, though – underneath the surface. And our national game breeds heroes who are worshipped as frantically as Babe

Ruth and Joe DiMaggio ever were. Nor do any athletes earn their hero worship in a harder field.

At the start of each season, a professional hockey player knows that he faces almost certain injury of a pretty spectacular kind. By the time he retires he has lost count of the stitches taken in various parts of his anatomy. Stick and skate gashes; broken jaws, cheekbones, teeth, collarbones, ribs, ankles, and legs; shoulder separations, sprains, and dislocations are so common in hockey that teams seldom take the ice at full strength. Any difference in ability between the best teams in the National Hockey League is so slight that the Stanley Cup is usually won by the club which enters the playoffs with the fewest injuries. Yet in the entire history of the NHL, only one player has died as the result of a rink accident, and only one other has come close to death.

The one who died was Howie Morenz, the greatest all-round forward and the most beloved hockey player the game has known. Morenz has been compared to Babe Ruth, but he was much more like Walter Johnson; he had Johnson's rare combination of speed, power, and gentleness, and there was something in his style that made everyone love him. I was in the Forum that January night in 1937 when his career ended. He had been playing marvellously that evening and the little smile on his lips showed that he was having a wonderful time. But once too often he charged into the corner relying on his ability to turn on a dime and come out with the puck. The point of one of his skates impaled itself in the boards. A defenceman, big Earl Siebert, accidentally crashed over the extended leg and broke it. Howie's head hit the ice with a sickening crack and he was carried out. Six weeks later, as a result of the brain injury, he died.

The all-but-fatal accident involved Ace Bailey and the great Eddie Shore, and Shore was almost as much a victim as the man he nearly killed. Yet, in spite of the censure Shore received, this was surely an accident. It was Shore's reputation for violence that made everyone assume that he had assaulted Bailey deliberately. And indeed, what the crowd saw that December night in Boston looked like a brutal, unprovoked attack. They saw Shore charge into Bailey at full speed and smash him to the ice. They saw big Red Horner, the Leafs' defenceman, drop his stick and slug Shore unconscious with his fist. But the crowd did not hear Shore murmur in anguish afterward that he had never even seen Ace Bailey, that he had been stunned by a body check and did not know he had crashed into him. Shore would have been held for manslaughter if Bailey had died, but fortunately Bailey recovered, and when he was well enough to talk he exonerated Shore. He himself had no idea what hit him.

There have been other Donnybrooks far worse than the Ace Bailey affair. The worst of them involved that legendary character Sprague Cleghorn, who played defence with his brother Odie for the Canadiens in the early 1920s. In 1923, in a playoff with the old Ottawa Senators, Sprague cross-checked Lionel Hitchman across the face and seriously injured him. And a few minutes before this event it was a miracle that Cy Denneny was not killed by another Canadien. This is how the staid Montreal *Gazette* described what happened to Denneny:

"Denneny scored from the boards on the south side of the rink and after the puck had lodged behind Vezina, the Ottawa wing started to coast around behind the net. Couture followed in behind and with his stick struck him over the back of the head, sending him rolling over and over on the ice to come finally to a stop twenty feet away."

Several riots interrupted this game. At one time twenty Montreal cops were fighting for their lives with the mob. Those who claim that modern hockey is rougher than it used to be are extremely forgetful.

But not even the old-time hockey player was a stumble-bum. Two famous veterans of the hockey wars, Lionel Conacher and Bucko McDonald, have been members of Canada's federal Parliament. (Bucko still is, but last spring in the annual softball game between the MP's and the Press Gallery, Conacher dropped dead of a heart attack.) A good many more have won prominence in business and the professions, and once their blood has cooled, they look back on their old hockey-playing selves in wonder. Kenny Reardon in his day was one of the most fearsome men in the league – he was once forced to post a thousand-dollar bond to keep the peace for the rest of the season. Not long ago he confessed with wry amusement that he could not understand how he had ever been like that.

It was the hot excitement of hockey that made him like that. A natural aristocrat like Lester Patrick, who did more to develop the game than any other single individual, contrived to manage a hockey team without losing either his temper or his sense of proportion, and his sons Lynn and Murray, now coaches, share a little of their father's detachment. But they are exceptions.

Far more typical among the coaches is Dick Irvin of the Canadiens, who feels about a losing team the way John Knox felt about sin. And of course there is Connie Smythe of the Leafs, who coined the phrase, "If you can't lick them outside in the alley, you can't lick them inside in the rink." Smythe was arrested for punching a fan in Boston the night Ace Bailey was injured. Smythe can be heard screaming at his team over the roar of fourteen thousand people in Maple Leaf Gardens, and if he had had the size and ability he would have been a terror on the iceways, for he never asked his boys to do anything he wouldn't have tried to do himself.

If the men who play hockey professionally are a projection of the emotions of millions of their countrymen, it is because all Canadian boys put on skates and begin to knock a pseudo puck around as soon as they can hold a stick. Inevitably they grow up projecting themselves into the jerseys of big-league giants.

In any small Canadian town – like Chicoutimi up the Saguenay River, Owen Sound on the windy shore of Georgian Bay, a tank village on the CPR tracks west of Lake Superior, or a collection of raw frame houses under a towering grain elevator on the prairies – the kids coming home from school are stick-handling along the streets. Years ago there wasn't much traffic and the snow was shiny-smooth from sleigh runners. Twenty years ago even an average player in the NHL was superior as a stick-handler to any but a handful of the men in the league today.

The first Canadian teams to play for American cities in the NHL circuit – Boston, New York, Chicago, and Detroit – contained superb stick-handlers and passers, and because of them hockey became a popular spectacle in the United States. There were the Cook brothers and Frankie Boucher of the New York Rangers, who swirled through a defence in a razzle-dazzle of elliptical curves. There was that glorious Canadien line led by Howie Morenz with Aurel Joliat on left wing and Billy Boucher on right. There was that powerhouse of a line that played for Toronto – Primeau, Conacher, and Jackson. A little later Detroit won the Stanley Cup with one of the lightest lines in hockey – Aurie, Barry, and Lewis – whose stick-handling and passing made them lethal. Even some of the old defencemen were rare puck-jugglers, men like Babe Siebert, King Clancy, and Hap Day.

In the little towns from which so many of those puck artists came, the kids were on the ponds or makeshift rinks as soon as school was out. Nobody skated without a stick in his hands, and if frostbitten feet had been a deterrent there would have been no hockey players. The boards of the rink were slapped together by the local carpenter, the goals and scrapers made by the blacksmith, and the rink cleared of snow by the kids themselves. On clear afternoons when frigid air pinched the nostrils and made noses run, when the sky changed from deep blue through pale blue to aquamarine and rose, those rinks were a focus for the yells of all the kids in town. You could see their bright-coloured jerseys weaving in and out, toques or peaked caps on their heads, and always there were one or two who would hold your eye. They were the ones who made their shoulders swerve one way while their feet went the other, who sliced through a melee with their heads up and the puck controlled as if their sticks were extensions of their arms.

Often there was a shack nearby where skates could be changed and hands warmed beside a hot stove. The stove was tended by a bad-tempered old man in galluses who sold chocolate bars and soft drinks. The air was hot and foul, and the old man's perpetual refrain was, "Shut thet door – and keep it shut!" To this day there are millions of Canadians who can't see a pot-bellied, rusty old stove without feeling nostalgia for a happy youth. It reminds a man of ice in the hair of his temples, of rime in his eyebrows, and of the lovely swollen feeling of throbbing feet after supper when he pretended to do his lessons. . . .

In any Canadian small town there used to be three public

buildings that were always recognizable. One was the railway station, another the post office, and the third was the skating-rink. Modern methods of freezing ice, as well as a preference for watching sport from the living-room instead of from ringside seats, have closed most of the old skating-rinks. But there are still a few around and they all look the same: big brown barns with sway-backed roofs. They were called hippodromes, coliseums, forums, arenas, or simply "the rink." Their roofs were intended only to keep snow off the ice and the rough benches on which spectators sat. Except on hockey nights the doors and windows were kept wide open, the interior temperature being considered ideal if no higher than ten above zero. Hockey was designed to be played on fast, hard ice; it slows down when the puck is sloshed about on a wet or sticky surface.

Of course the spectators in the days of those old rinks were almost as crazy as the players. They arrived wearing furs or heavy ulsters, stocking caps, two pairs of socks, and often carrying Hudson's Bay blankets. Even with this protection they were in danger of frostbite, for in prairie towns like Brandon or Prince Albert the night temperatures could easily fall to forty below. So the crowds stomped their feet and their breath steamed out in clouds to mingle with the fumes of the boiling coffee they swallowed between periods. And the players got more fun out of it than they do these days because there were few substitutions. They would have caught pneumonia if they had sat waiting on the benches for ten minutes at a time as some do now.

Players and spectators were close in body and spirit then because every spectator was a player himself. That is why hockey these last fifty years has taken such a grip on the imagination of Canadians that it seems a part of their lives. That is also why the small towns which have kept their rinks in repair still supply the best hockey players.

Look at their faces as they pour off the bench and melt into the game without stopping the play. Intense, strong, tough, and cocky – but also guileless and still amateurs at heart, carrying on the tradition of old-timers like Newsy Lalonde, who didn't so much play hockey for money as he accepted money to enable him to continue playing. In all its violent history, there has never been the slightest hint of a hockey game being fixed.

In the spring of 1954 when the Canadiens lost the final match of the Stanley Cup playoffs in overtime to Detroit, Elmer Lach (too old to be on the ice and knowing it) said, as he hung up his skates for good, that he would gladly give five years of his life to have scored just one more goal. Nobody thought he was insincere. Hockey breeds that sort of guileless passion in those who love the game.

From "Remembrance of Men Past"

MacLennan loved eccentric characters, and he collected, and retailed, stories about them with the same relish that is evident in this 1955 piece:

... Fifty years ago, even twenty-five, in my own province of Nova Scotia, survivors of the great age of eccentricity were all around us. I knew more than one Steerforth, three Mr. Lorrys, two Peggotys, and one Uriah Heep. Most of my father's friends had gone to school under at least one Creakle, and Barkis could be found wherever teamsters were in demand. I grew up thinking that eccentricity was a social asset, liking particularly the legend of Herbert Spencer, who carried to every dinner party (and he was a much-sought guest) a pair of ear-muffs, which he put on with ostentation whenever the conversation at the table began to bore him.

England was the home of the prime eccentrics, of course. It could afford to be. Dickens didn't invent the Veneerings or even the gnomes of the Pickwick Papers, nor had his business executives like Gradgrind and Murdstone been educated by smooth corporation life or trained in behaviour by their relations counsels. And Oxford was the place in all of England that contained the largest number of singular human beings in proportion to the population. The dons who teach in Oxford today are doubtless abler men than the ones I remember from twenty-five years ago. They are more courteous, more highly polished, more practical in the ways of the world. But I warrant that few of them will be as memorable to the undergraduates who encounter them as their predecessors are to us.

Not all the eccentrics in Oxford were dons. I knew a short,

bald-headed little merchant there who made and sold truly marvellous cigarettes. His business was two hundred years old and he owned plantations in Egypt. Rhodes Scholars from the United States tried to persuade him to increase his sales-volume by advertising and better marketing methods. He was horrified. "Sir, if I did that, how would I know that my cigarettes would be smoked by the proper people?"

I met an ex-prizefighter turned commercial traveller, who carried in his pocket a clipping of a portrait of Shakespeare. "I shows it to furriners," he explained, "and I asks 'em 'oo they can put up that kin stay in the same ring with Shykespeare."

I knew an undergraduate who had been run through the shoulder while fighting a duel in an Oxford garden, and an inn-keeper who wore buckled shoes and an eighteenth-century wig and was advertising nothing. I knew a cleric who composed witty and bawdy limericks, a colonel who gave me a free dinner because my college (some three hundred years ago) had melted down its plate for the coffers of Charles I; and a porter – formerly a sergeant of the Coldstreams – who remarked solemnly to an agnostic undergraduate, "You'd never do for the army, sir, without no religion. They wouldn't know properly 'ow to mark your cross when you got killed."

The rarest of Oxford's eccentrics, of course, were found among the dons. There was a scholar distinguished in the history of the drama who boasted he had never been inside a theatre in his life. There was a little philosopher who always stumbled over his gown, came stumbling into the lecture room, stumbling onto the podium, and never felt secure until he was standing on top of a table, from which he frequently lectured with his back to the room. There was a mathematician whose opening conversational gambit with strangers became celebrated – not only for the frequency with which it was used. "Whenever I see a naked woman I faint. Do you?"

The first don I worked under happened to be a man who deplored eccentricity in others and denounced it as the enemy of efficient work. He wore yellow celluloid collars, suits that would have looked gloomy on a banker, button boots, and a scrubby moustache he kept long enough to chew. He disappeared from my life because he always rode his bicycle on the wrong side of the street as a matter of principle, disapproving of the English habit of the left-hand drive. One day he was killed.

There was a life-fellow in another college who had been appointed before the compulsory retirement law was introduced and was therefore secure in the habits of a lifetime. As he grew older he conceived a violent antipathy to undergraduates. He left Oxford the day term began and came back two days after the beginning of each vac. One night, his failing eyes detecting movement at the back of the empty hall where he was dining alone, he summoned the butler.

"What's that down yonder? What's there, eh, eh?"

"Gentlemen, sir," the butler said, and explained they were science students who had permission to remain in residence until they completed their laboratory experiments.

"Then get me a screen," the old man cried. "A screen at once! Gentlemen in college! It will never do, it will never do at all!"

In still another college was an even stranger life-fellow who had been engaged for forty years in the composition of a book he intended to call *Universality and God*. He did no teaching and lived like a dormouse in a back room high under the college roof. During Michaelmas and Hilary only his servant saw him, but when gillyflowers scented the gardens in June the ancient scholar would sally forth. Wrapped in a winter overcoat, his neck and head swathed in scarves, a blackthorn in his hand, he would root in the college garden. When a fine, rich bit of earth had been overturned he would peer at it and then shake his stick at the worms. "You've not got me yet, you rogues! You've not got me yet!"

Men like these were laughed at, but they were also revered, for it takes character to become a character, and the stories of their idiosyncrasies were retold with affection.

Just before my time in the university, there had expired in Trinity College a scholar of fabulous learning called Robinson Ellis, whose monograph on Catullus was more than a hundred times longer than the poet's actual works, for Ellis believed he had contrived a system which enabled him to re-write the many poems of Catullus that are lost. People being what they are, his fame in the university rested on other quirks of his mind. He believed that the college servants were trying to starve him to death and he insisted on having double breakfasts delivered to his rooms. One he ate, the other he concealed behind his books, where his servant later found it and took it away.

Ellis was also obsessed by the fear that his reputation would be usurped by a formidable German scholar called Baehrens, whom he had been insulting in Latin textual introductions for nearly half a century. One day he entered a university lecture hall rubbing his hands and smiling.

"Gentlemen," he said in his quavering voice, "gentlemen – I have wonderful news for you today! Baehrens is dead." He chortled. "And I'm not!"

New College was the home of the celebrated Spooner, who had died just before I came up, but in my time it still had its characters. One was a don called Joachim, a world-shaking authority on Kant and metaphysical problems generally. I was ordered by my provost, whose sole eccentricity was having been born in the lee of Cape Wrath, to attend the lectures of Joachim. The provost warned me, however, that I must arrive early and get a seat directly under the lectern, because the old man was occasionally difficult to hear. I did as I was told.

Into the dim, chilly, half-empty hall crept the aged professor in a gown and carpet slippers. He laid a sheaf of yellowed papers on the lectern, peered at us through the tiniest spectacles I ever saw, and asked, "Can you hear me?"

Most of our hands went up and he dropped his voice.

"Who hears me now? he asked.

Only half the hands went up and his voice fell to a whisper.

"Anyone still hear?"

My hand and two others near the lectern were raised. He gave us a grim smile. Then for five minutes, while the other students picked up their notebooks and left the hall, I watched Joachim's mouth opening and closing without hearing a single sound more distinctive than a faint hiss or rattle of breath. When I was the only student who remained, he looked at me and spoke in a normal voice.

"Young man, you will kindly return to your provost and inform him that he has made the egregious error of underestimating me."

I knew, of course, that if Oxford students stop attending a

formal university lecture, the professor is not obliged to appear for further sessions.

Two of the most fabulous survivors of the age of eccentricity in my day were heads of colleges, McGrath of Queen's and the Bodger of John's, each a century old. It was so long since anyone had seen McGrath that the only relevant fact known of him was that two pro-provosts had died in his service, thwarted in their natural hope of succeeding him. But the Bodger (I never heard his real name) was one of the most sociable college chieftains in the university, for he endeavoured to entertain at his table every undergraduate in his college, working down the list from top to bottom and asking them seven at a time. The Bodger's hours of entertainment were at breakfast, and I say hours because the repasts that began at eight in the morning seldom ended before noon. The meal began with fruit, continued with porridge, proceeded to fish, established a solid basis with bacon and eggs and reached a climax with steak. When the remains of the last course had been cleared away, the old man and his guests nibbled toast and drank tea.

Several friends of mine attended the Bodger's breakfast parties, including one Canadian. They told me it was the old man's intention to talk to all his guests in turn, starting with the man on his left, and after each course he would ask his favourite questions – the man's name, birthplace, and subject. But as he invariably fell asleep after each course and snored till his servant woke him for the next one, he always forgot whom he had spoken to before. As a result the only man who was ever addressed was the one on his left.

The morning my Canadian friend breakfasted with the Bodger he had the seat of honour and by noon he had been asked his name, birthplace, and subject six times. When the Bodger took formal leave of the party at the door, he said to the Canadian, who probably had an indefinable difference about him in the old man's eyes, "So sorry I wasn't able to chat with you. Tell me – who are you? Where are you from? What are you reading?" He nodded his head as he listened to the answers. Then he smiled as his white beard went up and down. "How slow I am to be sure!" he said. "You are all from a strange place called Montreal. You all have the same name and you all read history. By Jove – you're all brothers!"

We took our eccentrics for granted in Oxford, thinking the university would breed them forever. So it is hard to explain to the boy who is searching for symbols in Dickens that human beings, in their eagerness to get along, have lost colour as they have become more efficient. To prove to him that it is not only Oxford where such curiosities abounded, I gave him finally the story of a don of Cambridge, that excellent if sober institution that helped colonize New England and lately has played such a useful role in developing nuclear bombs. The story is told by an eminent scientist now living in Montreal, who may have better ideas than I about the symbolism of Dickens.

In Cambridge, so he says, one of the old dons in his day was a metaphysician who always walked the streets sideways, scraping his back against the walls of buildings somewhat in the manner of a small boy trying to edge his way out of a room without being seen. When asked why he chose such a singular manner of locomotion, he eyed his questioner with the expression of a man who has never accustomed himself to the stupidity and lack of imagination of his fellow mortals.

"If I were to walk in the conventional manner," the philosopher replied, "how could I be sure it wouldn't occur to somebody to kick me in the rump?"

"Confessions of a Wood-Chopping Man"

From 1942 until the end of his life MacLennan owned a cottage in the Eastern Townships of Quebec. In another famous essay, "Everyone Knows the Rules," he called the place "for the purpose of non-identification, Ste. Elizabeth." It was, in fact, North Hatley, a beautiful little lake-side town whose population almost doubles each summer when the cottagers pour in from the eastern United States and from Montreal. In MacLennan's words, "We play tennis and sail together and are wise about the ways of the world."

North Hatley is in truth a place of much accumulated wisdom. Besides the interesting mix of Americans and Canadians, anglophones and francophones, it has been a place of some literary importance, sheltering not only MacLennan and the late Frank Scott, but also Ralph Gustafson, Ronald Sutherland, Douglas Jones, the late Blair Fraser and his son Graham, and occasional others of note.

MacLennan loved his North Hatley cottage and garden. He even enjoyed, as this 1956 essay shows, the hard work of felling trees there:

Pleasure, profit, and beauty from a single afternoon's exercise – what more could a puritan ask, especially when the profit will not be reaped till next year, and the beauty harvested for years to come. As for the pleasure, merely to be alive on an Indian-summer afternoon in my part of the country is as close to heaven as my imagination extends.

After the first frost has turned ferns to brown dust and the birds have flocked south, the woods around my house in the country are filled with the living presence of silence. My feet crunch outrageously in the dry undergrowth as I make my way to the heart of the grove. My jeans are stiff with ancient sweat and my jersey is out at the elbows, the red paint has long ago been rubbed off the bow of my Swedish saw and my axe blade, several ounces lighter than when I bought it nine years ago, is honed sharp enough to sever a hair on my forearm. Looking up to the sky through the leaf-patterns I shame my environment by the academic thought that this scene is the equal of Sainte-Chapelle, but the comparison lasts only a few seconds. A hard-wood copse in the Eastern Townships of Quebec in Indian summer can be compared to nothing else on this earth, being itself an absolute. By some recurring good fortune I am here; I am here with the axe, the saw, the wedge, and the determination to alter the landscape a little. It is a moment that involves every aspect of the slow change in my whole view of life over the last decade and a half.

I was born and raised in a part of Canada where nobody is able to change the landscape. Along the Atlantic coast of Nova Scotia you grow up with the conviction that everything in nature here is as it is forever, and that man, living with the shifting immutability of the ocean and the unshifting immuta-bility of granite rocks, can never dominate his fate, never play artist with nature, but must take life and the world as he finds them. The glacier that set the mould of the Nova Scotia coast (and the coast set the mould of the Nova Scotian character) so denuded the rocks of topsoil that for evermore only a spruce will thrive there. From childhood I accepted the belief that summer, spring, and fall are much the same. One is grateful for a spruce if it is the only tree one really knows, but since any spruce is much the same as any other, and since no spruce ever changes its colours, the trees of my childhood helped the granite and the ocean to confirm me in the belief that nature can neither be altered nor be improved.

It took me a good many years to respond to the soft luxuriance of the Eastern Townships, where the eye, the ear, and the sense of smell are played upon gently and with subtle variations. It took me no time at all, however, to learn that here the landscape can and must be altered from time to time because it is continually altering itself to your disadvantage. A house in the country for summer living must be tied to the earth by close plantings of shrubs and trees, to give protection from the winds and to take away its aspect of being a brash intruder. But a maple sapling grows eight feet a year in this rich, rainy land, and a small fir that looks like an incipient Christmas tree when you transplant it soon becomes a dense screen breeding swarms of blackflies. Where there was one butternut there is soon a grove, and within a decade the pasture in which your house was built has been taken over by a stand of maples, oaks, poplars, wild cherries, honey locusts, old apple trees, hornbeams, birches, beeches, and even some stray pines. Their roots are now under your cottage, their branches are joined over your roof, and they have made your home as dark as an animal's den.

The year I bought my house, I cut away every cedar, pine, and spruce that crowded it. This was an act with a double meaning for me. I intended to let the sun filter down through the branches of the great hardwoods farther back, and I also needed a symbol of emancipation from the stern acceptance of my youth, I suppose.

"You'll feel naked without some kind of protection, won't you?" said a neighbour. "Now there's only the garden and the lawn between you and the road."

He meant that *he* would; I felt as though cobwebs had been swept from a dirty window. What good to keep other people from looking in, if at the same time I was prevented from looking out? Anyway, I live high on a hill away from the village, on a dirt road that leads to nowhere, and the passers-by are few and friendly. Since my land slopes at a twenty-five-degree angle and the road is below the house, I can overlook any activity on the road and let my eye take in a view that extends for ten miles over a deep lake indented with bays that lap the feet of thrusting hills. I can look across wind-blown farms and red-pine headlands and the shining roofs of new cattle barns.

I began to cut in order to get sun and air into the house and I continued to cut in order to get sun and air into the surrounding woods. The second year I was mildly surprised to discover that the wood I cut had saved me many dollars. Then I bought a lot across the road and down the hill to protect our view. But the view gradually disappeared behind a wall of rapidly growing trees. They were a fine mixture of greens in summer and an unbelievable blend of colours in the fall, but living with them in front of me was like living behind a seventy-foot hedge.

So, over the years, those rapidly growing trees have given a pattern to my life in much the same way that his rotating wheatfields pattern the life of the farmer. Come the fall and I must get to work on them.

I have a neighbour who thinks it a crime to cut any oak, but what do you do if you have two oaks within six feet of one another? I run my hand over the smooth, olive-green trunk and feel the hard muscles inside the bark. An oak, especially a young one, feels human when your hand strokes it. But more than any tree in the forest, the oak needs room to grow. Its roots spread wide and lie close to the surface of the earth. I look up at this pair and see that they have grown like basketball players, tall, thin, and not much good for anything else but growing tall and thin. Their lowest branches are at least twenty-five feet above the ground, since it was always dark in here before I got busy cutting out the saplings, and the trees had to thrust high in order to reach the life-giving sun. I feel the trunks of both and decide that the spindlier one must go, to give the other a chance to fulfil the destiny of an oak.

So I go down on both knees, set the saw at the trunk of the victim, and get to work. In such a close-grained tree the opening made by the slim saw-blade is almost invisible once the saw has buried itself in the trunk. White dust spurts out, to become brown as the blade reaches the darker heart of the tree. Then comes the crack – hard, solid, vibrating up the entire length of the trunk and echoing through the silent copse. There is a shiver, a twitch in the pinky-brown plumage, a moment of hesitation. As I stand up and watch, one hand on the trunk, the tree nods in the direction I had intended it to fall, then goes down in a swooshing, stately plunge. There is a flash of scarlet as a maple is brushed on the way down. Inevitably the oak comes to rest at an angle, its cascading upper branches caught by the interlocking branches of neighbouring trees.

In the new silence I consider my next move. A fallen tree, even one as modest as this, creates a sizeable wreckage. I think of Mr. Gladstone, who used to slay giant oaks, Royal Navy oaks, to relieve his emotions. When Disraeli was extraordinarily witty or the Queen ordinarily rude, another oak on the estate of the Grand Old Man was doomed to fall. And then there was the labour of cleaning up the mess, a job that I know from experience must have taken days. So far as I can discover from my reading, the Prime Minister gave little thought to this aspect of forestry. He was able to sate his aggressions and stalk off, sweaty under the armpits but with his Victorian waistcoat still in place, while humbler men took over the long task of trimming the oak, sawing its trunk into logs, splitting them and trundling them into the woodshed. Humbler men without the need to sublimate a libido must have stacked and burned Mr. Gladstone's slash.

Perhaps the psychiatrist who lives below me on his own tree-enclosed acreage, hearing the crash of my falling oak, thinks I am ridding myself of aggressions, too. He may even think I am slaying a father-image. But no matter what he thinks, my oak has merely been severed at the base, it has not been transformed into cordwood.

It was cold last night. It was colder still at six this morning when I peered out at the thermometer and saw that the mercury stood at twenty-seven degrees. When I got out of bed at eight and built a fire there was still rime on the lawn. The day was fine and clear, but it was so cold my fireplace consumed ten logs before one o'clock. This year a short cord sells at seven dollars, a long cord at anything from fifteen to twenty, depending on what kind of wood it contains. No matter what my woodpile represents to a psychologist, it gives me an intense pleasure to use it for warmth, even though (as the countrywoman remarked yesterday when she came in to clean the house) it takes a lot of sweat to build a woodpile.

I think, sometimes, that Mr. Gladstone missed the best part of tree-cutting. Each fallen tree presents its own problems, and the man who walks off and leaves them is as bad a tree-butcher as the one who murders a copse with a power saw. This oak of mine is entangled with two other trees and of course the simplest thing to do is cut them both down so that all three are prone. But the tree supporting the oak on the left is a rowan, a fugitive from an old garden, probably, and under no circumstances, under absolutely none, will I cut a rowan tree in my own woods. The other is a rock maple, a tree which still fills me with wonder and joy because it was scarce in Nova Scotia, and in England almost non-existent. I always have a twinge of conscience when I cut down a maple. But here the maples grow like weeds and this particular one is so close to the rowan it will rob it of nutriment as both try to grow. So the maple goes, and the crack of its fall echoes over the hill.

Still the oak is suspended; when the maple went, its weight was taken by more stuff beyond. There is nothing for it but to cut the oak down to size in the only way left. I start sawing the trunk in eight-foot lengths, each cut about four and a half feet above the ground, which is as high as I can drive the saw. With the entire tree exerting hundreds of pounds of pressure on the saw blade, I must use the wedge. And this means that for the rest of the afternoon these two trees, the oak and the maple, are going to keep me busy.

Toward sunset the logs are piled and split and fragrant, the slash dragged off into a great angular pile to dry and await my pleasure on a future moist day. I come out of the copse and look to see what effect my work has made on the landscape. A little, and the beginning of a lot, because a splendid butternut has now been uncovered and must be given its chance. With that poplar out of the way the sun will slant deeply into the copse and I will have the beginnings of a woodland nave. A forest without sun is like a church without God; I reflect that the thought is corny, but I don't care. Disposing of the poplar will put no burden on my conscience. Along with a ragged spruce, it exists to be destroyed, for if the axe doesn't get to it the insects will, and after the insects will come the flickers and the pileated woodpeckers. Tomorrow afternoon's work is now planned, and it, in turn, will lead to the work of the day after and the day after that. Carving out the raw material of a forest to create a civilized wood is like making a picture or writing a book. One vista suggests another and there is no absolute end to it in a country like ours. But when the season's cutting is over after Thanksgiving, and I go muscle-bound back to the city, I feel as Melville did when he finished *Moby Dick*, as pure as the lamb.

From "A Disquisition on Elmer"

Only a very fine essayist could link a trigger-happy Arizona barfly with John Aylmer, the sixteenth-century English churchman. This 1957 essay shows MacLennan mixing history and anecdote to great effect. After noting his fascination with names in general and especially with given names in the United States (where "they tend to be either fantastic or to prove something about their owners") he comes to Elmer:

... Whether these changes of fashion in American nomenclature represent a decadence is a matter I leave to Arnold Toynbee, but the decadence has clearly not gone the whole way, for there is one American given-name which has survived all changes in fashion from Cotton Mather to Eisenhower. That is Elmer. There have always been Elmers in the United States, and there are none anywhere else except in a few Canadian families of United Empire Loyalist extraction.

Why Elmer? From the first time I heard the name I have wondered.

"I don't know," one Elmer said to me. "I guess there's always been an Elmer in our family."

"I never even thought about it," said another.

"Elmer is a rube name," said a New Yorker who wasn't called it. "Haven't you ever heard W. C. Fields' joke?"

As time passed, Elmer began to haunt me, nor did a search through historical records do anything but deepen the mystery of its origin. There aren't any Elmers. No Elmer (the surname, I mean) appears in the Testaments Old or New, none in the passenger list of the *Mayflower*, none among the Roman and Greek regicides, none among the signers of the Declaration, the early Abolitionists, or the Civil War generals. Moreover, none of the people of the name I have ever met seem to have the slightest notion of how the name got into their families.

Yet the idea persisted in my mind that Elmer, in the American beginning, stood for someone or something which seemed pretty important to the first Americans who bestowed it on their sons. It was basic; it was uniquely American and always had been. All the Elmers I knew had names derived from the British Isles. All of them seemed to be sectarian Protestants. There were more of them in the north than in the south, and more in the corn belt than anywhere else. Find the principle behind Elmer, I thought, and you will solve the riddle of Elmer.

If you stay with an idea long enough you are bound to learn something about it, and this is how I finally learned about Elmer.

A few years ago I drove across the United States west to east, and on the second day out of Los Angeles I stopped for the night in a small town on the Arizona plateau called Flagstaff. In the bar of the only hotel was a considerable crowd of people in western dress, both real and phony, and one of them who looked at least half-real was making a great deal of noise. He was huge, fat, and wore a ten-gallon hat; he was a braggart and his voice sounded like a cement mixer working unnecessarily hard. He left after half an hour.

Beside me at the bar while all the noise was going on had sat a tall, thin, silent man about sixty years old with a face eroded by wind and sand. He turned to me and said: "Yew like thet fella?"

I said I was a stranger and didn't know that fella.

"Yew don't hev to know a fella," the lean man said, "to hate his guts."

After this exchange he was silent for ten minutes. Then he turned to me again.

"Year ago," he said, "I shot thet fella. Sideways. Through the ass."

I expressed appropriate surprise and the man was silent for another five minutes. Then he spoke once more.

"Yew like them auto-mobiles with four-note hawns?"

"Not particularly."

"There's a lotta things I don't like, I guess."

Another silence ensued before he started again.

"Thet fella thet was in here, he had an auto-mobile with a four-note hawn. Used to go around town nights a-blowin' of his hawn and awakin' of people outer their beds and feelin' mighty big."

Another silence.

"Third night he done thet, I sed to my wife, 'I guess I don't hev to stand fer this.' So I tuk my rifle and I opened the window and there he was, a-leanin' on his car and a-blowin' on his four-noter and feelin' mighty big. So I tuk a bead and I guess thet stopped it."

Another silence, but a little shorter this time.

"Sideways," the thin man said reflectively. "More across the ass than through it. Didn't chip the bone any. Jest kinda stung him up a bit."

I looked at the grim face, the lantern jaws, the sand-pitted skin, the pale-blue eyes, the crisp white hair.

"One little thing I don't get here," I said. "You say you shot this man. How can the two of you drink in the same bar after that?"

Another silence.

"Maybe we couldn't at thet, if he knew who done it. But he don't. Folks knew though." Silence. "Folks was pleased." Silence. "I never did like them four-note hawns. There's a lot of things I never did like, I guess."

After this we got into a general conversation during which he learned I came from Canada and I learned that he didn't think the Russians were so tough. Finally he gave me his card and in large, uncompromisingly plain lettering I read the name of Elmer Z. Stebbins. So the hunt for Elmer was on again.

"No," he said, "I can't say I know where the Elmer come from. The zee is easy. It's for Zebadee and Zebadee is in the Bible."

"Were you born in Arizona?"

"Arkansas," he said. "My dad was born in Missouri and his dad come down from West Virginia, for our family keeps movin'. My grandad tol' me there are Stebbinses back east thet are big shots with dough, but us, we don't have dough and we never bin big shots. Guess we never stuck around long enough for the moss to grow. Take my son. A lot of things in Flagstaff he didn't like, so he moves on to L.A. Take his son. Wouldn't be serprised if his son ends up in Honnaloola."

"Is your son's name Elmer too?" I asked.

"How'd yew guess?"

"I don't want to seem curious, but did your family come west from New England?"

"How'd yew guess? Salem. My grandad was a great one fer history, and he tol' me us Stebbinses were original Americans from the start."

"And there's always been an Elmer?"

"I guess most of the time yew'd be about right about thet."

"It's a name I've always liked," I said. "And I've been wondering where it came from. I was wondering if you'd know."

His grim, impassive face looked into mine, pleased, but eager not to show it.

"Thet's mighty interestin' you bein' interested in thet. Elmer was a preacher, my grandad said, and a mighty fine one."

And so help me, Mr. Stebbins turned out to be right!

A few weeks ago I happened to be searching a little-read American reference book for a word to fit a double-crostic and suddenly – I would have missed it had I not been subconsciously primed – I saw what I had been looking for these twenty-five years. "Elmer:" the book said in black print. "See Aylmer." So I did see Aylmer.

John Aylmer, the man responsible for the fact that hundreds of thousands of American boys are called Elmer, was indeed a preacher, and his name (in the seventeenth century it would have been pronounced Elmer) was a famous one in the history of early church controversy. Born in 1521, born to trouble as the sparks of his own cantankerous character flew upward, he went to Cambridge and later became tutor to the unfortunate Lady Jane Grey, and Jane's father, the Marquis of Dorset, thought so highly of his work that he obtained for him the archdeaconry of Stow.

It was then that John Aylmer sealed the fate of those hundreds of thousands of unborn American boys. For he discovered there were a lot of things about the Established Church he did not like, one of them being the current view on the all-important matter of transubstantiation. He was against transubstantiation, and said so, and since being against transubstantiation at that time was a burning matter in England, Aylmer fled for his life to Calvin and Knox in Geneva. There were a lot of things he did not like in Geneva, one being John Knox himself, and by the time Mary Tudor died and Elizabeth ascended the throne, Aylmer was glad enough to escape from the Calvinists. He returned to England; in the course of time he was advanced to the see of London by the Queen, and in that capacity he made more enemies than any bishop in the history of that stormy diocese. He ended hostile to everyone, the Puritans included.

But what difference did that make to the founders of New England? John Aylmer had started the ball rolling that finally rolled across the sea into Massachusetts Bay. He had been an authentic puritan hero before the puritan movement even began. And besides, he had a name much more pleasant and pronounceable than Jedediah.

I was so fascinated by this discovery that I almost wrote to Elmer Z. Stebbins in Flagstaff to tell him about it, but I reflected that I would not be able to find him in Flagstaff.

"There's a lotta things about this town," he had told me before we parted, "thet I don't like."

"You'll be moving on?" I asked him.

"Guess so," said Elmer.

"Boy Meets Girl in Winnipeg and Who Cares?"

Only a few days before the publication of The Watch That Ends the Night, *MacLennan published this essay about the perils faced by those gamblers who write books for a living. The odds against success – certainly in Hollywood – are considerably raised if you are foolish enough, he suggests, to set your book in Canada:*

The writing profession has many advantages: no boss breathes down your neck, nobody cares if you are late to work so long as you are not late *with* work, you don't have to co-operate with anyone except yourself and maybe the occasional editor. Along with the uncaught criminal, the artist is, as Somerset Maugham long ago pointed out, one of the few remaining species of *homo sapiens* who can roughly be described as free. Not even the Russians have been able to organize him without making him useless.

For this freedom the writer pays, and with each passing year he pays more, because in any technological society freedom almost prices itself out of the market. The price you pay for freedom today is a total lack of security.

While a book is in train, life can be so exciting for the writer that he never thinks about money unless the bank tells him he is overdrawn, and he thinks about his security only in those ghastly moments when the book bogs down. But all this changes after the book is completed and sent off to the publishers. Publishers are more human than writers in their cycles: a writer's period of gestation may range from ten days (Erle Stanley Gardner) to five years (myself with the last novel) to the lifetime necessary for the man who intends to produce a masterpiece the moment he can get around to it. But publishers, from the time they receive a script to the time they deliver the first edition to the bookstores, usually consume from seven to nine months.

Nine months can seem pretty long to a waiting man, and during this period I always swear I will reform. I remember my father telling me not to gamble, and I realize that if I have not gambled with money (never having had enough to gamble with) I have certainly gambled with my life, and have done so deliberately with the odds against me. The writer's usual gamble is to bet on hitting the jackpot somewhere along the line, his idea being that if he keeps on writing long enough the probabilities are reasonable that he will do so at least once, and then he can invest the money and attain his security. In the old days this worked pretty well, and in one or two countries it still works up to a point for the very lucky few, in spite of the tax gatherers necessary for the support of the welfare state.

But in Canada the gamble doesn't work at all; in Canada the odds against the jackpot are what they would be in roulette if every tenth slot was a double-zero. I have known this for years, and yet I have contumaciously gone back to the tables again and again. While it is true that our population is rising fast, at least a third of it is not presumed to read English literature in its spare time. A best-seller in our market is exceptional if it tops 10,000, and the royalty on 10,000 copies is about $4,500. On the other hand in the United States, where the population now exceeds 170 million, all of them over five taught to read and write and all of them over two to look at television, a best-seller can not only hit the half-million mark but later, and for this very reason, be sold to the movies and television people for sums of money which fatten the tax gatherers as a dead elephant fattens the vultures that roost on Kilimanjaro. But even after the publicans have picked you, if you hit a jackpot like that you have a sizeable paycheque to bank.

This simple arithmetic I have always disregarded whenever I have been in train with a novel. To hell with figures, I say, while genius pretends to burn. I write English, I say, and the Americans read English, and as long as I build a better mousetrap the world is sure to beat that famous path to my famous door. Again and again American reviewers, who are more generous to outsiders than any other reviewers in the world, urge their readers to read Canadian books. But in spite of all this goodwill, grass still grows green and thick around the doorsteps of our better Canadian mousetrap builders.

Why shouldn't it? If we insisted on electing Mackenzie King for twenty-two years, why should Americans think us an interesting people? In any case, literature has always been mixed up with nationalisms and popular assumptions. Citizens of new countries are supposed to break sods instead of typewriters, and Europeans coming to live among them are supposed to furnish them with such culture as they can imbibe. A century ago Melville and Hawthorne had as hard a time crashing the international market as we Canadians have now, and it did their pockets little good, nor did they know about it during their lives, that in our day Harvard students turn out about a dozen theses a year on their work. In the last three generations the United States not only broke through into the international market; for a time it came close to capturing it. But the American writers who developed a mature native literature had an advantage the critics have seldom noted: a huge and growing native population. It was this native population which supported them in the years when they were growing up, for it is natural for people to find their own societies more interesting than the societies of strangers.

Facts such as these I have stubbornly disregarded for more than twenty years. I have known them perfectly; I have known them ever since I received a telegram informing me that two Hollywood studios were interested in my first novel. I saw dollar signs all over the Windsor Station the night I boarded that train for New York, and there were still more of them hanging from the skyscrapers when I drove in a taxi to the old Ritz-Carlton to meet the representative of the studio which was the more interested of the two. He was a man exceedingly affable, though somewhat boiled-looking about the eyelids, and before ordering a thirty-dollar lunch he gave me two cocktails. He also told me the deal was off.

"It's like this," the man explained. "This book of yours, it's about this town Halifax and who's ever heard of Halifax down here except as a word nicely brought-up kids say when what really they mean is hell? 'Go to Halifax' is what nicely brought-up kids down here say. Well, of course, this wouldn't make any difference if this was an ordinary book. We could work a switcheroo. But the trouble is in this book of yours Halifax gets itself blown up in the climax of the story. We fooled around with a switcheroo even on that. We thought of the Johnstown Flood, but that happened so long ago that who cares, so we canned the whole idea." He looked at me in sincere friendship and said: "It's tough, but that's how it is. All you've got to do next time is set the scene in the United States and *then* we'll be really interested."

Being naïve in those days, I asked what difference the locale of a story makes so long as the story is good.

"Well, take Paris," he said, "that's okay for one kind of story. Take London – that's okay for another kind. But take Canada – that's not okay because what do Americans think when they hear that word 'Canada' except cold weather and Mounties or maybe when they hear it they don't know what to think. Now this is not the way it ought to be and it's tough, but look at it like this. A boy meets a girl in Paris, one thing leads to another and they – well, it's interesting. But a boy meets a girl in Winnipeg and they swing into the same routine and who cares? I'm not saying it's not just as good in Winnipeg as it is in Paris. Maybe it's even better because in Winnipeg what else is there to do? But for the American public you've got to see it's a fact that Winnipeg kind of kills interest in the whole thing."

I protested (I was *very* naïve in those days) that my books tended to be serious, what you might call social novels.

"That's exactly what I've been trying to say," he explained. "The way you write, if you want a big market down here, you just haven't got much of a choice. The way you write you've got to make it American. Now let me tell you a little tale to illustrate that point."

One Monday morning on the Coast, he related, in the days of the silents when Hollywood magnates were real magnates and not Organization Men, one of the very biggest of these magnates padded into his office, seated himself behind his twelve-foot desk and pressed down all the buttons it contained. Within five minutes most of his executives, script men, continuity men, cameramen, directors, idea men, editors and press agents were arrayed before him. He advanced his dimpled chin, stared at each of them in turn, and barked:

"Why do I pay you guys one – two – three thousand dollars a week and from you what do I get but strictly nothing?"

After the necessary quarter-minute's silence had been observed, the magnate continued:

"Over the week-end I was with high-class people and they told me of a very wonderful book, the most wonderful story of this century, and from you what do I hear of this story but strictly nothing?"

After the necessary ten seconds of silence, the chief story editor asked if the title of the book might be revealed. It could be, and it was *The Well of Loneliness*. The editor shrugged and said he had read it long ago.

"Then why," stared the boss, "don't I see this *Well of Loneliness* in lights?"

The editor sighed and said it was impossible. The magnate scowled and said the word "impossible" was a word that nobody in his studio was permitted to understand. The editor agreed that this was true, but argued that the censors would not permit *The Well of Loneliness* to be shown in American family theatres, not even with the "Adults Only" sign on the door. The heroine of the book, he explained to the chief, was a Lesbian.

The dimpled chin advanced further across the desk, the wonderful little eyes gleamed.

"Why do I pay for brains when evidently brains is what you do not like to use? So the girl in this story is a Lesbian? So what if she's from Peru? So what if her home is in Costa Rica maybe? In this studio we make her an American!"

The man from Hollywood looked at me mournfully and said: "So now you see the way it is."

Oddly enough I saw exactly how it was, just as I see how it is now, for right here in Canada the situation is little different. Suppose you try to sell a serious social novel about Peru or Costa Rica in Canada, how many Canadians are going to storm the shops to buy that book?

Yet I, fully understanding this situation years ago, have continued to squander my dwindling hopes of security by continually writing books about Canadians living in their own country. Can anybody be stupider about his interests than that? Now, with still another long novel due this month (due as a matter of fact on Friday the Thirteenth of this month and no kidding) I feel like the gambler in the garden at Monte Carlo solemnly telling himself "Never, never again." For five years I have been assuring myself that this novel is by far the best thing I've ever done or dreamed of doing, that its Canadian setting is worked into it like shot silk, that here is a story that should sound just as good in London or New York as in Montreal. Maybe it will; maybe it will! But my Scotch instinct also says, "Maybe it won't!" And as I await the results with Scotch fatalism, I again remember the words of that man from Hollywood, and this time I swear I'm going to act on them the next time I write a novel.

"The thing for you to do," he said, "being a Canadian, is make the best of *both* your worlds. Mix up the English and Americans in the same package, and fix it so somehow this Englishman in this book comes over to the States with certain ideas and he changes them, understand, when he finds out about American women and democracy." He shook my hand warmly as we left the Ritz. "Now just one more little thing and it shouldn't be too hard to do. Try to work Lincoln into the story somehow. Work Lincoln in, you as a Canadian work Lincoln into it with this Englishman, and something very nice ought to come out."

He paused as we passed through the revolving door, wrinkled up his face into a confidential question-mark and spoke again:

"How inhibited are you on sex?" he asked me. "This last book of yours, it had some hints of sex but not half enough in my opinion."

"How much sex do you think I need?"

"Pretty well all you can put in. Of course, it's got to be moral. I mean, if people get it extra-curricularly they've got to pay for it, but you can describe them getting it, and while you're at it, let yourself go. A book with no sex, the reader feels cheated. But you know all that anyway.". . .

C H A P T E R · 8

The Watch That Ends The Night

From 1947 until her death in April 1957, Hugh MacLennan's wife Dorothy lived, as he wrote, "knowing that at any hour of any day she might die." His anguish as a husband informs what many see as his greatest novel, The Watch That Ends the Night. *Published in 1958, the book deals with the fragile Catherine and the two men who love her: the Norman Bethune-like surgeon, Jerome Martell, and the narrator, George Stewart:*

There are some stories into which the reader should be led gently, and I think this may be one of them.

One evening at the beginning of a cold February, the first winter of the Korean War, I left my classroom in the university and made my way along the corridor to the stair. It was five o'clock and the best time of my days that winter was about to begin. I love Montreal on a fine winter night and I was looking forward to the walk home along Sherbrooke Street with the evening star in the gap at the corner of Guy, then to a drink before my fire, to dinner and after dinner to a quiet evening with my wife, a little more work and a good night's sleep. That evening I was happy.

Now I suppose I should introduce myself. My name is George Stewart and I come from what might be called an old Montreal family. But I also come from an impoverished family and even now I think of myself as a product not only of Montreal but also of the depression, scarred by it like so many of my friends. For this intricate, fostering city was a bad place in the depression.

I have done various things for a living, but radio has been the only thing in which I have gained any reputation. For years before the Korean War I had been a political commentator over the radio and a writer of free-lance articles on political topics for our magazines. In a huge country like the United States a man with a reputation such as I had here would have been prosperous. But Canada is a country with a small population, and the pay for my kind of work is proportionate. Hundreds of thousands of Canadians knew my name from coast to coast, but most of them were better off than I was. I had never known financial security. But at least I managed to get by and was not in debt.

I have never felt safe. Who of my age could, unless he was stupid? Quite a few people thought me successful, but in my own eyes I was no more successful than the old Greek who pushed boulders up the hill knowing they would tumble down the moment they reached the top. Some people thought me calm, but inside I knew I was not. I have often heard myself described as a "mature" commentator, but I have never seemed mature to myself. The young seem more so because they know nothing of the 1930s. The young have the necessary self-confidence and ignorance to feel mature, and that is why I like them so much better than I like my own generation. Was there ever a crowd like ours? Was there ever a time when so many people tried, so pathetically, to feel responsible for all mankind? Was there ever a generation which yearned to belong, so unsuc-cessfully, to something larger than themselves?

That winter I truly thought I had begun to relax for the first time since I was a boy. I thought I had come to terms with myself and with the peculiar fate which controlled me owing to my wife. I even thought I might have become self-confident. And I had loved this part-time job in the university, because it had brought me into touch with the young.

These post-war students seemed to me a new breed on earth. They were so much freer in their souls than we had ever been, and so much easier in their emotions. Also, unless the world goes crazy again, they were luckier. For not one of them could remember the depression or what it had been like when Hitler was the most powerful man in the world. Not one of them was corroded by the knowledge that nobody wanted them. They all expected to get jobs and marry young and to raise families young, and now as I walked down the corridor I felt joy flood me as I heard the happy noise they made at the end of their day. A student asked me a question about my lecture; I gave him an answer and stopped at a window and looked out.

Powder snow lay deep and white on the slope of Mount Royal and was flecked with the foot and tail marks of the squirrels who lived on the mountain. On this clear winter evening after sunset there was a green blink in the sky, and as I looked up through the boles of the bare trees I saw a flash of bright colour and recognized a pheasant which also lived on the mountain and survived the winters on scraps thrown to him out of apartment windows by old ladies who loved him. This pale twilight bathing the city erased time: it called me back to the Montreal which once had been one of the true winter cities of the world, with iced toboggan slides on the mountain and snow-shoers in scarlet sashes and tuques and grey homespuns bright against the snow and shacks with rank coffee and acrid air where you warmed your half-frozen feet in front of Quebec heaters and felt young and clean and untroubled. It was gone now that we were learning to live like New Yorkers.

The porter was at the foot of the stair and I saw from his expression that he wanted to speak to me. He was an Englishman, a former Grenadier, and he had a ramrod back, waxed grey moustaches and a voice husky and formidable.

"A gentleman 'as been calling you, sir," he said in that voice of his. "Most important 'e said it was, sir, so I left you 'is number in your box."

I went into the staff room, took the number out of my box and waited for an elderly professor to finish using the phone. The number was unfamiliar, but from its exchange I knew it was located downtown and this suggested that it might be more important than an unknown lady who wanted me to give a political talk at a suburban women's club. So I sat and waited, looking out the window at the clean northern twilight feeling easy and relaxed.

Must one remember or is it better to forget? Certainly that winter it had seemed easier to forget than ever before. Sleep had come easily, and sometimes the nights were like quiet oceans where I woke after five hours of profound sleep and lay happy in the dawn. We lived in the heart of Montreal but inside our apartment home it was always quiet and we never seemed conscious of the city. Nor is anything quite like the silence of a northern city at dawn on winter morning. Occasionally there was a hiss or whisper and a brushing against the windows and I knew it was snow, but generally there was nothing but a throbbing stillness until the street cars began running up Côte des Neiges and I heard them as though they were winds blowing through old drains.

Must one remember or can one forget? Those trams of Montreal were history to me, and when the day came when they would be replaced by buses I had the feeling that history itself would disappear with them. Whenever I sat on one of their straw-yellow seats, hearing the bilingual conductor chant "Mountain Street – de la Montagne," I was apt to have a total recall and remember exactly how I had felt in those same cars when I sat reading the news from Mukden, Chapei, Addis Ababa, Guernica, Sudetenland, Eben Emael and Forges-les-Eaux. What a terrible lesson in geography my generation had learned! Those place-names of our lost passions and fears! No wonder there were moments when I felt like a survivor, for those names which could still send a shiver through me meant nothing to these students I taught three hours a week. Most of them had never heard of them.

Can one forget through another human being? That winter I loved so many things, and one of them was the thought of Catherine in the dawn. She was always asleep then in her separate room, but I would lie and be conscious of her presence. I would watch one of her paintings grow visible on the wall and some of the joy she had when she painted it became mine and I was so happy because she had discovered this wonderful thing before it was too late, and I was proud, too.

I had made Catherine the rock of my life. As a boy, at least for a time, I had been religious and believed that God cared for me personally. In the thirties I had said to myself: There is no God. Now I had Catherine and Catherine's fate and that winter, feeling confident of being equal to it, I said to myself: "What difference does it make if there is no God? Or, if God exists, why worry if He is indifferent to justice?"

For on account of Catherine I could not believe that if there is a God He is just. Catherine had a rheumatic heart which had handicapped her from childhood and it was not on account of her sins, or of her parents' sins, that the seeds of this obscure disease had singled her out among hundreds of thousands of others who went free. A rheumatic heart is fate palpable and unavoidable. It cannot be contended against, it cannot be side-stepped and until very recently it could not be cured. Twice within the last few years Catherine had nearly been killed by it, and for such time as remained to her she must live with the sword dangling over her head every minute of every day. So had she to live and so had I. And I was proud that winter because – so I believed – I could do so without begging for help from a Power which, if It existed, I could not respect because It had allowed this to happen to the woman I loved.

Now as I sat looking out the window at the twilight darkling on the snow, thinking idly as I have described – how many thoughts you can have while waiting to get to a telephone! – inevitably I remembered the man I always remember when I think about the 1930s, the man who would always epitomize that time to me. He at least I had all but forgotten. He had been dead for a decade now and I had put him behind me, I thought, forever. I had put him behind me as a grown man puts behind him his predecessor, his father. He had not been my actual father but for a time in the thirties, when I was spiritually and emotionally fatherless, I had virtually allowed him to become so.

The professor rose from the phone, smiled and apologized for delaying me, and left the room with his head on one side. I took his place and dialled, and immediately a harsh voice spoke to me in French: "L'hôtel Édouard Sept."

"What?" I said, and was sure the porter had copied the number wrong. I continued in French: "My name is George Stewart. Is there anyone there who wants to speak to me?"

"*Moment, s'vous plaît,*" and I was left with an idle line.

So I waited and wondered if I wasted my time in doing so, for it seemed inconceivable that anyone I knew would be staying at a place like that. Before the war I had known several who had frequented the Edward VII, for it had been a famous institution where respectable men had gone to sleep off a bender; it had been disreputable, but to its disreputableness there had been a certain *cachet* in pre-war Montreal. It had no *cachet* now, for the war had ruined it. During the war years it had rented its rooms to soldiers and their girls by the hour, and so many soldiers requiring penicillin had mentioned its name to battalion medical officers that the army had put it out of bounds for troops. Now it was a place you never heard mentioned unless somebody died or was arrested in it.

I heard a noise at the end of the line, heavy breathing and then a voice spoke which made my hair prickle.

"Is that George Stewart?"

No! the thought crashed through my stunned mind. No, this is impossible. Things never happen like this.

"Yes," I heard my own voice say, "this is George."

"Really you? Really old George?"

"Really me."

"This is Jerome. Jerome Martell."

"I know," I said. "I recognized your voice right away."

Then I began to shake and felt myself turning pale. Telepathy is more common than we care to believe. Jerome Martell was the man I just mentioned, the one I had thought dead for a decade.

CHAPTER II

I was shocked and startled into utter banality. "When did you get back?" I asked him.

"If you mean Montreal, I got back this morning. I've just been talking to Harry Blackwell."

Another name from the past and I said: "Good God!"

"He told me about you and Kate and I phoned your apartment."

"You mean, you've talked to Catherine?"

"No, there were so many George Stewarts and G. Stewarts I gave up after the fourth try and called Blackwell instead. He told me you had this university job. Look George – he told me you've all thought I was dead."

"That's right. We did."

"Kate, too?"

"What else could she think?"

A pause and then he said in the voice of a man who can be surprised by nothing.

"Truly, I thought I'd got word out."

"Word out of where?"

"I've been –" another pause, I heard his heavy breathing, and he went on. "I've been in Russia and I've been in China. I got out of China into Hong Kong and I spent a year there getting my health back. I wrote several letters from Hong Kong, but they were all returned. On the odds it would be surprising if Kate were still alive, but inside me I was sure she was. I had this inside feeling all the time about her. How long have you been married?"

I took out a packet of cigarettes, spilled one onto the table beside the phone, put it between my lips and lit it. My right hand shook when it snapped the lighter.

"I suppose this must be a shock," he said.

"That's one way of understating it."

"Harry Blackwell kept repeating, 'But it was in the papers you were dead!' That poor sorry little man, he always believed the papers."

For a moment the wire sang between us and then I said: "Harry has done pretty well lately. We all underrated him. We underrated so many people who have done well since the war."

Jerome did not seem to hear me. "Didn't even one of my letters get back?" he said.

"Nobody has had a single word from you since 1939."

Again the wire sang between us.

"Did Blackwell tell you *how* we thought you had died?" I asked.

"He just said it was in the papers I was dead."

"Does the name Lajoie mean a thing to you? A French aviator? Captain Lajoie?"

He waited a moment and said no.

"Well," I said, "this Captain Lajoie was over here for a time in the war and he said he knew you in the French underground. What he told us wasn't pretty."

"He might have known me under another name," Jerome said. "What did he say?"

"He said the Nazis spent two days torturing you and afterwards they hung up your body on a meat-hook in the square of a French market town."

"Was all that in the papers?"

"No, just that you'd been killed in the French underground. The *Gazette* wrote you a very nice obituary, considering what they thought of your politics."

There was another silence.

Then Jerome said: "Did everyone believe this story of the torture and the meat-hook?"

"Yes."

"Did Kate believe it?"

"Yes."

"Well," he said, "it came pretty close to being true. Did Kate believe it?"

"I said so, Jerome."

Looking out the window I saw the darkness visibly flooding down over the snow with its squirrel tracks, and now a light was on and there was a yellow track from it across one part of the snow. I felt numb, unreal, and heard myself say, "Where have you been? What have you been doing?"

"George, I can't tell you all that now. Russia – China – the war – everything. You see I was caught with the Spanish in France in 1939 when we came over the Pyrenees and my passport was stolen. When I was in Hong Kong I read a book about one of those French concentration camps written by a man called Arthur Koestler. Did you ever read that book?"

"Yes."

"Then you know what it was like." I heard him breathing so heavily that I wondered if he was sick. "When the Nazis came in, the French let me out and I had to go underground. I lasted till 1943 before they caught me. They didn't kill me because I was a doctor. They shipped me around for a while, but I ended in Poland after I was caught escaping."

"Auschwitz?"

"Yes," he said simply.

There was another silence and I felt even more unreal as I tried to imagine what he looked like.

"When the Russians came in they shipped me east. The

Russians wanted doctors too, and after a stretch in one of their arctic camps I was a surgeon in a Siberian town. They promised to let me go home but they never did. But they did let me go to China. It's too long a story and it's too commonplace. What happened to me has happened to millions of others. The Chinese let me out after I got sick. They let me out to Hong Kong." He paused, and then he said with an intense calm more powerful than any note of passion could possibly be, "All I ever wanted was to come home. All I lived for was to come home to Kate and Sally."

I felt as tired as a man after a fainting spell.

"How long did you say you and Kate have been married?"

"I didn't say, but we've been married nine years."

Another pause before he said: "How is she?"

At last I recovered something of myself, for this question was the one I was most frequently asked. Whenever I met a friend on the street his first question was apt to be, "How is Catherine?" I began to talk about her and with dramatic suddenness his tone changed to that of a doctor.

"What, precisely, are the symptoms now?"

For the next five minutes I recounted them, and from time to time he interrupted me with questions.

When I was done he asked: "Did I understand you to say *two* embolisms?"

"That's right." And noting the doubt in his voice I added: "She's had the best opinions, Jerome. Jack Christopher is her physician now."

"I guessed he would be. I'm glad he is."

But he was, at least partially, still the same Jerome, for he cross-questioned me further about her symptoms. I assured him that to look at her casually you would never guess she had even been sick, and I asked him if he was out of touch with recent medical developments. He said he supposed he was out of touch to an extent, but that he had worked for a year in a hospital in Hong Kong, having obtained the post through a chest surgeon he met there whom he had known years ago in Edinburgh. I explained to him about a new drug which had helped her, one which had been used for the first time in such cases here in Montreal, and he admitted that he had never heard of it. A professor entered the room to hunt for mail, inhibiting me by his presence, and looking out the window I saw that it had become totally dark.

"How's Sally?" I heard Jerome say.

"She's in her last year in the university."

"Tell me more about her, George."

It was then that I became haunted by the thought that I must know what he looked like if I was to continue talking to him. His age I knew – he was fifty-two. But what a fifty-two years of life he had spent! Was he white? Was he scarred? Did his eyes have that look of the men who had been in the camps? Did his face have that holy expression that sometimes comes from just the right amount of starvation?

I tried to describe Sally to him.

"Little Sal a biologist!" He gave a soft, wondering laugh. "Remember how I used to set up the microscope for her when she was a kid? The things she used to say when she looked through it!"

When he said this my eyes burned and I nearly wept. Those last words of his had jumped the years, had picked him up and brought him back alive as I had known him in those depression evenings in Montreal when he was the centre of rabid discussions in apartments when we sat on the floor and drank beer and talked politics and economics and dreaded the coming war and reviled Baldwin, Chamberlain and the capitalists. He was right in front of me now, Jerome Martell in the mid-thirties, ugly-handsome with muscular cheeks, a nose flattened by an old break, hair cropped short because it defied a brush, a bull-dog jaw, nostrils ardent like those of a horse, mouth strongly wide and sensual, but the eyes young, hungry and vulnerable, quick to shame as a boy's, charming with children and the weak, quarrelsome with the strong. There he was, that oddly pure sensualist so many experimenting women had desired, the man so many of us had thought was wonderful in those depression years when we were all outcasts.

"George," I heard him say, "you're probably thinking a lot you're not saying."

"I suppose you're doing the same."

"Does she hate me?"

"She never did."

"Then she hasn't changed! Then she's just the same! Then what I saw in my sleep was true! Does she still talk about me?"

"Not any more."

There was a long silence after I said this. Then I heard him whisper, "Kate! Kate!" And I heard him sob, and the pity of the moment was almost too much for me. I had never doubted that he loved her.

"I've got to see her, George. I've got to see her and Sally.". . .

Later, George Stewart tells how he became a teacher, in a passage that allows Hugh MacLennan to draw on his memories of servitude at Lower Canada College, his personal "Waterloo":

The road which brought me to Waterloo was too drab and long to waste time talking about. For ten years after my father lost his money I lived in Ontario, mostly in Toronto. My first job was in a bank and I stayed with it for five years during which, out of a small salary, I saved enough money for two years in the university. I left the university in order to work again, and the year I returned the depression settled in. When I obtained a degree I was twenty-seven years old.

During this long, drab hiatus three things happened to me, as they happened to millions of other young men at that time. I lost my faith in religion; I lost my faith in myself; I lost my faith in the integrity of human society.

My last year in the university ended and there was no job in Toronto. My degree was worthless and there was no job anywhere. So in late June I returned to Montreal, and lived with my parents because there was no other place to go. . . .

The summer I walked the sidewalks day after day, I searched the want-ads and soon gave up because no employer even bothered to advertise for help. I found nothing to do, absolutely nothing. I applied to every teachers' agency in Canada and to half a dozen in the United States. I made a few semi-friends about the town, but most of the time I was alone. And the sexual loneliness which had been growing in me became as sour as the Dead Sea.

Summer passed into autumn and the leaves began to fall. And then one evening in mid-October I came home and found a telegram. It was from a teachers' agency and informed me that a job was waiting for me at Waterloo School, the salary ninety dollars a month, room and board included, and that I was to report for duty immediately.

This was the middle of October and even the private schools had been in session for a month, so I was sure there must be a mistake. I wondered what to do and asked Father about it.

"Why, call them up long distance, of course, and find out."

"Long-distance calls cost money."

"But this is a job, George. You have to spend money before you can make it. I discovered that years ago."

I telephoned to Waterloo and after a wait of seven minutes an English voice, speaking as though all telephones were its personal enemies, boomed into my ear.

"Stewart, did you say? Of course you're wanted here. What's been keeping you, I'd like to know? Be here tomorrow morning."

Without giving me a chance to ask another question, the speaker hung up. I presumed that he was the headmaster of Waterloo, but as he had not introduced himself I did not know that his name was Dr. Lionel Bigbee, much less that his doctorate was purely imaginary, and that he called himself Doctor because he believed that all headmasters should be called Doctor for the sake of morale. I tried to recall what little I had heard of Waterloo, and the little I was able to remember did not sound so good. The only person I knew who had gone there was an eccentric who had been at Frobisher when I was in the middle school, and he had only gone to Waterloo because Frobisher had expelled him. His name was Adam Blore and he claimed to be a sculptor; for a living he sold carpets in Eaton's.

"My God," Adam whispered, when I called him up. "Have you been reduced to *that*?"

I mentioned the pay, the room and the food.

"You'll get beriberi from the food. Those Englishmen out there eat like convicts. They don't know any better. Those Englishmen out there never ate a decent meal in their lives. If old Bigbee hadn't expelled me, I'd have died of malnutrition."

The next day I got off the train at Lachance and was met by a gnome-like creature in a flat cap driving a Model-A Ford he called the Waterloo bus. He was Ti-Jean Laframboise and he drove me over three miles of bumpy dirt road and then up a weedy driveway to a building the like of which I never saw before or since.

Originally, I suppose, Waterloo School had been the house of a prosperous French-Canadian landowner. Now a cascade of marble steps poured down in front of it surmounted by a portico which in turn was decorated by four angels who gesticulated at one another and looked as though they had been stolen from a Catholic cemetery. Over the door was a shield with a coat of arms and the strange motto *Caveat Gallus.*

"Where did the steps come from?" I asked Laframboise.

"The Doctor put them in seven years ago. Him and me. They're beautiful."

After my luggage was inside, Laframboise led me upstairs and along a corridor that boomed like a sounding-board to a cell-like, rugless room where the pipes were exposed, the plaster flaking and the smell ratty.

"I guess this is your room," he said. "Now I guess you better see the Doctor."

I followed downstairs once more, then along another corridor where the stuffed heads of lions, tigers, impalas, rhinos and African buffalo stared at each other like family portraits in an English country house.

"Did the Doctor shoot these?" I asked Laframboise.

"He bought them at an auction. But you wait till you see his birds. They're beautiful."

He knocked on a door, a loud voice boomed, "Come in!" and I entered to make the acquaintance of the man described by hundreds of old boys of Waterloo as the greatest personality they had ever known in their lives.

Dr. Lionel Bigbee was as thin as a stork's neck and stood five feet five in his socks. But at that moment he was not standing; he was leaning back in a wooden chair with his feet on his desk, his left hand stroking a pink, bald, shining skull, a pair of watery blue eyes peering out from under tufted white brows, his right hand flapping as though I were a taxi and he were hailing it. He was entirely surrounded by stuffed birds. Quails and geese perched on the floor, on the window sill were an eagle and an owl, an albatross spread wings in one corner and a swarm of lesser fowl clustered on tables and shelves.

"Well Stewart," said Dr. Bigbee in a male alto boom, "you've taken your own good time getting here, I'm bound to say. You should have been here five weeks ago. What have you been up to? Missed your sailing?"

"I beg your pardon, sir?"

"I'm not seasick or any other kind of sick myself, but I notice a lot of men are. Were you?"

"I beg your pardon, sir."

"There's no chair for you, so don't look for one. The other chair's fractured and Laframboise is mending it. But standing never hurt a man. Speak up, Stewart. What have you got to say for yourself?"

I muttered that I was sorry, but that I had only heard from him the day before and did not understand what he meant by ships and seasickness. The Doctor listened, rubbed his skull and stared out the window.

"You aren't from home, not with that accent, Stewart."

"I beg your pardon, sir."

There was a knock and Laframboise entered with another wooden chair, which I sat on. I looked past the Doctor's head to bookshelves containing some battered school texts, the complete Oxford Dictionary from A to E, and five bound volumes of *Punch*, 1888 to 1892 inclusive. Behind the doctor was the room's sole decoration apart from the birds; it was an engraving of a seventeenth-century battleship firing a broadside.

The Doctor spoke: "These agencies aren't worth the price of a stamp. I know picking a new master's pretty much a matter of putting one's hand into the poke and coming out with what it grabs, but at least the agencies understand that I take my men from home." His blue eyes appraised me. "Where did you say you were from, Stewart?"

"Montreal."

"Mmmm," said the Doctor. His eyebrows jumped quickly up and down and settled themselves. "Well, I must have a master and you're here. I suppose you have some kind of a degree?"

I told him I had an honours degree in history from the University of Toronto.

"Mmmm," said the Doctor. "Well, you can't teach history here. Ponson does it in the uppers, McNish in the lowers.

Ponson's old Boer War and McNish is Royal Navy. The socialists axed him and the poor chap had to come out here. What else can you teach?"

I told him my French was pretty fair and that I could probably teach English as well, but the Doctor did not seem to listen.

"We'll find plenty for you to teach," he said as he stared sideways out the window. "Don't you worry on *that* score. Do you know any French?"

"Yes, sir," I repeated.

"Then I fancy you'll teach some French in the middle school where there are always gaps that need stopping. Far better not having a Frenchman for French, the boys can never understand a word he says. I expect you'll stop that particular gap very nicely." The Doctor swung around and his voice became confidential. "Let me tell you something, Stewart. When you've been in this profession as long as I have, you'll understand that the least important part of schoolmastering is teaching. Show the flag, set an example, give a tone. Can *you* remember anything you were taught in school? *I* can't. But I jolly well remember my school, and a jolly good school it was, too."

The Doctor took a silk handkerchief out of his sleeve and blew his nose with such violence that dust spurted from the head of the nearest owl. The he recrossed his legs on the desk, and with both hands clasped behind his head and his body tilted so far back he was almost prone, he rattled off the schedule, which he described as "Ponson's timetable," adding as he did so that Ponson was the kind of chap who understands timetables.

Rising bell was at 6:45, breakfast at 7:15, prayers at 7:45, and then there was a half-hour break.

"Bowels," said the Doctor. "Give 'em plenty of time to move 'em. The secret of a good school's a happy boy, and the secret of a happy boy's a comfortable intestine."

From 8:30 to 12:30, with a fifteen minutes' break in the middle, were classes. Then came lunch, followed by a half-hour break and then more classes till 3:30. These were followed by detention and/or games. If the master was on duty he took detention and if he was not he supervised games. If he was on duty he also patrolled corridors, attended the prefects' court where junior offenders were caned by senior boys, took the two-hour evening prep and when that was over he put the junior and middle schools to bed.

"Keep 'em on the hop and you have no moral problem," explained the Doctor. "But give a boy time to think and you know as well as the next man what he'll think about. Have you ever used a cane?"

"No, sir."

"Then go to Cutler – he's our sergeant-at-arms and an old Green Jacket – and ask him for one. Preaching at a boy, chivvying him, making him ashamed of himself, there's nothing worse for the character. But give him six of the best if he deserves it and you've made a friend for life."

The Doctor contemplated the eagle which stood on his window ledge and rubbed his head some more.

"Well, Stewart?" he said after a while, genially.

"Yes, sir?"

"I've noticed you've been admiring my ship-of-the-line." He jerked a lean thumb over his shoulder at the engraving of the seventeenth-century battleship and his voice became excessively cordial. "She's HMS *Terrible*, first of the name in the Navy List if I'm not mistaken. An ancestor of mine had her once, an ancestor on the maternal wing, Prisser, Admiral of the Blue. I don't expect you've ever heard of him. My full name actually is Prisser-hyphen-Bigbee, but Prisser won't do in a school for obvious reasons, so I drop both the Prisser *and* the hyphen out here. Did you ever notice the motto over the school door?"

"Yes, sir."

"It was Prisser's. *Caveat Gallus* – 'Let the French Beware!' I rather fancy with good reason, for they never came out to fight him. He watched 'em for years and they never came. I'd wanted a naval name for the school, but it wasn't as simple as it looked. Nobody out here's ever heard of Camperdown. If we called us The Saints in this province they'd think we were Roman Catholics. The Nile? Copenhagen? Obviously wouldn't do. Trafalgar naturally – but do you know, Stewart? In Montreal there's a *girls'* school called Trafalgar. So I settled on Waterloo willy-nilly, though it wasn't the Duke's best battle. Salamanca was that, but out here who's heard of Salamanca?"

With a crash the Doctor dropped both feet to the ground and rose towering among his birds, and with an expression disconcertingly roguish he pointed his finger at me and wagged it.

"Stewart, you're the first native, I mean the first man not from home we've ever had here. So go in and win."

"I'll do my best, sir."

"Of course you will. And by Easter, instead of being the wrong Stewart, you may have proved you're the *right* Stewart."

The encounter with Dr. Bigbee, and the staff and routines at the school, seem humorous to the reader now, and even, recollected in tranquillity, to George Stewart. Montreal, in the grip of the Depression, was not a subject for humour:

But during my actual time at Waterloo I saw nothing humorous about the place, and it was the weekends that kept me sane. Every fourth weekend I was on duty, sometimes I was down with a cold and often I was broke, but whenever I had a chance and could afford it, I fled from the place on Friday afternoon and went to Montreal.

Never before was Montreal as it was in the thirties and it will never be like that again. The unemployed used to flow in two rivers along St. Catherine Street, and I used to see eddies of them stopping in front of shop windows to stare at the goods they could not buy. There was a restaurant that used to roast chickens in its window over electrically operated spits, and there were always slavering men outside staring at the crinkling skin of the chickens and the sputtering fat. I remember how silent the unemployed were when they emerged after a snowfall to clean the streets, often without mittens on their hands, and how pitiful their cheap worn shoes looked as the snow wet them and turned the unpolished leather grey. And above all do I remember my own guilt as I saw them, for I had work and they had none.

In those days the streets of Montreal were a kind of truth to me and I roamed them. I learned them block by block from their smells and the types I saw, I came to love the shape of the city itself, its bold masses bulging hard against the sky and the purple semi-darkness of the lower town at evening when Mount Royal was still high and clear against bright sunsets. I loved the noise of the ships booming in the harbour and along the canal to the Lakes, and the quiet little areas some said were like London but which were actually indigenous to this wise, experienced, amiably cynical town.

Though I slept in my parents' flat in Notre Dame de Grâce, I seldom went there until after midnight when they were asleep; Sunday was the day I reserved for my parents, Sunday when I was tired. On Friday evenings when I arrived in town I checked my bag in the station and roamed. The streets were so candid and unashamed that they made everyone who walked them seem equal: housewives and office clerks and the thousands of unemployed, threadbare boys and girls in love with each other and whoremasters sliding around corners after silent girls and the hideous olive-green street cars of that period with their greying conductors half-sitting, half-standing in their cages at the back while the crowds read the bad news in the papers – all these people seemed part of a collective sameness which had a character entirely its own. In winter the city was more than ever itself. In winter when the snow slanted like black wires against the lights, or creaked under foot when the stars were hard overhead, I would see the young people in hundreds in their ski-clothes going down to the cheap special trains that took them north. And in those days you could see the hockey for fifty cents.

In my first year at Waterloo I spent nearly all my Montreal weekends alone, and it was the autumn of 1934 before I began to make friends in town. The first ones I met were through Adam Blore, the young sculptor who had been expelled from Waterloo and now sold carpets at Eaton's, the man who had told me I would get beriberi from the Waterloo food. With him began a chain which eventually led me to Jerome Martell and back to Catherine after all those years.

Jerome and Catherine take George to their lake-side cottage in the Laurentians, and the two men go out in a canoe:

... I looked at the cool serenity of the steely lake under that amazing sky and the silence held us.

"What made you decide to become a doctor, Jerome?"

"The war." His face changed again – I never knew a man

whose face changed so quickly as his – and became sad and haunted. "I was too good a soldier in the war, George. Before a battle I'd be so scared my throat was sand and my knees knocked together and I'd pray to be wounded before I went over the parapet. Anything not to have to do it. I'd walk out with the others and have no sensation in my legs from the hips down. But when we came up with them I'd go berserk. I killed eleven men with the bayonet, George."

"And that decided you to go into medicine?"

"Afterwards, yes. To kill a man with a rifle at a distance means nothing much unless you've got imagination. But the bayonet is murder. His face is right in front of you and he wants to live. His hands drop to the knife and get sliced. I killed eleven men that way."

He looked off into the distance and the expression on his face at that moment is with me still.

"I got one poor devil through the throat. I kicked him off it and he fell back into a shellhole. I took one step forward and the bullet smashed me in the thigh" – his right hand tapped the scar – "and I fell into the hole on top of him. He gurgled his life away before I could get off him, and then I had to spend ten hours in that hole with the body, for the machine guns were registered so close to the ground a rat couldn't have escaped. Well George, that was something. There'd be no wars if every soldier who killed a man with the bayonet had to spend ten hours immediately afterwards in a shellhole with his body. I took that kid's life away, and that's all he was – a kid. A frail blond boy who never had a chance against a man as strong as me."

Jerome stopped and looked out over the lake. "That's why this Spanish thing has got under my skin. The big war made no sense at all, but this Spanish thing does. If we can stop fascism there, we'll stop it for good and there won't be another big, senseless war."

We were silent for some time before Jerome resumed.

"I never really got over that last bayonet murder I committed. Afterwards in the hospital I was in a state of psychological shock and for weeks I couldn't speak. In the bed next to mine was a Jewish boy from Oshawa and his name was Aronson, and this boy had that funny understanding of people a lot of Jews have. 'Tell me about it,' he kept saying, 'and then maybe it will go away.' But I couldn't, because I couldn't talk. Finally, one day I did talk and I told him. 'It wasn't you who killed that soldier,' Aronson said. 'You were just an instrument. It was the system, the capitalistic system.' Then he explained to me how the system worked and for the first time I understood why every soldier who could think felt he was cheated and turned into a murderer for nothing. He changed my life, Aronson did."

Jerome tells George about his childhood – raised by his mother in a lumber camp deep in the New Brunswick backwoods. She was the camp cook, a solitary, man-hating woman, and he never knew her surname. One night, when Jerome was ten, one of his mother's sexual encounters took an unexpected turn:

. . . There was liquor that night, but in the magic of the evening, the purest kind of evening we ever have in this northern country, the men sipped at their liquor without swilling it and nobody got drunk. Jerome's mother came out in her apron and leaned in the doorway of the cookhouse listening to the singing; finally it fell dark and one by one the tired men got up and drifted off to the bunkhouse to sleep. When Jerome went to bed it was much later than his usual hour and the camp was so still the only sounds were the ringing of frogs and the slow sigh of the river in flood.

He guessed it was an hour before midnight when he woke in his mother's arms, his hands about her neck and his chest against her warm, heavy breasts. His face was still hot from the sun and his ears were swollen and hot from the blackfly bites and he woke so slowly it was only when the spaniel nuzzled and licked his face that he opened his eyes. He saw moonlight pouring into the kitchen in three separate shafts through the three high windows that faced the moon, and between those shafts of light he saw the Engineer standing still. The bedroom door opened, his mother stood there, and he heard her say, "What are you waiting for?" Then the man followed her in and the door closed.

This time the encounter was different. The Engineer he had feared so much began talking in a low, earnest stream of conversation, talking about himself and how lonely he was and how wretched was his life, and how different everything would be if she would go away with him. Jerome could only partly hear his words, and hardly any of them could he remember, but he knew that of all the lonely men in the camp this was the loneliest of all, and he yearned for some gentleness to come into his mother's voice in place of the withholding silence or the sneer he was afraid would come if the Engineer continued to talk like this. He wanted the Engineer to break through his mother's refusal to some kindness inside, to some safe kindness inside.

After a while the Engineer stopped talking and the usual noises began. They ceased almost at once and Jerome heard his mother's voice flare in a jeer of unspeakable contempt.

"So that's the best you can do! A kid could of done better!"

He heard the man groan and cry something out, and then he heard his mother mock and scorn him, and Jerome remembered thinking: Don't let her treat you like that, Engineer! Please, please, please do something to make her stop treating you like that!

The Engineer did. Suddenly his voice changed as the woman drove back his longing for tenderness into the pride and hatred Jerome had feared in him all winter. The man began to curse the woman in a stream of obscenity using every word Jerome had ever heard the men apply to the women they called whores. There was a short struggle, the pant of his mother's breath, then a loud smack as she hit him across the face and Jerome thought: Please, please don't let her do that again!

What happened next was as sudden as a bottle exploding. Jerome and the dog sprang up together at the scream of enraged fear that came from his mother. Something bumped and fell in the bedroom, there was a heave of bodies, then the crack – crack – crack of hard fists driven expertly home. This was followed by a yelp from the man, a gasp of pain, then a crunching shock more terrible than a fist blow. Then silence.

This silence, as abrupt and profound as the end of the world, was soon filled with a multitude of sweet noises. Mating frogs were singing high and happy in the night, so loud and high that the whole kitchen was filled with their joy. Then came another sound, the sobbing breath of a frightened man in agony.

Jerome put his hand on the knob of the bedroom door and pulled it open. He saw the Engineer bent double clutching his groin and he knew where his mother had hit him that last time. Beyond the Engineer's hunched body he saw his mother's legs and thighs naked in the moonlight, but the hunched man was between the boy and her face.

It was the dog who betrayed Jerome's presence. Whining into the room, the spaniel rubbed against the man's legs and made him turn. The Engineer gasped, his face came around distorted with his sick pain and was horrible with the knowledge of what he himself had just done. But he saw Jerome and recognized him, and the moment he saw him he plunged. The boy dodged back and the Engineer stumbled and hit the floor with a crash, his spanner rattling away from his right hand. Jerome saw that his pants were down about his lower legs and that it was these which had tripped him. On the floor the Engineer looked up, his mouth shut, his violence as silent as that of a fish in the sea. Jerome turned to run, escaped from the room, reached the kitchen door, felt the dog against his legs and had the presence of mind to push him back before he himself went out. He closed the door behind him and with his nightshirt fluttering and his feet bare he ran across the moonlit, chip-strewn clearing into the darkness of the forest. When he was in the trees the undergrowth began cutting his bare feet; he stopped, turned and lay flat.

Nothing moved in the clearing. The long cookhouse with the two metal pipes that served as chimneys stood silent, its sloping roof whitened by the moon, its walls dark, its windows glittering like gun-metal. He heard the sigh and gurgle of the river as it poured among the tree trunks along the flooded banks, but there was no sound of men and no light in any of the bunkhouses. He could not see the bunkhouse which was still occupied, but if there had been lights in it he would have seen their glimmer through the trees.

With the instinct of an animal Jerome got up and changed his position, slinking through the shadows among the stumps at the edge of the forest-fringe to a place he knew about thirty feet away. He found it, a depression in the ground about ten feet from the edge of the moonlight, and lay down and scooped pine needles over himself to conceal the whiteness of his shirt and skin. Lying flat with his chin in his hands and his elbows in the needles, he stared at the kitchen door and listened to the pounding of his heart.

The Engineer was only ten feet away when Jerome first saw him. He was skirting the forest-fringe with the spanner in his hand, staring into the darkness of the trees and stopping to take quick looks behind him. He wore no cap, his mackinaw shirt was open and in the moonlight Jerome saw the splash of dark hair rising out of his shirt to his throat. The man stopped directly in front of him and Jerome kept his head down, pressing his face into the needles, the needles itching in his hair. Once he lifted his eyes and saw the man's feet and noticed they were small feet even in those high leather boots. There was a crunch of bracken as the man entered the woods, one of his boots came down within a yard of Jerome's head, but the Engineer was staring into the total darkness of the forest and did not look down at his feet. In the cool air of the night Jerome could hear the man pant and thought he could feel the heat of his body. The boots turned and went back out of the forest into the clearing and as they crunched farther away Jerome looked up and saw the man's shoulders go around the corner of the cook-house and down the path to the bunkhouses.

"I knew for certain that he was after me. He was putting himself between me and the men asleep in the bunkhouse. He knew I couldn't get around through the woods without making a noise. He knew the path was the only way I could hope to go."

Jerome wondered if he ought to call out, but he knew how hard the men slept and he knew who would be the first to hear him. In any case he was too frightened to call. Except for that single jeering laugh of his mother and the man's single outburst of obscenity, what had been done that night had been done with the silence of animals killing each other in the dark.

Jerome lay still until he began to shiver and when the shivering came it was so violent it seemed to shake the ground. It was like being tied up in the cords of his own muscles shaking the earth so that everyone living on it must know where to find him.

Getting to his feet, he beat the pine needles off his nightshirt and scraped some more of them out of his hair. Others chafed the tender skin between his thighs, but these he disregarded as he stepped slowly out of the forest into the moonlight. He stopped, waiting for the man to appear and give chase, but the only sound he heard was the pounding of his own heart and the only man he saw was the man in the moon. He believed there was a man in the moon who saw everything and didn't care, who sat up there seeing and not caring and laughing to himself, and he thought he was laughing now. With his nightshirt fluttering, the boy ran across the clearing, opened the kitchen door and went in. This time he forgot about the dog, who jumped outside and ran away before Jerome could close the door.

Inside the bedroom the blind was drawn and the darkness was total. Jerome found the match-box, lit the lamp and turned to look. His mother's body lay like a sack under the blankets because the Engineer had covered her and pulled the blind before going out. Jerome lifted the blanket, put his hands to her face and felt the fingers of his right hand sink into a warm stickiness. He jerked them back as though he had put them into fire and stood frozen.

"The bad wound was on the left side of her head and her left eye was bruised by his fist. Her mouth was open and her clear eye was open and angry. She looked far angrier than frightened. My mother died in a rage."

Her body was not yet cold, but it had lost some of its warmth and the blood barely oozed now that the heart had ceased to pump it. Blood was dark and wet all over the pillow and wetly thick in her hair; her breasts were like chalk-white balloons when he tried to shift her body. It was only then that he knew absolutely that she was dead. He cried out to her, he beat her naked breasts with his palms to wake her and all the time he did this he understood she was dead. Knowing she was dead he called to her to come alive again and take care of him, yet all this while he was glad the Engineer had not been like the other men whom she had humiliated.

Then he froze once more, for a step creaked outside. He blew out the lamp and turned to run into the darkness of the cookhouse where there were tables to hide under, but he was too late. The kitchen door creaked open and he crawled under the bed and crouched there against the wall with the sag of the spring just over his head.

The man entered and when Jerome heard him sniff, he knew he was smelling the snuffed wick of the lamp. When the man lit a match it was like an explosion of sound and light simultaneously, but the man did not carry the match to the lamp. Jerome saw his boots standing by the bed as the light slowly died. Then darkness again. Then the Engineer let out a slow, choking sob and went away. Jerome heard his feet go away noisily, heard him bump into a chair in the kitchen, open the door and leave.

He crouched shivering with cold and fright, and he might have stayed there for hours if the dog had not returned to the room. The dog came under the bed whining and nuzzling, and Jerome felt his long, wet tongue licking his feet. The feeling of the dog's tongue horrified him and he rolled over and pushed the animal away, pressing his hands against its muzzle. The beast whined appreciatively and Jerome's hair bristled when he knew the dog was licking his mother's blood off his fingers. He hit the dog and heard him whine. He hit him as hard as he could on the muzzle and the dog let out a yelp and left him alone. Then Jerome came out from under the bed and stood up.

Years afterwards he told Catherine that this was the first of many occasions when a sudden, clear-headed coolness came to him after moments of paralysing terror. He was only ten years old, but he knew exactly what had happened and what else would happen if his mother's murderer caught him. He knew the murderer had left the bedroom because he was in terror of what he had done there, but he also knew he would be on the watch outside. The Engineer would almost certainly be watching by the kitchen door, for that was the natural way for Jerome to get out and it would also be the shortest route to the bunkhouse where the rest of the men were sleeping.

Jerome had to escape from the horror of that room where his mother lay dead. He took his clothes from the hooks where they hung: his shirt, stockings, pants, sweater and cap, and the heelless larrigans of cowhide he wore all year round. He took them out to the kitchen and dressed beside the stove which still was warm, with the dog nuzzling and whining, and he had to push the dog away several times as he pulled on his stockings.

After he was dressed he washed the remaining blood from his hands under the pump and dried them on a roller towel. Very clear in the head now, he opened the big ice chest where the food was and took out the first thing he found. It was a garland of blood sausage much too clumsy and big to carry, so he cut it into lengths and stuffed a length of sausage into each of the side pockets of his pants. He left the kitchen and entered the long eating-barn where the benches and trestle tables were, heading for the door at the far end, a door rarely used, and when he reached it he found it unbarred. He guessed that the Engineer had used this door when he had first gone into the clearing to search for him.

"It must have been the dog that saved me that first time. When I ran out into the clearing, the dog must have gone into the eating-barn and when the Engineer heard him moving there, he must have mistaken him for me. That was the mistake that gave me time to hide."

The dog was with Jerome now and this time Jerome made no error; he caught him by the long hairs at the back of his neck, held him while he stepped out, then pushed him inside and closed the door on him.

From this corner of the cookhouse the distance to the edge of the forest was no more than twenty yards and nobody was in sight as Jerome ran across it and disappeared into the trees. He worked his way silently through trees and deadfalls until a quick coolness touched his cheeks and he knew he was near the water on the edge of the northwest branch where his canoe was beached. In flood time the branch invaded the forest a distance of thirty yards or so, and now it was pouring through the trunks of the trees, gurgling and sighing as it strained through the scrub and deadfalls, and Jerome saw quick flashes of light as the moon struck here and there against the living water.

He worked his way along, his oiled larrigans keeping the moisture off his soles, but once his foot sank into a hole and the icy wetness poured in through the laceholes and his foot felt cold and soon went numb. After a few minutes he reached the place where the canoes and rowboats were beached, his own little canoe among them. The camp motorboat was moored to a jetty about a hundred yards downstream in the main river, but the canoes and rowboats were moored where the current was weak, and now he saw their snouts projecting out of the blackness of the woods into the moonlight. He stepped out, looked up to see the sky a wide-open dome with a moon in the middle of it and a vast circle of light shining around it.

"I knew I was going to make it. Every time afterwards when I was older, every time when I've been in danger and everything seemed hopeless, some moment like this always came. Suddenly I'd hear myself saying, 'You're going to make it. You're going to make it after all.'"

The short birch-bark canoe with the air cans under the thwarts was easy to lift; he turned it over and ran it out into the water. He found his own paddle made to fit his height, and with a single movement he pushed the canoe off and swung himself over into the stern seat, then crept forward and settled down just about midships, got the paddle working and guided the canoe past a tree trunk and clear of some fallen branches. The movement of the current kept pressing him inshore, but he paddled hard on the left into a backwash that took the canoe gently out, he changed sides and gave two hard thrusts on the right, and then the canoe floated silently out into the great wash of moonlight where the branch widened into the main course of the river. The current of the branch carried him far out from the shore and when he felt himself making leeway he knew he was in the central stream at last. He gave two more thrusts and pointed the bow downstream, and at once he began to move fast on a river wide, firm, silver and alive bearing him down past the silent camp, utterly alone for the first time in his life, bearing him down under that wide-open sky through the forest to the open sea which he knew was at its end.

Jerome paddled as he had been taught to paddle in a current, slowly and evenly, making long, steady sweeps of the paddle and after each stroke taking a short rest with the blade trailing behind like a steering oar. The river at this season and place was flowing at more than five miles an hour, breaking and gurgling in the shallows and sparkling in the moon, but out in the central current the flow was so satin-smooth the eddies were like whorls of polished glass. A thin mist lay patchily over water colder than the air, and the moon was enormous in the wide greenly shining sky.

"When I grew older and learned how human organisms behave," he said, "I knew I was in that queer state of euphoria that often comes after shock. The response of the adrenal glands to danger. But that's a mechanic's way of looking at it. It's just as real for a man to say, after he's escaped a danger to his life, that he feels twice as alive as he ever felt before. All that night I never thought of my mother. I just thought about the canoe and the river and I was so alert that everything I saw and did – everything – I still remember."

Steadily the tiny canoe went down the river between the trees, following the curves almost by itself in the current. Now that he was secure in the canoe, Jerome eased further back against the air-can lodged under the stern seat and got the head up and sank the stern to give more purchase for the current to take him along. Often he passed floating logs and once he came up with a raft of them lodged on a hidden rock and damming the current, the water washing over and making the whole raft pitch and heave as though things were alive under it. He paddled around, touched logs once or twice and when he was clear he found himself in a flotilla of individual logs that had shredded out from the raft and were going down by themselves. He kept on paddling down, occasionally rubbing against a travelling log and sometimes afraid of holing his canoe, but as the logs were going in the same direction there was little danger of this. There were no lights on the shore, no cabins or houses, there was nothing but the forest, the sky, the moon, the river, the canoe and the logs floating down to the sea.

"I had no sense of time that night, but I'd guess it was about one in the morning when I first heard the motorboat. I can still hear it. It was a primitive boat, nothing but an old high-bowed fishing boat with an engine installed. Its motor was always getting out of order and the Engineer was the only man in the camp who could do anything with it. When I first heard it, the boat was still around the bend I had just rounded, and its sound came to me muffled by trees."

Jerome was abnormally strong for his age, his shoulders powerful even then, and now fear gave him its added energy. He paddled hard toward the shore, but at this point the current was so swift that when he tried to move athwart it the canoe was swept hard alee, he knew it would take him minutes to reach the shore and that even if he did, the backwashes would sweep him into the current again. A hundred yards ahead was a small wooded island in the middle of the stream and he brought the bow about and paddled for his life, making the featherweight birch-bark craft jump to his strokes. The drub-drub-drub of the motorboat struck his ears solidly and looking back he saw its dark shape with the hunched outline of the Engineer sitting at the hand-wheel in the starboard forequarter. As Jerome drew in toward the island he saw that many logs had got there first. Instead of a beach there was a mat of logs bobbing in the press of the stream and he was panic-stricken, for the log mat spread in clear moonlight about twenty yards out from the shore, and he knew he could never get through it to hide in the trees. There were all kinds of logs there, long ones and pit-props mixed, some of them piled on top of others and the whole mat creaking in the current. "I had never seen this island before but in a vague way I knew about it. There were several islands like that in the river and they caught tons of logs every year. Once the drives had gone down, work gangs used to follow to clear the islands one by one. That was one reason why men were still left in the camp."

The canoe lifted, slid smoothly up onto some half-sunken logs, stopped dead, and there was nothing for Jerome to do but lie in the bottom and wait. He peered over the side smelling the wet logs and hearing the gurgle and lap of the stream, the canoe bobbing gently with the logs while the motorboat came straight on growing larger all the time, its drub-drub-drub filling the river and the man at the wheel looming up. Jerome was sure the man was staring straight at him, but when the boat was about twenty-five yards off the island the Engineer moved and Jerome saw the bows swing sharply off and an instant later the dark length of the boat went out of sight around the left side of the island.

"Then I knew what he was doing. He was running away. All the men knew about the railway track that crossed the river at the town just inside the estuary. It was the railway a man made for when he got into trouble or just wanted to get away. Sometimes a man left after a fight and sometimes he just left. Looking back on it, I know the Engineer was numb with his own fear. He may have been drinking and that may have been why he didn't see me. Or maybe he was just exhausted by what he had done and in the state of mind when a man can't think or see anything because he can't stand thinking or seeing anything and does one thing automatically after the other. I don't know. But he was certainly getting away as fast as he could and in the only way he knew. There was no telegraph or telephone and it would be morning by the time any of the men would find my mother and a good time would pass before they missed the Engineer and put two and two together. He'd have lots of start. He'd reach the railway long before any of the men could reach it, and once he was at the tracks he'd have his choice of trains moving east or west. I knew nothing about east or west so far as the railway was concerned, not then. I didn't know that east was down to Moncton and Halifax and a dead-end, and that west was up to Quebec and Montreal, and that he'd certainly go west. But I did know he'd be able to catch a train, for all the trains stopped in that town for water."

For a long time Jerome lay in the canoe listening to the diminishing throb of the engine. Such wind as there was came up the river and it must have been twenty minutes before the throbbing ceased. It would die away and return, die and throb up again, but at last there was no sound but the lap of the river and the slow, water-softened creak of the shifting logs.

With the passing of the motorboat Jerome's euphoria left him and he began to shiver and cry. He was chilled because at dawn the cold increased and his left foot, which he had soaked while moving through the trees, began to ache. He reached into his pocket and felt the stickiness of the blood sausage he had stored there; he took it out, washed it in the river, bit off a mouthful and ate it. The taste of blood made him feel sick but he went on eating until his shivering stopped and he felt new strength grow inside of him. He scooped water out of the river in his cupped hands and sucked it in through his teeth though it was so cold it made them ache. Meanwhile more logs from upstream were floating down and kept looming at him out of the dark water, hunching at him silently, pressing at him out of the dark as though they were the river's muscles forcing him out. The log mat was loose enough for him to get his paddle into the water and he changed position and pushed and paddled until at last the canoe gave a quick slip sideways, swerved broadside on to the stream and began to list against the mat of logs as he paddled hard to get clear toward the left-hand channel. A new log loomed at him about to ram but he fended it off, struck hard with the paddle as the canoe's bow yawed against the pressure of the stream, then the unseen hand of the current caught him, he struck with the paddle on the left, the bow shot around and again he was in the flow, passing the island so effortlessly that he was by before he knew it and now in a widening river he went on with the current pouring down through the forest to the sea.

After a time – how long he did not know for he had lost all sense of time – he became conscious that the world was lighter and opening up. Instead of seeing the forest as a dark mass on either side of him, he saw it clear and close with individual trees standing out. Now the western sky where the moon was had become darker than the east, soon there was more light in the east than there had been in the dome of moonlight under which he had sailed since leaving the camp, and looking over his shoulder he saw the moon low over the forest, its light a pallid copper-coloured lane along a river that had become steel grey. Colours appeared, a flush of pink in the east broke apart until it looked like the parallel bars of a gate across the pathway of the dawn, the bars merged, the colours grew stronger, they swelled into a cool conflagration that flushed up into the wide and real sky as the entire world opened up.

Now Jerome became aware of life all around him as birds called in the forest on either side of the river, he saw the white trunks of a stand of birch, and as the current at this point swerved in toward the shore, the carolling ring of bird calls was loud and near. A crow flew out from a pine top and its cawing racketed back and forth across the river echoing from shore to shore. The hammer of a hungry woodpecker whacked against a dead trunk while a larger bird, one of the blue herons called cranes in the Maritime Provinces, flew slantwise across the rising dawn and turned slowly, its long legs folded in under its body and trailing behind, its snaky head hanging down as it quested for fish with slow flaps of its wings heading upstream along the right bank. Jerome heard a snick and saw the flash of a trout's belly. He paddled on through clear water with hardly a log in sight and within ten minutes there were snicking flashes all around him as trout broke the surface to feed on early flies, the first run of the season in from the sea, quick, slim fish with bellies as bright as silver coins, firm and fierce from a winter of cold salt water as they drove up against the current to the beds where they had been spawned. Jerome saw the lazy roll of a salmon about ten feet from the canoe, the little humping of water as the fish turned and went down; he heard a splash behind him but when he looked over his shoulder there was only a ruffle of broken water; he paddled a few minutes more, the trout still snicking, and then directly in front of the canoe the river broke open and a huge salmon slashed out shining, paused in the air with its hard muscles bending its body like a sickle and dropped with a drenching splash, the canoe crossed the broken water, and Jerome looking over the side saw the last twisting tail-thrust as the big fish went down.

Still the tiny canoe throbbed down the stream, the boy in the stern, and around the next bend he saw a shack but no smoke from its chimney pipe. Now he was sleepy and tired and stopped paddling; he sat with the paddles across his knees and his head sunk forward.

"I must have slept like that for half an hour; when I woke the canoe was drifting slantwise and light was hurting my eyes."

It was the rising sun, a turmoil of gold like a tremendous excitement in heaven pouring its arrows into the forest and flashing them off the stream. His limbs dead and cold, Jerome straightened the bow of the canoe and let it drift in a current much slower now because here the river was deep and he felt the huge unseen pressure of the tide lower down. Close to the shore he passed a deer drinking on a sandspit and after a while he was afraid that if he fell asleep again he would lose his paddle. A small cape stood out with a sentinel pine, the canoe struck it with a soft crunch and Jerome crawled ashore and dragged half of it clear of the stream. Then he got back in and slept.

When he woke the sun was almost directly overhead, his nostrils were dry with heat and his body felt tired, hot, heavy and stiff. It was a May morning without a cloud in the sky and already the heat had made the balsam forest pungent.

"The time must have been somewhere between eight o'clock and nine. At that season of the year the sun rises about five, so I must have been asleep nearly three hours. If it hadn't been for the glare I suppose I'd have gone on sleeping all day. I was in the aftermath of shock. Even now I can't tell you how far I had come down the river, but I had been paddling with a fast current for at least four hours before I fell asleep.

"But I didn't think about distances when I woke up. I didn't even know what distances were. What I remember is how I felt. I felt black. I felt the way I felt that morning after I first killed a man in the war. I saw my mother's dead face hard and angry in front of mine. God, she was an angry woman, that mother of mine. I saw the Engineer with his spanner and when I tried to eat some of my sausage I nearly vomited it up. I had to get out of that forest and get off that river. Far away was where I wanted to go, and then I thought about the trains."

Though he did not know it, Jerome was now close to the sea and was paddling in a new kind of river. As it nears salt water that river becomes wide and is tidal for several miles. The town lies a distance inland and Jerome could not see the open water of the Gulf, but he could smell it and his cheeks felt a new salty moisture in the air. He became conscious of settlement along the shores – not a town, but a scattering of frame houses and large breaks in the forest where there were fields and cattle. He also became aware that paddling had turned into heavy, leaden work, for the river was much wider here than it had been at the camp, and its current was stopped by the pressure of an incoming tide from the sea. Jerome ached all over his body as he forced the canoe forward, he sobbed with exhaustion and shock and was drowned in his own sweat, he was on the point of giving up when he rounded a final bend and there, right in front of him, was the black iron bridge that carried the main railway line between Halifax and Montreal. Beyond it was a small wooden bridge for road traffic and beyond that the river seemed enormously wide. There was a town on Jerome's left, a small, drab town built almost entirely of wood, and through his sweat he remembered having been in it before, last fall when he came down in the steamboat with his mother and some men, the time she bought him his first ice cream. As his canoe drifted in toward the bridge he backed water and tried to ease toward the shore. He was so tired he cried. Then he almost dropped his paddle in terror, for a train appeared out of nowhere almost on top of him as it crossed the bridge.

"It was only a small work-train – an old-fashioned engine with two olive-grey cars and a caboose on the end. It made an awful racket though, for it crossed that iron bridge with me almost underneath it. Its exhausts were crashing as it got up speed and it belched smoke from the soft Cape Breton coal all the engines burned in those days. The whole river seemed to shake as it crossed the bridge, but by the time I passed under it the roaring had stopped and I heard the singing drone that rails make when a train goes away down a track. I looked up and saw a man on the platform of the caboose looking down at me and his face was shiny black. He was the first Negro I ever saw and I wondered if all the people in the world outside the camp were black like him."

Jerome forced himself into a last spurt of action and paddled the canoe across the current, making heavy leeway, toward a jetty on the left bank between the two bridges. He remembered it from the time when the steamboat had landed him there. The sight of the jetty also reminded him of the motorboat and he became terrified, for what if the Engineer were waiting for him on the wharf? But there was no sign of the motorboat either at the wharf or along the shore.

"He had either beached it above town or sunk it in the river. He'd have wanted to walk quietly into town at dawn before the people were up and hide somewhere near the tracks till a train stopped."

Two men in dungarees and peaked caps were sitting on the curb of the jetty watching Jerome as he paddled in, but neither of them moved as he swung against the landing stage. He climbed out and hung onto the canoe with no plan whatever. He was just doing one thing after another and the next thing he did was to take the painter and secure it to a mooring-post.

"Wheer'd yew git thet canoe from, son?"

A lean, unshaven face with a chicken throat was staring down at him from the curb of the wharf.

"It's mine."

"Littlest goddam canoe I ever seen," the man said and spat into the water.

Jerome climbed the ladder stiffly and as he reached the wharf the man made a lazy half-turn in his direction.

"Wheer'd yew come from, son?"

"I bin paddlin'."

The man spat again but did not answer and continued sitting with his legs dangling and his unshaven lantern jaws working steadily on his cud of tobacco. Jerome, afraid of everything and everyone and tired in every bone, walked shakily off the dock onto a dirt track that ran along the riverside of the little town. He reached the railway, bent down and touched one of the shiny rails and found it so hot it burned. When he reached the station he saw men unloading freight out of a solitary box-car and was surprised that none of them were Negroes. Jerome sat on a bench under the overhang of the station roof and ate one whole length of his blood sausage, and there he continued to sit an unknown length of time half-asleep and half-awake like the town itself, but feeling a little stronger now there was food in his stomach.

George Stewart recalls a visit to the socialist paradise of Russia, very like the visit by Hugh MacLennan in 1937:

Standing on the balcony of the Europa Hotel in Leningrad I had forgotten, for the time being, the intense little tragedy in which I had been involved the previous spring in Montreal. Now I was out in this huge, news-making, future-making – what? Who could understand Europe in 1937, or Russia then or ever? The provincial walls in which I had lived had crumbled and I was out in this alone. With me was a young American I had met on the train out of Helsinki the night before, and he had come all the way from Nebraska to see with his own eyes the shape of things to come. By noon of his first day in Russia he had seen enough to daze him, to terrify him with its unknown quantities, to smash to pieces the neat little walls of theory with which he had armoured himself. Now we were together, close and intimate in Russia though we barely knew each other's names.

The *nuit blanche* of Leningrad in late June made eerie the perpetual rustling of thousands of shoeless feet on the pavements below, the pavements laid out by the Czars which the communists had captured along with this hotel and the marble palaces nearby. We could just distinguish the human swarm in the *nuit blanche*, not the faces of individuals but the smock-wearing, shuffling swarm which flowed hour after hour without ceasing because, apparently, they had nothing else to do and no place to go.

"*Byprizorni*," the American kept muttering. "*Byprizorni*."

In the weird white night they swarmed like creatures mysteriously risen out of a Sargasso Sea, ourselves on the ship's bridge looking down, and after a day in the Leningrad streets we knew that every face, to us, was a variant of the same face we had stared at since leaving the Finland Station that morning: a face wrinkled, prematurely old, unsmiling, unblinking, the face of Tolstoy's peasant in a world he could not understand, scarred by years of cold and hunger, knowing a totality of unwantedness, the face of the millions too old, slow, ignorant and stupid for this new Soviet world.

"See Russia," said the American, "and let your theories die."

The thousands of feet shuffled with the sound of a restless sea that would never be still and never know a storm, and they shuffled like that because each one of them was wrapped in bandages and hemp, and they were wrapped in bandages and hemp because there were not enough shoes in Russia, and because the price of cheap shoes cost more than double the monthly pay of the average Soviet worker that year.

"Where do they come from? Where are they going?"

A voice with an English accent answered behind us: "They come from the land and they are going no place. These, my friends, are counter-revolutionaries. They are, or were, kulaks. They are the sons of serfs, and the Bolsheviks liberated them in 1917."

Near the end of the novel George Stewart emerges triumphant from a hospital vigil:

For something new and strange had begun to happen to me. Light seemed to be shining inside of me when I stepped outside and walked down the driveway toward the city. The weather had turned still warmer, and on the precipices of the mountain tiny rivulets of icy water were making musical sounds. Romeo Pronovost had been right: winter was ending and this night was lovely with the first sounds of spring, and where is spring more gaily virginal, colder or more fresh than in this northern land where it comes when there still is snow? The soft air was as sweet as a healthy childhood, and the sky was not merely a night sky but a radiance illuminating my fatigue. Such a sky I had not recognized since I was ten years old, and I remembered its wonder and how I had almost wept on account of it. The chaos which had been dark within me for days had disappeared and my soul was like a landscape with water when the fog goes and the moon comes out and all the promontories are clear and still. The whole city shone and seemed to have a voice and I heard it, the voice of them all, the lights shaking and standing up, the sky opening to receive that volume of sound and colour from underneath, all of it glad and good. As I walked along the familiar street chipped out of the rock of Mount Royal, with the city luminous below and the sky luminous above, there was music within me, so much that I myself was music and light, and I knew then that what she had upheld from childhood was not worthless, that she was more than a rat in a trap, that the loves she had known and inspired had not cancelled one another out, were not perishable absolutely, would not entirely end with her but would be translated into the mysterious directions of the spirit which breathed upon the void. I reached home, found Sally there, kissed her forehead and told her that all was well. Then with that music in my mind, Bach's music, I fell asleep and lay motionless until eight in the morning when I woke to see Catherine's painting on the wall, its colours singing, and the joy she had when she painted it was mine again.

CHAPTER · 9

Essays 1958–64

"Scotchman's Return"

Much of Each Man's Son *is concerned with Scottish heritage and its effects. MacLennan's 1958 visit back to the land of his forebears tells us more about its effect on him, and on millions of others. This essay was the first in the collection, to which it gave a name, that was published in 1960:*

Whenever I stop to think about it, the knowledge that I am three-quarters Scotch, and Highland at that, seems like a kind of doom from which I am too Scotch even to think of praying for deliverance. I can thank my father for this last-ditch neurosis. He was entirely Scotch; he was a living specimen of a most curious heritage. In spite of his medical knowledge, which was large; in spite of his quick, nervous vitality and tireless energy, he was never able to lay to rest the beasties which went bump in his mind at three o'clock in the morning. It mattered nothing that he was a third-generation Canadian who had never seen the Highlands before he visited them on leave in the First World War. He never needed to go there to understand whence he came or what he was. He was neither a Scot nor yet was he Scottish; he never used those genteel appellations which now are supposed to be *de rigueur*. He was simply Scotch. All the perplexity and doggedness of the race was in him, its loneliness, tenderness, and affection, its deceptive vitality, its quick flashes of violence, its dog-whistle sensitivity to sounds to which Anglo-Saxons are stone-deaf, its incapacity to tell its heart to foreigners save in terms foreigners do not comprehend, its resigned indifference to whether they comprehend or not. "It's not easy being Scotch," he told me more than once. To which I suppose another Scotchman might say: "It wasn't meant to be."

So far as I could tell, my father found it almost impossible to believe that anyone not Scotch is entirely real. Yet, at the same time, buried in the fastnesses of his complex mind was the contradictory notion that if a Scotchman ever amounts to anything important, he will not be any too real, either, for some beastie will come along and spoil him. As engineers keeping the ships going, as captains serving the owners of the lines, as surgeons, teachers, clergymen, and the like, as loyal seconds-in-command – in these niches the Scotch might expect to fare well. But you seldom found them on the summit, and if by reason of an accident one of them got there, something bad was pretty sure to happen. When Ramsay MacDonald became the first man with a Mac in his name to become a British Prime Minister, my father shook his head gloomily over MacDonald's picture on the front page of the paper, and when I asked him why, he said: "He won't do." He had an overweening admiration for the English so long as they stayed in England, and for the Royal Navy above all other English institutions. Indeed, one of his motives for becoming a doctor was an idea in the back of his youthful mind that as a surgeon he might become an R.N. officer. But he was no light Anglophile. I well remember a summer afternoon in the mid-twenties when a British squadron paid Halifax a courtesy call, and better still do I remember that the two leading ships were HMS *Hood* and HMS *Repulse*. As my father at that time was doing some work in the military hospital, he was called to perform an emergency operation on an officer of the *Repulse*, and the Commander of the ship later invited him to tea in the wardroom. He took me along, and as I also was brought up to love the Royal Navy, this was a great thrill to me. It turned out to be an experience almost traumatic.

No sooner had we taken our seats in the wardroom than the officer-of-the-watch entered, resplendent in the dress of the day carrying his cocked hat under his arm. He laid the hat beside him on the table, nodded to a steward for his tea, glanced at us, and when he saw we were civilians and natives, his lips parted in an expression of disdain in which, to quote a famous English author who has noted such expressions as carefully as Shelley the lips of Ozymandias, delicacy had no part. Ignoring my father, this officer inclined his eyes vaguely in my direction and said: "D'you live here?" "Yes, sir," I replied. "Beastly place," was his comment and then he fell silent. So did everyone else.

After several minutes the silence was broken by the racket of an R.C.A.F. training biplane stunting over the harbour and the arrogant disdain on the face of the former officer-of-the-watch was replaced by something very like a flush of anger. "So you have those wretched things over here, too?" he asked my father accusingly. I noted with some pride that my father did not reply to this officer, but instead turned to another man, who had been embarrassed by his colleague's behaviour, and asked mildly if the development of aircraft had made it necessary for the Navy to alter its battle tactics. This officer was beginning to reply in some detail when the officer-of-the-watch interrupted: "Do you," he asked my father, "seriously believe that a wretched little gnat like that aircraft could possibly threaten a ship like this?"

No, it was not a successful tea party, nor did it last much longer. My father rose as soon as he felt it courteous to do so, we were escorted to the ladder and handed down into the launch, and as the launch drove through the fog my father was informatively silent. After a while he said, as though excusing the officer's rudeness: "Of course, the weather has been depressing here and they've come up from New York." But before the launch touched the jetty he added: "All the same, he shouldn't have said that." I understood then that my father had not felt himself snubbed, but that the Scotch in him had been gravely concerned by the officer's *hubris* concerning the Air Force. A beastie had been alerted to keep a special eye on that slim, powerful, but extremely vulnerable battle-cruiser which was the last brain-child of the ferocious Admiral Jackie Fisher, the ship which Winston Churchill later described as having the brilliance and the fragility one is apt to associate with the children of very old men. Years later in the terrible December of 1941, when the news came from Malaya, I recalled that afternoon aboard *Repulse* with a thrill of sheer horror.

My father was also the reason why I never visited the Highlands when I was a student in the Old Country. Nor did he
think I should have done so. "You'll see them one of these days,"
he said. And he added as an afterthought: "If you're spared and
well." And he added as another afterthought: "When you do see
them you'll understand." Naturally he did not tell me what I
would understand, assuming I would know, but this comment
did nothing to foment a desire in me to travel north of the
Highland line.

But we can't escape ourselves forever, and more of ourselves
than we choose to admit is the accumulated weight of our
ancestors. As I grew older the thought of the Highlands began
to haunt me, and in the summer of 1958, after having lived for a
long time under a great strain, I decided to get a change and sail
to England on a freight ship. I landed in Manchester and of
course went south, but after spending a week in London, I went
north on the train to Edinburgh and on a Monday morning I
found myself in a car-rental agency in the Haymarket making a
deal for a Vauxhall.

Ahead of me was the only American I saw in the Old Country that year who behaved as Europeans desire Americans to
behave abroad. After complaining about the tastelessness of
British food, the harshness and skiddiness of British toilet
paper, and the absurdity of driving on the left-hand side of the
road, he finally came to the topic of the Edinburgh Sabbath
which he had just survived.

"Do you realize," he said to the car dealer, "that in the United
States there's not even a village as quiet as this town was yesterday?"

The Scotchman looked up at him, inwardly gratified but
outwardly glum.

"Ay!" he said, and assumed incorrectly that the American
understood that both himself and his country had been
rebuked.

When he turned to me after the American had departed, and
had identified my nationality by my driving licence, he allowed
himself the luxury of an irrelevant comment.

"Ye appear to have deeficult neighbours," he said.

"Perhaps you have difficult neighbours, too?"

"Ay!" he said, and seemed pleased, for an instant later he said "Ay" again.

More or less secure in the Vauxhall I headed north for Stirling and the Highland Line, and after a night by Loch Katrine struck north by Balquhidder, mistook my road to Glencoe and went too far west, and soon found myself beside Loch Awe. I also found myself, with some surprise and mortification, unwilling to perceive any beauty in this region because Loch Awe is in Campbell country, and in the near past of several centuries ago, the Campbell chiefs had been an anathema to the less successful clans they pillaged.

The roads in the Highlands, as those will know who have travelled them, are not only so narrow that in most sections two baby Austins are unable to pass, they are also infested with livestock. Sheep fall asleep on their narrow shoulders and cars must stop again and again while bullocks make up their minds whether or not to move out of the way. The roads were built by some English general, I think his name was Wade, who had the eighteenth-century English notion that if he built roads the communications between the clans would improve. Only lately have General Wade's roads been hard-topped, and never have they been widened except at regular intervals where cars may turn out to allow approaching cars to pass. They are adequately marked if you are familiar with them, but I was not familiar with them and again I lost my way. I went into the pub of a hamlet to ask where I was and discovered behind the bar an elderly gentleman with white hair and the demeanour of a Presbyterian elder, and beside the bar three workmen silently sipping ale.

"What's the name of this place?" I asked the publican.

"The Heather and Bull," he said.

"I meant, what's this community?"

"Mostly Protestant," he said, "but in recent years wi' a small smattering of Roman Catholics." He turned to one of the workmen: "John, how many Catholics now?"

"About eighteen per cent. Going on for twenty."

"They're risin' fast," said a third man.

"Ay!" said the publican. And turning to me he asked when I had left Canada.

"How on earth did you guess I'm a Canadian?"

"You are not English, that is certain, and you are not American. You still have some of the voice." He put out his hand: "God bless you!"

We talked of Scotland, Canada, and theology and I forgot what I had intended to ask him. An hour later, when I shook his hand and received my directions, his noble face was as solemn as a memory from childhood.

"You will be disappointed," he warned me. "Scotland is full of nothing but Irish now. Och, we have no dignity left."

An Anglo-Saxon or an American might assume a racial situation from this remark, but it was the sort of thing I grew up with, the sort of remark I have made myself, in different connotations, all my life. Its meaning was clear to me if to nobody else. The old gentleman was unburdening himself of a beastie which had nothing whatever to do with the Catholics, the Irish, or with anything, possibly, that he himself could put into words.

The next day I was in the true north of Scotland among the sheep, the heather, the whin, the mists, and the homes of the vanished races. Such sweeps of emptiness I never saw in Canada before I went to the Mackenzie River later in that same summer. But this Highland emptiness, only a few hundred miles above the massed population of England, is a far different thing from the emptiness of our own Northwest Territories. Above the sixtieth parallel in Canada you feel that nobody but God has ever been there before you, but in a deserted Highland glen you feel that everyone who ever mattered is dead and gone. Those glens are the most hauntingly lovely sights I have ever seen: they are vaster, more moving, more truly vacated than the southern abbeys ruined by Henry VIII. They are haunted by the lost loves and passions of a thousand years. Later that summer on the lower reaches of the Mackenzie, after talking to an Athabascan Indian with Celtic eyes and the name of McPherson, I remembered the wild loneliness of Lochaber and it occurred to me that only a man from a country as lonely and ghost-ridden as the Highlands could have had the insane determination to paddle a canoe through the Rocky Mountains and down La Grande Rivière-en-bas to the Beaufort Sea, and that nothing was more in the life-style of the Highlander than Alexander Mackenzie's feat in searching for the Northwest Passage in a canoe. After an achievement of incredible boldness and endurance, what, after all, did this Highlander find but nothing?

Yet, as a by-product, he and others like him surely found much of Canada, even though one of them, solitary on the Qu'Appelle or the Saskatchewan, admitting the grandeur of the woods and prairies of the New World, sang from a broken heart that he was an exile from his native land, and while making possible the existence of a country so vast that Scotland would be lost in it, regretted his inability to wield a claymore in defence of a barren glen presided over by an imbecile chief. The exiled Irish never forgave their landlords, but the exiled Highlanders pined for the scoundrel Pretender, and even regretted the proprietors who preferred sheep to humanity, enclosed their own people and drove them starving across the western ocean with such an uncomprehended yearning in their souls that some of them ended up in log cabins along the Athabasca and on the shores of James Bay.

In the parish of Kintail, whence some of my own people were driven a century and a half ago, I was told there are now barely four hundred inhabitants. In my ancestors' days there were more than twelve thousand.

"Where are they?" the minister said when I asked him. "Where indeed but in Canada? And some in Australia and New Zealand of course, but most of them in Canada."

With them they brought – no doubt of this – that nameless haunting guilt they never understood, and the feeling of failure, and the loneliness of all the warm-hearted, not very intelligent folk so outmoded by the Anglo-Saxon success that they knew they were helpless unless they lived as the Anglo-Saxons did, failures unless they learned to feel (or not to feel at all) as the Anglo-Saxons ordained. Had my father been clairvoyant when he told me I would understand when I went to the Highlands?

I'm not sure that I do understand or ever will understand what he wanted me to know. But one evening, watching a rainbow form over Loch Leven, the mists drop down the hills into rain, then watching the sky rent open and such a tumult of golden light pour forth that the mountains themselves moved and were transfigured, still moved and then were lifted up until they ceased to be mountains and turned themselves into an abstraction of sheer glory and gold – watching this I realized, or thought I did, why these desperate people had endured so long against the civilization of the south. Unlike Ulysses, they had failed to stop their ears when the Sirens sang, and the Sirens that sing in the Highlands, suddenly and when you least expect to hear them, have voices more dangerously beguiling than any in the Aegean Isles. Beauty is nearly the most dangerous thing on earth, and those who love her too much, or look too deeply into her eyes, pay the price for her, which often is an empty stomach and a life of misunderstanding.

So it was here, though an economist would point out that the land is barren and that in the early days the people lacked education and civilized techniques. But this practical attitude merely begs the question of why the people stayed so long: stayed, in fact, until they were driven out. These mountains are almost as useless to the cultivator as the upper reaches of the Laurentian Shield. The Gaelic tongue sounds soft and lovely, but compared with English and French it is a primitive means of communication. The ancestors of almost a quarter of modern Canada never did, and in their native glens they never could, develop even the rudiments of an urban culture. When they made the acquaintance of the English this must have sorely troubled their conscience, for they were religious, they were Christianized after a fashion, and the parable that meant most to them was the Parable of the Talents. Only a few of their chiefs could possibly be called intelligent, and the conduct of the chiefs of their only really successful clan (it shall be nameless here, though every Highlander knows the one I have in mind) was of the crafty peasant sort, the more base because it exploited the loyalty of a people who were already enslaved by their own conception of honour. But though these chiefs did well for themselves, they only became rich and famous after they had conspired with the English enemy. No leader, not even a genius, could have raised in the terrain of the Highlands a civilization capable of competing with England's. Yet the Highlanders held on to the glens; incredibly they held on to them until the end of the eighteenth century. Often I have said to myself that my grandfathers three times removed lived in a culture as primitive as Homer's, and last summer in the Highlands I knew that they really had.

Driving south through Glencoe where the Campbells massacred the Macdonalds, I remembered the first time I met Angus L. Macdonald, who then was Premier of Nova Scotia and previously had been Canada's Minister for the Navy. With a suddenness that would have been startling to anyone but another clansman, Mr. Macdonald turned to me in a company of people and from the depths of a mutual empathy he said: "To be a Celt is never to be far from tears."

But we Celts are withal a mercurial people also; our sorrowful moods pass like the mists on the braes and the sunlight strikes through when we least expect it. A week later I was in the most fatally civilized country in the world, Sweden, waiting for a Pan-American Clipper to take me home.

Just as I belong to the last Canadian generation raised with a Highland nostalgia, so also do I belong to the last which regards a transatlantic flight as a miracle. When I was a boy I saw the first tiny plane to fly the ocean, the American seaplane N.C. 4, which took a very long time moving by stages from Halifax to Sydney, to Bonavista Bay, to the Azores, and finally to Lisbon. Eight years later plane after plane set out on non-stop ventures and disappeared into the sea.

Now, eating a filet mignon and sipping champagne in the supreme luxury of this Pan-American aircraft, I looked down on the waste of seas which, together with the mountains of British Columbia, had divided the clansmen from their homes over a century ago. Sitting there idle I felt an unwarranted lift of joy and omnipotent power. The plane nuzzled into the stratospheric wind, she rolled as slowly and surely as a shark speeding through the water in which it was born, she went so fast that though she left Stockholm as late as 4:30 in the afternoon it was still bright daylight when she put down in a rainstorm in Keflavik. She took on fuel and set out again, I slept for an hour or two, wakened to a change in the propeller pitch, and learned we were circling Gander, which as usual was buried in fog. After an hour the pilot said over the intercom:

"The weather in Gander has deteriorated to zero-zero. We are now proceeding to New York. We will arrive in Idlewild at 7:40 Eastern Daylight Time. We will arrive on schedule."

Here, of course, was the supreme triumph of the civilization which, in wrecking the clansmen, had made it possible for me to think of Canada as home. The plane tore through the fog, the stewardess brought a delicious breakfast, and just as I was sipping my coffee the sun broke dazzlingly through the window into the cabin. I looked out and there, in a semicircle of sunshine, the only sunshine apparently in the whole northern hemisphere at that particular moment, lay Cape Breton Island. The plane sloped down to eight thousand feet and I saw beside the Bras d'Or lake the tiny speck which was the house where my mother and sister at that very moment lay asleep. We did reach New York on schedule and that same day I ate my lunch in the Medical Arts restaurant on the corner of Sherbrooke Street and Guy. The man next to me at the counter asked where I had been and I told him I had been in the Scottish Highlands.

"It must have been nice," he said.

"It was. But it's also nice to be home."

Am I wrong, or is it true that it is only now, after so many years of not knowing who we were or wanted to be, that we Canadians of Scotch descent are truly at home in the northern half of North America?

"Footsteps of Genius"

MacLennan's fascination with unusual characters is revealed in this essay about Einstein. Every student at Oxford or Princeton at the same time as the great scholar would have cherished their encounters with him. Perhaps it says more about MacLennan that he also sought out the company of the bootleggers mentioned here. The juxtaposition of Einstein and the bootleggers would have provided a lesser man with an irresistible title:

> Ah, did you once see Shelley plain
> And did he stop and speak to you
> And did you speak to him again?
> How strange it seems and new!

When I was a boy these lines of Browning thrilled me, for I was raised in the belief that everything we value, from Christianity to the pasteurization of milk, had come to us from a handful of men who had been singled out by the Divine Spirit and whom we described as geniuses. Merely to see a living genius was considered a privilege, and we agreed with Emerson that the search after great men should be a legitimate dream of youth. Certainly it was my dream when I grew up in Nova Scotia to meet and speak with a truly great man before I died.

The most undeniable genius of our century is Albert Einstein, and when I first left home for Europe the idea that I might see him in some public place was an exciting one. I was therefore thrilled, during the winter of my last year in Oxford, when Einstein came over from the Continent to deliver a series of lectures setting forth his latest theory of the nature of the universe. In those days there was much discussion about whether we lived in a finite or an infinite universe, and it was expected that the results of Einstein's latest researches would tell us, at least in general terms, where we were.

Few lectures Einstein ever gave can have been more frustrating to him than this Oxford series. His courtesy and modesty were legendary, but the press pestered him wherever he went, and university gossip had it that he was pained when he discovered that hardly anyone understood what he was talking about. The reporters who flooded the town had lean pickings. They had not expected to understand the equations, but they had hoped to find at least one or two scientists attending the lectures who would tell them in simple English whether the universe was curved or rectangular, expanding or static, finite or infinite. So far as I could discover from reading the press – as an undergraduate I was not admitted to the lectures, nor would I have learned anything if I had been – all they found out was that Einstein's hair was turning grey and that he liked to take long walks by himself.

It was his walking habit that brought us together for the first, though not for the last time. One day during Einstein's stay in Oxford I woke up at noon feeling as a young man does when he has helped celebrate a friend's twenty-first birthday the night before. After getting something to eat, I decided that only Spartan measures would rid me of my malaise, so I put on running shorts and shoes, two sweaters and a scarf and set out for a run around the three-mile path that circles the Christ Church meadows. In the narrow section where the path winds along the Cherwell between trees and shrubs I rounded a corner and all but ran into a strange and wonderful man.

"Please," Einstein said in a strong German accent, "can you tell me where I am?"

While I struggled for breath, he smiled: "I am entirely lost in the trees."

Two years later when I was at Princeton, Einstein left Europe with a price on his head and was spirited off his steamer at the mouth of New York harbour lest some of Fritz Kuehn's hoodlums make an attempt on his life. After a few days he arrived in Princeton to begin his long sojourn there. His arrival sent a flutter through the little town, which was not so accustomed to celebrities as Oxford was, and his walking habits soon made him a familiar figure. Princeton thinks extremely well of itself, but with the exception of the barbers, who were sure they could make an improvement in his appearance, neither town nor gown was too sophisticated not to feel flattered by his presence among them.

In those days some of my best friends were ex-bootleggers who had survived from the days of prohibition, a much respected body of men in Princeton because of their service to the community during the previous Republican administrations. They loved their town dearly. They regarded foreigners with contempt, and foreign country to them began on the other side of the Delaware River about a dozen miles away.

Late one night I was munching a hamburger in a diner, while my vocabulary was being enlarged by three bootleggers who leaned on the counter and told me things about the United States that are not recorded in either the press or the history books. Suddenly their gravel voices ceased, and looking over my shoulder I joined them in a long stare at an apparition in the doorway. He had vast brown eyes open in child-like enquiry, he had a wild mop of hair and he was wearing a baggy suit of clothes. When he saw us looking at him his face broke into a wonderful smile, his hands made the apologetic gesture of a man discovering himself an intruder in the wrong place, and while we stared he turned out of the shaft of light and disappeared into the dark.

Before the monosyllabic conversation within the diner could be resumed, a burly character wearing a truck-driver's cap came swaggering in, plunked himself down at the counter, demanded coffee, looked around at the rest of us and said, "Whaddya call this dump?"

Now it was apparent that this man was a genuine foreigner, for even if his base of operations had been as distant as Pennsylvania he must have known what Princeton was. He may have been new on the run, or he may have come east with a load from across the mountains, and as he slurped up his coffee I saw one of the bootleggers contemplating him with the professional expression of a butcher sizing up a carcass to estimate how much it weighs. This bootlegger was a simple man but a passionate one; insanely loyal to his friends, he was subject to dark movements in his soul which more than once I had heard emerge in a kind of poetry. Once in his speakeasy the lights had gone out and the moon, striking through the window, had illuminated his face in a manner utterly uncanny; his eyes had rolled white in the moon and he had broken into a stream of profanity which had no connection with the failure of his lighting system. When I asked him what the matter was, he had answered in what Evelyn Waugh would call a lapidary phrase: "That God-damn moon reminds me of jail," he said. So now as I saw him contemplating this truck-driver who had entered the place just after Einstein had left it, I was glad I was not in the truck-driver's shoes. Two years ago the bootlegger had served what he called a nine-spot for slugging an out-of-state revenue officer with a baseball bat.

"What goes on in this town," he said in a gravel voice while fixing the truck-driver with a slow stare, "is something a guy like you would not understand."

"Yeah?" and the word was not a question but a challenge.

"Did you see that old guy with the hair?"

"What old guy with what hair?"

"That old guy that was in here before you."

"I never saw any old guy." The truck-driver shrugged. "What goes on in this place nights?"

The bootlegger's stare remained in sullen fixation, and the truck-driver gave a look over his shoulders at the other men, who were silent in the way Americans of that type know how to be on certain occasions.

"Okay," he said, "so what's so special about this guy?"

The bootlegger shifted his weight and eased his shoulders under his suit: "You wouldn't know, but that old man is working on the next war. He's making photoelectric cells in this town, and when the war comes he's gonna let them loose, and when he lets them loose nuthin's gonna stand against them."

The truck-driver finished his coffee and rose: "That a fact?"

The bootlegger turned his thumb in slow motion in the direction of the door. "Okay, you can get going now. And next time you drive that load of junk through this town, you can keep right on going all the way through. In this town we're used to big shots."

A few nights later I happened to be walking through the campus with a young English physical chemist on the way to a Schoenberg recital at the McCarter Theatre. It was a windy night and under the elms it was very dark with only a few lights flickering where paths intersected and a few windows illuminated with graduate students behind them poring over drab details which would be compiled after a year or two in Ph.D. theses which nobody but the examiners would ever read. Near the Classics Seminary we came upon Einstein standing still and apparently waiting for us to overtake him.

"Please," he said, "I go to the concert but I am new here and now I do not know where I am."

The Englishman's voice quivered with delight as he remarked that we also were going to the concert and that perhaps Dr. Einstein would permit us to show him the way.

"But how," said Einstein in a genuine wonder, "do you know who I am?"

"Oh, sir!" said the Englishman.

"You are too kind," the genius said as he fell into step with us. "You two young men go together and you have things to talk about."

We assured him that what we had been talking about could wait for another occasion, and the three of us continued side by side through the windy darkness.

"Do you like Schoenberg?" Einstein asked us.

One of us murmured that we did not know, and the other of us added that this would be the first time we had ever heard his music.

"I have been told, sir," said the Englishman, "that one must be an exceptionally good mathematician to be able to understand Schoenberg's scale."

As though he had heard this for the first time, Einstein nodded with great emphasis and said: "But that is so true!" And then he said: "Unfortunately I am such a poor mathematician I do not understand him at all."

A great gust of wind went shrieking through the trees, a pattern of light tossed wildly in the shadows of waving branches, and rain began to fall.

> Ah, did you once see Shelley plain
> And did he stop and speak to you
> And did you speak to him again?
> How strange it seems and new!

From "Have You Had Many Wimbledons?"

A Maritime Singles Champion in 1929, MacLennan played tennis well and appreciated the subtleties of the game. He also appreciated the subtleties of encounters such as the one that led to his acquiring a ticket to Wimbledon, after he had travelled to the nearby Southfields station in the hope of just such a miracle. The world-famous tournament has, of course, long since recovered from the shock of its first black player, Althea Gibson, whose appearance so upset "the woman with the gorgeous skin."

Ten years after this 1958 essay appeared MacLennan noted: "One of the best things in my fifty years of life has been the game of tennis, chiefly because on the tennis court experience atones for a lot of lost youth."

. . . At Southfields station the train stopped and we got out into taxis, four strangers to each car, and were driven to the courts.

Opposite me from where I sat on a jump seat were three women, one looking like every English games mistress I ever saw, another apple-cheeked and elderly, the third thirtyish with gorgeous shoulders, a skin that looked like the petal of a white rose dipped in cream, but an expression which should have made, and probably had made, many a man pause before he tried to cultivate her acquaintance.

Suddenly this almost-beautiful creature spoke in a clipped voice: "Shall we have to see Gibson this afternoon?"

"She plays the Haydon child, doesn't she?" said the elderly lady.

"I expect she does. Last year when Gibson came over one was told one should like her because she couldn't help her colour. One tried. But of course it was impossible. Didn't you find her ghastly?"

"I thought she had great dignity," said the lady mildly.

"Did you really?" said the woman with the gorgeous skin. "How very odd!"

Then with a charming smile the lady said: "Have you had *many* Wimbledons?"

The woman with the gorgeous skin fell silent, the lady with the apple cheeks leaned back twinkling, definitely one up.

A moment later, after fumbling in her bag, she produced a sheaf of those thin little papers which are Wimbledon tickets.

"Oh dear," she said as though talking to herself, "here I am with extra tickets for the last three days. I got them in Worcestershire last winter from our club, expecting my sister to come, but my poor sister took ill, and now with this wretched weather it's been most frightfully difficult to know what to do with them."

Not believing that this was real, I leaned forward.

"Ma'am," I said, "if that's your problem, I'd just love to help you solve it."

"You mean you've come all the way out here without a ticket? How extraordinarily hopeful of you!"

I opened my wallet and produced a five-pound note.

"Oh, but they're worth nothing like that much."

The girl with the gorgeous skin said to me: "You seem to be in the most remarkable luck, I must say. But then, you Americans so often are."

"What an extraordinary thing for you to say!" said the elderly lady. "Really, I'd have thought that by this time *everyone* in England would know the difference." She twinkled at me charmingly: "I had quite a few Canadian boys with me during the war. They were very naughty with the girls, I'm afraid, but I did adore them, and a woman can't really mind if a man's naughty, can she?"

But I had noticed that she had made no offer to sell me her tickets, and I knew why. I could almost hear her thoughts. It would be such a bore, she was thinking, to have a mere tourist beside one for three days of Wimbledon. Much better an empty seat than that.

"Have you ever played at Wimbledon yourself?" I asked her.

"Oh yes. Very badly of course, but I played several times."

"I nearly played once," I said, and shamelessly I went on: "I was Oxford tennis secretary in a very lean year, and I could have got in on that."

"Then I expect we have quite a few friends in common?"

I mentioned a few well-known players of yesteryear, and she knew all of them, and as we got out of the taxi I understood that the unhoped-for had happened.

"No nonsense now about paying for these tickets," she said. "They've been paid for long ago and I won't hear of any non-sense about five-pound notes."

"We'll see about that later," I suggested.

"Well, we certainly shan't see about it now." We found our seats among the fifteen thousand spectators at Centre Court, and saw Ashley Cooper serve an ace against Mervin Rose. "Oh dear, these mechanical Australians! Why do they bother to play at all when one always knows what they're going to do? Ah well, perhaps the doubles will save the tournament."

"Why the doubles?" I asked her.

"Well, of course, in men's doubles tactics and imagination can still make a difference, don't you think?"

She was right about this, as she was right about so many things. . . .

. . . The men's doubles game still defies the science of the factory managers, and this year the three best teams in the doubles were amateurs. The defending champions, the ancient pair of Mulloy and Patty, were beaten in the best match of all in the quarter-finals by Krishnan and Kumar of India. The Indians, well-made but too short for a power service, had wrists like cobras and imaginations that sparkled. They gave all they had, they changed the pattern of their game at least half a dozen times in beating Mulloy and Patty, who were astute themselves, and they won in the fifth set. They were tired the next day, and the Swedish pair of Davidson and Schmidt beat them after another brilliant match to enter the finals against the finalists of the men's singles, Fraser and Cooper.

The men's doubles final was not as interesting as the previous two rounds, but for anyone who loves the game of tennis it was immensely satisfying. The two Swedes have tremendous services and massive overheads, but their ground game is weak and often they make errors the machines never commit. In singles neither of them would have a hope against Cooper and Fraser. But in doubles they proved that two amateurs, if inspired and in good condition, can upset the best-laid plans of the planners. Within ten minutes it occurred to the Swedes – you could see it on Davidson's face when he went over to speak to Schmidt – that although their opponents were perfect they were absolutely mindless. Everything the Australians did was flawless; it was also predictable. Serve, cross-court volley, down-the-centre volley, smash – the same strokes, the same positioning, the assumption that errorless power is all you need. But by the middle of the first set it became apparent that something was happening to them, that although they appeared to have the initiative they really lacked it, because the Swedes were thinking faster than ever. Davidson often flubbed a backhand and Schmidt's backhand, by championship standards, was hardly a stroke at all. Yet the Swedes were winning. They were winning because they were in places where they should not be even though they often played strokes which would warrant a man's expulsion from an Australian or Californian tennis factory. The Australians continued to play with mechanical perfection, disliking the game as most of them appear to do, and the Swedes became steadily more inventive. They took the first set easily, the second more easily still, and in the third Davidson, who is also an expert soccer player, was so relaxed he often trapped a loose ball with his toes, juggled it, and with careless exuberance back-heeled it across the net to Cooper or Fraser when the Australians needed another ball for the service. In the third set they handled the Australians as a pair of matadors handles a pair of bulls, and when it was over the crowd went home happy.

So did I, for as long as Wimbledon can produce tennis like this, as long as two amateurs can still win an event in the greatest of the tournaments, the game has a small chance of survival. But best of all, as usual, was the atmosphere of the place. The old lady and I sitting side by side for successive afternoons became fast friends, even though we knew we would never see each other again after the tournament was over. "I've enjoyed my Wimbledon very much this year," she said, and never did I feel I had been paid a nicer compliment.

But we did see each other again, if only for a few more hours. Going back to town in the Underground, it suddenly occurred to me to ask what she was doing that night. She twinkled and said "nothing," and when I asked her to dinner she twinkled again and said "yes." While she tidied up in her club I strolled down to the public house at the end of the street and relaxed at the bar with a pint and an old copy of the *News of the World*. At the appointed time I sallied back to the club, and together the elderly lady and I set out for Soho. In Greek Street we found a French restaurant and for the first night in weeks in a restaurant I actually tasted the food I ate. We drank a bottle of Beaune, and after the coffee she even consented to a glass of Rémy-Martin.

"This has been *very* nice," she decided as the taxi took us back to her club. "I thought it was charming of you to take me to that place. French cooking can be quite refreshing – for a change."

"It's the U.S. or Us"

One of MacLennan's greatest strengths was his willingness to tackle major issues. In Two Solitudes *he dealt boldly with English-French relations in Canada. In* The Precipice *he touched on national differences between Americans and Canadians, a theme to which he would return in telling Timothy Wellfleet's story in* Voices in Time.

But in this 1960 essay on the Americanization of Canada he was at his most direct:

The Americanization of Canada – by which I mean the swamping of our national purpose by that of the United States and of our habits by a state of mind totally American – has been such a subconscious process on our part, and such an unmalicious one on theirs, that no reasonable man could call it a conquest. It has been more like a seduction in which the lady keeps murmuring that she can't help herself. . . .

For surely anyone can see that from the standpoint of an American corporation man with holdings here, the setup is perfect. His Canadian branch is scrupulously careful to recruit Canadian labour to serve it. His handful of Canadian executives are well enough paid to swallow their chagrin whenever they realize that the company's policy will never be influenced by them except on the most minor of local levels. Nor have many of these executives had much choice in serving their American bosses. Often they had given years to a Canadian firm only to discover, in *their* middle age, that it had been swallowed by an American one. And in no respect are these postwar American business chiefs subtler than in their trigger-fast repudiation of any suggestion that Canada has become either a commercial colony or a political satellite.

But as foreigners see it, that is just what we are: a colony of a sort unknown to the history of Europe or Asia. No military might breathes on us from south of the border. None would, for the Americans are not that kind of people. None is needed, for the arrangement here, as my Washington acquaintance said, is one that could not make a modern power happier. What is happening to Canada is merely this: she is becoming, at least on the popular level, *a mental and spiritual colony of the United States*; a conditioned-reflex colony of that cluster of ideas, values, habits, and thought-patterns called by Mr. Harry Luce The American Way of Life.

What wonder, then, that the shrewd American with business here should not be delighted to see us make our own laws, administer our own courts, honour our queen, and elect our parliament and provincial legislatures? What wonder that he should cheer every time we declare our political independence, especially when, having done so, we usually vote in the UN precisely as Washington wants us to? Americans want us to retain our self-respect not only because they like us, but because they are shrewd.

"Give me the making of the songs of a nation, and I care not who makes its laws," said Andrew Fletcher of Saltoun some 250 years ago. Today that sprightly phrase might well be rewritten by an American organization man: "Give me the writing of a nation's advertising and propaganda, and I care not who governs its politics."

Yes, the setup is perfect. If American-made economic policies prosper here, nobody could be more pleased than the American boss if the Ottawa government takes credit for them. If they go sour, he knows that Canadians won't blame *him*. How can they, when they don't even know who he is? Instead, they will turn out the government in power in Ottawa and elect another, which will be in exactly the same position as regards the national destiny. It would take political leadership of a truly heroic and brilliant sort to combat the propaganda theme that has been pounded into us ever since the war. To think other than Americans do in economics and social values – why, if a man does that he is an egghead, or perhaps – "I wouldn't like to say this aloud but I've heard rumours" – perhaps he's even a Commie!

"I care not who makes a nation's laws . . ." Why indeed should any American care who makes ours when he sees the newsstand in his Canadian hotel, or visits our homes and looks at our choice of television programs? Most astonishing of all must appear to Americans the phenomenon of the "Canadian Editions" of some of their own most strident national journals. These emissaries of The Way of Life set themselves up here as *native* publications, and week after week they import into this country, absolutely free, an editorial content as one hundred per cent American as *Pravda*'s is one hundred per cent Russian.

Soon, unless this invasion of broadcast and printed words is checked, the sole authentic Canadian voice left will be the CBC's. That must be why the Canadian government has appointed a royal commission to examine this entire problem.

For our newspapers, except perhaps in the large cities, are to a great extent influenced by the American wire services to which they subscribe, and by the American syndicated columns they publish day after day.

Noting all these things, a Frenchman said to me in Europe a few years ago: "Canada disappoints me more than any other country I know. It could have been a marvellous land if it were not next door to the United States. Now, in many ways the United States *is* a marvellous land. But Canada is not. She is becoming a spiritual slum of the United States – a slum because you import the worst American examples and few of their best. You seem willing to take anything they give you." . . .

How has Canada come to this – if indeed she has?

I would say for the same reason the bulk of the Americans came to the same thing. And this brings me to a significant aspect of the psychological state today known vaguely as anti-Americanism.

This has nothing to do, I would say, with dislike of Americans as people or with hostility to the United States as a nation. Certainly it has nothing to do with the truly grand American tradition of Washington, Jefferson, the austere New Englanders of earlier times, the gentry of Virginia, or the homesteaders of the west. Indeed, the first anti-Americans – in this peculiarly modern sense of the word – were not foreigners. They were American patriots who were appalled by what they saw happening around them. They were men like Thoreau and Emerson in the last century; like Mencken, Sinclair Lewis, and the editors of *The New Yorker* in the present one. They were the ones who deplored that the culture of freedom should degenerate into a mass culture of mass appetites, later to be glorified into a conforming patriotism of a kind that Jefferson would have laughed to scorn and Washington would have rejected with an aristocratic shrug.

Of all the American diagnosticians of this phenomenon, the subtlest and most intelligent I have encountered was a man who died at seventy-two years of age some fifteen years ago. He was Albert Jay Nock, the author of a book little read but long remembered by those who did read it, *Memoirs of a Superfluous Man.*

It was Nock's thesis that a civilized person could not help being anti-American in this latter-day sense of the word because American mass-made tastes and habits were anti-him. At the end of a long life, Nock was able to say that for most of it he had been superfluous to American society. He was a man of deep culture, erudition, wisdom, and insight. He was of old American stock. But the philosophy he saw swamping his country desired nothing he had to offer it. It had subordinated every aspect of the national life to what Nock called economism: in other words, to the theory that man's chief end is merely to produce, distribute, consume, break records, and grow rich. Because of this philosophy he had seen most American universities degenerate into trade schools, American literature turn increasingly to sensationalism, American sexual attitudes become steadily more infantile, American business become more and more confined by the weight of its own colossal success. Nock foresaw the day when "the sheer unloveliness of the life produced by economism" would turn millions of people away from the United States merely in order to save their souls. Merely because – to quote Victor Hugo on Napoleon – a time must surely come when God would be bored with it all.

For years Albert Nock was curious to understand how this subordination of the nation's genius to materialism had come about. All the Americans he knew seemed to deplore it. When Sinclair Lewis created the character of Babbitt – that pathetic, amiable, self-cheating, perennial adolescent, who measured everything by money, automobiles, plumbing, and physical comfort – millions of Americans cheered. A generation later, Arthur Miller's play on much the same theme, *Death of a Salesman*, was acclaimed as a great American work of art. Why, despite such self-knowledge, did the process go unarrested?

Nock discovered the answer, finally, from the Wall Street financier Edward Epstean. Shaking his finger one day at Nock, Epstean said: "Can't you see it's a law of life? The average organism *always* satisfies its desires with the minimum of effort. Its most basic desire is animal comfort, *and in America we have made the average man our ideal.*"

So impressed was Nock by this insight that he thought it should be made a companion piece to Gresham's law, the one that says bad money drives good money out of the market. He called it Epstean's Law, and it explained the whole picture to him. Since the unthinking man can be manipulated, why not make him the apparent ideal of a democratic society? Why not flatter him, since then you will make him your consumer and his conspicuous and wasteful consumption will make you rich?

For my part I would modify Epstean's Law: The average organism, *if unchecked by education, religion, or a high ideal*, will behave just as Epstean said; nor need he be poor or belong to a lower social class to do so. Apply Epstean to history and he fits like a glove. Every decadent society has declined because it failed to resist the impulse to follow the course of least resistance. The bread and games of the Romans, the slave states, the French aristocrat who said *Après nous le déluge*, the British imperialists who bribed the pashas – the list is as long as history. On the other hand, every society that has grown vigorously has abjured the course of least resistance, including the United States in the days when Americans said "Root, hog, or die."

If so many foreigners today resent the United States, it is because she has become the great tempter, the more so since so many million Americans seem quite satisfied with their own surrender to Epstean's Law. Where is the Old American literature of revolt? Where is a statesman with the fierce integrity of Theodore Roosevelt or Woodrow Wilson? Adlai Stevenson, certainly. But look what the voters did to him! Who would not fear being captured by a culture whose citizens are so kindly, so sensitive and easily hurt, yet so apparently helpless in the grip of their own opinion industries? Who would not tremble, living beside such a nation, at the evidence that its present economic boom depends to a substantial extent on thoughtlessness? How can anyone deny that much American prosperity has been purchased at the price of an impoverishment of mind and soul? For the more thoughtless a person is, the more open he is to the suggestion of the advertiser that he constantly increase his physical needs, even though this may mean the mortgaging of his spiritual future. Whether the American economic system could endure with less huckstering may be a moot question, but the evidence suggests that few Americans believe it could. Therefore, huckstering is bound to increase, to become more shameless in its conditioning of our reflexes, to become still more successful in silencing any other effective voices but its own.

That is why anti-Americanism is bound to spread until the United States may find herself isolated. I wish Americans could realize this: ANTI-AMERICANISM TODAY IS SIMPLY ANTI-HUCKSTERISM. It is the last, and possibly a futile, expression of a desire to save one's soul from this fatal American harnessing of Epstean's Law to the economic system.

We Canadians, when Epstean's Law moved in on us after the war in a big way, fell as hard as Adam.

Why do we take so many of our opinions ready-made from the States? Simply because the American opinion industries were highly developed at a time when we had virtually none of our own. It was easier for our salesmen to accept American hand-me-downs than to develop techniques more in the character of the Canadian people.

Why do we accept so much of their sleaziest entertainment? Because they offer it at cut rates and if we accept it we are saved the effort of developing our own.

Why did we sell out our national resources in such a hurry? Because it was easier to get rich that way than to undergo the slower process of developing these resources, at least in part, by ourselves.

Well, we got pretty rich pretty fast, but does wealth assure us that we are going to have much hope of fulfilling our destiny as a nation, which we certainly cannot do so long as we believe that our prosperity depends on our becoming cheap copies of our neighbours?

Perhaps it would help if we asked ourselves what our national destiny might be, and then ask whether it is worth paying a price to achieve it.

During the past fifteen years there has been much soul-searching in Canada, and that is the other side of the picture to the gigantic sellout. We are beginning to discover a genuine national identity, and the image of no mean nation has begun to emerge. Here, under fearful difficulties of climate and history, our ancestors produced a stable nation out of elements that once had been enemies. With scant help from the British, and none from France, Canadians of the English-speaking provinces and Quebec developed a system of higher education that owed little, at least until recently, to American examples. We developed a federal political system at once more tolerant and subtler than the one that came out of the American Constitution, and if we do not recognize this ourselves, the new nations of Asia do. By refusing to subscribe to the American theory of the melting-pot, we permitted millions of new Canadians to retain a sense of their European pasts. Finally, we are a northern people with a poetry in us of an austere kind, with an art and a literature that already reflect a national character subtly different from the American and beginning to be recognized abroad. At present rates of increase, Canada will have forty million people at the end of the twentieth century. Who knows how valuable that nation may become to mankind?

Is this future to be thrown away simply because it is easier to sink into a colonial status and allow the Americans, with the best will in the world, to turn us into copies of themselves? Unless we break ourselves of the drug habit, this is what will happen.

The best and most immediate area to make a start of breaking the drug habit is in international politics. Most of our men on both sides of politics in Ottawa agree that under the eight-year Eisenhower trance the Western cause sank into contempt and almost into impotence. Whether the new president will be any better we cannot know: at the time of writing nothing has been said by either candidate that has not been aimed at vote-catching and, in the current American atmosphere, the simplest way of doing that (Epstean's Law again) has been to shout about how tough the candidate will be on communism.

Most informed Canadians believe this is childish. Russia must be lived with or none of us will live at all. Russia and China are already becoming hostile to each other, and mature leadership from the West could quickly exploit the rift. We are sick of the pretence, so useful to the Republicans in the 1952 election, that Chiang Kai-shek is democracy's great hope in the Far East. We consider the continuance of a defence policy based on nuclear terror so dangerous that only a lunatic could rely on it. We would like to see an end of testing weapons that can be used only if the user intends to commit suicide. We listen with horror to Pentagon voices soothingly telling the people that nuclear war need not be as dangerous as every honest scientist has told us it is.

Since our leaders believe this, why don't they say so aloud? The chief reason, I suspect, is a well-grounded fear of American anger. Naturally they must retain American friendship. But how true is the friend who believes his neighbour is endangering his own and everyone else's life, yet keeps quiet lest he hurt his feelings?

On a subtler level than politics, this country as a whole must foster and protect her own national voices, and give them a chance to survive against the huge brass band of American salesmanship that we import duty-free into the country. Many things have been done to encourage them, of which the Canada Council is perhaps the most original example. But there are far too many Epstean's Lawyers working for their own small profit against the country. Every time I see some false sneer at the CBC in the press, some reiteration of how bureaucratic it is and how much it costs the taxpayer, I want to ask: "What special interests do *you* represent?"

For, in the long run, nothing will save Canada's future but resistance to the army of conditioned-reflex salesmen who have followed the American economic investment into the country. It is not the investment that does the damage, it is these mental carpetbaggers. Therefore, all native activities that foster a resistance to Madison Avenue – art, literature, education, magazines, radio, television, motion pictures – these should deliberately, wherever possible, divorce themselves from American mass-models no matter how loud the advertisers scream.

Only let us not forget: it will cost quite a lot, and not all the cost will be monetary. Some of it will be psychological. For we genuinely like our neighbours and wince when we read the lies and abuse directed against them by Communists and people like the African nationalist who is supposed to have blamed the State Department for the tsetse fly. Americans are so easily hurt that if we repudiate even a fraction of their culture – even when it invades us – they will assume we dislike them and are jealous, and some will say we are biters of the hand that guards us. To express dislike of Americanism has become a kind of treason in the United States since the McCarthy era. Ever since then their television and public prints have been giving us this same idea, with the result that, like their own best men, we too hardly dare say aloud what we really think of the United States or of Madison Avenue.

From "The Scottish Touch; Cape Breton"

Many of MacLennan's best stories concerned the people of Cape Breton. In the course of a 1964 essay for Holiday *magazine entitled "The Scottish Touch: Cape Breton," the following section appears. It is one of the rare occasions when MacLennan's ribald sense of humour surfaced in print.*

Ironically, MacLennan was attacked in Canada for having too much sex in his novels. The chairman of Classics at McGill wrote of Two Solitudes: *"What must trouble many readers, both of this book and of* Barometer Rising, *is the generally quite unnecessary intrusion of sex." That criticism found its way into an editorial in the Montreal Gazette.*

My father never touched liquor; he admitted frankly that he was afraid of it, and I suppose this was another way of saying that he was afraid of himself. Most Celts have this secret fear, and no wonder. The clan system in the old country had so stupefied the race with loyalty that even after their chiefs had sold them out, most of the people pretended it wasn't so. Yet the clans had given all of them pride, and many of them the manners of gentry. Pride and manners were the only valuable chattels they took with them across the ocean in the starvation ships. One of the most courtly men I ever knew was born in a two-room hut on a Cape Breton upland farm. The man, who was supposed to be the strongest human being of the nineteenth century, a Cape Breton giant called Angus McAskill (just under eight feet tall, broad in proportion, and weighing four hundred and twenty-five pounds), when challenged to fight by an American pugilist, bowed and said in a soft, courteous voice: "But first we must shake hands, howeffer." When the fool put out his hand, the giant squeezed it so hard he broke every bone in it.

The clan names caused a social problem in Cape Breton when I was young, and to a lesser extent they still do. There were so many MacDonalds, MacNeils, MacLeans, MacKenzies, MacGillivrays, MacLeods, Grants, Camerons, and Chisholms, and so many of the boys were called Alec, Angus, Hector, Rory, Donald, Norman, and John, that neighbours had a hard time identifying each other in conversation. People did as they do in Wales: they resorted to nicknames, and often the nicknames descended through the families to the third or fourth generation.

A miner went on Saturday to draw his pay, and because his wife had forestalled him by buying groceries at the company store, all Sandy received was three cents: from that day, he and his family were known as the Big Pays. A boy in school could not understand what his teacher meant by the word "quadruped," which had cropped up in a spelling-book. In desperation his teacher asked him: "What has a cow got four of that I have two of?" The boy's answer explained why a village labourer, sixty years afterward, went through life by the name of Neilly Tits. There were Wild Anguses, Red Rories, and Black Normans all over the place; there were even a few unfortunate girls known as Big Annie. . . .

CHAPTER · 10

The Return of the Sphinx

The Return of the Sphinx marks the return of Alan Ainslie, the young MacNeil boy adopted by the Ainslies in Each Man's Son, *now risen to the Cabinet in Ottawa. It was published in 1967, the celebratory year of Canada's Centennial, and the novel's predictions of revolutionary violence in Quebec were not warmly received.*

The novel's Oedipal theme concerns Ainslie, his dead wife Constance, his separatist son Daniel, and his daughter Chantal. In this scene his oldest friend, Gabriel Fleury, is alarmed to find that Chantal and he are attracted to one another, and thinks of her father:

In 1943 the age-gap between them had been much more marked than it was now, when it hardly seemed to exist. In 1943 Gabriel was barely out of his youth; not so much timid (this at last he understood, though he had not understood it then) as empathetic and therefore diffident with others and more terrified by the war than most of them were. Ainslie was then in his thirties; he was already a veteran of some twenty-five missions and to young Gabriel he had seemed a confident, almost a senior, commander. The rest of the crew were boys, but ten years of disciplined work in External Affairs had printed on Alan Ainslie's face the signs of proved authority which other men recognize instinctively. Gabriel knew nothing of Canadians then and had thought of them vaguely as a rougher version of Americans. Alan's manners had taken him aback for, without him even being aware of it, they had verged on courtliness. Gabriel had been posted to this crew because all the aviators except Alan were French Canadians and the previous navigator was in hospital with a ruptured appendix. The moment Alan saw the *France* shoulder-flash he addressed Gabriel in excellent French with an accent Gabriel could not place, and when Gabriel answered him in his public-school English he switched back into English immediately. "One's apt to be nervous the first time out. Speaking for myself I was scared to death. But tonight is nothing but a milk run. I think you're going to enjoy it."

Gabriel almost did enjoy it; it was the only operation he didn't actually hate. In the half-light of dawn flying home over the North Sea with little Joe Lacombe telling bawdy stories over the intercom, Joe sitting behind his tail guns all alone back there chattering in what seemed to Gabriel at the time the most barbarous French he had ever heard, a French so barbarous he told himself it was impossible for French ever to be turned into this – and then he remembered that in Brittany Joe Lacombe would have no trouble at all – Gabriel Fleury at that moment felt himself immortal and would have embraced the gay little French Canadian if he had been able to reach him. It had been an easy operation so far as enemy action was concerned, but there had been heavy cross-winds and he had been the one responsible for getting them over their target on time, and the others in the crew went out of their way to be complimentary. "It looks like we got ourselves a navigator, boys," said Lacombe from the tail of the aircraft. "It looks like we got ourselves a navigator that can navigate us right up Hitler's arse." And Alan Ainslie, gloved hands gripping the controls, had winked at Gabriel who had come up with another course-direction and said into the mouthpiece, "If that's what he's going to do to us, let's throw him overboard right away."

The next afternoon Alan invited Gabriel into his quarters and after they had talked awhile, he showed him photographs of his family. One was of a tiny male baby only a few months old whom Alan said he had never seen; the other was of an enchanting girl-child who looked to be about six. Now the being that child had become was in his arms and it was hard to believe it.

"Your father was marvellous in the war," he said to her. "When I first saw him I thought he was a natural officer, but he wasn't that at all once I knew him better. He didn't have the instinct for it. That's why he was never even made a wing commander in spite of his record."

"You and Dad always come back to the war, don't you? Often I think you're sorry it ended."

"At least we believed in heaven then. We called it peace."

"Where have all the husbands gone?" She crooned the song to him. "Long time passing. Where have all the husbands gone? Long time ago. Where have all the husbands gone? They're gone soldiers, every one. Oh, when will they ever learn? Oh, when will they ever learn?"

With an effort of will he disengaged himself from her and again went to the open door. Behind him he heard her crooning another verse of her song and he did not know whether he felt frightened, horrified or merely ridiculous. When he turned to her and their eyes met, her face was wide open to him.

"Gabriel dear, please don't turn me away tonight. If you do, I won't go home to that empty place, you know. If I must leave you, I think I'll go down to one of the railway stations where there are lights and people."

Is this emotional blackmail? he wondered. Or am I simply out of tune with what's happened in the world? He glanced at his watch and saw it was nearly midnight, but in this city no European bells tolled the hour out of the past's continuum. Instead he heard the wail of a police-car siren.

"Chantal, I'm too old for you and that's final. For heaven's sake, why can't you like men your own age?"

She looked at him helplessly, but his back was still toward her. "Because all the ones I've ever met are children."

He turned and she was still crouched on the floor and her eyes were looking at him as though saying she knew that his words were no more than the routine gestures of a gentleman.

"Why?" he demanded. "Why can't you? You and me – it's not right. You know it isn't."

She gave a little shrug. "I had hopes a little while ago. He's a nice enough boy. Good-looking and sensitive and full of all the things he wants to do and knows he can't. But what can a girl do with a man who's likely to break down and weep after he's made love to her? He's the son of that Tarnley man you said you met this afternoon."

Gabriel felt a flick of pain and anger and was humiliated to realize that he was jealous.

"Poor Guy," she was saying, "he's like so many of them. He hasn't a chance. His father had it all laid out for him on the line. They all had it all laid out for him on the line. None of them ever gave him a chance."

"None of whom ever gave him a chance?"

"They. Just 'they.'"

His legs felt as if they were made of uranium.

"Chantal, I'm tired out. Stay if you want to, but I've got to go to bed. There's a bed made up in the spare room and you'll find pyjamas in the drawer of the dresser there. They'll be too big for you, but at least they're pyjamas. You'll even find a toothbrush in the room next to it."

"All right, Gabriel dear."

Fifteen minutes later she presented herself to him to say good-night, tiny in pyjamas so big for her that she had to hold them up to keep from tripping.

"These smell of lavender," she said. "Did you know they do?"

"You'd better go back and turn off the light and go to sleep."

But for him, half an hour later, sleep was a continent away and his eyes were open in the dark and his nerves were so tight that his whole body felt encased in a strait-jacket. That uncontrollable memory of his – that awful memory of his. Now he was walking up Guy Street beside Constance and the thing was coming at them down the slope of Côte des Neiges and people were staring or running. It was a double-zero coming down the hill with broken brakes – actually a truck with a trailer. Traffic was crossing normally from east to west and from west to east and this thing smashed through the double lines and automobiles burst up and to right and left as it came through them, the truck now detached from its trailer, an automobile impaled on its radiator. It was the trailer that did the important work. It went wild – no control but its own momentum, it began to lurch and it went over on the two wheels of the left side and came straight at them, snaking and falling over as it came. There was no place to go because they were up against the wall of a building and when it reached them it went all the way over and came down. He tried to shield Constance but something knocked him over and the thing smashed down flat on the sidewalk a few inches from his face while he lay on his side with his back pressed by reflex against the wall. Lying there he saw the engine part of the apparatus running wild down the hill, smashing into one car after another, and he crawled to his feet with blood all over him which he realized was not his own. He saw Constance's body without a head. What had been her head was under the trailer and was still joined to her shoulders. She had not been decapitated; her head had merely been squashed flat. Five minutes earlier the two of them had met by chance on the corner below and she had suggested that he join her for coffee in the little restaurant here. Two more steps and they would have been inside its door.

It took police and workmen more than two hours to hoist the truck upright and get what was left of Constance's head clear of its oppressor. Gabriel had stayed there. The trailer with its load was too heavy to move and it took more than an hour for the workmen and police to empty it. The load consisted of tons of processed cheese in cartons, and his mind was sufficiently detached to observe that this processed cheese had been scientifically and internationally processed to look cheesier than real cheese. Several dozen cartons had broken open and their contents were spread on the pavement glistening in the sun with whatever it is that holds processed cheese together and makes it glisten.

It was only after the ambulance carried her off that Gabriel left the scene to tell Alan about it. Alan was in his office a quarter of a mile away winding up the affairs of his magazine. He guessed what had happened the moment he saw Gabriel's face and bloodstained clothes, and his face went green before it clamped shut in the expression Gabriel had seen on it that night over the German city when Alan sat in the flames, holding the plane up while the rest of them bailed out.

People still talked about the senselessness of that accident; Gabriel did himself. But what was so senseless about it, after all? Mathematical odds were surely available to cover that sort of thing. Before each weekend the press published the mathematical prognosis for fatalities on the road and they were always right to within a few decimal points. If not me, why not you? It was all entered into the book of human statistics now. Whenever he saw a jetliner hovering in over the city he eyed it speculatively and wondered if this was the one that was going to crash.

He was trying to get the sight of Constance's death out of his mind when the wind began to blow; it blew with pressure from the south and the venetian blind began rattling and he got out of bed and adjusted it. Too restless to sleep he put on his slippers and walked on tiptoe into the living-room and again he went out the French doors into the garden. The warm, moist air smelled of tropical waters, the garden quivered nervously and the stars seemed a little clearer than they had been before. After a while he went back inside and was groping toward his room when a flicker of whiteness appeared before him.

"I really tried to sleep," Chantal said.

"I know. I couldn't, either."

The white shadow was still there.

"Gabriel dear, I'm not thinking of forever. You know that, don't you?"

He was speechless.

"You and Dad and so many of you felt you had to think of forever, and it's been so hard and tragic for you all."

"I know."

She was white and silent.

"When did you first want this with me?" he asked her.

"Years ago, I suppose, though I didn't really know it then."

Afterwards he honestly did not believe he could have helped himself. She was so blindingly young to him and he also had loved her for years, and probably in this way without daring to admit it. A silvery light filtered through the half-open venetian blind and the warm air continued to flood the city. Then in his mind he saw the waves of a Laurentian lake running through the dark like ranks of white cavalry horses while the spruces and pines bent and the whole empty north gave tongue. Then again he was a boy on a ground sheet in an almond grove near Aix wakened by the mistral and for a half-awake, half-asleep second he was mistaking hummocks of earth for the slumbering forms of the Roman legionaries who had camped there the night before Gaius Marius so handled the matter with the Teuton horde that not even a messenger survived to take the news home to the yellow-haired women who had stayed behind in the German forests. "What is love?" said jesting Pilate and would not stay for an answer. With these words garbled in his mind, Gabriel Fleury lay with the new-found, new-lost girl in his arms and was afraid to think what he had done. "I have never yet found a hiding-place for my heart," he thought. "I will never dare to." But she was peaceful there; he could feel from her breathing that she was happy there, at ease there, and that for her this had been good. She had been so shy until the passion had seized her but then she had lost herself and now she was just beginning to come back to herself again. She stirred against him and sighed and this time he sought to lose himself in her and he did lose himself more than he ever had with any woman in his life but the traitor thoughts went on, "She's very experienced at this," and he hated himself for the idea and, "Why not?" he asked himself, "Indeed why not?" and again he thought, "I have just said no to death," and this was answered by, "How pompous can you be?" and finally he prayed to a God in whom he did not believe to give him some kind of sureness that he had done her no harm and he was still trying to pray when he fell asleep.

Much of the novel is set in Ottawa, where the memorable figure of Moses Bulstrode, suggested by John Diefenbaker, dominates the city:

Alan Ainslie left the concentration of offices sardonically known in the capital as The Department Store ever since the Prime Minister had permitted Moses Bulstrode to become – there was only one word for it and that word was used at least a hundred times a day in the capital – the "bottleneck" through which the plans and decisions of a variety of departments had to pour. The Old Gentleman had been an admirer of C. D. Howe, had considered him the greatest co-ordinator of departmental work in the country's history, and it was with Howe's example in mind that he had placed Bulstrode where he now was. But Bulstrode – as was also repeated a hundred times daily in the capital – was no C. D. Howe. After spending nearly two hours with him, Ainslie felt as though his normal conditioned-reflexes had broken down.

A quarter to five on the hottest Saturday afternoon in seven years and the city looked empty. But not quite. A young man in an Ascot topper, a morning coat with a gardenia in the button-hole and grey gloves in his left hand was bowing to Ainslie from the centre of one of the parliamentary lawns.

"Good afternoon, Mr. Minister. I've just come from a wedding. Where did you come from? The bride, Mr. Minister, had been the great and good friend of all eight ushers, including me, and my heart is broken, Mr. Minister."

This country is getting very queer, Ainslie thought as he walked past. Very queer, and everything I learned in my life seems to disqualify me from being effective in it. His old civil-service friends blamed all of his troubles on Moses Bulstrode, but this was an exaggeration. He would have been in a bad enough position without Bulstrode. Since the Prime Minister had also appointed Bulstrode as House Leader, capital gossip was blaming most of the country's troubles on him as well, and Bulstrode himself talked at times as though he were the Prime Minister in fact.

The man invited attention, though for most of his life he had obtained very little of it. To begin with, his appearance was extraordinary. He had a face and head that reminded many men of Roman emperors; he also had huge hands that could twist horseshoes and a torso that made children think of bears. This mighty body was supported by a pair of unusually short legs, so that however imperial he looked when seated behind a desk, the moment he rose and walked he appeared top-heavy and low-slung. He had a twanging voice and eyes and eyebrows that had a tendency to flicker and jump up and down and a habit of staring at people. But he also possessed, as Ainslie and others had recently found out, a strange but enormously effective animal power.

Ainslie was suddenly accosted by a bald-headed, square-jawed man who had emerged from a doorway in the East Block. His name was McCartney and he accosted Ainslie in a voice very close to a snarl.

"That was a nice effort of yours this morning. What do you think you're doing – giving your French-Canadian friends the idea the rest of us are scared to death of them?"

You hard-nosed bastard, Ainslie thought, and looked at the man without answering.

"I just asked you a question."

"Sorry, I didn't understand that you had."

The older man flushed. "All right, Ainslie – you keep on talking like that and see how long you last here. Some of us who've been here for years appreciate a little thing called loyalty. Those punks burned old Moses in effigy and you treated them like heroes."

Ainslie lifted a shoulder and walked away. This was a sour Parliament and a sour government. Conditions in the country would have produced sourness in any case, but the Prime Minister's refusal to lead, combined with the general belief that he was on the verge of retirement, had split the government into half a dozen factions, all of them scheming with an eye to the succession. Bulstrode had the fanatical support of most of the veteran back-benchers who saw hopes for themselves if he ever did succeed in becoming the leader, while the more sophisticated ministers detested him. Bulstrode increased the frustrations of everyone by reducing all issues to personalities because he was unable to think in abstractions. He seemed incapable of relaxing tension, and Ainslie, remembering the contradiction between his forehead and his mouth, thought that if he had to sustain inside of himself the conflicts this man had to live with, he would be torn in pieces inside of a week.

It was said of Bulstrode that he loved power but did not know what to do with it when he had it. Ainslie simply did not know. He did not even pretend to understand the man, and he had an idea that Bulstrode was much more intelligent than most people believed he was. He was certainly adept at changing the subject if it ever seemed likely to take him into areas where he did not wish to do anything. After Ainslie had spent half an hour explaining what it would signify in Quebec if the government made the federal civil service bilingual, Bulstrode had suddenly leaned across the desk at him and said, "You know, Alan, the first time I met you I knew we had something very deep in common. You know what I'm referring to, of course?"

Off his guard, Ainslie had said he had no idea.

"We both saw our parents killed before our eyes when we were little children."

Ainslie had gasped and turned pale, and his first reaction was to believe the man was clairvoyant. Then he remembered that Bulstrode was one of the few men in the government with access to the secret files of the RCMP. There was no malice in Bulstrode's interruption, quite the contrary.

"A thing like that," he had continued, "changes a man's view of everything. But of course in the case of my parents it was an accident. There's no question it was an accident."

A recent article in a national newspaper supplement had told the whole country about this accident. As an infant Bulstrode had been carried like a papoose on his mother's back over the Chilkoot Pass into the Klondike with his father bent double beside them under a hundredweight and a half of provisions and gear. Long after the Gold Rush petered out, his father had lingered in the Yukon searching for the mother-lode. One day an avalanche carried the family cabin down a mountainside and buried it in snow. It was four days later before a pair of wandering prospectors saw some protruding wreckage, dug themselves inside and found both of Bulstrode's parents dead and the little boy half-conscious with his legs broken. They dragged him on a sledge through mountain passes to Dawson City and there a rough-handed doctor set the legs as best he could. But though they were strong enough, they had never grown normally.

The second chapter in Bulstrode's saga was almost as strange as the first. He had only one relative in the world, a preacher-uncle who lived in an Ontario bush-town. Months after the accident, this uncle appeared in Dawson. He was a sombre man with a heavy beard – the newspaper supplement had published an old-fashioned picture of him. He took young Moses home and raised him as his own son in a house where the only literature was the Bible, religious tracts and *The Dictionary of National Biography*, and Bulstrode claimed that he had read them so often he practically knew them by heart. Tom McCartney, the man who had snarled at Ainslie, who worshipped Bulstrode, was fond of saying, "If you want to know what makes old Moses tick, it's those books he read when he was a kid. The kind of people he took for heroes were the kings and judges of Israel and men like Wellington and Gladstone. That's why when he looks around here, all he sees is pretty small potatoes."

In the bush-town Bulstrode had done more than read his uncle's modest little library; he had also taken strongman's courses by correspondence and at nineteen years old he joined a circus and competed with Sandow and Louis Cyr. He had never married and his name had never been mentioned in connection with any woman. He did not drink, but on Saturday nights he made a ritual of smoking a single large cigar. Though he lived almost like a monk, his mouth was heavy and sensual. Was this why, when he was angry, he was apt to vibrate like an over-heated boiler?

At any rate, here he was now and Ainslie had to deal with him, and after two hours with him he believed he would never learn how. He decided not to return to his office and walked toward the hotel where he was staying until he could move back into the rooms he had rented when he had first come up to the capital. The Ottawa valley was so humid in this heat wave that his brain felt as though wrapped in wool that had been dipped in hot water. He strolled into the little park behind the hotel, found an empty bench and sat gazing out across the toy-sized locks of the Rideau Canal. From this position it made him think of a combination of Westminster, Edinburgh Castle and a châ-teau of the Loire. But not even here could he get Bulstrode out of his mind.

"What gives the French Canadians this idea they've had it so tough?" Bulstrode had suddenly demanded. "It was twenty times tougher in the Yukon than it ever was in Quebec."

When Ainslie had tried to get the subject back to the point of interruption, Bulstrode had continued as though he had not spoken.

"It was the cold up there. You know, the only place in the world lower temperatures have been recorded are around the Yenisei River in Siberia. I've seen spirit thermometers frozen solid. I've seen snow turned into concrete ribs by the wind. We had wolves too. One winter they were starving and they used to howl around our cabin at night – and the nights lasted most of the twenty-four hours. Poor Father! To cheer us up he used to play us tunes on his mouth organ. He knew all kinds of tunes – hymn tunes, jigs, march music. Mother used to love them and so did I. But wolves or no wolves, Father always went out prospecting. Many a time Mother and I wondered if he'd ever come back alive. Can you imagine what it was like for a little boy to try to sleep knowing the wolves were out there waiting to eat his father?"

When he finally got back to the subject, Ainslie made his biggest effort of the day.

"I tell you, Mr. Minister, no people in history has ever tried to break with a strict Catholicism without turning to nationalism or some other kind of ism as a surrogate religion. As I see it, that is the essence of the situation in Quebec today. The problem there isn't economic, it's psychological. That's why these little things I try to remind you of are so important. What's happening in Quebec – whatever it turns out to be to a large extent is going to depend on the rest of us – is something deeper than we've ever seen before in Canada. It's a genuine revolution in a way of life, and I don't have to remind you that all revolutions have neurotic roots."

While he was saying this, Bulstrode picked up a paper from his desk and began reading it. He was still reading it half a minute after Ainslie finished. Then he took off his glasses and rubbed his eyes.

Young Daniel Ainslie, Alan's son, is gaining fame as the host of a French television show not unlike This Hour Has Seven Days. *He is, however, being manipulated by a separatist intellectual, Aimé Latendresse:*

It was a dark, low-ceilinged *boîte* murky with breathed air and cigarette smoke and throbbing like the inside of a drum. Its name was "*Le Cachot*" and it had been designed to resemble the interior of a medieval dungeon, with barred windows and heavy iron grilles and walls faked to look like thick granite blocks. There was a patch of empty floor where girls and boys twisted to the hammering racket of a juke-box and here they called it "*Le Separatwist*." There was also a small bar and a folk-singer who sat on it with a guitar in the intermissions of the juke-box and sang nationalist folk-songs of his own composition.

When the *chanteur* had finished his first round of songs, Daniel looked around at the young men and girls, the men with long hair or with short hair brushed forward like his own, crouched over the tables with beer and their girls. Why do the English have to be so much bigger than us physically? But aren't the little brown men of Viet Nam doing better in the jungles than the big Americans?

Aimé Latendresse leaned across the table toward him. "Did you hear the news about your father tonight?"

Daniel nodded glumly.

"That royal commission is nothing but pinky stamps from a chain grocery store. It's worse than a deliberate insult."

"It was Bulstrode," Daniel said. "It wasn't my father, it was Bulstrode."

Latendresse eyed him. "Your father was present. He took his seat in the House. By saying nothing, he consented. He approved."

Daniel remembered the night and morning at the lake and how beautiful it had been. Were there two Quebecs now – the old Quebec of the country and the new Quebec of Montreal and places like this?

"They're saying he's sold out to Bulstrode," Latendresse said.

Suddenly, and for the first time, Daniel dared ask himself if he really liked this man he had admired so much.

"Whatever else he does or doesn't do," he said, "my father's not on sale to anyone."

"I wasn't talking about money." Latendresse's lips moved in a thin, intellectual smile. "At any rate, it's now more important than ever for you to arrange a debate on your television show between him and me."

"I told you last week he'd never accept that."

"I don't agree with you. Evidently you don't understand how impossible his position has become now."

"Why is it so impossible?"

Latendresse smiled contemptuously. "Not even the official press of Quebec – not even *La Presse* – will accept this. Unless your father repudiates Bulstrode, even the Quebec bourgeois establishment will reject him. Bulstrode is a living impertinence to all of us." The opaque eyes narrowed. "A man like your father would not be influenced by criticism coming from the English – he'd be too proud for that. But if our side attacks him it would provoke a different behaviour. He has nothing else, nowhere else to go. So far as French Canada's concerned, he's already *parti-pris*. He'll want to justify himself to us some way or other."

"My father's not an ordinary politician," Daniel said shortly. "He's never even tried to think like one."

"Anyway, arrange a debate – no, 'discussion' would be a wiser word – between him and me. Call it a friendly discussion between the both of us on your show."

Daniel squinted through the smoke of the Gitane. "Supposing he agrees, what kind of line will you take, Aimé?"

"The important thing for us now is to obtain a forum with somebody in an official public position. That will signify that we are officially recognized."

Now what Daniel was feeling for Latendresse was hostility but, though his instinct knew it, his mind still refused to accept it.

"The technique of revolution can now be called a science," Latendresse went on in his emotionless voice. "It makes no difference what group you belong to or what your ideology is. The techniques are all similar. A political movement is like a car parked near the crest of a hill. First, the brakes must be released. Then the car must be put into neutral gear. Then she must be pushed. The first pushes are the hardest, but once the car is over the crest of the hill our task is to get it to that point."

Daniel looked away from Latendresse and around the room. The singer was seated at a table surrounded by little girls and, as Daniel felt Latendresse's cold eyes on him, he wondered if he had become suspect because he was only half-French.

"Where will it end?" he heard himself say.

"I don't understand your question."

"This car you speak about – after it is pushed over the crest of the hill, where will it go? Where will it end?"

Latendresse contemplated him without expression. Finally he said, "A number of people in Paris are with us now. De Gaulle has made a lot of difference. He knows as well as I do that the

French language is in danger everywhere. He also understands that there is room for judo in politics. If a country is as strong as America, its strength can be used to defeat itself. And of course, the chief American iron-ore reserve is here with us."

Does he think I don't know all that? Daniel thought.

He said, "I don't know what I can do. My father was in town last night looking for me. I wasn't home and I didn't find out about it till this morning when my sister told me. He wants to see me very much, she said. I was thinking of going up to Ottawa tomorrow or the day after."

"Could you make studio arrangements in Ottawa?"

"I don't know. I suppose so."

"Then I will go up with you. We could do the show there."

"No," Daniel said. "I must talk with him first. I don't know what he's thinking these days. It's months since I've seen him."

Latendresse looked away and Daniel realized that for himself as a human being this man not only had no feelings, he did not even have an ordinary consciousness of his existence.

"Do you believe," he said, avoiding the eyes of Latendresse, "that my father would be accepted into the movement if he wished to join it?"

Latendresse's smile was ironic. "That's an interesting idea, that one."

"He loves Quebec, he really does. Other people besides – besides us French can love Quebec. He was very fond of my mother's family and they were very fond of him. You must understand that, Aimé. After what Bulstrode's done to him – and Bulstrode's simply doing it on account of the rural Ontario and western voters – my father's very unselfish, you know. He's brave too. Did you know he won the DFC in the war?"

Latendresse's eyebrows lifted. "What does that mean, the DFC?"

Daniel was silent and stared ahead of his nose.

"Anyway," Latendresse said, "I'll be expecting to hear from you inside a few days. The interview between you and me is for Thursday night, isn't it?"

"I told you it was for Thursday night, didn't I?"

Latendresse nodded, left Daniel and joined a group at another table at the far end of the room near the singer. Watching him go away, Daniel thought he looked as incongruous in this setting as a priest would be.

Daniel smoked, glanced at the untouched glass of Cinzano in front of him and relaxed a little. A friend in a group at another table beckoned to him and as he went over he noticed a single man of indeterminate age sitting by himself in a corner near the door. This man had a half-empty glass of beer in front of him. With leisurely movements the man got up and strolled out the door and Daniel noticed that he had left his beer unfinished on the table.

Gabriel Fleury finds himself drawn into the dramas of the Ainslie family, dramas that are more than domestic ones:

In the cold air of the Monday morning after the storm Gabriel Fleury walked through streets thundering with pneumatic drills and dusty from excavations and building materials. These days central Montreal reminded him of London after a blitz. Old buildings going down and new ones going up and his own firm making a fortune out of it. His firm was very proud of having gone totally modern, but to him all they were doing was to standardize ideas that had been formulated by *avant-garde* architects half a century ago. A generation from now, he predicted, these styles would be hated, but it would then be too late to change what they had done to the city.

When he entered his office, the windows reaching from floor to ceiling, he felt himself in a glass cage. The chrome and glass of buildings similar to his own glittered in the sun of a new weather that made the heat and humidity of the weekend seem as remote as his memories of Indo-China. He found it hard to be interested in his work that morning and wondered if the time was not at hand when computers could do it better than himself and then, his mind roaming, he wondered whether computers and social-science surveys had replaced God in the modern superego.

He was happy but at the same time anxious and worried. He ached for Chantal; his tenderness for her filled his soul, but the fatal arithmetic of their ages – or was it so fatal after all? – troubled him profoundly. Of course she wanted children; no woman could have given herself as she had done without being deeply maternal. His conscience was troubled because what he had done ran contrary to his idea of the rightness of things. His chief objection to modern morality, including some of Chantal's, was that it was sentimental. They seemed to have forgotten that morality's only use is self-protection. In their blind way even his own exasperating family had understood that, at least apart from their attitude toward the military.

He looked out the window and saw a white ship moving slowly up the river to its dock and tried to think of his position coldly, particularly in relation to Alan Ainslie. Surely it was the priority that no matter what he did or wished to do, he should not betray his friend. But was he actually doing this? There were regions in Alan he had never penetrated. Did Alan suffer from a kind of unconscious egoism that comes more easily to the unsophisticated than to somebody like himself? If so, it was never an egoism that wished to dominate others; it was larger than that; it sought a more ambitious identity. Alan himself had said of his father, "He told me I must school myself to belong to civilization." In Alan's mind was the belief that neither he nor his country had as yet proved themselves worthy of civilization. A very odd point of view in a time when the usual question asked was, "Is society worthy of me?" But in a personal crisis with Chantal or Daniel involved, how would Alan behave? At this point Gabriel was puzzled by a curious secrecy in a man who in most other ways was recklessly frank, and then he remembered the time they were shot down over the German city. It had been a traumatic experience for both of them.

When the plane staggered, screamed and caught fire, Alan had instantly taken command and ordered the others to jump. Gabriel had lurched forward to him and been met by a slap in the face by the back of Alan's gloved hand. He was sitting there with the flames coming around him holding the plane's head up. Gabriel had gone back and jumped and the plane had lurched off in flames above him.

Swinging in his harness Gabriel came down through the semi-darkness with the tracers spitting past him and underneath the fires of the city growing rapidly larger in his eyes. He tried to manipulate the chute away from them, but the turbulence caused by the heat of the fires made it impossible to do so.

He hit the pavement in a public square beside the statue of a soldier on horseback and sprained an ankle, unharnessed himself and lay flat at the base of the statue while the earth heaved and the air roared with exploding bombs, and spent bullets and flak fragments rattled like hail. Soon it was over and he heard the planes going away and the rushing noise of the burning town. He tried to remember the map of the city he had studied before the raid, but it was an old city with crooked streets and a number of public squares and he had no idea which one of these he had fallen into. He hobbled across to the sidewalk and around the nearest corner and walked straight into the arms of a German patrol. They recognized his uniform and seized him, one soldier hit him under the eye and shouted obscenities. Gabriel answered in broken German and the *Feldwebel* in charge of the patrol shouted to shut up and then shouted, "*Marsch!*" He hobbled in the middle of the patrol back to the square and across it into a burning street where he saw for the first time what an Allied bombing raid could do. "*Neunzig Kinder getötet hier! Neunzig Kinder!*" Apparently one of the buildings they had hit had been a children's hospital. He was marched through a swarm of men and women whose eyes were staring and horrified, whose faces were smoke-blackened, but no harm was done to him and within an hour he was in a guarded truck *en route* to a prison camp.

There he found Joe Lacombe and some of the others but he did not know for two months what had happened to Alan Ainslie and only then when Ainslie himself appeared in the camp. He walked on a crutch and his face was in bandages and he had only one eye. He had fallen into another part of the city, had been shot through the left thigh and thrown into the fire of a burning building. A German patrol had hauled him out and Alan said to Gabriel, "All this about the German discipline is absolutely true. One of the soldiers who hauled me out of that fire is still in the hospital himself." More than this Alan never mentioned to anyone about what happened to him after he came down in his parachute into the German city. . . .

Gabriel got up and looked out the window and saw, far below, the crawling lines of pedestrians and automobile tops moving like objects on an assembly line. He wondered how many of the people down there had been in the war and what each one remembered of it. Then he returned to his desk, picked up the phone and telephoned to the gallery where Chantal worked and felt a loosening behind his knees when he heard her voice. She wanted to see him again that night but he forced himself to refuse.

"Have you heard from your – from Alan?" he asked her.

She told him of her phone conversation with her father and that he had come down from Ottawa on Saturday night and found his home empty.

"I told him I'd spent the night at your flat."

Gabriel controlled his breathing with difficulty. "Yes?"

"He was so relieved. He'd been worried sick about me. Now of course it's Daniel he's worried about."

"So you told him about Daniel? I think you were right."

"I didn't have to tell him. He knew – and from the worst source possible. He was told about Daniel by your old friend, Joe Lacombe."

"You mean, the RCMP are onto him already?"

"Of course he hasn't committed any crime yet. It's just that they know about him. I hope to God the newspapers don't find out, or Dad will be crucified. Daniel came home finally – yesterday morning when I was still with you, as a matter of fact. Then he drove up to the lake. It was a crazy wild-goose chase Sunday, for Dad had the same idea and got there first. Something happened to Daniel's car and he didn't arrive till late and by then Dad had left. They must have passed each other on the autoroute going in opposite directions. Daniel stayed the night at the camp and I haven't even seen him yet. I just talked to him over the phone. He promised to call Dad this evening – that's something anyway."

After a few more words Gabriel said he had to go back to work.

Essays 1968–72

"The Maritimes"

After The Return of the Sphinx *MacLennan devoted himself less to personal essays and more to sweeping retrospectives or wide-ranging studies of current affairs. An exception to this trend is this brief look at the area from which he sprang, and whose intonations his speech always retained – the Maritimes:*

During the thirty-four years I have been based in Montreal, years during which I have travelled all over Canada, I have sought, as writers do, for the exact combination of words which might express the general view other Canadians have of the Maritime Provinces. The best I can think of is "exasperated affection."

Affection, because it is hard to dislike people of whom you cannot be jealous and who live in such varied and lovely scenery. Exasperation, because the whole pattern of Maritime life makes the rich and successful ask themselves what wealth and success are really worth. With a few bad pockets of degrading poverty excepted, like the Negro quarter of Halifax and some northern counties of New Brunswick, the Maritimes are just about the happiest regions in North America, though their official standard of living is low. Nowhere else do you see so many children naturally laughing just because it feels good to be alive, or so many ruddy old people living contentedly beyond ninety. Nowhere else do you meet more people undisturbed because so much of their latent energies are not being used.

Nowhere do you find such polite taxi drivers and policemen. The Maritimes give the lie to the philosophy that the richer a man is the happier, though they have produced some men of formidable wealth like Cyrus Eaton, Sir James Dunn, Isaac Killam, Lord Beaverbrook and K. C. Irving. With the exception of Mr. Irving, of course, they all had to leave the Maritimes to succeed and no wonder. These provinces make so little economic sense that Prime Minister Trudeau, who loves them, said that if Canada were no more than an economic union, it would be the duty of a federal government to sell them.

The worst mistake anyone could make about this region is to assume that it is much of a muchness. The only two common denominators the Maritimes share are the sea and their inability to create a really large industry. Both denominators contribute to the general happiness of the people, though the latter is certainly the cause of their large emigration rate. The sea is the ancient home of all living creatures, and a mighty eroder of psychic insecurities, unless it hits you with a hurricane. Pure air contributes more to natural happiness than most people guess, and pure air and big industry have been divorced long ago. Whenever I return to Nova Scotia, which I do at least twice a year, the air is so pure it smells peculiar.

These denominators apart, the Maritimes contain within themselves a greater human variety than any other part of Canada except the two major megalopolises. No two regions of the Maritimes are ever monotonously the same for any distance. The landscapes along the St. John River vary almost from mile to mile. The seawater at Cheticamp in Cape Breton is about twenty degrees warmer in summer than the seawater in Ingonish only an hour and a half's drive away. The Gulf shore of New Brunswick is quite different from the shore along the Fundy. A Cape Bretoner not only thinks differently from a mainland Nova Scotian; he talks with a different accent. Your Lunenburger or Acadian are as different from Her Majesty's Yankees in the Annapolis Valley as a Pennsylvania Dutchman from an oldline New Englander, or a French Canadian of the lower river from a citizen of Brockville. If you intimate to an Islander that you can see no more difference between him and anyone else anywhere, you will lose a friend.

They don't even vote together in the Maritimes in federal elections. New Brunswick splits its votes regularly, the Island keeps switching from one side to the other with an uncanny ability to pick the winner each time. Nova Scotia votes solid Liberal for an entire generation, then swings about and votes solid Tory for the next. One of these days the Maritimes may coalesce into a single province, but I won't live half long enough to see it happen. For one thing, where would they put the capital? . . .

"Trudeau and Nixon"

The events of October 1970 that led to the declaration of the War Measures Act hit MacLennan hard. He saw his beloved Quebec in turmoil, and for a while even felt himself in danger. This essay, commissioned by Peter C. Newman for Maclean's, *appeared in February 1972, and speaks of those dark days. But it speaks mostly of Pierre Trudeau, whom MacLennan knew slightly and admired greatly, and of Richard Nixon, whom he regarded without enthusiasm. It draws a classicist's parallels between the American Empire and that of Ancient Rome. And, as always, it shows MacLennan's uncanny ability to predict the themes of future debates. How many other 1972 essays on politics include the words "ecology" and "nonrenewable resources"?*

In the last 18 months Canadians have learned that they can't hide from the 20th century. Remorselessly it teaches us those lethal lessons that break the hearts of small-l liberals: that good intentions do more harm than good if they ignore the nature of the human animal; that nice guys deserve to lose if they insist that their niceness deserves a fat reward; that no welfare state can fare well if it aims at nothing more than care of the physical; that nothing costs more mental sacrifice than freedom; that in a culture cut loose from its roots it is often difficult to tell the difference between a politician and a Mafia *capo*; that most of our liberal leaders can think of nothing else but to tranquilize the violence that always erupts when a culture betrays or outgrows its original content.

In such a time the usual cautions are useless. The only caution that can save is the caution of a wary fighter circling the ring against a much stronger man, knowing the gamblers have all laid their bets against him. Canada is in the ring now. Not the next 10 years, not even the next five, but the next two are likely to decide whether we shall win enough decisions to survive and create some spark of new life on this self-devastated continent or be processed into its mass as our old farmers' cheeses have been homogenized into products that look, in their cellophane, so much cheesier than any natural cheese there ever was.

In such a time the character and personality of the national leader are far more important than in seasons when the winds blow soft. He becomes a target, a focus, a catalyst, more than a mere man.

So it is impossible to detach Pierre Trudeau the man from Pierre Trudeau the prime minister, besieged by a multitude of interconnected and often contradictory forces which have grown out of past history, insane economics, the uncertain future of technology and American pressures impersonally aimed at a total economic and political take-over of our whole country. Can he serve as a focus and a force to release in us the saving energies that have been lulled to sleep ever since the Second World War?

Over against Trudeau stands another man whom history has by the throat, so it becomes impossible to see Trudeau solely within the cage and pressures of his office at home. He must also be seen within the cage and pressures that have imprisoned Richard Nixon.

When Pierre Trudeau was a private citizen, which seems only yesterday, I met him several times and flattered myself we were at least casual friends. But soon after he became prime minister, I heard people who had known him for 30 years admit with chagrin that they did not know him now. If Trudeau has become an unknown quantity to his old friends, the explanation may be a simple one. He is rare in many respects, but in none more than in this: he had to reach his late forties before discovering that the only job that really fitted him was the highest and loneliest in the land.

Though I was never an intimate friend of Trudeau's in those early days, I can at least say that thus far my estimate of the private man is still in accord with my estimate of the public one. The first time we met, I thought he had the clearest, most succinct mind I had ever encountered. When he assumed office in 1968, I was sure he would try to expose some of his ruthless clarity to the Canadian people, who had been conditioned by years of Mackenzie King to believe that haziness is the supreme mark of the mature statesman. I expected him to force certain issues so that Canadians would have to stand up and be counted for or against their leader's ideas of how this country must think and act if it is to survive.

He wasted no time in doing just that. Indeed, he set to work while he was still minister of justice. He saw very clearly that his first task was to defuse or at least isolate the paralyzing argument between Quebec and the rest of the country, because if this continued the country would fall helplessly into the waiting arms of the multi-national corporations. He saw that he must make the confrontation visible, and this he did in his show-down with Daniel Johnson at the federal-provincial conference. For a day and a half he sat mute while Johnson seemed to be running off with the show. What Johnson wanted was an impossibility, an associated state of Quebec which would be both inside and outside Canada. Then suddenly Trudeau turned and knocked Johnson cold with a single unforgettable stare and a single contemptuous question which demanded of Johnson what right *he* had to assume that a French Canadian elected to the Quebec legislature was any truer spokesman for his people than a French Canadian elected to the federal parliament? All along Trudeau had been sure that Quebec's intellectuals did not speak for Quebec's core and that Quebec's core wished to stay in Confederation. This could explain why he has been tough with intellectuals to the point of contempt.

His next move was to call the federal election for the day after Saint-Jean Baptiste and then to appear on the dignitaries' platform in Montreal during the parade. This was a direct, deliberate challenge to the separatists and they could not and did not ignore it. Several million Canadians saw him on television that night keeping his seat at the risk of his life and staring down the mob. The next day the nation not only gave him a plurality, but Quebec came close to giving him a clean sweep.

None of us had been accustomed to a leader with this athlete's combination of daring, preparation and fine calculation of the balances. But there was more than this in Trudeau and in the fall of 1970 a purely accidental meeting with him drove me to the personal conclusion that our Prime Minister is probably a genius.

My wife and I had been to a late wedding reception at the Ritz-Carlton in Montreal, and when it was over and I was hunting for a taxi I suddenly saw Trudeau with his back against the hotel wall engaged in what seemed to be hot discussion with some youths in jeans, who had apparently buttonholed him on the sidewalk. We caught sight of each other, he came over, I presented my wife to him and he spoke with her, then he went back to the kids. Something was coming out of his eyes with sudden, inexplicable force. Light shone out of them in contrast to the glaucous opacity seen in the eyes of so many politicians. But when I tell you it was a good light, let me tell you also it was a Gioconda light of such subtle and curious intensity I doubt if even the painter of Mona Lisa herself could have captured it. It had its impact on me and on those boys, who were very different from me. Some might call it charisma. I saw it as a reflection of a kind of genius.

This chance meeting occurred exactly nine days and nine hours before James Cross was kidnapped. In the month following, the nation and such of the world as was interested discovered that our Prime Minister's apparent casualness is usually a mask for highly concentrated action. In those horrible days when we all hung close to our radios, Trudeau seemed almost to be idle. Soon afterward we learned he was far from that. He was preparing to send troops into Montreal and was massing them; he was consulting legal experts and we may never know how many times he was on the phone to Premier Bourassa. Then he struck – like lightning, at three o'clock in the morning.

Well, I've gone out on the end of a long limb in this guess that Pierre Trudeau is a genius, so perhaps I should give my own idea of what I mean when I use the word. My idea of a genius is a person who can reach a destination without having traveled there, which is pretty well what Trudeau did when he reached No. 24 Sussex Drive.

Now it is the essence of genius that it is often dangerous. It changes worlds as Einstein learned to his grief. Most dangerous of all is the genius in politics, of whom the greatest example is Napoleon. The statesmen who have best served their countries have been those whose boldness was tempered by exceptional judgment, and since it is only in revolutionary times that a genius has a chance in politics it is worth noting that the greatest ones have been those who were able to convert revolution into evolution.

These have been so rare you can count them on the fingers of your hand. In ancient times the supreme examples were Moses, Solon and Augustus Caesar. In modern times, Queen Elizabeth I of England and George Washington, with the possible additions of Tito and Mao. Both Elizabeth and Washington functioned in the eyes of epic revolutions and both of them contrived workable harmonies between revolution and the old human tradition.

It is obvious that Canada, and especially Quebec, has been in the throes of a multi-sided revolution for a number of years. The winds of change blow into all quarters of our lives and confound our morals, values, politics and economics. I think that Trudeau has understood the nature of this multi-sided revolution better than any of our other public men. From the evidence of his speeches and actions before and during his public career, it is clear that he has worked relentlessly to convert revolution into evolution.

I think, though I cannot be sure, that for a long time he has known that the decisive catalyst in the Canadian revolution had to be the United States. When several years ago he declared his anxiety about the wash-over of American problems into Canada, I'm pretty sure he was thinking of something more substantial than drugs and student activists. Even two years ago he must have been preparing for what any clear-sighted man knew was sure to come – a showdown with the United States over the entire question of the independence we had been brainwashed into presuming we possessed. This surely explains his urgency in forcing Quebeckers to move from ambiguity into clear positions on the older question of Quebec separation.

Now Trudeau finds himself polarized in the posture he

defined for himself and the rest of us. Most intellectuals detest him, or profess to detest him, especially in Quebec. Small-l liberals and socialists like him no better, as they proved during and after the kidnapping crisis. Businessmen locked in traditional attitudes toward the United States and the multinational corporations fear him most of all because they sense he will not shrink from a political confrontation with our neighbour if he is driven to it. As for the press and the media, they have been frustrated by the unfathomable quality in the man, and if he has any avoidable and obvious weakness it is his evident amusement in keeping the press off balance whenever he can.

Last August, of course, our smouldering crisis with the United States at last came into the open so blatantly that not even a people trained in double vision could pretend any longer it was not a crisis. God knows they had had plenty of warning in recent years of what to expect: the way the State Department bullied the report of the O'Leary Commission on Publications out of existence; Nixon's bland proposal in 1970 of the resources-energies package deal which, if implemented, would have left us in effective control of perhaps 5 % of our energies and resources; the flamboyant passage of SS Manhattan through our Arctic waters; the alarms sounded by American scientists that their native supplies of oil, water and energy were shrinking to the danger point; the sudden swamping of our universities by a flood of American teachers and academic bureaucrats who often behaved as if they owned them and almost invariably appointed Americans to the staffs in preference to Canadians.

When Nixon finally pressed the button on August 15, many Canadians made the old pathetic plea, "Say it isn't so, Dick." They tried to pretend, though Trudeau didn't, that this was just one of those temporary things. Having been trained since the war to become great wasters themselves, they could not bring themselves to admit that an economy based upon built-in obsolescence and technological waste on the gigantic scale required by the Pentagon had somehow to be paid for, probably because they knew they would have to pay some of these bills themselves. But what they understood least of all was the profound change that came over the collective mentality of the American people during the 1960s.

The changes the Americans are passing through are different in kind from ours. They are undergoing a shocked reappraisal of themselves as the last, best hope of mankind, the universal world benefactor elected by Manifest Destiny, a people so confident of succeeding in anything they attempt that Lyndon Johnson believed he could create what he called The Great Society at home while at the same time offering unstinted American aid and troops to any region of the world that felt itself threatened by what he called Communism.

I would like to step back for a few minutes into ancient history, not because I believe that history repeats itself literally but because men and their politics change so little that history often develops similar patterns.

It so happens that a politico-military defeat astonishingly similar to the American one in Vietnam has happened before, and in an empire which still called itself a republic, an empire to which the United States has often been compared by Americans themselves. I mean Rome in the time when Augustus considered himself not as a supreme monarch but simply as the chief executive and commander-in-chief of the army.

The Rome of Augustus also believed in Manifest Destiny. Not since her infancy had Rome lost a war. The Roman people ruled, if loosely, over the countries now known as Italy, France, Belgium, the Netherlands, Spain, Portugal, Algeria, Tunisia, Egypt, Israel, Syria, the Lebanon, Greece, some of Turkey, the Adriatic coast of Yugoslavia and the islands of the Mediterranean. Their garrisons were firmly entrenched on the left bank of the Rhine and the right bank of the Danube and soon they would round out their empire by the occupation of Britain.

In 9 A.D. the Roman general Quintilius Varus crossed the Rhine with three legions, his mission to set up in the heart of Germany a Romanized state. But something went wrong with Varus' mission. Perhaps it was Roman arrogance; probably it was the territorial imperative. At any rate, in dense forests where traditional Roman tactics could not function, the German chief Arminius, a supposed ally of Rome, turned on Varus and annihilated him and his entire army. When the news reached

Augustus, that man of icy control nearly broke. He paced his floors crying, "Quintilius Varus, Quintilius Varus, give me back my legions!"

Five years later Augustus died. In a long reign he had made order out of the total revolutionary chaos he had inherited. He had created the Roman Peace. But he had been forced to make two decisions whose ultimate effects were to be of catastrophic importance.

The first, based on his experience that no empire can be successfully or economically defended by conscripted troops, was the creation of a permanent professional army and a permanent praetorian guard. Thirty-seven years after Augustus' death, the guard and the army began the practice of making and breaking emperors. The second decision was the direct result of Varus' defeat in Germany. It was to establish a policy based on the curtailment of further territorial expansion. The chief task of Augustus' successors was to stabilize and hold the frontiers along the Rhine, the Danube, the Black Sea and the Sahara.

From our present point of view, the most interesting decision was the latter. It meant that Roman energies turned inward, that Roman bureaucrats and businessmen concentrated their efforts within the Roman area of direct influence and control. This meant a deliberate effort to Romanize all those diverse, gifted, territorially based peoples of the ancient world, to make them accept Roman customs, Roman methods, Roman values. The result was not so much a Romanization as a homogenization into a weary decadence leading to the end we all know.

To return to the present. It seems that what Germany was to the Rome of Augustus, Asia has become to the America of Nixon – the final, impenetrable frontier. What else is the overall meaning of Nixon's about-face policy save a disguised admission that the American politico-economic empire has reached its limits of expansion? What can follow from this admission save a concentrated effort to establish the United States as the economic and cultural master of all her associates? Even more could be in the cards. Shortly before Nixon became President, he suggested that a time might come when America would have to develop a professional army. Should that happen, the President would of course be the Commander-in-Chief. The Roman word for that was *Imperator*. Has Nixon, then, been driven by events to emulate Augustus?

Outwardly, any comparison between the patrician Augustus and Richard Nixon belongs more to the theatre of the absurd than to history. For two decades the cartoonists and journalists of his own country have been depicting Nixon as the all-American hall-room boy, an uptight upward-mobile straight out of McGuffey and Horatio Alger, but streamlined, eager-beavering his way to the top with his mouth on a slant and what looks to be a bulge of muscle on the side of his right jaw. Yet this man is far more than a complex of caricatures. Until he finally reached the White House it was legitimate to believe that Nixon felt guilty; that his brand of small-town puritanism had made him identify failure of ambition with sin. But now, in the greatest political comeback in American history, he has arrived where those famous train whistles of his youth summoned him long ago from the little western town where he grew up. He has at last earned the right to a tragic fate. Not many men can claim that much.

In his case the tragic flaw could be his uncritical acceptance of the old American myth based on the direct road from the log cabin to the presidency. In nothing he has so far said or done has Nixon given any indication of the kind of mature political and human philosophy that animates the mind of Pierre Trudeau. It is hard to imagine that he has ever pondered the wisdom and the un-wisdom of Plato. Billy Graham would mean much more to him than the ancient Greek. It is all too possible to believe that he would never have read the abridged version of Arnold Toynbee's *Study Of History* if *Time* magazine had not run a cover story on Toynbee. As Vice-President he had things thrown at him by students in Venezuela, but he never walked through a country in revolution as Trudeau did in his younger days in China. He never paddled canoes through wilderness rivers, or scuba-dived with Cousteau, or studied the movements of fish, birds and wild animals in their native habitats. He never learned the art of gaiety with charming girls or the warmth and goodness of a variety of mature women. Nixon is no Trudeau.

Neither is he the villain his domestic enemies say that he is. His face reveals him as a lonely, puzzled man more certain of his need to be great than of his real power to become so. He holds the levers of enormous power and knows it. But which one to pull? It is not impossible to imagine him as one of those puzzled later Roman emperors, born in a remote province, who had longed for the purple and stopped at little to get it, only to discover that the Empire was hardly worth the effort; that it had become so big, so constipated in its mind, so adulterated in its moral and genetic inheritance that nobody could govern or even understand it any more. Such an emperor, and in the long Roman anguish there were many, always sought a confident adviser.

This adviser Nixon seems to have found in Secretary of the Treasury John Connally of Texas, whose countenance fits perfectly among the Roman imperial busts in the Uffizi Gallery in Florence. Having been taught to believe that the American nation is divine, Nixon will wish to be head of it as long as he can. In his acceptance speech in Miami in 1968 he said that neither Washington nor Lincoln had to face the problems the next President would have to face: and he was right. So there stands Nixon on the bridge of an eyeless juggernaut, surrounded by banks of computers, driving into a future he has not been prepared to understand, while in the juggernaut's bowels the turbines throb, fuelled by greed insatiable.

He has told us that Arnold Toynbee was an inspiration to him. Well, it was Toynbee's nightmare after the Second World War that the whole world might turn into a universal state like the Roman Empire, carrying within itself the sure seeds of decay and ruin. This cannot happen now on a world scale because the United States is balanced by Russia, Europe and China. Against Russia and China, the United States has maintained a standoff, but on neither of them has it been able to impose its will. Europe owes it a vast debt, and in recent years some of this debt has been collected. Now, the logic of events could force the United States to resign herself to the role of a Fortress Western Hemisphere, and this could become a military-economic universal state behind the securest of all possible frontiers, the Atlantic and Pacific Oceans. In such a system Canada could simply disappear.

Since it is to the interest of Canadians and Americans unborn that no such state should exist, least of all one based upon suicidal technological waste, Canada's survival as an individual nation takes on far more than a selfish importance. I am sure Trudeau recognizes this, for his patriotism has never been parochial. In the face of this challenge he will either be broken or emerge as one of the world's few great and beneficent statesmen.

His success or failure will depend to no small degree on his fellow countrymen. Will enough of us be able to understand just what is involved in this challenge? Will we have the acumen to resist the hidden pressures which already are being brought to bear? Will we yield to the mean but all too human temptation to further the whispering campaign already set in motion against both Trudeau and Canada? Will we have the guts and tenacity to take risks which only five years ago were unthinkable because they then seemed unnecessary?

We can begin by assessing coolly our position; first of all by admitting that Washington has taken Canada so thoroughly for granted that Nixon and his friends thought we were already in the bag. How otherwise explain his now famous statement that Japan was the closest trading partner of the United States? When Trudeau finally asked Nixon whether he was out to obliterate Canadian nationhood, his answer was a sincere no – inspired perhaps by the belief that we had already obliterated it ourselves. And after C. D. Howe and our vacillations of the Sixties who could blame him?

We may assume further that Washington is following what looks down there like inexorable logic. Connally himself laid it on the line. The U.S.A. must come first because it is the richest and the strongest and is tired of being everybody's whipping boy. It cannot (though this has not yet been stated publicly) remain for long the richest and the strongest without assuming essential control over Canada's energy resources and much of her water. Therefore Washington's economic pressures, which are regarded there as gentle, are intended to bring little Canada to its senses.

But there is another logic much more fundamental than any that has revealed itself to John Connally, and that is the logic of ecology and the human future.

To trade resources with a neighbor is one thing, but it is another thing entirely if the neighbor is going to use them to promote what his own best scientists have told him is a long-term suicide course. This is pretty well what the multi-national corporations and technocrats have been doing. If they continue at their present rate of consumption and waste they will exhaust most of the continent's non-renewable resources within the lifetime of children now being born.

To base our national sovereignty, worthless as a thing in itself, on a resistance to demands of this nature will give Canada a moral ground that could be formidable. To insist that cultural differences are life-giving and that cultural homogenization is life-destroying is merely to insist that we should not be expected by anyone, no matter what his power, to assent willingly to behave like history's fools.

I feel pretty sure that Pierre Trudeau understands these things much more precisely than I do. His move toward Russia was clearly intended to balance the onrush of the American technological juggernaut. It was the boldest move made by any Canadian leader since Macdonald.

Trudeau is now the target of many people, some hidden, some known; some naïve, some professional. He is resented by many of his own countrymen as bold and brilliant men have always been. He is fallible because he is human and he has already made mistakes; he is sure to make more. But I cannot believe that any other living man is more likely to release in Canadians the will to survive.

CHAPTER · 1 2

Rivers of Canada

It can be claimed that MacLennan first began to write about rivers when he produced the unforgettable opening to Two Solitudes. That passage prompted a wise editor at Maclean's to commission him to write a series on Canada's rivers. In July 1958 he travelled down the Mackenzie, and for the next two years he continued his coast-to-coast journeys, getting to know the rivers and the land that embraced them. In the summer of 1959 his visit to the Fraser River served as a honeymoon.

His second wife, Frances Aline Walker, was an old friend. "Tota," as everyone called her, had known the MacLennans as a couple in both Montreal and North Hatley. After Dorothy's death the friendship with Hugh deepened until in May 1959 they were married. It was a marriage that was to last, in sickness and in health, until his death in 1990.

"The real Hugh," Tota told Elspeth Cameron, "is found in his Seven Rivers of Canada." That book, published in 1961, was an expanded version of the magazine series. Later, in 1974, a further expansion and revision produced the heavily illustrated book Rivers of Canada. Because of its lavish format, that "coffee-table book" may not have been read as closely as it deserved. The excerpts that appear here demonstrate MacLennan's love of the land and his ability to weave geography, history, philosophy, and anecdote into an apparently pre-ordained pattern. The sections dealing with the Saskatchewan and the Fraser need no introduction. The opening section, however, comes from the early, historical part of the book. After demonstrating the importance of rivers to the early French exploration of North America *and to the fur trade that sustained the little French colony on the St. Lawrence, MacLennan deals with the Treaty of Paris in 1783. Not only did it establish the United States as a separate country; the boundaries it set cut off the Montreal-based traders – most of them Highland Scots – from all but the most distant fur country:*

... From this time until the North West Company was absorbed by the Hudson's Bay Company in 1821, the Montreal traders met one of the most remarkable challenges in the history of commerce. As they depended on the far northwest for their furs, they were now committed to an operation in which the supply lines were stretched to a limit which would make any normal, hard-headed man of commerce turn pale. The pelts had to be paid for in trade goods conveyed three-quarters of the way across the continent in birch-bark canoes. The pay loads had to be paddled and portaged back to Montreal over a distance of some three thousand miles. The market, nearly all of it in Europe, was still another three thousand miles to the east across the Atlantic Ocean.

Speed and efficiency of the highest kind, supported by an *esprit de corps* among the canoemen as intense as that of a championship hockey team, were the sole possible replies to a challenge so stern. The travel schedules set for the voyageurs seem incredible to the modern imagination.

Leaving Lachine in "brigades" of three to four canoes, with an experienced guide in the leading craft, the voyageurs from Montreal first set out for the Grand River, as the Ottawa was then called. At Ste. Anne de Bellevue they always stopped to pray in the chapel to the saint who protects travellers on water, and this rite gave rise to Thomas Moore's famous poem:

> Faintly as tolls the evening chime
> Our voices keep tune and our oars keep time,
> Soon as the woods on the shore look dim
> We'll sing at St. Ann's our parting hymn,
> Row, brothers, row! The stream runs fast,
> The rapids are near and the daylight's past ...

This poem, written in soft music by a cultivated visitor to Canada, using the word "oars" instead of "paddles," depreciates its subject. The Homer of the *Iliad* might have risen to the experience of the voyageurs, but not the sweet poet of Ireland.

After paddling and portaging the Ottawa as far as Mattawa, the canoes turned south toward Lake Nipissing, crossed it, and descended the French River into Georgian Bay. Then they paddled west along the North Channel above Manitoulin Island, working in the dead or choppy waters of the lake and often losing several days if the winds were contrary. They called the wind *la vieille* (the old woman), and if she was behind them they could raise a sail. But if she was heavy against them – and the prevailing winds in the region are contrary to west-bound canoes – they often had to put up on the shore because the high, steep waves of the inland lakes would break the backs of their canoes. When they went to Michilimackinac they were expected to reach their destination within a period of from thirty-five to forty days, and the same time was expected when they were bound for Grand Portage and Fort William. This voyage was accomplished with canoes fully loaded with trade goods, and there were thirty-six portages between Lachine and the Lakehead, some of them longer than a "league." In the voyageur's language, a "league" was roughly two miles. If express canoes without cargo were used, as they sometimes were on special occasions, the time was much faster. A letter survives dated in Montreal on May 6, 1817, which was received at Rainy Lake beyond Fort William on June 3.

What these voyages involved in hardship, labour, and moral stamina can no more be revealed by the historian's method of stating the facts than the truth of a battle can be conveyed by the communiqué issued by the high command after the fighting is over and the dead have been counted. From Julius Caesar to the P.R.s of the Pentagon, the truth of life and death has always been hidden behind facts and statistics. That is the trouble with history. It is probably an unavoidable trouble, but it certainly explains why so few people learn much from it.

"Our men moved their camp, marched twenty miles, and at night they placed their camp in a suitable place" – how many of us welcomed lines like these when we studied the *Gallic Wars* in school! They occurred so often we did not have to pause to work out the grammar. But they told us nothing of the realities.

On every step of that twenty-mile march, probably through hostile country, the legionaries had to carry their weapons and food, their armour and personal necessities, a total weight close to a hundred pounds per man. When the "suitable place" was reached, it was usually on a hill with a forest nearby. While one detachment marked out the lines of the camp, another dug a trench about it and still another went into the woods to cut trees. After the trunks had been trimmed, sawn up, and sharpened at one end, they were dragged to the suitable place and staked into the ground just behind the lip of the trench. Only after all this work was done could the soldier wrap himself in his cloak and fall asleep on the ground.

A similar recovery of reality is essential if any modern man is to understand the truth about life on the Canadian rivers in the voyaging days.

A ROUTINE VOYAGE

On May 25, 1793, a young Scot called John Macdonell set out from Lachine on his first voyage with a brigade of the North West Company. He has left a diary of that voyage written in the usual terse language of the communiqué, and he has also recorded, with the distances distinctly stated, the nature of each of the thirty-six portages between Montreal and Grand Portage – here the carrying-place was nine miles long – as well as the character of the streams and lakes. With the help of the imagination, the record is a fascinating one, the more so because this was a routine voyage.

On this stage of the journey into the west, the larger canoes carried loads varying from three to four tons and were manned by crews of eight or ten men. The middle men, using short paddles, sat two abreast while the bowman and steersman were placed higher and were equipped with paddles much longer. The Montreal canoe was thirty-five to forty feet long made entirely of the bark of yellow birch placed over ribs of thin white cedar with thwarts numbering between four and nine and boards four inches wide secured just below the gunwales as seats for the paddlemen. The bark was secured by melted pine gum, and after a heavy rapid or a day's paddling the seams had to be regummed to prevent leaking. The canoe used by Alexander Mackenzie, and specially designed for his exploration of the Rockies, was so light that it could be carried by two men. But the weight of a large canoe out of Montreal was much greater than this, and required at least four men on the portage. The whole operation of portaging brings up an interesting calculation in the mathematics of labour, sweat, and tired muscles.

Superlatives have bothered me all through the writing of this book, but I cannot avoid them without diminishing what seems to me the truth. Every new thing I have learned about the Canadian voyageur seems to me more incredible than the last. His deeds originated the Paul Bunyan myths of the American northwest, and Paul Bunyan was an inheritor of Hercules and Mercury in folklore. But the true and proved facts concerning the life of the voyageur are such that I can only say that if I, physically, am a man, he, physically, was a superman.

On portages the load that had to be moved, divided up among the crew, usually totalled more than four hundred pounds per man not counting the canoe. Every man of the crew was expected to carry at least two "pieces" of goods, each weighing ninety pounds, but so great was the emulation among them that some individuals often carried three pieces or even four. They did not walk with these loads: *they carried them at a dog trot* bent half-double with the pieces on their backs and secured there by a leather band, called a tumpline, which was passed around their foreheads. More than one traveller conveyed by voyageurs in the canoes has testified that without any load at all he could barely move as fast as these men did with two hundred pounds on their backs. Finally, because they worked at the height of the insect season, the voyageurs were encased over the carrying-places in humming, stinging envelopes of mosquitoes and blackflies.

In addition to the portaging there was the tracking of canoes against heavy currents and the running of rapids. The rapids were always risky, and crosses marked the graves of drowned voyageurs on the banks, clusters of them all the way from the Long Sault on the Ottawa to the mouth of the Winnipeg River. Tracking could be a nightmare. The men had to get out and haul by ropes attached to bow and stern (two ropes were essential to prevent the canoe from yawing in against the shore) and this meant slithering over wet rocks slimy with vegetable growth, stumbling over the usual litter of fallen trees, and sometimes wading breast high in the stream. As I know from personal experience, the silt along the banks of the Assiniboine, Saskatchewan, and Mackenzie is deep and soft, and after rain it has the consistency of porridge and sometimes the texture of axle grease. Along the Fraser when the men had to do a great deal of tracking under appalling difficulties, they wore out a pair of moccasins a day and had to make themselves new ones. While tracking canoes, the men were more plagued by insects even than when they portaged, because there were usually more of them along the water's edge. So paddling in a free river or in an open lake came as a marvellous release, and when the men swung into the stroke they broke into song. That was when time was made up. The mileage from Montreal to Georgian Bay was little more than the mileage from the mouth of French River through the Sault to the head of Lake Superior, and here the figures of John Macdonell tell their own story. It took his brigade thirty-one days to reach Lake Huron from Ste. Anne. But though they lost a day through a storm on the lake, they reached Grand Portage from French River in just under ten days! Look at the map, remember that most of the time they were travelling against the wind, and try to believe that this was merely a routine voyage!

At Grand Portage or Fort William the Montreal men ended their runs. The company's agent met the wintering partners from the northwest, and the trade goods were forwarded over the height of land by a special body of men to the company's fort on Rainy Lake, the eastern terminus of *les vrais hommes du nord* who had come down across the plains from the Athabaska country. At Grand Portage or Fort William the Montreal crews had a brief time for carousing and eating, then they reloaded their canoes with the furs and set out on the return trail to Montreal with the pay loads. If they did not get back before winter, they were frozen in and had to survive as best they could. A failure to return in time also meant a disastrous financial loss to the company.

THE TRUE NORTHMEN

At Rainy Lake the true Northmen took over, and these were the elite of the service. They paddled through Lake of the Woods and by a series of smaller lakes and interconnecting streams (the Winnipeg River was exhaustingly cursed by rapids) into Lake Winnipeg itself. In earlier times canoe parties used to paddle from there up the Red River into Minnesota toward the sources of the Mississippi, but after the American Revolution the goal was the northwestern edge of the North American map, Lake Athabaska and the Peace River country. The Saskatchewan and Athabaskan brigades paddled north up Lake Winnipeg to the mouth of the Saskatchewan River and then – after some very severe portages – they worked up against the current of the North Branch to Cumberland Lake and thence to Frog Portage, which made a bridge to the Churchill River. This powerful stream, against which they also had to paddle, led them to the Methy Portage (or Portage LaLoche), a very tough one with a sharp height of land at the end of it. The Methy took them to the Clearwater, a tributary of the Athabaska, and then they coasted down that great river of the northwest into Lake Athabaska and reached their chief northwestern base at Fort Chipewyan. In the later years of the North West Company the brigades went even beyond this. They paddled up to Fort Vermilion on the Peace, and later still the fur-traders established themselves in forts on the Fraser and the Columbia.

This final leap across two-fifths of Ontario, across Manitoba, Saskatchewan, and some or all of Alberta, all of it trending north, was a race against time even more intense than the run from Montreal to the head of Lake Superior. So close was the margin between the meeting with the Montreal canoes and the coming of frost that a delay of a few days might ruin a whole voyage. According to Alexander Mackenzie, the Athabaskan brigades generally left Rainy Lake on the first of August, and had to reach Chipewyan inside two months.

THE CANOES AND THE MEN

By the time the North West Company was established, the art of canoe-handling had so matured on the rivers that the French Canadians were much more mobile than the men of the Hudson's Bay Company. British as they were, the Bay men clung for a long time to wooden *bateaux*. The Nor'Westers used two types of canoe which they called the *canot du maître* and the *canot du nord*, the former for the run out of Montreal, the latter, which was lighter and carried less than a ton and a half of cargo, for the run west of Fort William where the streams were shallower and tracking was more frequent. The *canot du nord* often carried a crew of no more than five men.

But the *canot du maître* was a considerable craft. It had a wide beam, a remarkably high strake, and high, curved bows. It was gaily painted and travelled with a pennant blowing out from its stern and often with the picture of an Indian's head on its bows. A variety of pictures of these larger canoes survive and one of them has a feature which – at least to me – was more interesting than the canoe itself.

This was no less a personage than Sir George Simpson, the "Big Bourgeois" of the Hudson's Bay Company, the chief destroyer of the Nor'Westers, and in his old age one of the richest men in Montreal. After the Bay absorbed the North West Company they not only employed the skilled Canadian voyageurs; even before that time they had adopted the classic Canadian canoes. In this picture Simpson sits in the middle wearing a top hat of massive proportions, as did many of the bourgeois (this was the old French name for the proprietor or company partner) while *en voyage*. The top hat was a mark of their quality and station. In Simpson's canoe the paddlemen are seated as usual two abreast and the bowman and steersman are in their usual places. But directly behind Simpson, who wears a grim expression on one of the most haughty faces in Canadian history, are a pair of undersized, wild-looking characters blowing bagpipes.

The presence of these pipers in Simpson's canoe gives the Big Bourgeois an extra dimension. People who worked for him knew that he was the toughest employer there ever was in a notoriously tough trade. He pinched pennies, he was ruthless, he squeezed out of his servants the last ounce of work, he paid them as little as he possibly could. One knows that Simpson understood the value of every square foot of every canoe or York boat in the service of his company. And yet, there sits that pair of private pipers! The Scotch are a peculiar people, and never more so than when they try to out-English the English in cold calculation after they have gone into business and made a success of it. But the old wildness never quite leaves the pure Scot. Behind the granite features of George Simpson, underneath his brutal surface callousness, the primitive heat burned, and hence that pair of pipers. Without them, the *canot du maître* could have carried at least two hundred more pounds of trade goods. Yet Simpson sacrificed money for the pipers, and I like to think of him sitting there in his stove-pipe hat, the mosquitoes buzzing in his hair, the canoe swaying down a rapid through the forest wilderness, and that pair of wee pipers behind him blowing his ears off.

But there were no pipers, no luxuries, for the average *engagé* – the paid voyageur of the fur-trading companies. Day after day from dawn to dusk, sometimes for eighteen hours daily, they drove those loaded canoes back and forth across the continent. As they paddled they sang the old French songs and some others of their own making. In favouring currents they could swing the stroke easily, but in adverse currents or dead water their paddles bit hard. The average rate of stroking was forty to the minute, but often they stroked at the rate of one per second, in perfect time and with only a few stops in the course of the day. The stops were called "a pipe," and their length depended on the state of the men. Travellers carried in canoes have testified that after twelve hours' paddling, with only three rests of ten to fifteen minutes each, those incredible French Canadians refused to stop because they were still "fresh." Their sense of competition with one another was Homeric. Duncan McGillivray once witnessed a race in Lake Winnipeg between Athabaska men and a rival brigade. The men paddled all out *for forty-eight consecutive hours without once leaving their canoes!* A steersman collapsed into sleep, fell overboard, and would have been drowned had not his own canoe gone back to pick him up; he was sinking under the weight of his clothes and in a state of shock from the frigid water. In this race as the men stroked, the guides cut off hunks of pemmican and thrust them into the mouths of the paddlers.

What manner of men were these – giants? Actually, they were built more like gnomes. In 1826 an American, Thomas L. Mc-Kenney, visited the trading routes of Canada and described the voyageurs as follows:

> They are short, thick set, and active, and never tire. A Canadian, if born to be a labourer, deems himself to be very unfortunate if he should chance to grow over five feet five, or six inches – and if he shall reach five feet ten or eleven, it forever excludes him from the privilege of becoming voyageur. There is no room for the legs of such people in these canoes. But if he shall stop growing at about five feet four inches, and be gifted with a good voice, and lungs that never tire, he is considered as having been born under a most favourable star.

Freedom, T. E. Lawrence wrote, is man's second need: here is the sole explanation of those men's willingness to engage in a trade like this, which in time was sure to break them. Though there were many instances of river men keeping on working into late middle-age, the voyageurs as a rule died young. They were lucky if they were not double-ruptured and suffering from spastic backs before they were forty. But at least they were free from the forelock-tugging kind of poverty their class had to endure in Europe. They had the pride of champions which is the surest of all proofs of an inner sense of personal value. Freedom has always been the most expensive possession in the world, and the price for it has been paid in different coin from age to age. In the early days of Canada, the coin was hardship and endurance.

DAILY FARE

The food the men ate on the rivers makes the diet of a modern Canadian work camp seem like the fare of a Roman emperor of the decadence. On the eastern run to the Lakehead the voyageurs were called *mangeurs de lard*, or pork-eaters, and the French word gives us a good idea of the quality of the pork. In the west pemmican was the staple diet, and no more nourishing one was ever invented, but even with wild rice added, boiled pemmican at the end of sixteen hours of labour is not much to look forward to. If the schedule was not too exacting, the men fished and hunted and searched for birds' eggs, but if food ran out they would eat anything. Often they literally ate crow. The poor French voyageur, especially in the early days, usually had nothing better to eat than a kind of hominy made of split dried peas or corn impregnated with fat.

But of all the ordeals faced by the river men, that of the winterer was the worst. He was the one who had to stay out in the wilderness perhaps two thousand miles from his base. The Indians brought him furs, and though he often had an Indian wife, he sometimes was entirely alone. If game was abundant he ate well, and there was usually plenty of fish preserved from the fall through the winter. But if game failed or fish rotted, starvation or dysentery was his fate. If he fell sick there was no help for him, and his loneliness was total in a six-months winter when the prairie was nothing but a white death.

Narrow this life was, uncivilized and uneducated, but on the whole it was less brutalizing than the life in the lumber camps in the Victorian era. At the principal bases of the Hudson's Bay Company all the men were required to attend prayers regularly. There is a poignant memorandum dating from the early eighteenth-century records of the Bay which enjoins the company's servants "to live lovingly with one another not to swear or quarrel but to live peaceably without drunkenness or profaneness." The Nor'Westers had a rougher tradition but more personal independence within the service; less consciousness, perhaps, that they were suffering a thankless exploitation by rich men who never troubled themselves to know at what price of human stamina and hardship the profits were earned. Nearly all the Montreal partners in the company had served at least some time on the rivers. The French-Canadian voyageur, though not fond of washing *en route*, was a considerable dandy whenever he neared a post. Even though the only women in the post were savages, he washed and put on his best clothes. He

had a Gallic courtesy to counteract his almost incredible tough-
ness, and Francis Parkman writes feelingly of the human quality
of his *Canadien* guides along the Missouri. As for the Highlanders in the service of the fur trade, one of them wrote the "Lone
Shieling" poem, possibly the most haunting verses ever composed in Canada.

THE END OF THE FUR TRADE

The fur trade failed in the end; it was doomed the moment the
settlers began moving into the west to farm. Long before that
time there were men engaged in it who had seen the writing on
the wall. Sometimes when I walk up the avenue of the McGill
campus and reach the Founder's tomb, I think back on the life
he led and the shrewd Lowland caution which prompted James
McGill to take his money out of the fur trade in time. He had
never been a true voyageur, merely a poor boy from Scotland
who had entered the only Canadian trade which offered him a
living. He had earned his place in the Beaver Club by a winter
spent alone near the headwaters of the Mississippi, but he got
off the rivers before the life on them broke him. McGill lacked
the transcendent imagination of Simon McTavish and the last-
ditch loyalty of William McGillivray, but he had much common
sense. Unlike most of his old colleagues in the fur trade, he did
not die broke. His life had taught him that civilization could
never grow in Canada under the conditions he had known in
his youth. Though he was well off by colonial standards, he
would never have been accounted an especially rich man in
England. He left just enough to make it possible to found a
college. Until a few years ago, McGill University lay like a quiet
pattern of order in the roaring tumult of modern Montreal; it is
still the most important visible monument to the North West
Company's great adventure.

For the economic contribution of the fur trade after the
American Revolution has surely been exaggerated. It is a common argument that furs saved the country from being absorbed
by the United States because they provided an east-west trade,
all Canadian, in a continent where the normal lines of economic communication run north and south with the greater

power and population of the United States sucking the wealth of Canada southward. I cannot believe this. The fur trade may have bridged an economic gap for a number of years, but the true reason why it saved Canada from absorption was not economic. It was political, and none of the explorers understood this as well as did David Thompson, who detested Lord Ashburton for surrendering to the United States land which he himself had won by the rights of prior exploration.

Not only did the voyageurs explore most of North America; after 1783 they staked out Canadian – or, at that time, British – claims to the whole northwestern hinterland from the head of the Lakes to the Pacific. When the tide of homesteaders fanned out from the railheads in the American mid-west in the nineteenth century, the Canadian west would surely have been occupied by them, and subsequently claimed as American territory by the American government, had not the ancient rights of prior exploration, which the Americans respected, bound the land to Canada. The lonely posts were on the plains, in the Fraser and Columbia valleys, on the Pacific coast, and the Union Jack flew over all of them. Yet only a handful of men achieved this result. At the height of its power the North West Company may have employed as many as five thousand men, but less than two thousand were in service in the field between Montreal and Chipewyan. It was not their numbers that counted, but what they did. And in the long run what was done by the dreamers mattered the most.

David Thompson was probably the greatest geographer ever developed in North America; without his work, backed by Simon Fraser's voyage down the river which bears his name, it is hard to believe that British Columbia would now be a Canadian province. And of course there was Alexander Mackenzie, the boldest of all the Canadian explorers after La Vérendrye, but David Thompson, the most accurate and thorough of all individual surveyors in continental history, was the key man.

A dozen years before Lewis and Clark, Mackenzie reached the Pacific through North America. He threaded to the end the Northwest Passage. Its reality bore no resemblance to the European dream of a great gorge which would float sailing ships from the Old World through the continental land mass of the New. It was simply the chain of rivers, lakes, and portages which enabled canoes from Montreal to move all the way from the St. Lawrence across Canada to the northern and western oceans.

"Alexander Mackenzie, from Canada, by land, the twenty-second of July, one thousand seven hundred and ninety-three" – this celebrated understatement, scrawled in a mixture of vermilion and grease on a rock in Dean Channel after Mackenzie's passage down the Bella Coola, wrote *finis* to a quest begun exactly three hundred and one years earlier when Christopher Columbus set out across the Atlantic from Palos. The reality found by Mackenzie served only to dissipate the dream. But it introduced a new reality, just as Columbus's lost quest drew an entire hemisphere into the story of civilization. How strange that a Canadian birch-bark canoe without a name, last in a long succession of canoes from Champlain's first one, should have earned a place in the company of ships like the *Santa Maria* and the *Golden Hind*!

The Saskatchewan

Of all the major rivers of this continent, the Saskatchewan seems to me the loneliest-looking. By this I mean the concept of it, the image of it considered as a whole, for like any body of moving water the river in section after section can be sprightly and full of grace. In many places where I have sat beside it, the Saskatchewan made me think of a smooth body pulsing with life, a depth in it, a quiet tirelessness, and Marjorie Wilkins Campbell has written well of the beauty of the foam which washes down along its surface like white lace.

Yet surely the Saskatchewan, when we think of it as a whole, has within its image the great solitude of the prairie it crosses. Endlessly winding, seldom dramatic between the Rockies and the final spasm at Grand Rapids, the twin branches flow through the central plain in a huge, wavering Y.

Often the Saskatchewan passes through bush and parkland, and these were the regions most prized by the fur-traders. But more often it winds through naked plains, and the feeling of loneliness is in proportion to the bareness of the land. The river is always below the surface of the prairie and it seldom floods, for its trenches are extremely deep. For hundreds of miles the trenches of the two branches channel the waters easterly: hundreds of miles of tan, monotonous water with weeds and wildflowers rife along the escarpments when sand-bars protrude from the channels in late summer; hundreds of miles of greenish-white ice against the flat white of the plain in the six-month winter which seems so interminable that the people in the river towns hold sweepstakes on the hour and minute of the spring break-up. When finally the break-up comes it is the most awaited moment in the seasonal life of the Saskatchewan. The ice cracks, the floes pile up a dozen feet high, and occasionally bizarre things can happen. Not long ago in Saskatoon a bewildered deer was carried through the heart of the town on an ice pan while thousands of people watched. Then, after a pause, comes the time of high water when the twin branches race with foam as they carry eastward the run-off from billions of tons of Rocky Mountain snow.

The lonely feeling given by the Saskatchewan is different from what is felt on the Mackenzie because here there are so many people. It is the nature of the prairie landscape that a human being, a house, a grain elevator, a moving train, even a village etched against the sky, serves only to enhance the sense of space. Standing on the banks of the Saskatchewan, seeing it come out of one horizon on its way into another, many a newcomer must have felt he could go no farther into this enormousness without losing all sense of who he was. The western Missouri used to give a similar sensation to many an American homesteader. But though the Missouri is a greater river than the Saskatchewan, it lies farther south; it does not have that final northern quality of making you feel you are on the edge of nothing human. Stepping off a train onto the wooden platform of one of those stark little Saskatchewan river towns, many a settler must have walked down to the river and watched the water coming out of the prairie into the town – so tiny and alone in that vast space – and then watched it going out again into the prairie, and wondered if he would ever be equal to his life in such a land. Some prairie people are indignant when easterners use the word "stark" to describe their towns. They shouldn't be. The very fact that towns like Prince Albert exist and thrive in a place where recently there was nothing but grass is a triumph. Can towns becomes cities in two lifetimes?

For along most of the Saskatchewan, whether on the North Branch or the South, the world has been reduced to what W. O. Mitchell called the least common denominator of nature, land and sky. There is also the effect of the weather. It shifts constantly and with it the moods of sky and land, and the river reflects all these moods with total fidelity. Few sights in Canada are more peaceful than the mirroring of the pastel sky-hues on the Saskatchewan on a fine summer day; none more chilling than an eddy of snow in January when the thermometer stands at forty or fifty below and the ice is too hard for a curling-stone. The winds here are visible: in summer you see them as a throbbing radiance along a sea of grass, in winter as a drifting lace of ice crystals along a sea of snow.

My doctor father used to say that nature is usually just, that what she takes with one hand she gives with the other. The Saskatchewan country can be so bleakly stern it shrivels the soul; it can also intoxicate with a deluge of prolific loveliness that makes an English June seem insipid by comparison. In the spring the voice of the turtle is not heard much in this land, but the voices and movement of a myriad of other birds, many of them waterfowl, make hundreds of miles of clear atmosphere quiver with sound and flash with colour and the very sky thrill with the larks. The sloughs teem, the land deprived by the long winter goes mad with the lust of recreating the life the frost has killed. Moses would have understood this land. Had civilized men lived along the Saskatchewan three millenniums ago, the prairie country would have burgeoned with psalmists and prophets.

The Saskatchewan is not a simple stream but a system of waters having a combined length greater than that of the St. Lawrence or the Danube and draining a basin of 150,000 square miles, which includes much of the Alberta and Saskatchewan farmlands, a small corner of Montana, and (including the Nelson) much of northern Manitoba. The North Saskatchewan has a total drop from its glacial source of more than 7,000 feet, the South Branch a total drop of just over a mile. The river is seldom more than twelve feet deep, with many shoals and rapids, and after Prince Albert its average flow amounts to 56 million tons a day. To compare this with a man-made object, we can say that the daily tonnage of water carried by the lower Saskatchewan is sixty-four times greater than the tonnage of the SS *Queen Elizabeth*, the largest liner ever built.

After the twin branches leave the Rockies, the most dramatic moment in their course occurs at Grand Rapids, just before the stream discharges into Lake Winnipeg. Here the river, five hundred feet wide between twenty-five-foot walls, flowing at a velocity of ten miles an hour, drops seventy-five feet over a distance of three miles.

In 1964 a dam was completed on the Grand Rapids section which produced the ninth-largest man-made body of water in the world. In June of that year, to celebrate the completion of the dam, the engineers made an experimental shut-off which stopped the rapids entirely. The pools at the river mouth were filled with pickerel, northern pike, bass, goldeyes, and sturgeons, and on that single day one commercial fisherman made a haul worth $1,400. The next day the gates were opened and the Saskatchewan flowed, under control, into Lake Winnipeg again.

Its strategic course as the principal prairie water route has made the Saskatchewan the second most indispensable of all the rivers which have played a part in Canadian history. The voyageurs followed one branch northwest across the plains toward Portage LaTraite and the Methy, while the other branch carried them southwest and into the Rockies by way of Bow Pass.

THE NORTH SASKATCHEWAN

Though most of the Saskatchewan flows through the plains, its waters rise in one of the most spectacular regions of North America. The North Branch, fathered by the Columbia Icefield, comes out of the glacier on Mount Saskatchewan, and when you stand on the little bridge over the North Fork and look at the lithe, frigid stream, not glacial-green but milky from limestone, so narrow in August that a broad-jumper could clear it, you can have a strange sensation when you think how far this water has to go.

The analogy between rivers and lives has been overworked,

but only because it is unavoidable. The beginnings of both move us more than we care to admit because they show that all things are subject to accident. A chance in the human genes, a drunken driver, a virus so small it is invisible through a microscope, and a human life is stunted or killed. A tilt in the landscape, the proximity of a larger stream, and what might have been a famous river is only a tributary brook.

But this milky, cold brook we see bubbling down from Mount Saskatchewan survives to claim mastery over hundreds of brooks and even a few sizeable rivers. In the mountains it does not have the firm confidence of the young Athabaska, which finds the broad Jasper Valley soon in its career. In the mountains the North Branch is a nervous river. Its grey-green waters flicker down between Mounts Amery and Coleman, its wide gravel washes are littered with the bleaching bones of dead trees carried off in spring floods, and it finds or carves a narrow course through the ranges. It flows down to Rocky Mountain House where it takes in the Brazeau and Clearwater, then it swells in to the plain and flows on toward Edmonton, having gathered in several other mountain streams as it goes.

When the North Saskatchewan twists under the escarpments of Alberta's largest city, it is a master stream flecked with foam and haunted with wildfowl; it is about a hundred and forty feet wide under the bridges and the trench in places is deeper than a hundred feet. Its surface looks like tan silk, its current is visible with the life of the mountains still within it, its sound is a lisping whisper. But that this is already a river of the plains is proved by the amount of silt it carries. Floundering through ragweed and mud the colour and texture of axle-grease, I made the primitive test of holding a silver quarter under the river's surface. As it disappeared at a depth of three inches, I presumed that even here the river carries more sediment than the Red. And yet it does not look so sleek and muddy, and its flow, of course, is more powerful.

From Edmonton the North Branch winds out into the plain through horizon after horizon with here and there a tiny village stark on its banks, and here and there a clump of cottonwood or birch. After crossing the provincial border above Lloyd-minster – when the first homesteaders arrived in the North

Bend they found the prairie grass so rich and tangled they could scarcely walk in it – the river journeys some ten horizons farther into North Battleford. Here it takes in the Battle, bends south and then north to Prince Albert, above it the limitless sky, about and beyond it the empty land.

A little past Prince Albert, at The Forks, the North Branch finally meets its great partner from the south. Then the united Saskatchewan flows through the wilderness into Manitoba, past The Pas into Cedar Lake. Here through the ages it has deposited so much silt that Alexander Mackenzie, when he saw the region two centuries ago, predicted that in time all this watery expanse would turn into forest.

After Cedar Lake the Saskatchewan's journey is nearly done. With a swift rush of rapids, the waters swirl into the northwestern bulge of Lake Winnipeg at a point some three hundred and forty miles east of The Forks. Eventually some Saskatchewan water leaks out into the Nelson and reaches the brine of Hudson Bay, but it is wrong to claim, as some do, that the Nelson is a continuation of this river. Though in a sense it may be argued that it is now a part of the Saskatchewan's system, the Nelson, as was mentioned before, is one of the survivors of Lake Agassiz.

THE SOUTH BRANCH

The sources of the South Branch, which is sometimes considered a tributary of the North, are just as interesting as those of its partner and considerably more varied. The primary source is Bow Lake from which the Bow River pours so gaily down the pass through Banff to Calgary and beyond. Its confluence in southern Alberta with the Oldman, whose waters come from a number of mountain sources, is taken as the beginning of the South Saskatchewan proper. This was the great river of the buffalo plains in the early days, but because (unlike the North Branch) none of it passes through forest country after leaving the Rockies, it was never of great interest to the fur-traders. The South Branch was not prolific in amphibious animals. It flows easterly past Medicine Hat, then northeast across the provincial boundary where it gathers in the Red Deer, then up through the prairie past Saskatoon and Batoche to The Forks. The total length of the South Branch from Bow Lake to The Forks is 860 miles, and the total drop is about 4,700 feet. Bow Lake is one of the highest in the Rockies, and is still frozen in early June.

Between them the two branches of this river, together with their final run as a united stream, have a length just under 2,000 miles. Between them they embrace most of the farm land of Alberta and Saskatchewan. . . .

THE COURAGE OF THE HOMESTEADERS

"How can they?" I once heard an American woman say as she stared at the wind flattening the prairie grass beyond the Edmonton airport. "How can they *want* to live in a country like this?"

On winter days when forty-mile-an-hour gales tear across the prairie snows, this writer from gentle Nova Scotia has often had the same thought. There is no use in pretending that the Saskatchewan River country is a kind one to its people even now; half a century ago it was as cruel as the pole. This is one of the sternest terrains I know inhabited by people living normal civilized lives. But the very fact that it *is* inhabited by civilized people has an historical significance most of us forget in these comfortable times.

If anyone wishes to know what life was like a century ago in Europe for the underprivileged – what life was like a full fifty years after the Selkirk Highlanders came to Manitoba – the best place to go is not to England, central Europe, or even Montreal; it is to the Saskatchewan River country. Look at those millions of acres of sectional farms and the lonely little river towns where the farmers come in on Saturdays. Look at the early photographs of Saskatoon, which became a community only in 1882, and imagine yourself starting a life there at that time. Stand on the banks of the Saskatchewan and *feel* the river passing through that gigantic lonely land, and then ask yourself what must have been in the minds of the first homesteaders who came west from settled Ontario, or who crossed the ocean and then travelled two-thirds of the way across Canada to *this*! I remember the feeling of fear it gave me as a boy when my mother told me of a relative who had gone to Saskatchewan from Nova Scotia, and how she had watched her son walking alone across the prairie to school until he became a dot on the horizon.

In most ways, I have often thought, the courage of the home-steaders was greater than that of the voyageurs, for they had their families with them. How many fathers must have quailed at the responsibility they had assumed, at the results of their own ignorance, when all they could provide in the way of a house was a hole dug in the ground and roofed with sods! It is all very well to make jokes about the prairie that broke the plough so long as you make them in the East about certain glum novels of pioneering hardships. To make them in the West is like joking about rope in the house of the hanged man, for the hardships of this country are fresh in the memories of everyone over sixty. I have met a cultivated, brilliant woman (her father was consid-ered "county" in England) who spent her first year in Canada among the primitive comforts of a Saskatchewan sod hut.

It seems to me, since seeing the West, that the development of this Saskatchewan River country is an implicit refutation of all our sentimental images of the human past, for behind it was nothing more nor less than two basic needs which pre-twentieth-century society denied to everyone save a privileged few. Those needs were things the praisers of times past lack the experience – the experience, not the imagination – to compre-hend: sufficient food, and sufficient freedom to raise your chil-dren, if not yourself, to the full stature of human beings. In Sutherlandshire a century and a quarter ago, after the lord's agents had burned the crofters out of their homes, they forbade them to eat the mussels on the shore because they were the lord's property. Thousands of the descendants of the evicted are on the plains of Saskatchewan today. Despair, no less than courage, is behind that province.

Or think how it was in middle and eastern Europe only a short while ago when whole families stampeded the immigrant ships. In Poland a century ago – perhaps more recently in back-ward regions – a landlord could possess a peasant girl merely by demanding her, and think himself magnanimous if he sent her family a sack of potatoes. Wars, press gangs, and the lash lay behind many a homesteading family. Those who came to the United States may have believed the streets were paved with gold, but not one in a thousand who came to the Saskatchewan River country sought anything more than a home. If anyone were to ask me now what is the main common denominator which has held this nation together, I would answer very simply: a desire for a home, and a determination to keep it. *Ici, nous sommes chez nous* – the phrase is constantly used today in French Canada without sentimentality and without embarrassment.

The volume of effort expended by the Saskatchewan homesteaders can be estimated by looking at Saskatchewan life today and reflecting how quickly civilization has been established there. Drought and long distances, harsh winters and unpredictable rainfalls were always against the people. The deep trench of the river made it useless for water in dry seasons, yet civilization grew so fast it is hard for us to comprehend the advance. In the year when the Governors of the Hudson's Bay Company sold out their land rights in the West to the Canadian government, my own father was beginning school. Queen Victoria had been a widow for more than a decade when the Land Act was finally passed. Only twenty-two years before I myself was born, Riel and Dumont made their last stand at Batoche. Only two years before I was born, Saskatchewan became a province.

All of this was possible because of the homesteaders and the driving need that took them there. Between 1876 and 1900 the silence of the prairie was split by the creaking of thousands of Red River carts as the families moved in: during that period some 88,000 entries were filed. In 1905 alone, spurred by Clifford Sifton's policy of opening the plains to "the man in the sheepskin coat with the broad wife," no fewer than 30,000 entries were made in the Saskatchewan country, and many of these newcomers knew no English. By that time the homestead acreage came close to the five million mark.

This would have signified little had the people been concerned only with wheat-growing. But not only did they crave an education, they craved a good one. Montreal had been settled for two centuries before it had a university, but the University of Saskatchewan was established five years after the land on which it stands had been incorporated within the province. A professor I met in Saskatoon, originally a Nova Scotian and a man still full of vigour, told me of the morning when he and one or two colleagues saw their first students appear, and that the first subjects they taught them were Latin and Greek. Fifty years later the University of Saskatchewan was one of the best in the country.

AGAINST THE CURRENT

"As for me and my house," Sinclair Ross quotes on the flyleaf of his novel of Saskatchewan in the depression years, "we will serve the Lord."

In the context of Sinclair Ross's story, this was not a pious quotation. A great bitterness lay behind it. The sufferings of the Saskatchewan people in the depression years when the dust storms blew, the memories of hardships which constantly renewed themselves, the narrowness of strict religions made all the more severe because people in little places cannot escape one another, the corrosions caused by aggression buried deep because they were too dangerous to release – all these elements were in Ross's novel of Saskatchewan. But endurance was also there, even endurance in religion. The God of tigers and lambs, of bacilli and penicillin, of drought and plenty had to be served. Otherwise the people would have perished.

These days when I visit Saskatchewan I remember how students from the farms starved during the depression years in order to get an education. I think how the people co-operated, and thereby upheld the dignity of their species. I feel that here I have made at least a brief acquaintance with the kind of unconscious force which Tolstoy believed is decisive in history. And flying home over the Saskatchewan River, sometimes I have felt I could almost see those ghostly canoe brigades, tiny in that vast and tawny setting, paddling firmly upward against the current of the stream.

The Fraser

Here occurred the climax of two centuries of canoe exploration in North America. No easterner, least of all one from the Maritime Provinces, is ever likely to feel at home beside the Fraser River. It is alien to everything he knows, and so is its land. Great men have passed through its story, but they did not grow out of the country on which, for brief moments, they partially imposed their wills. Wild and amazing experiences have been recorded in some of the little towns along the Black Canyon and up tributaries like the Thompson, the Lillooet, and the Quesnel, but some of these towns are ghosts today and the descendants of the men who once thronged and brawled in them live elsewhere. It took the people of Switzerland many centuries to establish a real human relationship with the Alps. It will take Canadians of the scientific age at least half as long to do the same with the Rocky Mountains.

This is the most exciting country in Canada, and I don't see how anyone could visit any part of it without longing to return. Its beauty makes you catch your breath. But it was a westerner, Bruce Hutchison, who remarked that the beauty of the most spectacular parts of the Fraser River is that of a nightmare. This is the savagest of all the major rivers of America. It is probably the savagest in the world.

The Fraser is a mountain system, and though the area of its drainage basin is little more than 90,000 miles, here the figures are deceptively low because northern mountains catch huge quantities of snow, especially if they are close to an ocean like the Pacific. The Fraser's total length is 850 miles, its course the shape of the letter S drawn by a man in *delirium tremens*. It rises at 52° 45′ north latitude in two small branches fed by Mount Robson's glacier just west of the Divide, and the moment these feeder streams unite, they find a course in which to run. There in the absolute wilderness of the northern Rockies the drama of the Fraser begins.

Though the ultimate destination lies hundreds of miles to the southwest, the Fraser begins its career by charging northwest in a wide, wavering curve along the Rocky Mountain Trench. After about two hundred miles the rushing waters encounter the northern spur of the Cariboo Mountains, they sweep in a fierce arc around them, then they plunge directly south. Twisting furiously, with only a few brief interludes of relative calm, the Fraser roars for four hundred miles down to the little town of Hope, which began its existence as a Hudson's Bay Company post and was well named, as so many of these posts were, when one considers what awaited a traveller going north before the roads were built. At Hope the Fraser at last breaks out of its mountain trap.

To the geographer what happens here is one of the most exciting natural spectacles in Canada. Within a distance of a mile the entire character of the river changes and this tyranno-saurus of a stream turns sweet and gentle. In a broad valley shining in the sun, with a width the same as the St. John's below Fredericton, the Fraser winds calmly through the loveliest farm-ing valley in the land. The air is balmy, the cattle are as sleek as in a Cambridgeshire meadow, the snow peaks Olympian in the safe distance. During these last eighty miles the river traverses most of human British Columbia, for it is in this beautiful corner, and in the twin cities at the estuary, that the bulk of British Columbians live. At the end of its course the Fraser is old King Lear with the rage gone. But before the ocean swallows it, receiving its water through a surprisingly small delta, the river makes one final assertion of its true character. For miles it stains the clean brine of Georgia Strait with the dirty yellow silt it has torn out of the mountains all the way from the top of the Cariboo to the canyon's end at Hope.

"If a river could flow on the moon," I thought as I flew over the Black Canyon, "it would probably look like this."

The idea is not so far-fetched as it looks, because from twenty thousand feet a lot of the land around the central Fraser seems just as chaotic and devoid of purpose as the moon's surface. Those lofty, snow-clad peaks which inspire you when you stare at them from the ground are harsh, barren ridges of rock where nothing lives. The valleys where the elk browse and the little streams cascade are cruel scars. From the air the Rocky Moun-tains are seldom beautiful.

Yet the air is the best place to study the Fraser if you wish to understand the logic of its course. On the ground, travelling that fantastic highway which has grown out of the old Cariboo Road, the river seems to be coming at you from all directions and the road beside it twists like a spiral stair so that on a dull day, without the sun to tell you your course, you often don't know whether you are travelling north or south. But from the air the twists in the river are seen to be perfectly logical.

The necessity of every river is to get down to sea level by the shortest route possible, and this may vary from a gentle winding in a set direction to a tortured course through every point of the compass until the goal has been reached. The Fraser's terrain is the toughest of any major river in America, possibly of any in the world, and so is its problem.

From the air you see how it solves it. As all of its course save the final eighty miles lies in a mountain labyrinth where the peaks and ranges literally jostle one another, the Fraser must outflank ridge after ridge, and in some places bore its way through sheer walls of rock. From the air you see it like a very yellow, very thin snake that looks as if it had died after having had a convulsion in a rock trap. From the air there is no life in the Fraser, and it does not look like a river at all.

On the ground it explodes with life, and there is a marvellous variety in the spectacle through which it flows. Here the colours are so bold and strong – sage green, orange of sandstone, viridian of hemlock and fir, blue of translucent skies, Wimbledon green on the rare benches where the cattle graze – that a visitor from the east feels he has been translated into a larger, brighter, more exciting existence. The wild flowers are lovely along the Fraser, the wind sounds as though the mountains were breathing, the dawns and sunsets are such that you can only stare at them in silent wonder. Then you look down the steep trench – in many places you look down thousands of feet – and you see the intruder. That furious, frothing water scandalously yellow against the green – where did it come from and how did it get here?

This savage thing! On all the major rivers you expect the occasional turbulence, and you assume that all mountain streams are cataracts. Rivers like the St. Lawrence quickly calm down after their rapids, and mountain streams like the Kicking Horse are shallow and short. But the Fraser is neither short nor shallow. It is all of thirty miles longer than the Rhine, and it flows with cataract force for more than six hundred miles with only a few interludes of relative quiet. In a sense the Fraser does not flow at all: it seethes along with whirlpools so fierce that a log going down it may circle the same spot for days as though caught in a liquid merry-go-round. It roars like an ocean in storm, but ocean storms blow themselves out while the Fraser's roar is forever.

This is the most remorseless force of nature in Canada, and its effect on the person who travels beside it is curious. As you drive north in your car you twist for hour after hour around one hairpin bend after another. Some of these curves around abutments of the cliff can turn the knees of a height-shy traveller to water and I, personally, am glad I was able to travel from Lytton to Lillooet before the road was improved to the width of a super-highway. Past Yale, past Spuzzum and Boston Bar, up through Lytton to Lillooet that curving highway took us, sometimes through little tunnels in the cliff itself, once or twice around a narrow bend with an unguarded edge and a drop of thousands of feet straight down – the road is almost as exciting as the river itself, and you remember that in some of these towns, now quiet and half alive, thousands of desperate men once lived as dangerously as soldiers in war when they panned this river for gold. A little beyond Lytton the road leaves the river, and if you wish to follow the water you must abandon your car and take to the Pacific Great Eastern Railway. Miles higher up to the north, the road and river rejoin at Macalister.

All this time and all these miles the Fraser has been working on you. Sometimes you are so close to the water that its yellow malevolence boils into your subconscious, but most of the time you are so high that it looks as static as it does from the air. Almost never does it seem to belong where it is. Yet it is there, and after you have spent several days beside it, the Fraser intrudes into yourself also, and you are apt to see it in your sleep.

THE RIVER AS CREATOR

The Fraser River, which seems absolutely hostile to man and all his works, has been as important to British Columbia as the St. Lawrence has been to Quebec. This is another of the amazing facts about it. In his book on the river, Bruce Hutchison argues that the Fraser has practically created the province. So, in a sense, it has, and in a manner awe-inspiring to people from quieter regions.

Fraser salmon, which supported an Indian culture long before the white man came, today gives British Columbia a richer fishing industry than that of the three Maritime Provinces combined. The life-cycle of the sockeye salmon is one of those natural dramas so suggestive that the very symbolism of it cuts too close to the human knuckle for mental comfort. The story of the salmon's fight up the river to spawn and die has been told so often and well that I will not repeat it here. Everyone – at least everyone in British Columbia – knows about the fish ladders at Hell's Gate, about the river visibly bulging with life when the big runs come in, about the tributaries turning blood-red as the fish expire while giving life to a new generation, about the bears that wade into the shallows to eat them, about the males fighting with each other for the privilege of dying beside the females of their choice, about the stench which pollutes the wilderness when the bodies decompose. In the upper reaches the salmon are often too far gone in the death process to be eaten by humans, and the great catches are made in the sea when the fish are bright and strong swimming in toward the estuary, or in the lowermost reaches near Mission before the final death-rush begins.

Fraser gold, discovered in 1856 or 1857 (the exact date is uncertain), caused an epic of suffering worse even than the record of the Klondike. Terrible though the Chilkoot was, it was not so cruel as the Fraser rapids down which those heroic fools tried to flounder on rafts. The amount of gold taken out of the sand-bars and lodes at Yale, Boston Bar, Barkerville, and up the Thompson and Lillooet was trivial compared to the hardship and heroism that paid for it, nor were the individual fortunes more permanent than gold-rush fortunes anywhere else.

But the Fraser gold has two by-products of infinite importance to British Columbia. The river in the end carried thousands of disappointed miners down to the estuary where they were deposited like so much sediment with neither the will nor the means to return. Many stayed permanently, and added themselves to the nucleus of humanity which built Vancouver into our third city within three generations. The second by-product was the Cariboo Road.

In 1861 Governor James Douglas, one of the most dynamic men in Canadian history, realized that unless help on a huge scale were provided for the obsessed lunatics digging and panning up the Fraser Canyon, thousands of them would die of famine and cold. He therefore ordered his Royal Engineers to build a route into the interior, and the result was the most spectacularly dangerous highway in America. When the engineers finished their work, the Cariboo Road was a ledge in the cliff sides three hundred and eighty-five miles long and eighteen feet wide. In places the drop from the unguarded lip was thousands of feet, and many a horse and mule, and quite a few men also, hurtled off and down to the end of their troubles. One imaginative teamster even introduced camels to the Cariboo, thinking they would be more sure-footed than horses and mules, but their smell so frightened the other pack animals that the camels were taken off the road.

So far as the original stampeders were concerned, this famous road probably did more harm than good: it provided an excuse for thousands more to join the hordes of gold-fevered men already working there. But when the stampede petered out and the hurdy-gurdy girls and the chisellers went south, when the roaring shack towns turned into bleaching ghost towns, the road was there and remained. It led saner men into the interior who built logging camps and established the great ranches which make British Columbia's Dry Belt a rival in stock-raising to the American Southwest.

HAULING STEAMBOATS

The world knows little of the Fraser's history – nor does eastern Canada, for that matter – and I would guess there are two reasons for this ignorance. In the first place, nobody can imagine what the river is like unless he has seen it with his own eyes, for there is nothing else resembling it on this continent, and I doubt if there is anything else resembling it in the world. In the second place, modern people everywhere have been conditioned to think of post-voyageur explorations and settlements in the far west in the patterns established in the United States. From Francis Parkman's *The Oregon Trail* to the latest covered-wagon television show, the American story has been told and retold countless times. The story of British Columbia's exploration and settlement has hardly been heard at all.

It was quite different, owing to the tradition of Canadian exploration and the nature of the British Columbian terrain.

Though the passes through the American Rockies are sometimes difficult, horses and mules could usually negotiate them.
But there is nothing in the American west like the nightmare of
the Fraser Canyon. Before the building of the Cariboo Road,
the pioneers of British Columbia still had to depend on the
canoe or on boats, and use them on a river which no human
being in his senses would try to navigate unless he had to. Later,
when they built roads, they had to blast them out of sheer cliffs.

Incredibly, steamboats were used for a time in the canyon
itself, and this fact alone points up the harshness of the Canadian experience in the early days of the coastal province. If
anyone stands on the road above Hell's Gate – better still, if he
descends to the edge of the river itself at that point – he finds it
impossible to believe that anyone would even try to drive a
steamboat up-river against that ferocious torrent. But as the
alternative was back-breaking labour, men not only tried, they
actually succeeded in using steamboats for a while. They
dragged them up by means of winches on the ships with hundreds of men heaving on cables as they toiled along the ledges
above the water. Many of the men on the ropes were Chinese,
and perhaps some of them had worked on the Yangtse or the
Yellow River in their native land. The ships' engines roared,
sometimes the boilers exploded from excess of pressure, but they
were hauled up the canyon against that cataract.

The pioneers of British Columbia, and later the technicians
and engineers, circumvented the river's obstacles even though
they could not tame the river itself. The challenges they met
were never adequately described by them, nor do I think that
anyone now can tell their story as it truly was. But to some
extent we can guess at it by acquainting ourselves with the river
itself, and by looking at some of its vital facts.

SNOW TO THE SEA

The mountains through which the Fraser finds or carves a path
are far from the world's highest, but they cover a huge area and
are extremely varied. For miles above Lytton the river passes
through the so-called Dry Belt of British Columbia where the
traveller is astonished to encounter the sagebrush, tumbleweed,

and county-sized ranches associated with the American Southwest, and is warned against rattlesnakes on the rocky trails.
Little rain falls here, and if all the Fraser's course lay through
country like this, its volume of flow would be moderate. But all
of its course does not lie through country like this.

Many of the ranges sloping in chaos in the general direction of
the Fraser are exposed to moist Pacific winds, and in winter they
collect billions of tons of snow. By mid-June most of this snow
has turned into water and the water runs. The Fraser, draining
an area of 91,600 square miles, has to carry all this run-off to the
sea. A geographer once told me that the mere statement of these
facts tells you all you need to know about the nature of the river.
It does, I suppose, to a man with a geographer's imagination. But
I myself had to see it to believe it.

"When you reach Lytton," a British Columbian told me in
Montreal, "be sure to stand on that little bridge where the
Thompson enters. It's a wonderful sight. Thompson water is
blue-green and Fraser water is yellow gumbo. You can see them
both together – two separate streams in the same course."

I thought I understood what he meant, for the year previous I
had been on the Mackenzie and seen the phenomenon of the
Liard's brown water flowing along the left bank while the clean
Mackenzie water keeps to the right. The two streams are distin-
guishable side by side for nearly two hundred miles below Fort
Simpson. It takes the Mackenzie, one of the most powerful
streams in the land, all this distance to absorb its chief tributary.

When I stood on the Lytton bridge the sight was indeed
wonderful, but it bore no resemblance to anything I had
expected. The Thompson is the Fraser's chief tributary, a major
stream in its own right, a mountain stream also, and it does not
so much enter the Fraser as smash its way into it like a liquid
battering-ram. From the bridge I saw its water plunging into the
Fraser just as the man said, blue-green into the Fraser's yellow
froth. Then it completely disappeared. The Fraser swallowed
the Thompson in less than a hundred yards!

As soon as you pass beyond Lytton on the way up-river, you
see evidence of the Fraser's power in what it has done to the
land. Above Lillooet it has carved out a minor Grand Canyon.
Farther up in the plateaux of the ranching country it is almost

subterranean: you travel for miles across the ranges and think no water is anywhere and then suddenly you come to the trench and stare far, far down and there is that infernal yellow line frothing along.

But it is at Hell's Gate, its passage made still more narrow by rock-falls from railway blasting, that the prolonged violence of the river reaches its climax, and the best way I can think of describing its ferocity here is by making some comparisons with the St. Lawrence.

The mean flow of the St. Lawrence is 543,000 cubic feet per second, the Fraser's 92,600. But the width of the St. Lawrence in the Seaway section where the Victoria Bridge crosses to Montreal, *before* it has received the Richelieu, the St. Maurice, or any substantial weight of the Ottawa, is more than a mile and a half. The width of the Fraser at Hell's Gate, *after* it has received the Nechako, the Blackwater, the Chilcotin, the Quesnel, the Lillooet, the Thompson, and nearly all its less famous tributaries, is hardly more than fifty yards! This means that a good fly fisherman can cast a line across a river carrying one-fifth the flow of the St. Lawrence!

But there are days on the Fraser which are not average, days which come after steady sunshine and a succession of warm nights have melted the mountain snows in a rush. Then the Fraser becomes incredible.

During the flood of 1948 a flow of 543,000 cubic feet per second was recorded on the Fraser; in the worse flood of 1894, the flow was estimated at 600,000 cubic feet per second. In other words, there was at least one recorded occasion when 57,000 more cubic feet of water per second went through the gap at Hell's Gate than passes on an average day between Quebec and Lévis!

What this meant to the gentle valley below Hope amounted on both occasions to a national catastrophe. Thousands of acres were awash, barns and houses were carried away, cattle were drowned, and the bodies of cows were seen floating in the yellow smear spread for miles into the Strait of Georgia. But in the Black Canyon little was changed because its walls are so sheer and its trough so deep it could hold all the rivers of North

America without overflowing. In the twisted gorge the Fraser boiled and roared at prodigious depths and at velocities exceeding thirty knots. It churned millions of tons of sand in its whirlpools, its backwashes tossed giant logs like splinters end over end, it killed thousands of salmon by exhausting the life out of them or by hurling them clear of the water against rocks which broke their spines. It wore several more inches off the little islands which survive in the channel shaped like the pre-Dreadnaught battleships of the German Kaiser's High Seas Fleet.

I was not on the Fraser when these violent events occurred, but if I had flown over the canyon at those times, I would have seen nothing out of the ordinary at ten thousand feet.

BIRCH-BARK AND FOAM

This river was navigated – at least most of it was – by human beings in canoes of the North West Company, and of all the facts connected with the Fraser, this single one is the most impressive to anyone who knows the region. It was later navigated – if you can apply such a technical word to an insanely ignorant venture – by a few stampeders who built themselves rafts intending to float down the current, found themselves trapped in the canyon, and clung to the rafts because this was all they could do. But no stampeder truly navigated the Fraser any more than the logs do. Nor, for that matter, did the Frenchman who swam the river in 1958 swim it in the sense that experts swim the English Channel or Lake Ontario. Equipped with a frogman's outfit, he also was carried down like a log.

But voyageurs legitimately navigated nearly all of it. First, Alexander Mackenzie entered its upper waters in 1793 when he cut through the mountains by way of the Peace on the journey which led him to Dean Channel and the coast. When he launched his canoe on the western side of the Divide he was not sure whether the river would lead him, but he soon discovered that this was the worst river in his experience. His canoe was wrecked in the upper canyon by Fort George and he and his men were nearly drowned. They patched their canoe and continued, but at the point now called Alexandria, Mackenzie decided he had had enough. Besides being a magnificent river man, he had a poet's intuition: he abandoned the river in the nick of time and went overland to the Bella Coola. A few more miles and he would have passed the point of no return.

Fifteen years later in 1808 a different type of Scot, the stolid, factual Simon Fraser, following in the path of the man he referred to tauntingly in his journal as "Sir A. M. K." (the explorer's jealousy again), passed the point where Mackenzie left the river, and kept on going. Like Mackenzie before him, Fraser also was ignorant of the river's nature and even of what river it was. He believed it was the Columbia, and he had entered it with the specific mission of exploring it to the mouth in order to establish British rights to the entire Columbia region. When he entered the Black Canyon and the waters whirled him, he knew he must go through or perish. The result was the climax of the long story of the fur-trading voyages which began when Étienne Brûlé went up the Ottawa to the Chaudière Falls. Fraser's was the most terrible and wonderful inland voyage in the history of North America.

Tiny in their birch-bark canoes, the voyageurs stared up thousands of feet at the walls of that canyon. The river roared so loud they could not hear each other speak, it twisted so fast they could not prepare themselves for what lay around the next bend. When they watched the walls of the canyon flashing past, they must have realized that no canoe, for that matter no ship hitherto built, had ever travelled for such a length of time at such a speed and survived. They were spun like tops in the whirlpools, and when backwashes swept them ashore, they portaged over cliffs thousands of feet high, for they could not survive if they stayed still – their food was running out – and they did not believe it possible to return. Finally they reached Hell's Gate, which inspired the most celebrated passage in Fraser's journal:

"I have been for a long period in the Rocky Mountains, but have never seen anything like this country. It is so wild I cannot find words to describe it at times. We had to pass where no human being should venture; yet in those places there is a regular pathway impressed, or rather indented on the very rocks by frequent travelling."

This so-called pathway had been made by Indians who had been in the region so long that the village now called Lytton claims to be the oldest permanently settled place in North America. Fraser and his men, their canoes abandoned on the shore, crawled sideways with their packs along the cliff, hanging on to twisted vines "formed like a ladder or the shrouds of a ship." Somehow they got through, and lower down they bought Indian dugouts and so reached the ocean.

It was typical of Simon Fraser that when he reached the delta he was as disappointed as Mackenzie had been when he came to the larger delta on the Beaufort Sea. Whatever else this awful river might be, Fraser knew it was not the Columbia. Not being able to foresee the future, he assumed that his mission was a failure and turned back.

The return journey was in some ways worse than the passage going down, though at least its dangers could no longer surprise them. The Indians turned hostile and bombarded them with rocks which they dropped from the cliffs above. Their supplies were nearly gone, their clothing in rags, their shoes holed and torn, their bodies exhausted, and their minds dazed with hardship and danger. Simon Fraser was not an especially attractive character, but his dogged courage was rock-like, and his powers of leadership must surely have been as great as Mackenzie's. At the moment of their bottom despair, this normally undramatic man made his Scottish and *Canadien* voyageurs join hands and take this oath:

"I solemnly swear before Almighty God that I shall sooner perish than forsake any of our crew during the present voyage."

They got through. On the northern end of Hell's Gate they found their abandoned canoes intact, and those amazing men dragged and paddled them north the way they had come. They reached Fort George in thirty-four days. This last statement should be repeated: Simon Fraser and his party, fighting their way back against that river, reached Fort George in thirty-four days!

While this voyage was taking place, the North West Company's geographer, David Thompson, was on the river which

Fraser had at first believed he was on himself, and three years later Thompson explored the Columbia to its mouth.

Out of Fraser's voyage grew the story of British Columbia, which unfolded so rapidly in the next one hundred and fifty years that British Columbians themselves seem unable to realize how astonishing their advance has been. It took generations for eastern cities like Quebec and Halifax to grow, but Vancouver and the little towns of the lower Fraser Valley leaped up in a moment of time. As late as the First World War, the sole university in the province was little more than an extension department of McGill; today it is larger than McGill and one of the best institutions in the country. Vancouver is now Canada's third city; a century hence it will probably be her first, as the Pacific replaces the Atlantic in human importance.

But progress, not even with the instruments of a growing science behind it, can never change the character of British Columbia's chief river unless they dam it. Should that happen – and it well may if only because of American demands for Canadian water – the world's richest salmon fishery will disappear. At the time I write this, the men who wish to dam the Fraser have been rejected and the river is still itself. So long as it is allowed to remain so, and so long as mountain snows melt, the Fraser will roar and foam and will still be the narrowest and most savage of all the major rivers of this continent.

"Two Solitudes: Thirty-three Years Later"

As the first person to apply Rilke's phrase to Quebec and English Canada, MacLennan was regularly asked for his opinions on how the "two solitudes" regarded one another. This 1978 essay followed the election of the Parti Québécois, which altered the balance of power in Canada and called the country's future into question. As always, MacLennan took the long view:

If Canada holds together, the victory of René Lévesque on November 15, 1976, will possibly be regarded as one of the luckier events in our peculiar history. Lévesque succeeded in doing something no other Canadian politician has ever done. A nation which had always been polarized psychologically is now, thanks to him, polarized politically. He has managed to wake up English Canada to a few realities about this nation of ours. Now, a year later, he is waking up a great many Québécois to what *they* may lose if they continue to hide behind the myths told them in the past by some of their priests and in the present by the Parti Québécois.

History is so ironical she is apt to make cynics out of the few people who take her seriously. Hardly anything planned by politicians, especially revolutionary politicians, ever turns out the way they expected. If I were a horse player, I would wager that Canada will survive, if for no better reason than that none of our politicians has ever been able even to suggest a formula for taking her apart without ruining everyone, including themselves. If the country comes through this present crisis, the old story of Quebec and the rest of us is not going to fall asleep.

What would the newspapers, other media, and the demagogues do without it? But there would be a reasonable chance that Canada will become less schizophrenic than she is now, and if this happens, then some historians in the future will be naming Lévesque as one of her saviours.

I listened to the election results on November 15 in the company of some old French-Canadian friends who are staunch federalists, and we agreed, however reluctantly, that it could have been much worse. . . . It brought some Canadian realities into such an open and naked daylight that not even the ghost of Mackenzie King could ignore them. It proved that the Quebec hierarchy no longer had the power to crush a movement it had appeared to foster, and in the process break the hearts of devout followers who had believed the Church was behind them all the way.

Now, slightly more than a year later, English-Canadian leaders are forced to admit that no nation created out of such divergent traditions and loyalties as ours can be governed satisfactorily by a simple majority vote which, in great issues in the past, has automatically overwhelmed Quebec. The economic prospects and problems are, of course, very grim. The psychological hang-ups are even worse. But as these had been there for decades, like sacs of pus under the skin, many Quebec Anglophones – caught between the upper and nether millstones of Lord Durham's two nations warring in the bosom of a single state – were relieved when finally the sacs burst.

Speaking on a purely personal level, I soon had cause to regret Lévesque's victory. Because of a novel I published thirty-three years ago, I suddenly found myself jerked backward into a period of thought and writing I believed I had put behind me long ago.

A week after the Péquiste victory, a letter arrived from a character in my native province. I had never met him, had never even heard of him, but I noted that his name denoted an Ulster ancestry. This is what he said:

> When the true history of Canada is written, you will be named as the Father of Separation. Everything started from that book you called *Two Solitudes*. I hated it when I

first read it and I hate it worse now. I wonder how you can
sleep at night.

Since then numerous friendly journalists and acquaintances
have been asking me what I think of our present crisis. Why me?
I truly wondered. I am an extremely private person, and what
could I tell them except that all I know about our politics today
is what I read in the papers and hear (though rarely) on the TV.
Still, what did I know? They, too, had come to me because of
that old novel *Two Solitudes*. In this book the most dramatic part
of the action occurs between the autumn of 1917 and the spring
of 1919 – roughly sixty years ago. When we consider what has
happened in the world since then, those sixty years seem longer
than three centuries.

Last fall I read in a Toronto newspaper column that an
unnamed gentleman, identified only as "a Canadian economic
nationalist," had dismissed my book as valueless and out of date
in the year of its publication, which was 1945. Would that the
gentleman were right! If he was thinking solely in economic
terms, he was absolutely right. So were those Victorian historians who used to insist that the reason why Mark Antony
became involved with Cleopatra was to get hold of the Egyptian
wheat crop and use it to pay his troops and bribe the Roman
electorate with free corn. Certainly this was Antony's original
idea. But shortly after he stepped ashore in Alexandria another
factor entered the equation and – as Somerset Maugham once
remarked – there soon grew up between Antony and Cleopatra
something more interesting than an economic situation.

Between Quebec and the rest of Canada there is also something more interesting than an economic situation. And as I live
in Quebec, and am a member of a minority which is gleefully
being instructed by Quebec politicians in what it feels like to be
in a minority – after all, two centuries of experience have given
them plenty of time to get up their homework – I ask you to take
my word for it that *Two Solitudes* is not considered entirely *passé*
in *la belle province*, and for a reason that has always been at the
root of Canada's problem as a nation.

What has divided Canada in the past has not been language,
though certainly language contributed to the division. It has

been the point of view of the élites and rulers on both sides of the linguistic fence.

The collective mind of English Canada, the United States, and only to a slightly lesser degree of England, is pragmatic. As external conditions change, the pragmatist, who can seldom spare the time to see a situation in its entirety, puts the past behind him. He lives in the present and he builds a future he refuses to face until he comes to it.

But in Quebec it was not like this. Until only a few years ago, the education of the French-Canadian élite rested its philosophy on the teachings of St. Thomas Aquinas, who created the most complete and interrelated synthesis in the entire history of learning, and behind him was Aristotle, who had died more than a thousand years before St. Thomas was born. This is one more reason why Quebec refuses to forget her past. About the same time that Henry Ford, that supreme pragmatist, announced *ex cathedra* from Willow Run that "History is the bunk," the famous Canon Groulx was pounding into the heads of his students at l'Université de Montréal the slogan "*Notre maître, le passé.*" It fell upon ears that had been well prepared. Quebec has not forgotten the Conquest. She has not forgotten 1837. She has not forgotten Louis Riel. She has not forgotten and will never forget what was done to her in 1917 by the Anglophone majority. This habit of mind is enshrined in the motto on her crest: *Je me souviens.* (And in this year 1978 that motto will be printed on the licence plates of every car registered in the province.)

Economically, of course, the Quebec of today has hardly a corner left in which Thomas Aquinas could rest his head. It is very different even morally from the society described in the first half of my old novel. The new breed of Québécois is now a city-dweller, and he is doing his best to forget what it used to be like down on the farm when *sa mère* had ten children and was pregnant with the eleventh, and M. *le Curé* was the fountain of all wisdom in the village.

But these external changes have not entirely changed Quebec's ancient attitudes or her inherited emotions. The younger, middle-class products of her belated industrial revolution – Bourassa's crowd, who described themselves as technocrats,

Lévesque's enthusiasts, who think they are planning a political revolution according to the most sophisticated formulas in the revolutionary textbooks – are emotionally still so involved with the past emotions of French Canada that a single word in the wrong place – or in the right place – can trigger them off. In this sense they are correct in calling Quebec a true nation. The tragedy – or the comedy, depending on your point of view – comes from their inability to understand the Anglo-American pragmatic experience, while at the same time the pragmatists are just as incapable of putting themselves into the emotions of a people that loves Pepsi-Cola, fast cars, and Florida vacations, yet can be turned on by the *chansons* of their modern pop singers like Gilles Vigneault, Pauline Julien, and Monique Leyrac. Lévesque has said many times that he can't lose when all those singers and poets who have been conducting a passionately paranoic love affair with their nation are behind him.

I wonder, however, whether this necessarily portends what Lévesque thinks it does.

I am almost entirely of Highland-Scotch ancestry, and like many others who used to call themselves Scotch-Canadians I also have long memories, even what Freud called "memory traces in the subconscious." I am a descendant of enclosed or evicted crofters – at least that's what I suppose my forebears were, though I can't be sure because nearly all the parish records in the Highlands disappeared. But at any rate I have never had any difficulty in understanding the apparent contradictions within the modern, prosperous French-Canadian bourgeois. For I have seen, and so have thousands of others in this land, how quickly some of our stern-faced Scotch-Canadian bankers and business men can turn into entirely different personalities when the pipes play Jacobite music. In 1703 Andrew Fletcher of Saltoun wrote a famous sentence: "Give me the makings of the songs of a nation and I care not who makes its laws." Alas, it wasn't so in Scotland any more than in Poland, Hungary, Czechoslovakia, and a great many other weak nations. Only forty-three years after Fletcher wrote that sentence, historical events in Scotland proved that it was the losers who had made the best songs and the winners who had made the best deals. And which of them chose the better part is still an open question.

To return again to that old novel of mine: I had forgotten it until recent events made me reread it. The title had been used so often by politicians, especially in Quebec, that I had almost come to believe that it was a political novel. I rediscovered that it is nothing of the kind. It is a fairly simple tale of people living together in a region where religious traditions made it impossible for them to know one another. (The idea behind what used to be called the *Entente Cordiale* was simply this: in order to avoid trouble, avoid one another.) The history taught the French-Canadian children was diametrically opposite to the history taught the English-Canadian children. The two did, however, share a common denominator: each was equally false. In the middle, the politicians contrived and the operators operated with great benefit to themselves, and what was visible in Quebec was also visible in the entire nation. To the average Québécois, English Canada was another world. To the average citizen in the Anglophone provinces, Quebec was generally referred to as "The French-Canadian Problem."

Yet Canada in those days was generally a stable society economically – much more so than she is now – because both the French and the English used to be thrifty. The old Hapsburg Empire of Middle Europe was also a stable society economically while it was still a going concern. Some years ago I was much taken by Arthur Lower's comparison of Canada to Austria-Hungary. In Middle Europe there was a confederation of various ethnic groups dominated politically, and to a lesser extent economically, by the Teutons. The various lesser components of the Empire spoke different languages and were diligently taught to detest one another; the only area in which they shared an emotional agreement was a mutual detestation of the Teutonic majority. Two religions – Roman Catholic on one side, Greek Orthodox on the other – had collectively hated one another for more than one thousand years. So I used to ask myself, as Arthur Lower asked himself, whether Canada was anything more than a latter-day version of this.

Under the surface the resemblances are not really close. In Canada we live in what still is a new world. No Mongols or Turks ever invaded our territories and butchered or enslaved our ancestors. No archdukes supported their luxurious living by selling able-bodied young men as soldiers to foreign armies. True, the federal government in 1917 imposed conscription on Quebec, and it is futile to deny that English Canada, and especially the Conservative Party, has been paying for that ever since. But not even our two conscription crises put us in the same class as the succession states of the Holy Roman Empire. We are still adolescents here, and while this may be embarrassing to our *amour propre*, hopefully it has also some advantages. The hatreds of adults are usually implacable (as that prime American adolescent, Woodrow Wilson, discovered at Versailles in 1919), but quarrels between adolescents can often turn into friendship after a good squabble.

There is evidence that something of that sort is happening in Quebec right now. If Canada is in a state of genuine hostility, why is it that on a person-to-person basis the Francophones and Anglophones of Quebec have never been so cordial to one another as they are now? One reason is that at long last most Quebec Anglophones are not only learning French, but are associating so much more with their *concitoyens* that they have a chance to speak it naturally.

There seems to me more to it even than this. In the Coliseum in Quebec City – not too far from the provincial assembly where reigns at present that curious government of ex-professors, ex-journalists, ex-psychiatrists, ex-priests, and *prêtres manquées* – why there, only a few weeks ago, did a crowd of six thousand Québécois roar their support for junior Team Canada against the Soviets, although there wasn't a single Québécois on the line-up? . . . But at any rate, this crisis of ours, which certainly is serious – the ridiculous can often be serious – has few of the earmarks of crisis as they understand the word in Europe and the Middle East.

I am no sage and no political scientist and I profoundly mistrust abstractions when they are applied either to human beings or to what Dr. Camille Laurin calls *la collectivité*. One of the more unedifying characteristics of the fanatical nationalist is that he has no sense of humour whatever. Thank God there is still a lot of that commodity in modern Quebec. A popular nickname for Dr. Laurin is *la mère supérieure*, probably because of his priestly gestures and the holy forbearance of his manner when he psychoanalyses *la collectivité* in public. As you all know, the surname of René Lévesque means "bishop," and last spring a French-Canadian student said to me with a grin, "*Plus ça change, plus c'est la même chose; en dépit de la victoire du Parti Québécois, il est encore impossible d'échapper des évêques.*"

No, I prefer human beings to abstractions about them, especially in a country like Canada where people have only recently begun to think seriously about what this whole country amounts to. It is to many of these abstractions that we owe our present state of confusion; perhaps a better word for it would be paralysis. It is because of abstractions that English-Canadian and French-Canadian nationalisms don't speak the same language. And once again it might behoove even a pragmatist to look back into the past and understand why.

Modern nationalism is a nineteenth-century phenomenon, and it arose as a defence mechanism against the exploitation of unorganized ethnic groups by highly organized imperial powers like the France of Louis XIV and Napoleon, the Austria of a long succession of Emperors, the Russia of a variety of Tsars. In our century it spread into Asia and Africa and over the years it became mixed up with nineteenth-century ideologies like socialism, communism, and anarchism. Within our own memory, socialism fused with nationalism to produce the tyrannies of Mussolini and Hitler. Whenever nationalism is elevated to the status of a lay religion, it produces fanatical loyalties which in turn produce fanatical hatreds. And on this word "loyalty" I would like to turn back to the Canada in which I was born – specifically to the Quebec of the middle Depression years.

Like most Anglophones living in Quebec who were not born there (and at present these may account for as much as half of the English-speaking minority), I came to Montreal because it was the only place I could find a job. The year was 1935, the job was schoolteaching, the pay was $1,000 a year. Ten years later it had risen to $1,925 a year after taxes. I was fairly typical of most young Anglophone Quebeckers in those years. I knew hardly anyone who had what might be called "money." "Security" was a word which had vanished from the vocabulary of everyone I knew. Yet even then in Francophone Quebec the myth persisted that the English were rich and the French were hewers of wood and drawers of water.

I had expected to learn French within a few years – as I already had German – but I soon discovered, as did so many others, how hard it was for an adult Anglophone to begin learning French in Quebec. I was married and had to work ten to twelve hours a day. . . . The worst difficulty was that the French people we met all spoke perfect or almost perfect English. However, this did not excuse the native-born Anglophone Quebeckers from learning French (many did, actually) because a better school system would have made it obligatory. But once again that ghastly division made by the rival religions which isolated the two ethnic groups from one another. In Montreal the majority of perfectly bilingual Anglophones lived in the working-class districts, and though they went to English schools, they played and fought in the streets with their French neighbours.

. . . The Montreal I first saw in 1935 had, so far as I knew, no counterpart anywhere on earth. It was the visible replica of the Canada of years ago. Though its human atmosphere was much more personal than it is now, there was something here that was unnatural, and what was unnatural was what was unnatural in the nation itself. Here the two cultures of Canada, without even planning it, had evidently decided that the best way to coexist was to ignore the existence of one another. The Francophones said the Anglos were too arrogant to make friends with them. The Anglophones said the French clergy forbade their people to make friends with the heretics. But hardly anyone said these things in the presence of the other group. Montreal was perhaps the politest city in the world then.

The absurdity of this situation was visible to everyone except the natives. It was even visible geographically. The "British Empire" extended west and northwest from Guy Street to the rich farmland of Montreal Island. . . . The "French Fact" began at Bleury Street and extended indefinitely east and northeast, embracing in the process one of the most gifted Jewish communities in North America. Between these two distinct territories, for that is what they were, was a common ground, a kind of miniature Belgium, along the two-mile stretch of Ste. Catherine Street, where the two so-called founding races of Canada encountered each other in small shops owned by French Canadians and Jews and in four large department stores owned by Anglophone companies, two of them based in Toronto.

On the steep streets that ran up the slope of Mount Royal between University Street and Côte des Neiges were the massive mansions, each one with its conservatory, owned by the descendants of the railway builders, the bankers, the brewers, and the merchants of the nineteenth century, who still controlled more money power than could be found in any other part of Canada. Most, though not all, of them were Anglophones.

. . . This was the Montreal of only yesterday, and one quickly learned to accept that its loyalties were totally divided. It is humiliating to remember that until the end of the Hitler War the really passionate loyalties felt in Canada had all been born in Europe and had emigrated here with the various waves of settlement. . . . Arthur Lower was accurate when he wrote that in those days Ottawa was little more than a centre of administration. Canada's spiritual capitals were in Rome and London, and had it not been for the restraining influence of the Vatican, the conscription crises of 1917 and 1944 would have rived this country apart.

And so I come to the Hitler War, when once again "two race-legends woke remembering ancient loyalties and ancient enmities." It was only then that I understood just how traumatically shocked French Canada had been by the imposition of conscription in 1917. It was then that my conception of *Two Solitudes* emerged.

Its genesis came to me in a dream in which I saw a tall, angular blond man arguing with a stocky darker man. They were shouting at each other more in frustration than in hatred, and in the dream a voice suddenly said, "Don't you see it? They're both deaf."

It was the Hitler War which quite literally abolished the Canada of the nineteenth century. By the time it was over, loyalty to Britain had become meaningless because the Empire had gone into liquidation. It was then, though half-heartedly, that English Canada at least began to accept that now this nation was alone and would have to grow up whether she wanted to or not.

It was an idea that took a long time to percolate. So far as the English-French relationship was concerned, the 1950s were lost years. . . . English Canada completely forgot about Quebec and plunged into the huge commercial boom without even realizing that she was now in process of making herself a commercial colony of multi-national conglomerates, and was developing an enormously high standard of living by selling her natural resources.

Quebec? With Duplessis in the saddle, the tycoons thought they had nothing to worry about. He gave them what they wanted and they gave him what he wanted. But underneath the deceptively calm surface an enormous change, a truly revolutionary change, had at last occurred in Quebec. For the first time in her history she developed a large, affluent, ambitious, educated middle class. And if Marx was ever right about anything, he was right when he said that it is from a rising middle class that revolutions come.

At the time I was writing *Two Solitudes*, another writer was also busy in Montreal. This was Gabrielle Roy and she, like myself, had come from another province – from the St. Boniface settlement in Manitoba. With intuitive clairvoyance, Gabrielle Roy put much of the future character of Quebec into a single book, *Bonheur d'Occasion*. . . . In the character of Jean Lévesque, who saw in the war boom a chance finally to make a break with a poverty-ridden past, this novel not only prophesied the rise of the ambitious French-Canadian man of affairs with his house in Outremont or Westmount, his Cadillac, his cottage in the Laurentians, and his vacation in Florida; it also foresaw in the character of Emmanuel Letourneau the thoughtful, independent, kindly, sceptical Québécois of the Silent Revolution.

If only by implication, it forecast in the deprived characters of the Saint-Henri slum the violent gangsters of today and the political terrorists of a few years ago, who very easily may turn to terrorism again in the near future.

And finally, by quietly indicating that the Church could no longer give Quebec comfort and security, but that education might give it more than that, this book, seeing through a glass darkly, made it easier to understand the mentality of the Parti Québécois.

But Gabrielle Roy did not foresee – nobody did then – that within little more than a decade the authority of the Quebec Catholic Church would suddenly collapse. This collapse resulted directly, and inevitably, in the rise of the separatist movement.

Although Quebec's lower clergy had always been nationalistic, many of its members resentful even of the Irish Catholics who spoke English, the Quebec hierarchy had always looked to the Vatican, and in all previous political crises produced by nationalistic passions, the hierarchy had come down on the side of Confederation, not because it loved the English, but because its highly intelligent *monseigneurs* and bishops understood very well that nationalism can very quickly become a religion which by its very nature will be hostile to a universal Catholic Church governed ultimately by the Vatican. And this is exactly what happened at the end of the 1950s after French-Canadian intellectuals travelled widely in France, Algeria, and indeed all over the world.

But no individual, much less a large percentage of an ethnic population, can abandon a religion as strong as Catholicism without feeling a terrible loss. It is therefore easy to see how the separatist movement, without its leaders consciously realizing it, attempted to convert the old clerical pattern into politics:

• The young élite would replace the old priests as the guiding authority of the people;

• The concept of life as a pilgrim's progress to the heavenly kingdom imperceptibly shifted into the belief that the Christian heaven could be replaced by the political independence of Quebec;

• Satan, previously identified with materialism, reappeared to the fanatical young nationalist in the person of Quebec federalists who warn them of the economic consequences that would follow the fracture of the Canadian nation.

Such is the situation we find ourselves in today, and of course it is in a state of constant transition. For a variety of reasons, English Canada has been forced to sit on the sidelines while the contest for the nation's future is being fought by French Canadians – Pierre Trudeau and his federalists against René Lévesque and his separatists.

Politics are nearly always a generation or two behind realities, and I would guess that whatever final resolution we come to in Canada may well be determined by events and pressures outside the country. How long will the oil last? How long can the United States and our own federal government continue printing paper money and putting the entire economy into hock to the Arabs? How long before many of us conclude that nobody, and no nation, is today the master of his own destiny, and try to live with it? How long before enough people accept that fast solutions never work?

In conclusion I would like to quote a few sentences written long ago by Montaigne – sentences I would like to see framed on the wall of every politician in the world:

> Le monde est inepte à se guérir. Il est si impatient de ce qui le presse, qu'il ne vise que s'en défaire, sans regarder à quel prix. Le bien ne succède pas nécessairement au mal. Un autre mal lui peut succéder, et pire.

Voices in Time

Published in 1980, Voices in Time *is set in the post-Orwellian future. In 2039 an old man named John Wellfleet is contacted by André Gervais, who is trying to put together a picture of life before* The Destructions. *A cache of papers has been discovered telling some of Wellfleet's story and that of his family. Many of the papers deal with his cousin Timothy, born in 1938 and raised while his father was fighting with the army in Europe. Here in Chapter 8 John Wellfleet tells Timothy's story:*

I have told you how it was for him when he was a child and quite a lot about him when he was at the height of his television career. André was informed by the Diagram that the crack-up occurred when I was in my late twenties. But did it? My own idea is that it began with Timothy's crowd, and Timothy was twenty years older than me. His age group was greatly disliked by ours, especially after they began copying the way we dressed and poached on our girls. We called them "the thirty-year-olders." I think now that we were as unfair to them as they were to the generation above them. We simply did not understand how much baloney had been jammed down their throats. As Timothy put it, "Instant marriage, instant family, instant coffee, instant jobs, and a trained consumer for the rest of your life." The programming of their ideas was changed as smoothly as the gears in the automatic transmissions of the automobiles of the time. No wonder poor old Timothy raved so frantically against the System. And with this clumsy introduction, I must ask you to bear with a short interlude while I take you back to what

Timothy called "Those stone-dead years when I was doing my best to be like everyone else."

Before leaving school, in a craving to please his father and make him his friend, Timothy decided that he wanted to go to the Royal Military College instead of to a regular university. Nothing he ever did made his father so happy. Colonel Wellfleet had himself been an RMC man; so had his own father, one of his brothers, and two of his uncles in that older time when RMC was the prime stamping-ground of the Anglophone establishment, its traditions and even its uniform straight out of nineteenth-century Sandhurst, most of its instructors burly, mustachioed ex-sergeants of famous English Guards regiments. Timothy spent two years there.

At times he could be fair even to people he disliked, and he admitted that the RMC he attended was not particularly exclusive, that the cadets really did come from what the Commandant called "every walk of life," and that the navy and the air force were there in addition to the army. But the very thought of anyone like Timothy in a military college ridicules itself.

When his third year lapsed around he told his father that all he had learned at RMC was to keep a tidy room and a straight back. Later on it mortified him to know that the sergeants had trained his reflexes so thoroughly that he could never get over the habit of sitting and standing like a soldier.

When he told his father he intended to drop out of RMC he expected an explosion, but Colonel Wellfleet merely seemed lonely and sad. What was the matter with RMC – had it fallen off? Timothy said there was nothing the matter with it if you liked the army.

"But you've known all along that RMC doesn't commit you to a military career. It's a training for almost anything."

"Oh sure, it's a training all right. Look at my shoulders."

His father rubbed his chin, glanced at his watch, and picked up the phone.

"I'm going to have a word with your Commandant. He and I did a spell in Staff College in the early days of the war."

Timothy sat still and erect during the conversation that followed over the telephone. Finally his father nodded and said, "Thanks, Cuffy, for being so frank with me. Next time you're in

town give me a buzz and we'll have lunch and a splash together."
He hung up, relit his pipe, puffed on it thoughtfully, and
between puffs went into a soliloquy.

The Commandant had agreed that RMC was not the right
place for the boy. Timothy had made no trouble, in fact he had
put out a real effort, but he just wasn't the type. A long puff and
a cloud of fragrant smoke from the imported Erinmore.

"I'd hoped it wouldn't come to this," the Colonel said finally,
"but I'm afraid it has. You've become a problem."

A bank? No, that would never suit him. Another puff. What
about investments? A long pause.

"From your expression I gather you're against investments,
but you never know in advance about investments. I suggest
that you take an aptitude test. Sometimes the most unlikely
people turn out to be good at investments. I knew a man who
wasted ten years of his life trying to be a painter. It took him all
that long to find out he had no talent. Then he took an aptitude
test and the test pointed to investments. Do you know what?
That man astonished everyone, including himself. Inside five
years he was a millionaire."

"Where is he now?"

"Dead, I'm sorry to say. As a matter of fact he committed
suicide. Nobody ever understood why. He seemed to have a
happy family. Nice wife and two splendid young sons. Queer
things happen these days."

"Father," said Timothy, "I don't think I want to go into investments."

His father sighed. "Something tells me you're right."

The Colonel continued to think aloud. Insurance? He shook
his head. Real estate? There was a strong gambling element
there and it could be stimulating but – "No, you haven't the
instinct. I've seen you play cards. Any ideas of your own?"

"I'd been thinking of becoming a teacher."

"The last refuge of the undecided," said the Colonel. Then
once more he surprised Timothy. "But hold on a moment.
There might be a great deal in that idea. One of the most
successful men this city ever knew began as a schoolmaster and
he taught tough subjects – Latin and Greek. He told my father
something that made a great impression on me. Six years with

schoolboys had taught him two priceless lessons, he said. First, he always knew when someone was lying. Secondly, he discovered that boys are just like grown men most of the time and that it was from boys that he learned what most people really want. So there you have two things – to recognize when people are lying and to know what they really want – especially if they're ashamed of what they want." The Colonel was warming to the idea. "And here's another consideration. These days teachers are being paid much more than they used to be paid. More than most of them are worth, in my opinion. But if that's what you want, give it a crack." A longer pause. "But of course you know yourself there's another problem here. You'll have to go to a university first. That will mean you've already wasted two years." He shrugged. "Oh well, what difference need that make? I lost more than five years in the war."

So the Colonel staked his son and Timothy enrolled for joint honours in Sociology and Political Science, which were prestige subjects in those days. He acquainted himself with a variety of girls, most of them of his own social class, and in his final year he fixed on a plump, rosy-cheeked blonde called Enid. Subsequently he found it "dismally funny the kind of ethics we used to have." Apparently the young people of his class were frank with each other verbally, if frank in few other ways. "I was too dumb then to know that Enid was even dumber. She had the hang-up, all right. She'd love to sleep with me – *sleep*, for God's sake! – but only if we first announced our engagement. So like a bloody fool I got publicly engaged for no better reason than that I was crazy for a regular lay."

But Timothy's father was delighted, because Enid's parents were old family friends. Marriage made it essential for Timothy to get a job even though his father was happy to stake the happy couple, but Greg Wellfleet was looking toward the future. Toward grandchildren and the future of his grandchildren. He therefore told Timothy that he must forget all about schoolteaching and that it was too bad he'd wasted all that time with Sociology and Political Science when he might have been studying Commerce. Once again he invited Timothy into his library and this time he didn't tell him he was a problem. He said he had the solution, but he took a long time to get around to saying what it was.

"Then it was that at last I found myself watching Father with a sad wonder. Then it was that I understood what had happened to him. I felt a great pity for Father. He no longer could recognize the world he was living in. He had become an exile in it. Instead of renewing his youth, he had become a well-heeled hangover from an age that had blown itself out. That young wife of his had only accelerated his aging. She was even blinder than he to the real world. I found myself thinking even then – long before I met Esther – what would he have been like if he had possessed the kind of courage to defy the stuffed shirts he had grown up with and marry some lusty immigrant girl who might have laid to rest that mighty animal in his loins and heart? You poor old bastard, I thought, while he was planning my future. The only time you were free to be yourself was in the war. You brave, sad, gallant man. Harnessed to a youthful replica of the poison that began to kill you when you were only twenty-two. Why did you *refuse* to understand me? Now your wealth is just another burden for your tired, frustrated shoulders to carry. I know a poet who lives with a long succession of girls and has no shame at all. He lets them support him. People swarm after him for his autograph. But you do have honour, and the only autograph anyone wants from you is your signature at the bottom of a cheque. You brave, sad man. So old before your time when your body and soul yearn to be young. Helping to liberate Holland didn't liberate you after all, for you came home to that bitch of a mother of mine and then you must have gone into a panic. Now there's no place for you in a world a-borning because it won't offer a man like you even a corner of itself to weep in. So here you are, a proved hero, searching the maps and travel agencies for some tropical island where you can escape the taxes and fence yourself in with others as rich and hopeless as yourself.

"As though I had been reading his thoughts, Father suddenly said, 'Your stepmother and I have been thinking of settling in Nassau.' So I said, 'Don't do it.' He said, 'Why not?' and looked at me hard. 'If you go there,' I said, 'the blacks will spit on your shadow when you pass.' And he said, 'I've nothing against the blacks. Why would they do that?' Then he turned away from me and said, 'I think I've found the solution for your problem.'"

The solution turned out to be an advertising agency which

one of the Colonel's wartime friends, in fact his Adjutant, had inherited from his own father, who had also been a previous colonel of the regiment. So Timothy started to work in a business house which was respected, self-respecting, and dignified. Mr. Campbell was an obstinate man of high character who believed, and told Timothy at their first meeting, what while it was legitimate for an advertising man to dramatize the products he promoted, he must be as careful of the long-time truth as the editor of a first-class responsible newspaper.

"All the ads that's fit to print?" Timothy suggested.

Mr. Campbell gave him a stern glance to indicate that he did not appreciate flippant young men.

Looking back, Timothy marvelled that Mr. Campbell lasted as long as he did, for "His ethics were frozen in the prewar days when Canada was a dull and on the whole honest country with a dollar worth a hundred cents instead of twenty-five and when it was fatal to oversell anything from a detergent to a politician." When Mr. Campbell reached the end of his road, a bright young account executive smilingly described him as a time-adjustment casualty.

"So was the whole country a time-adjustment casualty, for what happened to it was as swift as a dream-sequence. For twenty years our dreaming capitalists had been selling out their companies to huge American combines which were wide-awake; or rather, the combines had been suavely and systematically engrossing them just as they had engrossed the smaller businesses in their own countries. One of them finally engrossed us. Mr. Campbell was retired with a generous block of the company stock, we became known as Campbell of Canada, Ltd., and just how limited we were we soon found out.

"Up from Madison Avenue came a thirty-five-year-old product of Phillips Andover and the Harvard Business School to modernize and reorganize us. His name was Melvin K. Goodwillie and it would have been hard to find a friendlier fellow. The moment he met me he said 'Hi!' and immediately called us all by our first names, including men twenty years older than himself. Soon he was sending us down in relays to New York to take what he called immersion programs in techniques which were more or less new to us, and there we met men as alert and friendly as Goodwillie himself, including the boss of the whole multinational whose name was Taylor W. Truscott. He also called us by our first names at first sight – silver hair with natural waves in it, a fast smile, a thin mouth, and pale blue eyes so alert to opportunity they could see around corners."

Mr. Truscott's message was that he welcomed this opportunity to expand into Canada because there the advertising industry still retained a dignified image, "and we intend to keep it that way."

In order to dignify the image still further, Goodwillie was ordered to move the agency into the most prestigious (according to Timothy, one of Goodwillie's favourite words) tower in the city. In those days, as well I remember, you could hardly go anywhere without hearing some kind of music, and on the floors where the typists worked, piped-in music whispered softly from nine till five. On the floors where the account executives worked, the carpeting went from wall to wall and the windows from floor to ceiling "so that we could get the right perspective by looking down like Gullivers from thirty-eight floors onto the Lilliputian consumers swarming below." Silk screens depicting rural and mountain scenery in Canada adorned the walls and Goodwillie announced a poetry award of a thousand dollars for annual competition. Finally came the day when Goodwillie buzzed Timothy to come to the executive suite to witness the installation of what he called his *pièce de résistance*. He was just beginning a crash program in learning French.

Timothy arrived to see four husky French Canadians with the shoulders of ancient *voyageurs* manhandling into the suite the biggest Quebec armoire he had ever seen in his life.

Goodwillie beamed. "Genuine seventeenth century," he said.

The wood looked slightly dry-rotted, and when Timothy touched it and examined it closely he realized that it had been deliberately and carefully scorched and then stained.

"Mel," he said, "where did you find this eleven-dollar bill?"

Goodwillie laughed. "No hard feelings, man, but you guys don't even know your own town. You've lived here all your life and you never knew there's a business on Craig Street that manufactures antiques to order. This piece is perfect Louis Quatorze."

The next day Goodwillie summoned Timothy once more. "I just thought you'd like to see it operational. Just watch."

He pressed a button on the left side of the antique and out swung a tray bearing iced Coca-Cola, Seven-Up, two tins of tomato juice, six uniform glasses, and a bottle opener.

"*Pour l'heure du cocktail*. I had a small refrigerator installed inside of it. From now on, we hold our business luncheons in the executive suite." Goodwillie grinned. "Of course, this tray is for abstainers. You always have to watch out for them. More than one account's been lost by offering a drink to a dry." Pressing a button on the right side he said, "This is for real." Out swung a much larger tray bearing gin, vodka, Scotch, rye, and mixed martinis, also soda and tonic waters, eight glasses of varying shapes and sizes, and another bottle opener.

"*Les apéritifs*," said Goodwillie.

In those days Timothy wrote that Goodwillie wore Brooks Brothers pink on social occasions and nothing but charcoal black, thin ties, white shirts, and gold cufflinks when he was on the job. He also sported a crew cut. A few years later he was wearing unmatched jackets and pants, enormous ties, bushy sideburns, long hair carefully tailored, and a goatee "that looked Christawful on Goodwillie because he didn't have the right face for it."

But that Goodwillie was smart Timothy never doubted. Under his leadership Campbell of Canada boomed as it never had before. What most intrigued Timothy was that Goodwillie was sincere. When he described himself as "really dedicated to this country," he meant it. When he said, as he often did, that he had taken Thomas Jefferson for his model in life, he meant it. And when he said that Timothy's work for the agency was right on, he meant that, too.

"And what a thought *that* was to carry around. And what did it say about my character that Mr. Campbell had never trusted me while Goodwillie kept telling me I was by far the best idea-man in the whole outfit."

Glowing reports of Timothy's work went down to New York, Goodwillie explaining that in Timothy the company had acquired just what it most wanted, a smart native with a natural instinct for the industry who knew how to readjust the usual

Madison Avenue presentations so that they had a genuine Canadian look.

"That's one thing we've learned," Goodwillie said, "that the British never learned. You must never give a guy the idea you're invading his territory. The British never thought about this and that explains why they lost their empire."

Besides John and Timothy Wellfleet the novel's third central character is Conrad Dehmel, who becomes Timothy's stepfather. Born in Germany in 1910, Dehmel is a decent individual caught up in the whole people's decline into the "barbarism" spoken of in Hugh MacLennan's thesis. One telling scene Conrad remembers from his early life is at the end of 1918:

Grandfather lived long enough to see the soldiers marching home in good order after their defeat and I was standing beside him on the sidewalk with the silent people watching. Now you must understand that Freiburg was always a quiet city, a gracious city close to France and Switzerland, with no heavy industry or conflicts between capital and labour. It was the only place I knew and for me it was the centre of the world. The soldiers marched in their worn, patched, and muddy uniforms and broken boots and the crowd had pity for them. But suddenly a man in the rear began to shout, "Nein! Nein! Nein! – Feige!" I felt a shiver pass through the crowd and this was ugly, for many of these watching people had lost sons and husbands and lovers and these returning, beaten soldiers at least were still alive, but to call them cowards was shameful. The man in the rear continued his shouting and I looked at him and his face was crazed. He was shaking his fist at the soldiers and a few in the crowd were with him. I heard a woman say, "He had four sons and they were all killed." But when I looked at Grandfather, and heard the murmur increasing in the crowd, his face frightened me. It was not merely that his face was emaciated with hunger but that the last dregs of hope had been drained out of it.

"These people will obey orders again," I heard him mutter. "When the orders are given, yes, they will obey them again. They have learned nothing and they will forget nothing."

Born the son of a naval officer, Conrad becomes a scholar and pursues his historical studies in England. Despite the warnings of his Jewish lover, Hanna Erlich, he returns to a Germany where the Nazi Party is ascendant:

Berlin was hard and naked under a full moon and there were few people on the streets near his hotel. Suddenly he heard loud voices and just ahead of him some big men in brown shirts and breeches were erupting onto the sidewalk from an underground rathskeller. They were all in early middle age, thick through the chest and hips, and the bellies of three of them bulged out over their belts. He smelled stale beer and they stared at him with stupid and automatic hostility as he passed. The original wave of the movement, he thought, the first of the bully boys, the beefsteaks brown outside and red inside. Suddenly he was seeing history instead of reading about it. Smelling it, too. Unseen behind these goons would be the young ones coming up, lean, hard, cold, and trained.

The hotel lobby was empty except for the night porter. Conrad said good night and asked for his key. Only then did he notice behind the desk a coloured photograph of the Leader and under it was printed a jingle:

> Trittst du als Deutscher hier hinein
> Soll stets dein Gruss Heil Hitler sein.

The porter was bigger than any one of the Brown Shirts he had passed on his way here: a brutal body, an ex-bouncer for sure, in the last war probably a corporal and now a *Blockwart*. He must have weighed at least 110 kilograms and Conrad took in the beetling eyebrows, the thick-fleshed face creased into a permanent scowl, the square moustache, the shaven head the colour of cement with a few veins showing living between the skin and the bone. A single spike of pepper-and-salt hair jutted up from his scalp just over the centre of the forehead. With the key in his hand he stared at Conrad.

"Heil Hitler!" he barked.

"Danke, gute Nacht."

The porter's mouth opened so wide that Conrad saw its red roof. His thick thumb jerked backwards over his shoulder in the direction of the Leader's picture and he bellowed, "Heil Hitler!"

Conrad looked back at him levelly, but he felt the fear of the civilized man in the presence of the barbarian. Before Hitler had taken charge, it would have been inconceivable that a man like this porter could have talked like this to a gentleman. But Conrad was also his father's son. I, who had no father I ever knew, could I ever have responded to a man like this as he did?

"You will speak to me properly," Conrad said.

The porter stared at him.

"You are insolent," Conrad said. "I have just returned from London. I have not been in Germany for a long time. What's the matter with you?"

The porter looked at him and laughed sneeringly. "Your passport!"

"I presented my passport when I registered. I left it in my room."

The porter bent over the register and Conrad watched his thumb travel backward over the list of guests and finally stop. Then he looked up with a smile and the smile was not pleasant.

"Sie sind Herr Dehmel?"

"Herr Doktor Dehmel."

"A German name and a German passport. Heil Hitler!"

They looked at each other and Conrad shrugged. "If you insist."

"Then say it."

"Adolf Hitler is the Chancellor of Germany. Didn't you know that? Now, give me the key."

The porter looked at him dumbly and handed the key over. Conrad went to the elevator cage, pulled open the folding metal door, went inside, closed it, and creaked slowly up to the third floor. He was unnerved because he had felt such a useless fury against the man, and when he rose and turned on the light he took his diary out of his suitcase and sat down at the little table. This is what he wrote:

"Hanna was right and I was blind. I have come home to the unthinkable. You can smell the fear and the rottenness. It reeks like the smell of stale boiled cabbage in a slum. It is unthinkable to know that it is dangerous to be writing these words. Hanna was right again. I knew more than I know now about the reality of history when I was a child and Father came home after the great battle. Now history has stepped out of the books and documents and is looking me over. I can smell her breath but I can't read what's in her eyes. I'm afraid of her. I'm afraid of myself. I'm afraid she will make me know I'm a coward."

Conrad Dehmel's nephew, John Wellfleet, recalls the later collapse of civilization, preceded by the Great Fear:

Some time ago I tried to write about the Great Fear, but I don't think I was successful in describing it. What I wrote was true so far as it went, but what were the actual facts?

Right up to the beginning of the Fear, the Bureaucracy continued to smile at us. Their computers computed us, their pollsters polled us, their con men conned us. They even conned themselves. Behind them moved in the shadows those faceless men who juggled what they called the world's economy. Slowly, we came to realize that the true power was seldom in the hands of our governments, but there was always plenty of beer and sex, the stadiums were crowded, and the action spilled out into the living-rooms of everyone with a television set, which in my country meant about ninety per cent of the population. The Deer Park of the old French king had become democratized and it was at least more salubrious than the original one, for most of us washed and didn't have to use civet to drown our body odours. Decadent? We were constantly called so. Yet I'm reasonably sure that it wasn't decadence that brought on the Great Fear.

About ten years after Uncle Conrad's death, whole peoples in what the journalists called the Third World began to erupt. We saw them on our screens, mobs as large as a million or more, packed body to body like swarming insects, some of them blasting off with the guns our businessmen had sold to their former chiefs. We knew nothing about these people, but anyone could see they were screaming support for the usual Saviour who was promising them a new life. All this would not have mattered to us if they weren't sitting on top of an ocean of oil. Without oil our System could no longer continue as a System. So naturally their Saviours thought they had us by the balls.

They pretty well did. Soon our money went out of control.

People who had laboured for years when money was worth something now found themselves desperate. A murmur circled the world multiplied by hundreds of millions of murmurs – "What is going to happen to me? What can I do?" All we could think of doing was to blame the politicians we ourselves had elected. Now that it was clear to us that our leaders were as helpless as ourselves, we felt we were living in a vacuum and it was in the vacuum that the Great Fear was spawned.

Nature, I was told in school, abhors a vacuum. Soon a handful of unknown individuals silently moved into it. They had taken a hard look at our bureaucracies and had decided they would be gutless because for years we had insisted that they be gutless. These operators began a new kind of terrorism that made our old-fashioned kidnappers, skyjackers, and bombers look like bush-leaguers. It was obvious that they were highly educated, because no ignorant person could have done what they did.

The first cell built and planted a bomb in a great city and demanded an enormous ransom in gold and diamonds. They gave the Bureaucracy a time limit of only twenty-four hours to pay up. If the Bureaucracy refused, they said the bomb would be exploded by remote control, the city destroyed, and perhaps a million people would be killed. The communiqué issued by this cell was so precise in its scientific details that the experts knew they weren't the usual run of kooks. Later, when the bomb was found and disarmed, it turned out to be exactly as the communiqué had described it.

A half-hour before the ultimatum expired, the Bureaucracy surrendered. Its front man came onto the screens and informed the world that the crisis was over, but this time he was too scared and shaken to smile at us. I happened to be in Paris at the time, sitting with a girlfriend in a brasserie and looking at the screen. The French people were tense and silent, some of them were white-faced, and the atmosphere in the little brasserie was acid with fear. The front man's speech was translated into French, but what interested me most was his face. He looked like an ordinary, well-intentioned man who had just discovered that the ground on which he thought he had stood all his life had vanished from under his feet. All I can remember of his speech is something like this: "While it is intolerable, and in the future must not be tolerated, for a great civilization to be blackmailed in this fashion, the facts speak for themselves. We were given no time to track these people down. We were presented with a brutal choice between gold and diamonds and the lives of a million people. What else should we have done?"

Most of us agreed that there was nothing else they should have done.

During the next year there were bomb blackmails in five more metros and only in the fifth did a bureaucracy refuse to surrender. The bomb exploded and killed half a million people. The bureaucracy that had defied the terrorists was execrated and forced to resign. Then we were all on the roller coaster. Money did not merely decline, it collapsed, and what we called the Western world went into hysteria. This was the climax of the Great Fear.

God knows my friends and I had despised the Smiling Bureaucracy. To jeer at our so-called rulers was part of what we called our Life Style, but never would we elect a bureaucracy that would compel us to change our ways. As I said to André soon after I met him, who will stop the music when everyone is having a ball?

But there were others who thought differently; there were millions of others who thought very differently. Suddenly people like us discovered that we had become targets. Those unknown millions we had dismissed as red-necks felt against us a rage deeper than anything they had felt against the bombers. Furious voices spewed out hatred and loathing against my whole generation. We were the spoiled brats who had been responsible for all their woes. We were the ones who had destroyed their authority over their children and foisted our own laziness and sensuality onto everyone else. We were the ones who had insisted on abolishing capital punishment, had sneered at the police, had sympathized with the murderer and not with his victim, had pretended that crime is the fault of society as a whole and not of the criminal.

They turned with especial fury against our women and some of them bellowed from street corners that they were all whores. Their hatred was soul-shrivelling. These people who roared for law and order – and they craved order far more than they craved law – now took to bombs and guns themselves. Their first target was the Smiling Bureaucracy, which had ceased smiling for some time now. Even in my own small nation two cabinet ministers were assassinated. They also went berserk against others – against the men who had made millions by saturating us with sex magazines; against the millionaire kings of the rock music; against actresses who had become sex symbols. Some of them were beaten up. A girl who had been advertised as "The most luscious sexboat in the world" was found in her New York apartment with her throat cut. I met a man who claimed to have known her and he told me the whole thing was crazy. She was just an ordinary girl of humble parentage who had been conned into the act by some agents who had pocketed about ninety per cent of the profits.

Though at the time I did not understand it, I know now that this was no ordinary political revolution. It was an upboiling of subterranean wrath that had been seething for years. Against this fury the Smiling Bureaucracy was helpless and was swept into the discard, to be replaced by what I have called the Second Bureaucracy. This was a coalition of several so-called governments and after a summit meeting of its front men it was given international powers. It cracked down everywhere. Millions of private homes were searched, hundreds of thousands were thrown into jails without trial, and the masses applauded. When two of the blackmailing cells were caught, the authorities announced that they were composed entirely of intellectuals. They were publicly executed. These executions did not happen in my country, but we saw them on our screens.

I could not believe that what was happening was real, neither could my friends. One day Joanne and I were walking hand in hand in the city and she was wearing slacks. She was so graceful in them, they outlined her exquisite little figure so precisely, that it was a joy merely to look at her. Suddenly a police siren screamed, a car slammed to a stop beside us, two cops jumped out and grabbed Joanne. When she struggled, one of them slapped her face so hard he broke her glasses and without them she was half blind. When I tried to help her, the other cop back-elbowed me, cracked my septum, and knocked me rolling. By the time I got to my feet with my nose gouting blood, they were driving off with Joanne in their car.

I knew where their station was and fifteen minutes later I arrived on foot with my nose still bleeding. I was confronted by the same pair of cops who had arrested Joanne, both of them with sneering grins on their square faces. Without a word they frog-marched me into a back room, pushed me down onto a wooden chair, and shaved off my beard with cold water and ordinary kitchen soap. Then they cut my hair so short it was only a fuzz on my skull. They made me look at myself in the glass and for the first time they laughed. Then they jostled me out the doorway and sent me stumbling into the outer room where I saw Joanne very pale and dressed in a long, drab skirt and a smock of some coarse brown material.

"How does your little friend look now?" one of my two cops said and guffawed. As his fist was clenched I knew he was hoping I would answer him back. However, to keep the record straight, I must admit this much: Our local cops had become mean and rough with their fists and sometimes their boots, but they never went in for the systematic, refined tortures that were commonplace in some other countries.

They released us with jeers. Holding my arm, Joanne walked with me to her apartment where she kept another pair of glasses. Her hands were cold and she could not stop shivering. She was like a woman frozen and I was like a man frozen.

The kind of life we had always known now closed down like a summer bungalow when the winter comes. International travel was banned except for some of the Bureaucracy and the huge tourist industry ceased. Strict morality laws were passed. Sexual promiscuity was forbidden, though this was a law they were not too successful in enforcing. To be found with drugs of any kind meant a prison sentence. To be caught selling hard drugs was death. But this was not the end. Indeed, the Great Fear abated now that the mass of the people believed they were under an authority strong enough to rule them.

When the end finally came I was incredibly fortunate, if to survive was really a good fortune. I had a cottage in the hills outside Metro and in it were all my books, most of which I still have. I was planting vegetables when the earth where I was kneeling hit me with a shock that struck up through my knees to the top of my skull. I got to my feet and staggered about as the earth continued to pulsate against my soles. I thought it was an earthquake. Then far off in the area of Metro I saw towers of flame and smoke rising into the high sky. Soon came a surging sound roaring in a profound bass as though the firmament had become a colossal, sonorous drum. I don't know how many minutes passed before the shock waves of air arrived. They knocked me off my feet. I saw the trees bending, screeching as though in a terrible agony as the wind tore them and broke them. Distant flames continued to billow up into the sky and with them a vast smoke that covered thousands of square kilometres. The darkness for a time was so intense that the sun was entirely eclipsed and so it remained for several hours. Toward evening the sun reappeared as a lustreless disk in the sky.

In reconstructing the events of his century, John Wellfleet comes to see that the Destructions were a world-wide extension of what happened to Conrad Dehmel's Germany: "Now I am forced to link up my own experience of total destruction with his, and Germany's the touchstone."

In Germany in 1944 Conrad is persuaded by Admiral Canaris that his only hope of saving Hanna and her father is to do the unthinkable: he must join the Gestapo:

The next day in Munich I was inducted into the Gestapo. My fingerprints were taken and checked against those on the dossier which Krafft had ready on his desk. He asked me a series of routine questions about my past career and turned me over to a doctor for a medical examination. The doctor stabbed a thick finger up my rectum with such violence I nearly screamed from pain and shock. He grinned at me.

"So you're not a homosexual. What a pity! However" – he was still grinning – "it was a necessary medical examination."

Later that day I was fitted for the black uniform and the next morning my training began. It occupied me entirely and I discovered it would take a good deal longer than Canaris had expected. For more than six weeks I studied manuals, listened to lectures, spent four hours a day in rugged and exhausting physical exercises, underwent weapons training, and was instructed in various methods of making arrests. I had been in the Gestapo for more than two weeks before the western Allies landed in France. The first communiqués were vague and made light of the situation and I was afraid it was another failure like Dieppe.

The pace of the training became faster and harsher. One morning a senior officer barked at me to stand at attention. I did so, and without warning he slapped me hard across the face with the back of his hand. It was a test, of course, and as I had heard about it I did not flinch. Later I was put into a section of twenty young men with blank faces and powerful bodies and taught some routine methods of quick killing. Finally I received a summons to appear before Krafft once more.

"You have done quite well," he said. "At least adequately well. I will now tell you what lies ahead."

Here Canaris had been accurate. My work with the Gestapo would be purely bureaucratic. I would be assigned to a small district in Hungary where I was to order a compilation of the names and addresses of all the Jews living there. Those still at liberty I was to have arrested and finally I was to make arrangements with the railway officials for the trains that would take them to the gas chambers and the ovens in Poland. When I asked when I was to leave for Hungary, Krafft became irritable.

"The damned bombing is causing delays everywhere. In France alone we've lost thousands of freight cars and hundreds of locomotives. Anyway, your training is not complete. You must still pass your final stage."

He did not tell me what the final stage was and for another week I was put through even more exhausting physical drills and weapons training. It was now midsummer and the weather was hot and humid. I worried constantly about Hanna and her father because time was passing and I was afraid they had already been arrested. If there was any reliable news about the battle in France we were not told of it. The first real information came to me by chance at the mess table when a senior officer joined Krafft and I overheard the conversation. This officer looked tired, strained, and very worried. He had just returned from Normandy.

"It's not good," I heard him say. "We knew the English and the Canadians would be tough but we thought the Americans would be soft. We were wrong about that. Of course, none of them are in our class, but that fool Goering has left us without an air force. Their planes are over us like an umbrella from dawn till dark. The bombing is unbelievable. The fighting is worse than anything I ever saw in Russia."

I kept my eyes fixed on my plate. So the invasion was successful. So Hanna and her father might have a chance if they were still free. I myself might have a chance. And surely the British and the Americans would know there were men like Canaris in Germany who could do away with Hitler and make peace with the West before the Russians came in and tore what was left of the country to pieces.

When the visiting officer departed I finally made my gamble. I told Krafft that I had just learned that my mother, who was in Freiburg, had been diagnosed for cancer. I wanted to speak with her physician to learn the exact nature of her case. As she might have little time left, I begged for a few days' leave to visit her before going to Hungary. Krafft looked at me with suspicion.

"Your final sessions begin tomorrow. You will have three of them on successive days."

I asked him what they would consist of and he said casually, "Interrogations."

Stephanie, those next three days were the second most horrible I ever spent in my life. The sessions I attended lasted from four to six hours and I had to watch what they did to the victims strapped to a bloodstained table and I had to hear their screams. I had to look on with a frozen face, for Krafft kept watching me. If I had protested, fainted, or vomited I would have been disgraced in Krafft's eyes, and any chance of rescuing Hanna would have vanished.

After the final session Krafft became very friendly. He clapped me on the back and called me *ein ganzer Kerl* (a fine boy) and told me he now trusted me completely. He also said I might have four days' leave to visit my mother in Freiburg.

"Give your respected mother my greetings," he said. Then he added reflectively, "Those interrogations weren't much. Those men broke very quickly."

"Two of them screamed in French and one of them screamed in Czech."

"Did they? The difficult ones were the Germans in the early days. Communists. Swine of course, but they were at least Germans. Most of them died before they talked. What a waste!" He smiled at me. "You'll enjoy your work in Hungary. I think you'll enjoy it very much."

I hoped to get some more information about the battle in France but he was indifferent.

"The Führer will soon take personal charge of the situation and settle it. So now, on your way to Freiburg! Report to our barracks when you arrive and if you need anything, they'll provide it." He then gave me requisitions for a Volkswagen and gasoline and shook my hand. "Heil Hitler," he said. "Heil Hitler," I said.

The Colour of Canada

Like Rivers of Canada, this heavily illustrated book about the country had a complex history. Originally published as part of the Centennial celebrations in 1967, it proved to be so popular that MacLennan revised it in 1972, in 1978, and finally in 1982. That edition continues to be a perennial favourite. The selection of essays that follow – many of them so brief that they serve as captions to the photographs in the book – are themselves like prose snapshots that catch the spirit of each place as the book sweeps us across Canada in the path of the sun from east to west:

From the Introduction:

. . . We still have the land; we are still its tenants. The land is our overwhelming common denominator. A land of dramatic contrasts with an undeveloped frontier – much of it probably undevelopable – almost as large as Europe: great rivers, only a few of them polluted so far; thousands of lakes; and three oceans flanking the whole. Stupidly, we overcrowd three urban areas, a buck being still sacred with us. But the plane which leaves Vancouver air terminal flies over virgin mountains within ten or fifteen minutes. The cars streaming out of Montreal and Toronto can usually reach the wilderness in less than two hours. When you stand on a high point in Quebec City you can see only a few miles away the ramparts of the Laurentian Shield.

This land is far more important than we are. To know it is to be young and ancient all at once. Its virginity is our visible link with the beginnings of the race and the millions of New Canadians who have come here have found constant reminders of their homes in older countries.

In 1937 when I went through Scandinavia to Russia, I said in Denmark, "But this is like Prince Edward Island"; in Sweden, "How like New Brunswick this is!" In Finland, "Just like Quebec fifteen miles north of the river, or Ontario above Simcoe." In Russia and Poland I thought inevitably of the prairie provinces. A few years ago, sailing from Athens along the coast of Argolis, had I not known I was in the Aegean I could easily have mistaken that rocky shore for the coasts of Cape Breton or Newfoundland. British Columbia is our Norway. And one dawn on the Mackenzie, waking in the wheelhouse of a dredge moored at Wrigley Harbour, the sun striking like a searchlight across the river under a mass of clouds, wild ducks and geese arrowing off the water – this was North America when the first white men saw it!

In this book we discover Canada somewhat as the explorers, settlers, and *voyageurs* discovered it. We begin at the rocky harbours of Newfoundland and Nova Scotia, glance at the gentle farmland of Prince Edward Island in summer and winter, at the old Loyalist city of Saint John and some of the lovely rivers of New Brunswick. We come to Gaspé, go up the St. Lawrence past modern Quebec and Montreal, enter briefly the Eastern Townships, then pass through the water gap leading to the Great Lakes and Ontario. We look at the new Toronto and a variety of scenes in Ontario before leaping across the Shield to the Prairies – space apparently limitless under shifting skies all the way to the Rocky Mountains. We go through the mountains to the coast where a sea bird flies out from the land over the Pacific . . .

The Maritimes

Newfoundland has always been a stepping-stone between the hemispheres. Vikings were here before Cabot; Englishmen, Frenchmen, Spaniards, Portuguese shared the fishing rights before the Pilgrims landed in Massachusetts. The Labrador Current washes the island, makes it chilly and foggy; the storms are terrifying. Steamers following the Great Circle from New

York to Europe pass in sight of Cape Race, and the *Titanic* was only the most famous of the ones that failed to finish the voyage. In little boats the fishermen of Newfoundland put out to the rescue in North Atlantic winter gales. Alcock and Brown left Newfoundland in 1919 on the first non-stop transatlantic flight. During World War II, Gander was the last airport of Ferry Command. Now, after centuries of heroic isolation, Newfoundland is part of Canada, and of the continent, the oldest and newest province.

The ancient sea still washes the Maritimes, but almost gone is the life when the sea and the small family farms nourished the people. Less than a century ago Maritimers built, sailed, and manned one-fifth of the merchant fleets of the entire world. The Cunard and White Star Lines were born here. But modern technology doomed both them and the old life-pattern. Now thousands of shore lots have been bought cheap by foreigners desperate to escape the hideousness that made their cities rich.

Louisbourg was the loneliest, foggiest, most expensively fortified outpost of any European power in North America. Garrisoned by French troops, ill-defended by the French navy, unsupported by such *habitant* colonists as made the defence of Quebec an epic, Louisbourg fell to Britain and the New Englanders in the War of the Austrian Succession, was restored to France when the war ended, and was refortified at such cost that Louis XV complained that he would soon see the bastions of Louisbourg rising over the horizon. The city fell for the second and last time in the Seven Years War, and this opened Wolfe's way to Quebec. The British razed the city and fortifications to the ground, and left the site to the fog, the rain, the cold, and the sea birds.

ALONG THE CABOT TRAIL

No scenic highway in North America compresses into such a short length (roughly 300 kilometres) such an astonishing variety: cliffs, ocean vistas, highland glens, river meadows, and a short stretch of the Bras d'Or Lakes. Frigid seas and greyish-pink granite on the Atlantic shore; along the Gulf of St.

Lawrence, sienna-red cliffs and warm water in summer, Mediterranean light on fine days, and, from Cap Rouge, a view like the one from Taormina on the eastern coast of Sicily. The people are mostly of Highland Scottish or French ancestry, and even now some Gaelic and French lingers.

New Brunswick is a land of rivers, all of them beautiful and none gigantic. Rich farms and quiet market towns grew slowly along the banks of the St. John, Kennebecasis, and Petitcodiac, and some of the old houses are jewels. Fredericton is surely one of the most dignified little cities in North America, with an exquisite cathedral and our oldest university. Until recently, the St. John was the best salmon river on the eastern side of the continent. Dams almost abolished the salmon, and the great rafts of lumber no longer come down from northern New Brunswick and northern Maine to form masses of bobbing logs several miles square at Maugerville. Concrete finally destroyed the river's meaning, but not its beauty. This was the country where Sir Charles G. D. Roberts wrote his nature stories. In the northeast of the province, the Miramichi and the Restigouche are famous salmon streams still.

Into Quebec

When national and provincial borders were established in North America at the end of the eighteenth century, the decisive factor was often the movement of flowing water. Madawaska County in northern New Brunswick has a panhandle jutting into Maine because the St. John River flows into the Atlantic. The height of land between New Brunswick and Quebec is shared on the principle that such parts as drain into the Atlantic belong to New Brunswick, while those that drain into the St. Lawrence are in Quebec.

Human flow obeys no such geographic laws. Northern New Brunswick is mostly French-speaking today because thousands of French Canadians seeped over the height of land to work in the forests and lumber plants of New Brunswick, or to fish the waters along the shores of the St. Lawrence Gulf. St. Léonard and Edmundston are now as "French" as La Tuque. But along the Gulf Shore, many of the French-speaking New Brunswick-ers are of the Acadian stock that has been there for centuries.

Northeastern New Brunswick is forest land threaded by famous rivers: the Miramichi, the Restigouche, and the Matape-dia, which feed millions of logs down to the sawmills and pulp companies at the estuary, and which abounded in salmon until the factory ships discovered the meeting-place of the salmon in the Atlantic and vacuumed up almost nine-tenths of them. The Trans-Canada Highway, leaving Edmundston, mounts slowly up past Lake Témiscouata and descends the height of land to reach the St. Lawrence at Rivière du Loup, which looks across to the mountains stretching northeast from Murray Bay. The other road, paralleled by the tracks of the CNR, skirts Bay Chaleur with a magnificent view of the Gaspé mountains, then winds through a hundred miles of the Matapedia Valley and reaches the St. Lawrence just below Father Point, where the out-going vessels ship their pilots. Here the St. Lawrence is only nominally a river; it is really a firth of the sea – salt water deep enough to enable German submarines to operate in it during 1942, cold winds from the icebergs trapped in Belle Isle, and sometimes schools of white porpoises playing about the cutwa-ters of hurrying ships.

It has been said that Quebec's Eastern Townships remind every-one of some other place they know and love. This region was originally marked out by Lord Dorchester as land for Loyalists from New England. The descendants of the old settlers still speak in Yankee twangs, but now the region is predominantly French-speaking as French Canadians have moved in from more crowded areas to farm the land. Hence some of the place names: Saint-Adolphe de Dudswell, St. Paul d'Abbotsford, Stukely Sud, and Ham Sud. Americans have called the Town-ships "a geographical extension of New England" – it depends upon the point of view. There are splendid lakes like Massa-wippi, Memphremagog, Orford. Hills, almost but not quite mountains, loom over the pasture lands and farms, and in the autumn they blaze or glow with the scarlet of maples, the yel-low of birches, the copper of oaks, the pastel russet-red of butternuts. The St. Francis is the principal river and on its banks is the third-largest city in Quebec. Sherbrooke, once centred on an English garrison (when Lord Palmerston became Colonial Secretary his first order was to strengthen it against a possible American invasion), is now largely French-speaking.

Ontario

Ottawa was the most unlikely spot anyone could imagine for a national capital. A century ago it was an overgrown lumber village noted for its drunken brawls and cholera epidemics. The decision to make it the capital of the new nation was made for the reason that most important Canadian decisions are made: no other choice seemed possible. Kingston was too close to the American border, which then was not unfortified. Montreal was too "French"; Toronto too "English." Ottawa had twin advantages: the Rideau Canal linked it to Kingston; the river to Montreal and the St. Lawrence.

Ontarians are really the most astonishing people in Canada. Stratford, for years dependent on its locomotive factories, its most famous citizen the hockey player Howie Morenz, as the result of a dream in the mind of Tom Patterson, the genius of Sir Tyrone Guthrie, and the unlocked talents of Canadian actors from all over the country, is now the Shakespearean centre of the continent, with thousands of people coming from everywhere each summer season to see the plays as the Elizabethans saw them. One leaves the theatre after the evening performance. The sky is clear, the people move slowly, the waters of the Avon reflect the lights:

> . . . look, how the floor of heaven
> Is thick inlaid with patines of bright gold:
> There's not the smallest orb which thou behold'st
> But in his motion like an angel sings. . . .

The North begins in Ontario at Georgian Bay, but in summer it's warm enough for rattlesnakes. Naked rock formations stand magnificent against the sky, and in the tremendous autumn storms the blowing maple leaves stain the air. It was here that Tom Thomson and his colleagues of the Group of Seven first painted the Canadian northland as it truly is, and thereby enabled millions of their countrymen to see the nature of their land.

The Prairies

From Ottawa to the Prairies along the line of the Canadian Pacific you travel for a night, a day, and most of the night following, and nearly all of this journey is through the empty land of the Shield, the train wiggling like a mechanical snake around little lakes, with aspens and spruce blurring past the windows. Before sunset in summer you reach Lake Superior and it is like coming upon an ocean. Port Arthur and Fort William, now united under the tremendous name of Thunder Bay . . . then into the Shield again and at dawn you are at Kenora and the Lake-of-the-Woods. Living in a few hours through that appalling terrain, you may think back and try to imagine the miracle of the voyageurs who reached Fort William, birchbark canoes, four tons of trade goods, and thirty-six portages, thirty-six to forty days after leaving Montreal.

Then the rocks thin out. Suddenly you see black earth appearing and then you are in a land-ocean, the black prairie of Manitoba; on the horizon is a grain elevator and the onion dome of a Ukrainian church.

The breaching of the frontier between Ontario and the West is still the greatest achievement in the history of Canada. In this age of masses and abstractions, let it not be forgotten that this was the work of a very few men, that guts and imagination working together are the expression of the Divine in human life.

The towns with their grain elevators are like ships in this land-sea. Also, just as at sea, the weather dominates. The movement of clouds, their rapid changes of colour, make the wind visible. When the wheat is ripe, it writhes in the wind, it boils in the wind, ominously gold under the darkened sky, Van Gogh's wheatfield near Arles on a colossal scale.

Who Has Seen the Wind – the verb is the decisive word in the title of W. O. Mitchell's wonderful novel of a boy growing up on the prairie, discovering life, love, cruelty, fear, and God in the movement of grain, in the sound of the wind, in the prairie birds and animals. A land which might have produced Hebraic prophets looking up to that appalling sky and asking the Creator, "What is man, that thou art mindful of him," and more than once coming to the conclusion that He is not. Mitchell's phrase that here life is reduced to "the common denominator of sky and Saskatchewan prairie" serves better than reams of analysis to explain the feeling of prairie people that their life is unique, that the people in the East and on the Pacific Coast can never really understand them. It explains the almost perpetual political opposition of the prairie provinces to whatever is the ruling party in the central Canadian government.

When you travel across the far western prairie, the dramatic moment comes, not when you see the skyline of the Rockies, but when you reach the visible tilt where the prairie begins to rise. The foothills begin, rolling like the smaller waves that herald the titanic seas of a hurricane.

British Columbia

The natural division between the Prairies and the cordilleran West is the most dramatic of them all. The Great Divide in the so-called Canadian Rockies marks the line of demarcation between Alberta and British Columbia. This is the range of mountains that separates the waters flowing easterly to reach the Atlantic through Hudson Bay, and westerly to reach the Pacific. In the case of the Peace and Athabasca rivers, the waters drain through the Mackenzie Basin to the Arctic. The Columbia Icefield, straddling the divide, is the source of major rivers that reach all three oceans.

The piercing of the vast ranges of the British Columbia mountains by the railways was Canada's greatest single response to the physical challenge of her environment. The success of Confederation depended upon it. In our time, the bulldozer has enabled the magnificently scenic Trans-Canada Highway to make it possible for automobiles to pass through the ranges on comfortable grades all the way to the coast.

The prairie begins its transformation into foothill and then to mountain once you have passed the 110th meridian of longitude. Farther south, in Colorado, the moment arrives some eight meridians of longitude farther east, the Canadian prairie being wider than the American because the Rockies swerve easterly south of the border. After the swells of the foothills come the waves of the Rockies, grey, minareted, the earth in tempest all the way to the Pacific. Yet, in the troughs of these waves are the absolute stillness of the valleys and the perfect reflection of the mighty rocks in placid, glacier-fed lakes.

Victoria, capital of British Columbia, was founded in 1843 as a Hudson's Bay Company's trading-post known as Fort Camosun, later renamed Victoria in honour of the Queen. Its suburb, Esquimalt, is the western base of the Canadian Navy. It became the capital of the province in 1866, five years before British Columbia joined Canada as the sixth province (one year after Manitoba). When we remember that, in 1870, Victoria was divided from "Canada" by more than two thousand miles of Shield country, prairies almost empty of humanity, by hundreds of miles of mountains, the boldness of this decision takes the breath away. As a Canadian newspaper recently pointed out, if computers had existed a century ago such a decision would never have been made. All the evidence that men could have fed into it would have said "no" to it. . . .

In Honour of
Margaret Laurence

One of MacLennan's last public appearances was at Kingston in 1987, when he addressed the Writers' Union of Canada. Some months previously MacLennan had celebrated his eightieth birthday at a private dinner arranged by friends and attended by a select group including Pierre Trudeau. In Kingston he was obviously frail and the crowded room was stiflingly hot. Yet what he had to say was a fascinating blend of reminiscence and tribute to the other great writer for whom the lecture series was named:

It is a very great honour you have done me in asking me to give the first of the Margaret Laurence Lectures. Profoundly, I wish it were not so. It seems a grim jest of God that she should be gone and I should be here, for I was born some eighteen years before she came into the world. I came from the extreme eastern tip of Canada before Newfoundland joined us. Margaret was born in the dead centre some two thousand miles to the west. Both of us were of Scottish origin, though her surname, Wemyss, indicates that she was a scion of a prominent family from County Angus, while I was a Highlander from the North. Both of us were born in dying small towns. Both of us went abroad before we began to write. Both of us, in trying to discover ourselves, had first to discover some of the historical and psychological truths of the huge, undefined nation into which we were born.

Though I met Margaret very seldom during her lifetime, it was always like meeting someone whose professionalism I sensed so naturally that I took it for granted, as she, I believe, took me for granted. She had the inner generosity of a person whose life had been very difficult, and her work was at once a deliverance from herself and a triumph within herself. Toward the end, when apparently the whole nation held her in honour, she had to go to law to prevent a handful of self-righteous hypocrites from banning her books from the schools of Ontario. It upset her profoundly to have to take off the gloves and fight them in the courts, and though she won the battle, she must have suffered some psychological damage from it, and it is quite possible that if this outrage had not occurred, she would still be alive.

In the last months of Margaret's life, when I knew she had terminal cancer, I telephoned her every second week and always found her calm, a little more husky of voice than when I first met her, but acceptant and even tranquil. She knew she had done her work and that it was good; she had rounded it off; she had gone out from the prairie small town into the great outer world, including the Horn of Africa and southern England. Then, as naturally and inevitably as a Pacific salmon swimming back to its original spawning-bed, she returned and tackled the little Manitoba town where she had grown up. She re-created it under the name of Manawaka and in so doing, like Ulysses when he returned to Ithaca, she slew quite a few demons.

The southeastern corner of Manitoba is one of the most historic regions of this entire country, and its history is much better known in Quebec than in Ontario. This is because of the early *voyageurs* who, over a century and a half, explored in canoes the whole nation from Montreal to the Pacific and the Mackenzie delta, as well as the Mississippi valley down to New Orleans. La Vérendrye, born in Trois-Rivières in 1685 – which happened to be also the birth-year of Handel and Johann Sebastian Bach – returning from service in the War of the Spanish Succession, set out for the west with a party of fifty men, including three of his own sons. He established Fort Rouge on the banks of the Red River and continued west, perhaps to a sight of the Rockies. Later, after the English conquest of New France, the name was changed to Fort Garry and now, of course, it is Winnipeg.

After La Vérendrye, there appeared on the plains in increasing numbers the *Métis*, most of them children of French fathers and Indian mothers. Colbert, the great finance minister of

Louis XIV, laid it down that French settlers in America should mate with the native peoples, and this surely explains the astonishing endurance of the original *voyageurs*. Later on, the Scottish Highlanders of the North West Company and the HBC followed to some extent the same practice, though most of them had legitimate wives at home in Montreal. This fundamental part of the Canadian story was glossed over until very recently, but only a few days ago, at Percé in the Gaspé, President Mitterrand of France alluded to it openly, saying that many French-Canadian expressions were derived from the Indian languages.

In modern times, when at last a true Canadian literature developed, Manitoba gave us in Gabrielle Roy the finest of French-Canadian novelists, and she was a *Métis* from Saint-Boniface. Later on Margaret Laurence gave us that wonderful *Métis* character Jules Tonnerre. The great achievement of these two women writers was to tell hundreds of thousands of Canadians who they were.

I shall never forget a reading Margaret gave in McGill during the period I used to call "our time of troubles," when Spock-marked student politicians, many of them Americans, were raging against the American Empire which was committing suicide in Vietnam and involving much of the world in the general catastrophe. Margaret came into the campus like a wave of peace. She had an enormous audience of many ages, and though the acoustics were bad in the hall, she held them entirely with her. Waves of affection seemed to surge around her, and no wonder. For here was a woman of profound understanding of the human condition.

Academics have been trained for a long time to put their confidence in pure reason, and the American Republic was to a large extent founded on the theories of eighteenth-century philosophers, especially Locke, and, to a lesser extent, Rousseau. Locke has a great deal to answer for. This childless philosopher asserted that the infant new to earth and sky is born with a mind which is a *tabula rasa* – a blank sheet of paper, to be written on by the hand of experience. Every woman who has minded a baby understands that this is total nonsense, but sensible women were not listened to in the Age of Reason. Perhaps at last men are beginning to listen to them, the young ones at least. Writers like Margaret Laurence understood in their bones the truth of a sentence written by a great Frenchman long before the Age of Reason, which has triumphed in our time in the H-bomb and the Cold War. "Il est bon," wrote Malherbe, "et plus souvent qu'on ne le pense, de savoir de n'avoir pas de l'esprit."

The French Canadians and the *Métis* knew this truth in their bones, and that is how they managed to survive and stay sane for two centuries after the American Revolution.

I shall now leave Margaret Laurence in peace, and speak a little of my own experience as a writer in this country.

Seven and a half years ago I finished my last novel, *Voices in Time*, and knew it would be the last novel I would ever write. It occupied some ten years of my life and it exhausted me. Becoming a great variety of characters can be a soul-bending experience. I realized that I had reached the stage when I must try to deal with the most inexplicable character I had any knowledge of, myself. Two and a half months ago I became, to my dismay, eighty years old, which is fifteen years beyond the legal age described by that appalling modern expression "a senior citizen." Two weeks ago a group of high school students from Moncton came to see me (in addition to other writers in central Canada), and a fifteen-year-old boy asked me as practical a question as I ever heard. "You're eighty years old," he said, "and that's an awful thing. What does it feel like to know that you'll soon be dead?"

Now, how could anyone answer a question like that? . . .

There was much laughter in the packed room at this point, and MacLennan looked up and grinned, pleased by the success of his joke. He died suddenly at home in Montreal on November 7, 1990.

This book was selected and edited by
Douglas Gibson, the Publisher at McClelland & Stewart.
It is part of a select series
of titles under his personal imprint,
which are listed overleaf.

OTHER TITLES FROM
[DOUGLAS GIBSON BOOKS]
PUBLISHED BY McCLELLAND & STEWART INC.

THE PROGRESS OF LOVE *by* Alice Munro
"Probably the best collection of stories – the most confident and, at the same time, the most adventurous – ever written by a Canadian." *Saturday Night*
Fiction, 6 x 9, 320 pages, hardcover

THE RADIANT WAY *by* Margaret Drabble
"*The Radiant Way* does for Thatcher's England what *Middlemarch* did for Victorian England . . . Essential reading!" *Margaret Atwood*
Fiction, 6 x 9, 400 pages, hardcover

DANCING ON THE SHORE A Celebration of Life at Annapolis Basin *by* Harold Horwood, *Foreword by* Farley Mowat
"A Canadian *Walden*" (*Windsor Star*) that "will reward, provoke, challenge and enchant its readers." (*Books in Canada*)
Nature/Ecology, 5 1/8 x 8 1/4, 224 pages, 16 wood engravings, trade paperback

NO KIDDING Inside the World of Teenage Girls *by* Myrna Kostash
This frank, informative look at teenage girls today "should join Dr. Spock on every parent's bookshelf." *Maclean's*
Women/Journalism, 4 1/4 x 7, 320 pages, notes, paperback

THE HONORARY PATRON A Novel *by* Jack Hodgins
The Governor General's Award-winner's thoughtful and satisfying third novel mixes comedy and wisdom, "and it's magic." *Ottawa Citizen*
Fiction, 4 1/4 x 7, 336 pages, paperback

RITTER IN RESIDENCE A Comic Collection *by* Erika Ritter
This collection by the noted playwright, broadcaster, and humorist reveals "a wonderfully funny view of our world." *Globe and Mail*
Humour, 4 1/4 x 7, 200 pages, paperback

THE LIFE OF A RIVER *by* Andy Russell
This yarning history of the Oldman river area shows "a sensitivity towards the earth . . . that is universally applicable." *Kingston Whig-Standard*
History/Ecology, 4 1/4 x 7, 184 pages, paperback

THE INSIDERS Power, Money, and Secrets in Ottawa *by* John Sawatsky
Investigative journalism at its best, this Ottawa exposé is "packed with insider information about the political process." *Globe and Mail*
Politics/Business, 4 1/4 x 7, 368 pages, photos, paperback

PADDLE TO THE AMAZON The Ultimate 12,000-Mile Canoe Adventure *by* Don Starkell, *edited by* Charles Wilkins
"This real-life adventure book . . . must be ranked among the classics of the literature of survival." *Montreal Gazette*
Adventure, 4 1/4 x 7, 320 pages, maps, photos, paperback

OTHER TITLES FROM
⟦DOUGLAS GIBSON BOOKS⟧
PUBLISHED BY McCLELLAND & STEWART INC.

ALL IN THE SAME BOAT Family Cruising Around the Atlantic *by* Fiona McCall and Paul Howard
"A lovely adventure that is a modern-day Swiss Family Robinson story . . . a winner."
Toronto Sun   Travel/Adventure, 5 3/4 x 8 3/4, 256 pages, maps, trade paperback

WELCOME TO FLANDERS FIELDS The First Canadian Battle of the Great War: Ypres, 1915 *by* Daniel G. Dancocks
"A magnificent chronicle of a terrible battle . . . Daniel Dancocks is spellbinding throughout." *Globe and Mail*
                    Military/History, 4 1/4 x 7, 304 pages, photos, maps, paperback

NEXT-YEAR COUNTRY Voices of Prairie People *by* Barry Broadfoot
"There's something mesmerizing about these authentic Canadian voices . . . a three-generation rural history of the prairie provinces, with a brief glimpse of the bleak future." *Globe and Mail*
                    Oral history, 5 3/8 x 8 3/4, 400 pages, trade paperback

UNDERCOVER AGENT How One Honest Man Took On the Drug Mob . . . And Then the Mounties *by* Leonard Mitchell and Peter Rehak
"It's the stuff of spy novels – only for real . . . how a family man in a tiny fishing community helped make what at the time was North America's biggest drug bust." Saint John *Telegraph-Journal*
                    Non-fiction/Criminology, 4 1/4 x 7, 176 pages, paperback

THE PRIVATE VOICE A Journal of Reflections *by* Peter Gzowski
"A fascinating book that is cheerfully anecdotal, painfully honest, agonizingly self-doubting and compulsively readable." *Toronto Sun*
                    Autobiography, 5 1/2 x 8 1/2, 320 pages, photos, trade paperback

LADYBUG, LADYBUG . . . *by* W. O. Mitchell
"Mitchell slowly and subtly threads together the elements of this richly detailed and wonderful tale . . . the outcome is spectacular . . . *Ladybug, Ladybug* is certainly among the great ones!" *Windsor Star   Fiction, 4 1/4 x 7, 288 pages, paperback*

AT THE COTTAGE A Fearless Look at Canada's Summer Obsession *by* Charles Gordon
"A delightful reminder of why none of us addicted to cottage life will ever give it up." *Hamilton Spectator   Humour, 5 3/8 x 8 3/4, 224 pages, trade paperback*

ACCORDING TO JAKE AND THE KID: A Collection of New Stories *by* W. O. Mitchell
"This one's classic Mitchell. Humorous, gentle, wistful, it's 16 new short stories about life through the eyes of Jake, a farmhand, and the kid, whose mom owns the farm." *Saskatoon Star-Phoenix   Fiction, 4 1/4 x 7, 280 pages, paperback*